How Do You Want It

The Story of Southeast Trina

How Do You Want It

The Story of Southeast Trina

Darrell King

www.urbanbooks.net

Urban Books
1119 Straight Path
West Babylon, NY 11704

ISBN-13: 978-1-60162-025-5
ISBN-10: 1-60162-025-X

First Printing November 2007
Printed in the United States of America

10 9 8 7 6 5 4 3 2 1

*This is a work of fiction. Any references or similarities to actual events, real
people, living, or dead, or to real locales are intended to give the novel a sense of
reality. Any similarity to other names, characters, places, and incidents is entirely coincidental.*

Submit Wholesale Orders to:
Kensington Publishing Corp.
C/O Penguin Group (USA) Inc.
Attention: Order Processing
405 Murray Hill Parkway
East Rutherford, NJ 07073-2316
Phone: 1-800-526-0275
Fax: 1-800-227-9604

Dedication

This novel is dedicated to Mrs. LaVonia Cogdell, who has provided my family and I with Inspiration, guidance and much love.

Acknowledgments

I'd like to thank the creator of the universe first of all for life and this gift in which I'm blessed with. I want to thank my wife Sonya (Redd) for being in my corner from day one, my daughter, India, K'Linn, Peolandria and Angel, and my son, Darrell Jr. a.k.a. D. Young (up-and coming Hip Hop star). All my peeps from the National Archives (You know who you are!) my Mom and Dad, my brothers all my cousins in the dirty, dirty. Mike Williams of Exclusive Magazine (*Exmagonline.com*), you da bomb boy! My literary peeps K'wan (my road dawg for life!), my man KooKoo, Waz up my dude! Still can't see me on that Madden! Danielle Santiago, T.N. Baker, Tracey Brown, Karibu Book stores, *Coast2Coastreaders.com*, Urban-lit, my agent Joylynn Jossel (Thank You!), Earth Jallow (A True Nubian Queen!), Delores Thornton
(Queen of promotion!), Carl Weber & the Urban Books family. And I would also like to thank Victor Martin and Eric Gray. Anyone else who I forgot-you know who you are & you are loved.

Prologue
The Farms

Young Katrina Ricks was blessed with both ravishing beauty and a voluptuous, eye-catching shape. However, for the sixteen-year-old Barry Farms Dwellings resident, her shapely form was a curse more than anything else, for it was this same hour-glass figure that brought her such pain and trouble. Katrina, or "Trina" as she was commonly known in the neighborhood, was often the target of her stepfather's sexual abuse while her hardworking mother, Lucinda Ricks, was away at work on the night shift at Greater Southeast Community Hospital.

A typical night in Trina's home would feature a drunken or drugged up Maynard Middleton skulking into his stepdaughter's bedroom, snatching her up, wrestling her from her bed and forcing her legs apart as she kicked and screamed for him to stop.

"Get up, girl," Maynard would snarl. "You know what time it is."

He'd then proceed to do the unthinkable, forcing himself into her, thrusting sometimes so violently that it caused Trina to bleed.

"Stop it! No!" Trina would cry out to no avail.

The more the sobbing teenager begged her stepfather to stop, the more it seemed to spur him on. When he would finally climax, he would withdraw himself, gather the crumpled clothing that he had managed to remove before the assault, and proceed to exit with a smirk on his face.

As Trina, soiled and emotionally traumatized, sat naked within her darkened room, she would whimper softly and ponder just how much she hated her stepfather and life itself for dealing her such a cruel fate. Maynard would further incite both fear and anger in the girl by threatening her with bodily harm if she were to go to the police or tell her relatives about his sexual abuse against her, especially if she parted her lips to tell her mother.

"I swear to God, if you tell a soul, I'll cut your mother's fuckin' throat right in front of your face and then kill you before the police even think about taking me to jail," Maynard would threaten with the look of death in his eyes.

So Trina never dared tell anyone, not even her mother. After all, Lucinda wouldn't have believed her anyway—at least that's what Maynard had planted in Trina's head, telling her repeatedly that her mother loved him more and she was just some "stupid kid."

The brutal inhumanity sixteen-year-old Trina was forced to endure sparked a burning hatred, deep and bitter, for not only her stepfather, but for men in general whom she at an early age began to think of as vile oppressors of women. She observed how the neighborhood women, her own mother included, allowed the men in their lives to degrade them and their children, often with little or no resistance.

Trina also knew several other teenaged girls from her neighborhood, who like herself, had been victims of chronic sexual abuse. Yet their mothers acted as though nothing ever happened, or in some cases, even ended up putting the blame on their victimized daughters for inviting the rapes. Blaming them for wearing skirts that were too tight, jeans that were too short, make-up—flaunting their hot asses in front of their men, just asking for it. This was totally unacceptable and disgusting to Trina and she made a solemn vow that she would never again be weak-willed, nor would she ever submit to anyone again in her life—man or woman.

The year was 1984 and Trina had discovered that she was pregnant for the third time by her stepfather. During the first two pregnancies, both in 1983, Maynard took Trina to a Southeast area abortion clinic and paid for the procedures.

"Either I'ma kill the little bastard or the doctor gonna kill it," Maynard would always tell Trina on the way to the clinic. "This way is easier, don't you think?"

Trina would just sit silently in the car, holding in her tears of anger, wishing she could keep her baby, the one thing she thought would probably never hurt or disappoint her. Well, this time Trina was determined to carry her unborn child to term, and through much hiding and wearing baggy, oversized clothing, she delivered a healthy seven pound, eight ounce baby girl on June 30th, 1984.

Both Maynard and Trina's mother were furious when it was discovered that their daughter had given birth.

"Who's the gotdamn daddy?" Lucinda would shout at her daughter, her hands clutching Trina's shoulders, trying to shake the truth out of her.

Trina never disclosed the identity of her child's father to Lucinda and that brought great relief to Maynard, the culprit. Yet both adults would soon find out that motherhood wasn't the only thing that would make living with Trina quite different now.

By the fall of '84, Trina became much more rowdy and disrespectful to both teachers and fellow students at Ballou Senior High. She had gotten suspended a total of nine times during the month of October alone for fighting, using profanity, and threatening teachers with bodily harm. By February 25, 1985, she was expelled from school for good after smashing a boy in the face with a brick after he fondled her breasts in the back of the school as they were practicing for band on the black top.

Late one frosty night in late March '85, Maynard attempted to begin his predatory activities once more in his wife's absence. For quite some time Maynard had decided to forgo his usual sexual attacks on his stepdaughter as neighborhood girl-friends of hers had begun coming over to visit, hang out or sleep over. On this particular evening, the young mother, now 17, sat upon the edge of her bed bottle-feeding her precious little Porsche. The teenager calmly burped the infant before gently laying her down into her soft cushioned crib. She then took off her earrings and tied her long braided hair into a quickly done ponytail.

Trina immediately went over to the dresser drawer and removed an eight-inch steak knife from the top drawer. Since giving birth to her daughter she had slept with the concealed weapon. She might not have been able to protect herself over the years, but she'd damn sure protect her daughter. The deadly blade glistened as the light from the living room spilled into Trina's room as Maynard slowly opened the door. Unwittingly, the 41-year old entered as always, removing his pants and then his shirt, soon standing naked in the doorway beyond.

Trina feigned sleep upon her bed as she gripped the cold handle of the steak knife more tightly, preparing herself for Maynard's approach. As expected, the molester got into Trina's bed behind her and began to fondle her aggressively. Suddenly Trina turned to meet him with a surprisingly passionate wet kiss upon the lips.

"Die, you bitch ass muthafucka!" Trina hissed as she withdrew her moist lips from him simultaneously plunging the steak knife deep within Maynard's abdomen.

Chapter 1
Blue Plains

By the time the DC cops arrived, along with the paramedics, Maynard Middleton was dead. His naked body was sprawled out upon Trina's blood-soaked bed. Trina was taken into custody and led away to jail. She was charged with 2nd degree murder; because she was a minor, she was sentenced to a twelve month stay in Juvie, before having it shaved down to three, compliments of her older sister, Rita Ann. Katrina Ricks ended up housed at the Blue Plains Boys and Girls Village learning much more mischief than morality, more evil than education. It was here that the lovely teenager developed her first lesbian love affair as well as the brutal street smarts and thug mentality that would eventually transform her into the Beltway region's most ruthless drug lord.

In the afternoon Trina took a series of senior high classes, subsequently attending one of the various work details around the girls' dormitory before heading to the break room for some leisure time. However, on this particular day, Trina would make a beeline for the classroom of Sophia Carlin, a twenty-two year old Virginian from Richmond. Ms. Carlin was a tall, shapely, butter honey complexioned ex-model who now worked part-time as a Washington Redskin's cheerleader and part-time as a Blue Plains teacher. Trina loved the woman's deep dimples and long gorgeous legs. From the hallway Trina had watched those thick, well-formed legs and that plump, round ass as Ms. Carlin gracefully walked down the hall and out towards the parking lot. Of all places, Ms. Carlin's parking space was below Trina's dorm window; however her gold-colored Saab wasn't parked there today. Ms. Carlin went outside to get a whiff of fresh air before returning to her classroom. Unbeknownst to her, Trina was admiring Ms. Carlin's every move. Her beauty captivated Trina as the looks of even the most handsome boy never had.

Trina reached out for the doorknob leading into Classroom 2C, turning it slowly and easing inside. As the afternoon bell sounded, the surrounding hallways became a veritable sea of loudly chattering and laughing teens of various ages and races, though mostly black. Trina closed the door gently behind her with a soft click of the latch as she locked it from inside. Silently Trina watched as Ms. Carlin tidied up the messy classroom flitting from one corner to the other. As she moved about the room frantically cleaning, the sweet aromatic smell of expensive imported perfume wafted out towards Trina's nostrils. Ms. Carlin paused for a minute or so in front of the big blackboard. Trina drank deep lustful thoughts of the beautiful lady before her—a sexy, brick house of a woman fiercely dressed in a dazzling dark blue Dolce & Gabana pantsuit that accentuated her luscious curves nicely without losing its smart professional look. She would have her this day, she thought to herself as she began walking toward the Algebra teacher.

"That's some good smellin' perfume right there . . . what is it? Chanel #5 or some shit like that?" Trina asked, trying to thinking of something else to say in order to strike up a conversation.

Ms. Carlin spun around, shocked. She slowly smiled, placing a slender hand to her ample breasts. Trina smiled also as she surveyed the beautiful oval face that sported those delightfully deep dimples at each cheek. Trina didn't even care if Ms. Carlin's long flowing honey blond locks were as fake as her green contacts. To Trina this woman was a magnificent jewel to be adored and pampered.

"Girl! . . . You 'bout scared me half to death!! I didn't know anybody was even here. So, whassup? How can I be of assistance to you today, Miss Ricks?"

Trina moved in closer to the young Algebra teacher and placed her hand on top of Ms. Carlin's.

"I ain't tryin' to scare you, so that's my bad, walkin' up on you like that, but I been peepin' you . . . and I'm tryin' to get with 'cha. Know what I'm sayin'?" Ms. Carlin smiled wide and big showing a beautiful set of pearly whites.

"Oh, really? So you mean like a lesbian-type deal here?" she asked inquisitively. Her seductive bedroom eyes were boring intensely into Trina's inquiring ones, as Ms. Carlin searched for any signs of teenage playfulness or insecurity.

"Well I must say I'm rather flattered to be found attractive by you, Ms. Ricks, because in fact I am somewhat bi-curious and you are quite a desirable young lady yourself. But I am involved; as a matter of fact, I am engaged. And to be perfectly honest, I just don't do side flings. So I guess that's that."

"I don't care who ya man is, even though for real. I know you fucks with Lil' Mo' Gentry from out Anacostia. That's aiight though. What he don't know, won't hurt 'im. You feelin' me, Boo?"

Trina boldly took both of Sophia Carlin's hands into hers and pulled the young teacher in close to her. At that particular moment, as the two young women gazed adoringly into each other's eyes, Trina experienced a feeling she never felt before—she felt on top of the world. Trina was convinced that this was truly her first love. But even she couldn't escape the fact that she was treading on dangerous ground messing with the fiancée of one the area's most infamous and deadly criminals, Maurice Lil' Mo' Gentry. The Lincoln Heights cocaine dealer was one of the District's most powerful and ruthless men. A 25-year-old-power hungry baller who stood a little over 5'11", and weighed a hefty 256 lbs had the city locked down. The District was the hot-headed gangsta's drug empire, created through several years of bloody gangland killings, bribery, and secret alliances with shady city politicians who allowed him to flood the Chocolate City with an unbelievable influx of crack and PCP. As a result, Lil' Mo' netted several million dollars during the mid-eighties.

Gentry's iron-fisted reign went unchallenged and his brutality was legendary even among the other drug crews within the violent projects in and around DC. So Trina knew that she would have to be very careful or she could easily end up as another bullet-riddled statistic of the nation's murder capital.

"How do you know Maurice?" Sophia asked with surprise and curiosity as she backed away slightly, removing her diamond-studded hands from Trina's.

"C'mon now. Ur'ry body know that nigga Lil' Mo'."

As a matter of fact, Lil' Mo' had dated Trina's older sister, Rita Ann, when they both were high schoolers, but he was both short-tempered as well as a skirt chaser; as a result the love affair was short-lived Rita Ann took a whippin from numerous arguments and fisticuffs. "She got pregnant by him like twice . . . she got rid o' them joints though," Trina related. "But I do know one thing, that the nigga ain't shit for real. All he do is fuck around with other broads and beat on women. That's the simple fact my sister stopped fuckin' with his dumb-ass. Now I know da nigga caked up and all, ya know givin' you ice and all that type shit, but check this out, I can give you something that he can't. I can give you love, baby girl."

Sophia Carlin grinned slightly, shaking her head while staring at the love struck teen. A series of irritatingly loud honks from the outside parking lot caught Ms. Carlin's attention. "Look, I'm really sorry sweetie, but I gotta cut this conversation short. My ride is here and I don't want to keep him waiting," Ms. Carlin said, quickly snatching up her purse along with a small box of textbooks and test papers. Trina abruptly took the box from her teacher's arm and accompanied Ms. Carlin down the hall through the exit doors and out into the parking lot. Trina paused and looked on in silent anger as Sophia Carlin eased onto the plush passenger's seat of a magnificent gold and ivory colored Bentley Continental. Trina seethed with jealousy as Ms. Carlin embraced her bad boy beau, Maurice Gentry, warmly as she planted a long sensuous kiss upon his thick fleshy lips.

The notorious cocaine dealer immediately recognized Trina and acknowledged her with a slight nod of the head. Trina hated Lil' Mo' Gentry and did not return his greeting, but instead rolled her eyes and flashed him a mean smirk, which merely caused the usually quick-tempered Lil' Mo' to chuckle lightly to himself. As Trina placed the box of school supplies down onto the backseat, she smelled the fresh crisp scent of expensive leather upholstery which merged with the sweet aroma of vanilla musk that wafted out through the vehicle's air vents.

Maurice Gentry was rocking a handsome LeCoq Sportif red and white sweat suit accented with a huge 24 carat gold herringbone chain that sparkled brilliantly around his thick neck; diamond-laden jewelry adorned his wrists, fingers, and left earlobe. Lying down upon the platform between the driver's and passenger's seats was a shiny black stainless steel Beretta 9mm handgun with a full clip inserted into the handle. As Trina glanced at the hardware, she could only imagine how many lives Lil' Mo' had claimed with that particular weapon.

Trina waved goodbye to Sophia as she and Lil' Mo' Gentry pulled out of the parking lot en route to their upper northwest row house.

Before rolling away from the juvenile detention center, Lil'

Mo' yelled out towards Trina, "Hey Shorty, tell Rita I said Whassup, aiight? And, oh yeah, take this and get yo ass to a hairdresser, cuz ya shit's all over ya muthafuckin' head, young!"

Gentry laughed tossing a hundred dollar bill out the window towards Trina. She flipped Gentry her middle finger as the majestic automatic cruised slowly around the curb and through the partially rusted iron gates. Trina looked down at the wrinkled bill that occasionally took flight along with the trash littering the pavement in the brisk mid-April gusts. Reluctantly she walked over a few feet, near a pair of lonely park benches and snatched up the Benjamin before the blustery winds took it into the surrounding thickets. The girl felt embarrassed, like a sucker for going after the money that had been tossed to her like scraps to a begging dog. But she realized that she indeed needed the money.

Trina caught a whiff of the strong odor of marijuana and followed it over to where a couple of kids from her dorm wing were passing around a thick blunt, hidden from the view of facility officials behind an old decrepit greenhouse. Trina was welcomed with much laughter and hugs by the pot smoking teens who freely shared their weed with the new arrival. While the other girls giggled foolishly and spoke of the latest gossip, fashion, and the most desirable boys next door, young Trina's mind, though dulled now by the intoxicating effect of the cannabis could think of nothing other than the lovely, long-legged beauty known as Sophia Carlin. She had never before been in love with anyone male or female. Of course there had been two or three boys back in Ballou High School she would have considered talking to. And other than her horrible sexual abuse at the hands of her late stepfather, she'd only had two other sexual encounters: one with a Nigerian cabdriver who paid her two hundred dollars for a one-night stand and the other with an eighteen year old Blue Plains juvenile who paid her his entire monthly allowance for a five minute blowjob inside of a seldom used storage room.

At an early age Trina realized that for the most part men used women for sex and discarded them conveniently when they saw fit. So Trina planned to use a similar tactic on the men in her life. If they wanted to lay, they would have to pay. Yet no matter how handsome the boys at the detention center were, none of them seemed to move her romantically. She was remarkably mature for her tender age; the hardships she had experienced had forced her to grow up rather quickly. Just looking at Trina in comparison to her adolescent peers, she seemed to be in her twenties with her well-developed hips, breasts, impressive height, and rotund ass which made the average pair of jeans appear to be painted on.

The 17-year-old juvenile delinquent had acquired more knowledge of the hood and its various vices than she ever wanted to learn. Daily she was in the company of young con artists, dope pushers, swindlers and stick-up kids who during her stay at the Blue Plains Boys & Girls Village educated her in the criminal arts of stacking paper. Before long she was a pro herself, bringing in a couple hundred dollars per week from inmates and staff, even administrators. Her income was derived from card and dice games, turning tricks, and stealing. Of all forbidden capers the teenage criminal pulled off, none netted more profits than theft. She was such an accomplished thief that even the Director of the facility fell victim to her sticky fingers. Locked doors, even those that were double-bolted, presented little, if any, trouble for Trina and her crew of young burglars. Offices, dorm rooms, even staff members and visitors' vehicles in the designated parking lots were routinely burglarized. This continued for weeks until the center beefed up security and placed more cameras throughout the building and its surrounding areas.

One night as Trina sat Indian-style upon her bunk bed counting her ill-gotten money, her bunkie hopped down from off of the top bunk and plopped down on the bottom bed beside Trina.

Darrell King

"Young!" the high-pitched voice whispered in Trina's ear as she separated the stolen jewelry from the money and other goods. Trina looked over her shoulder into the high yellow, freckled face, partially covered with a mass of beaded dirty blond braids, which the girl continuously brushed away from her big moist gray eyes.

"Whassup?" Trina asked curiously.

"I just got off the phone with my brother right? Tell me why he said him and his peoples 'bout to run up on these niggas out in Maryland that be hustlin' in Glass Manor apartments and shit's right! He said after they get that work up off them bammas, they gonna break us off some o' that. So, whassup? You aiight with that?" the invading bunkie excitedly questioned.

"Oh, hell yeah! When is ya folks gonna drop that off?"

"My brotha said he's gonna holla at me this weekend when I get out on my weekend pass. So when I come back I'm gonna be holdin'."

"Aiight, that'll work!" Trina said smiling broadly, briskly rubbing her palms together in anticipation of more stolen goodies. "But looka here, Shonda . . . don't fuck around and get ya self caught up out here on these streets, you ain't got nutthin' but a coupla months left to go in this bitch. Please don't fuck that up over some ole dumb shit, aiight?"

The other girl gave Trina a quick smirk.

"Oh naw, young! Never that, trust me. I'm gonna be aiight, don't worry 'bout that. You just calm ya nerves and sit back. When I get back on Monday, I'm gonna bless you, aiight?"

"Aiight, then Shorty, I got you. Now go get yo lil' young ass back to bed . . . good night."

Trina hugged and kissed her roommate gently on the cheek before Shonda hopped back up top upon her own bunk. Trina then stored her valuables away into a large shoebox and stuffed it beneath her bunk and turned off the soft glow of the desk lamp before she settled herself under the covers for a much-needed rest.

To all the other young female juvenile delinquents, Trina served as a surrogate mother. At seventeen, she was a lot older than most of her peers and she was the most aggressive as well as courageous of the entire bunch. The girls acknowledged that Trina had the guts, knowledge and go-hard attitude needed to lead them and no one challenged that. Most of the young females housed at the Blue Plains Boys and Girls Village had brothers, boyfriends, or baby daddies who routinely sold drugs and involved themselves in other illegal activities such as car-jackings, armed robberies, and car thefts.

The drug dealing crews of DC were among the Nation's most ruthless. Killings in Washington, DC, reached levels that were unbelievable for a city of its moderate size. Yet the obsessive desire among fiends for the brief euphoria of crack cocaine was undeniable and many crack dealers became wealthy due to demand on the streets.

Trina was determined to get her share of the wealth, one way or the other. She felt that life had shitted on her one time too many and she would take command of her circumstances from now on. However, she was not interested in the petty nickel & dime earnings that the little fake ass ballers in juvey bragged about. She wanted to be a "Big Baller" like Maurice Gentry, someone who commanded respect and instilled fear among the residents of the hood. Due to her past insecurities and issues brought about by both sexual abuse and poverty, she had made up within her young mind that she would neither be broke or abused again in life . . . ever. In the meantime she was a juvenile delinquent with a murder charge on her record. Yet she kept a shoebox filled with stacks of hundred dollar bills as well as hundreds of dollars worth of stolen jewelry. She dressed much better than the other youngsters, rocking the latest fashions of the day, attracting both envy and admiration among her peers.

Almost everyone, administrators included, wondered how Trina stayed so well off with no outside assistance and volun-

teering for few, if any, side jobs at the facility. Still Trina remained silent about her extracurricular activities and steadily
attended to her studies and mandatory chores, thus remaining
a model inmate to the administrators. Early one Saturday morning as the girls sat around lazily watching cable TV in the lounge,
several rough looking security guards burst into the lounge area
barking orders for the girls to get up against the wall. Several
of the more defiant ghetto girls refused to be physically searched
so they were forced up against the wall by the burly ill-tempered guards. Seconds later it seemed as though the lounge
area was crawling with rental cops. Realizing that her shit was
air tight, Trina calmly assumed the position up against the wall
as the guards went about the business of frisking the belliger-
ent teenagers, patting hips and asses, and going into pockets.
Some were mean, mugging and yelling, and occasionally slapped
cuffs on the more overly contentious teens. As she expected,
the security guards pretty much went easy on her.

"All y'all lil' smart ass bitches 'bout to get dealt wit, cept for
my girl Trina, you can go ahead and bounce baby girl."

"What the fuck you mean she can bounce? She ain't nobody,
she just as guilty as the rest o' these lil broads up in here," said
another heavyset ugly guard who opposed Lieutenant Cooper.

"Look here, Nigga!" snapped Cooper, "If I say let her go,
then that's what the fuck I mean. I'm yo boss, playa, you ain't
mine . . . got it? So do what the fuck I tell you to do!"

Trina quickly winked at the lieutenant and said "Thanks,
Boo," as she eased past the officer who had recently frisked
her. As she breezed passed Lieutenant Cooper, she swiftly
slipped a fifty-dollar bill into his pants pocket. Later that same
day Trina invited the security staff to her dorm room and
handed out hundred dollar bills and twenty dollar bags of
marijuana for all of them. The guards, accompanied by Trina's
personal favorite, Lt. Cooper, gladly accepted their "thank
you" gifts and departed.

It didn't take long for Trina to realize that establishing and maintaining a favorable relationship with the law, whoever they might be, would benefit her greatly. She also realized the advantage of possible blackmail from delivering unto the guards such perks as drugs and sexual favors. Trina was a master of blackmail as well as thievery. She seldom accepted favors from anyone, especially men, knowing full well that there would be a cost to pay down the road. Trina preferred to have others indebted to her rather than the other way around. Trina plopped backward upon her bunk realizing that the dramatic events of the early morning hours had drained her, bringing on a slight headache. She prepared herself to take a refreshing shower before retiring to bed.

The long weeks spent in isolation in the juvenile detention center were tedious, gloomy, and boring as hell, except for the occasional excitements such as a fist fight, joking around, or flirting with an especially fine guard or administrator. Lights were out at 11:00 pm every night and the mandatory chores were monotonous and drawn out. Most youngsters simply waited out the long, dreary months until they finally got their walking papers.

It was now May 28, 1985, and the day was gloomy and rainy. The old broken-down building had taken on water damage, flooding the hallways and several of the dorm rooms and forcing the girls, including Trina, to seek refuge upon the upper levels of the facility. The upper tiers of the Blue Plains Boys and Girls Village were littered with boxes of textbooks, cleaning supplies, and unused office furniture. Occasionally the juvenile inmates would congregate there to get high, have sex or sharpen homemade weapons.

This particular day the teens were allowed legal access to the upper room until the cleaning crew took care of the flooded rooms. Over four or five dozen chattering teenage girls huddled together in the dusty attic area conversing about everything from shoes and skirts to quickies behind the greenhouse out back. To most of the girls this dark area was well known for of its isolation and usefulness for secretive activities, yet to others it was a dark brooding place, which brought about a deep gnawing sense of uneasiness and dread.

To Trina this was a place of business—a setting for crap games, prostitution and scheming. It had served as sort of an office for Trina and her little hood rats. As Trina sat alone in a dark corner listening to her Walkman, Shonda beckoned her over to an even darker corner where they could talk privately. It was there that Shonda both made good on her promise to deliver the goods she had promised as well as hipping her to some good news from the streets.

"Trina, my peoples told me that yo sista, Rita, done got in good wit a rack o' them lawyers and shit down at the District Court House. Word on the street is you'se 'bout to get up outta here round about next month and shit. I ain't know yo folks had pull like that . . . you luckier than a muthafucka. I wish it was me 'bout to walk through them doors."

Trina smiled weakly but she never did let emotions get the best of her. She would have to see it in order to believe it. But sure enough by June 21, 1985, Katrina Ricks was released from the Blue Plains Boys and Girls Village after only three months, totally unheard of for a young offender with a murder charge.

Chapter 2

Out in the Streets

At first Trina was assigned to a youth halfway house for teen girls in Lanham, Maryland, but through her defense lawyers, she subsequently was placed into the custody of her older sister, Rita Ann Ricks, who worked as an 8th District Homicide Detective for the Washington DC Metropolitan Police. Detective Ricks would be responsible for her younger sibling until Trina's 18th birthday. It was a task which the detective knew would prove challenging at best.

Trina reached her mother's little modest green and white Barry Farms rowhouse around noon on a hot, sticky Saturday in June. She had been out drinking and partying with friends celebrating her freedom up until the wee hours of the morning. They would complete the celebration at a Marlow Heights IHOP before her rowdy friends dropped Trina off in front of her mother's house. Trina stumbled and staggered her way down the cracked, trash-littered sidewalk pass the scores of giggling neighborhood children who rode here and there alongside her on oversized bicycles and scooters.

Finally she entered the rusted metal gates of her mom's

home, and proceeded up the dandelion-covered walkway towards the screen-covered door beyond, which the sound of a
television could be heard coming from the living room, along
with a ringing phone. Before Trina could ring the doorbell,
the screen door swung opened wide to reveal Rita Ann Ricks
standing in the doorway. The DC Detective motioned for her
sister to step in as she promptly ended her brief phone conversation and sat upon the large leather couch in the living room.
Rita who was still dressed for duty in a dark gray pair of slacks,
black patent leather pumps and a simple off-white blouse. Her
thick wavy hair was pulled back in a neat bun which showed
the hard lines and sharp creases upon the face of a woman who
had seen and dealt with far too much death for her 28 years.

Rita Ann gently patted a spot on the couch so that Trina
might have a seat beside her sister. Trina noticed a police-
issued cartridge belt and gun holster that held a silver
nickel-plated .38 caliber revolver hanging loosely from an old
sturdy coatrack up in the corner of the room. Rita Ann took up
the remote lying upon the magazine-covered coffee table and
switched off the TV. She then immediately took out a pack of
Virginia Slims and patted out a cancer stick, which she lit and
dragged deep, exhaling a billowing stream of smoke that
added to the already grayish white haze within the room. She
had put on weight of late—maybe five or ten pounds, yet still
her body, like most of the Ricks women, remained curvy especially in the hips, ass and thighs. She kept a mostly serious
look on her heavily lined and angular face which had lost
much of its soft girlish good looks, a genetic gift of the Ricks
family. As children the two sisters had never been close, they
had little in common due to the huge generation gap between
them and for the most part Rita Ann was very rarely home.
She was a straight A Ballou High Student who also involved
herself in team sports and often busied herself with school
politics and part-time jobs. When the older of the two sisters

was home, little attention, if any, was paid to her younger sibling. Finally at age nineteen, Rita Ann moved out of Barry Farms Dwellings for good, settling in with her two best friends in Takoma Park, Maryland, during her senior year at Howard University.

"You absolutely reek of alcohol, Trina. Where in hell have you been and what have you been doing?" Rita demanded angrily.

"That ain't none o' you muhfuckin' bidness for real . . . shit, you ain't my mother, so don't even come at a bitch like that, Joe!" Trina snapped with equal fury.

Rita Ann took a final quick drag on what was left of the cigarette before grinding it out in the ash-filled porcelain tray on the table.

She rose to her feet and bent over so she was nose-to-nose with her little sister. "Look here, Ms. Missy! I don't know who the fuck you think you are or what it is you think the world owes you, but guess what? I'm not one of your little ghetto ass girlfriends. I'll smack the shit outta you and not give a second thought about it. I see kids your age lying dead out on the streets of this city every fuckin' week! But I'm not gonna let that happen to you. Who do you think took care of your little daughter when you were away at Blue Plains? Me and ma . . . . that's who! I know that you went through a lot and I really want to help you cuz I know that I never did bond with you like I should have back in the day, but that was then and this is now. And I'm not now or ever gonna let you carry me . . . ever! You got that?" Rita Ann was fuming.

Trina hung her head somewhat, absorbing everything her sister had said before raising her face towards Rita Ann. Clearing her throat softly she apologized, "Sorry Rita, I ain't mean to go on you like that. I just got a lot o' shit on my mind. That's all. Don't get in yo feelings over that dumb shit though, we straight, aiight?"

Rita Ann relaxed, backed away and sat back down beside Trina on the living room couch. "You and them lil' ole hood rats hanging out at the Black Hole again, huh?"

"A girl gotta get her groove and her flirt on, ya know? Plus all the ballin' ass niggas be out Georgia Avenue on the weekends, know what I'm sayin'?"

"Ballin' ass niggas? So, you're into drug dealers, is that what you're telling me?"

"You damn right!" Trina answered bluntly. "Niggas wanna fuck bitches plain and simple, so I ain't mad at the niggas 'bout that . . . I like to fuck too, just as much as a male does 'cept I ain't layin' up wit no man just to go home wit' a wet ass and no money. If a nigga wanna go up in this coochie, he betta come wit' some paper. And it betta be long . . . just like his dick!"

Trina snickered for a minute until she noticed that her sentiments hadn't come off to the more serious Rita Ann as funny.

"You're really playing around with fire. You know that? Out here prostituting yourself, hanging around with low life ghetto skanks not to mention rubbing elbows with dope pushing scum that I routinely put behind bars. Do you even think about what the hell you're doing to yourself, to your family or your community? I mean you're a mother now. You gotta do better than what you're doing with your life. If not for you do it for that gorgeous little angel of a daughter you have. Because I swear to you, if you don't slow your roll you're gonna end up as another sad statistic . . . either in prison or six feet under. I'm trying to tell you. Oh, yeah, and while we're on the subject, what's this I hear about you hanging out around Orleans Place and Simple City with that crack dealer Raymond Edwards? You intimate with him too? Cuz word on the street is you out here on the grind slangin' rocks . . . please tell me it ain't so."

Trina's attractive hazel-colored eyes narrowed into evil-looking slits as they zeroed straight into those of her sister's.

"I said, tell me that what I'm hearing out on the street is a fucking lie, Trina! Tell me that you're not selling drugs."

"Well, it seems like you know everything. I mean you the po-po, you got dry snitchers, and everything out here on these streets. You tell me. Am I?"

Rita Ann quickly took out yet another cigarette lighting up in order to calm her nerves. But even her trusty nicotine fix was failing to sedate her.

"I don't understand. I fuckin' bent over backward in order to pull strings to get your little black ass out of juvenile lock-up, you were looking at three years minimum not to mention an additional two in a women's prison after you turned twenty-one. A total of five years in the DC penal system, that's the type of life that you were about to have to deal with. Now as for Raymond Edwards, several close friends of mine in the department, 7th District to be exact, are now hot on the trail of that piece of shit. He has over thirteen murders to his name in Southeast alone, not to mention the rest of the city. Edwards is a cold-blooded killer who continues to poison this community with his crack cocaine. I've got two investigative leads on him right now as we speak. And so help me God, I'm not gonna stop until I land that animal in prison. So, please, please, I beg of you . . . don't make me put the powers of the DC Police Department against my own flesh and blood because Sweetheart trust and believe I take my gig seriously. Before I allow Raymond Edwards or others like him to shit on my city any longer, I'll see everybody associated with them locked up for a long time . . . even you!"

Trina ran her long, manicured fingers through her braided hair uncomfortably as she stood for the first time since she had come into the house. "Don't worry 'bout what the fuck I be out here doin'. You need to worry about them lil' stick 'em up kids runnin' around jackin' niggas for their whips and shit out at Congress Place, or them jokers pullin' drive-bys and wild'n out up on Trinidad Avenue. How 'bout that?"

Rita Ann once more stood up in her sister's face, fuming with anger. "If any of your hoodlum friends even think about coming around here and causing trouble for our mother behind some ill shit you've done out here, you're gonna be in some real deep shit!"

Trina nonchalantly moved towards the door and stopped just before she pushed opened the screen and turned to look back at Rita Ann. "You think I'm gonna sit here and let you talk shit to me just cuz you my sister and cuz you bailed me outta Blue Plains? Bitch, you got me fucked up for real. I don't give a fuck about all that preachin' shit you doin' cuz I'm gonna get mine regardless. Where were you when I was gettin' raped by Maynard every other night and shit, huh? Where were you at then? Where were you when I was pregnant with Porsche and when I had her after nine painful ass hours of labor, huh, Rita? Where in the fuck were you? . . . Yeah, I thought so . . . you ain't got shit to say 'bout that though, right? Oh, I forgot, you were too busy doin' you, huh? Didn't have time for lil' ole me. Whatever, Young! Don't ever preach to me 'bout what I need to be doing. You shoulda thought about that back them. I'll be back to see my mother and my child. Have a nice day . . . holla."

Little did Trina realize that it would be quite some time before she would see her older sister again. Rita Ann had recently received a letter from the FBI in response to the application she had sent off months earlier. Overjoyed by this latest spate of good fortune, Rita Ann would gladly leave D.C. for the intense, psychological and physical training that the Bureau, for decades, deemed necessary for its agents. Therefore, she would be far away for an extended period of time. Rita Ann had indeed known of her younger sibling's hellish plight though she did little to bring comfort or protection to Trina, due to her own desire to free herself from the misery of their dysfunctional home.

Trina sashayed outside into the humid evening air of the Farms, feeling a sense of smug satisfaction over the hard-hitting parting remarks she hoped would induce strong guilt in her sister. Trina easily flagged down one of her many homies driving past her mother's home and caught a ride over to Orleans Place. Trina decided that she'd have her own car and apartment by the beginning of July once she'd gotten her money right which she damn well intended on doing sooner rather than later. Trina returned to her mother's later on that night around 12:30 a.m. She greeted her joyous mother warmly and had a bite to eat before retiring to her old bedroom for the night. She cradled her chubby gurgling bundle of joy close to her bosom and wept softly. She had been away from her precious little daughter no more than three months, yet it seemed like an eternity.

Trina snuggled and played with little Porsche who was now nearly a year old. The adorable toddler cooed, giggled and made several determined but awkward attempts at walking across the carpet towards her mother, only to decide that crawling would serve her better. Trina could not believe how quickly her baby had grown in the three short months of her absence. Little Porsche Ricks resembled both her and her mother, thought Trina, which suited her fine, since it would've destroyed her to have Porsche even remotely look like her rapist father. After playing with Porsche for quite some time, Trina bathed, changed, and fed her daughter and tucked her into her crib to sleep. The calm, quiet of the Ricks' household was a strange but welcome change from the drunken, dope-fueled discord that Maynard brought to it when he was alive.

Being in her own bedroom again brought back immediate

bittersweet memories even though her mother had redecorated it wonderfully since the night of the murder. Still it was her own, not the rowdy raucous zoo that was the Boys and Girls Village from which she'd just come from . . . constant noise, fighting, cussing. She looked upwards toward Heaven, closed her eyes and smiled, appreciative of the fact that she was home at last. She undressed, showered and quickly climbed into the big comfortable sleigh bed her mother had prepared for her. Because she'd seen the headlights of her sister's unmarked squad car pulling up on the curb, Trina grumbled irritably to herself as she pulled the cool, cottony sheets over her naked body. She was still very upset with Rita Ann and didn't want to be awake while she was present in the house. Everything would be all right as long as Rita Ann left her alone was Trina's thought as she drifted off to sleep.

Her dreams were filled with sweet visions of the lovely Sophia Carlin. The surreal trappings of the dream world erotically filled Trina with lust as she felt the soft wet tongue of the long-legged beauty circling her erect clitoris tasting the moist, hot sweetness of her pink gap. Trina wrapped her dark, thick thighs around her teacher's head grinding her bushy mound rhythmically into Carlin's face covering her mouth, nose and chin with the dripping stickiness of her multiple orgasms. As she collapsed backwards upon the sweat-soaked pillow, Sophia Carlin looked up from between her legs and smiled devilishly, all the while licking Trina's trickling pussy juice from her sexy, full red lips, then slowly she faded like a mirage from sight. Trina stirred in her sleep, then awoke to the early morning sunrays entering through the rose-colored Venetian blinds just above Trina's bed. Trina arose to find a wide circular wet spot beneath her that caused her to laugh softly to herself. She had a serious lovejones for another female and she couldn't deny it, nor would she. She was determined to have Sophia Carlin for herself—it didn't matter if she wasn't into cheating nor did it matter to Trina that she was engaged to perhaps the most dangerous and feared criminal in the greater Washington, DC, area. She could not have cared less. She wanted what she wanted and she was determined to get it . . . no matter what the cost.

Chapter 3

What's Mine is Mine &
What's Yours is Mine

At approximately 5:30 p.m., Katrina Ricks approached the large iron gates of the Blue Plains Boys and Girls Village at 500 C Street, Southwest, DC. She was cool and calm behind the wheel of a big white 1985 Ford Crown Victoria. She felt the rush of pride and importance as the guards at the gate raced out of their booth to greet her with loving hugs and kisses and to admire the fresh Crown Vic with the dark tinted windows and fancy spoiler kit. After brief greetings were exchanged, Trina, waved her diamond clustered hand to the two officers and proceeded on through the open gates.

Trina had been drinking Strawberry Daiquiris with her friends earlier in the day so she felt somewhat tipsy and knew that she'd have to drive carefully so as not to bring any added trouble to herself. She was tempted to either steal or jack some unsuspecting fool for his ride, but abandoned that idea after one of her more mature-minded girlfriends offered her the keys to her brother's car. Trina gladly accepted her friend's favor for she couldn't risk another charge. Still she'd have to be careful. She had no license or registration plus the whip that she pushed had been used in God knows how many drive-bys, stick-ups, and other heinous crimes. Yet it was well worth the risk to drive away with Sophia Carlin riding shotgun beside her. Even if she didn't know it yet, she would be going out with Trina for the evening.

In the back pocket of her tight fitting black denims was a wad of bills totaling $655 all of what she'd brought with her from her burglary spree at Blue Plains. She also sported a few of the gold pieces she'd stolen as well, in order to accentuate her 'hood diva' look. Early on as she filled the tank on her way to see Sophia Carlin, Trina discovered a silver nickel-plated Ruger semi-automatic lying beside a similarly colored clip loaded with deadly hollow tip shells inside the Go-Go cassette-filled glove compartment. Though hesitant at first, Trina took the pistol into her hands, running her long fingers across the cold smooth finish of the muzzle and grip.

"Dude won't be needin' this for a minute," Trina said to herself as she pushed the loaded clip into the grip of the weapon, concealing it snuggly in the front of her jeans before pulling her shirt over the top of it. Thus she'd be ready for any type of drama should anything happen to pop off. She also knew the imminent danger of involving herself with the bun-bun of Maurice Gentry; she'd convinced herself that having protection was of prime importance.

After only five minutes in the parking lot, Trina looked over to see Sophia Carlin strolling with an armful of books and papers across the lot towards the girls' dormitory, sexy and luscious as always with an enormous Gucci purse swinging back and forth from her slender shoulder. Trina honked her horn twice and caught the young teacher's attention.

Ms. Carlin pranced over smiling broadly, "Oh, my God! Miss Ricks, look at you! I didn't recognize you at first. I thought you were one of the building contractors trying to be fresh or something. Anyway, how've you been?" Sophia Carlin exclaimed as she embraced her former student.

"Oh I'm aiight, I'm aiight, ya know . . . just handlin' my business, takin' care o' my lil' daughter and everything. Ya know, basically maintaining," Trina answered taking the books from Sophia's arms and placing them on top of the hood. "But enough 'bout me. I'm here to take you out this evening before you turn in for the night. You ain't gotta worry 'bout payin' for shit cuz I got that, and I ain't takin' no for an answer. So, whassup?"

"Well" Sophia said with a mock surprise, "it seems as though our little rendezvous was planned ahead of time without my knowledge or approval."

Trina's almond shaped, hazel eyes narrowed in anger and she pulled the older woman to her planting a passionate open-mouthed kiss upon Sophia's red-painted lips.

"Look, young, I'm tired of bullshittin'! I want you badder than a muhfucka! I ain't never felt like this 'bout nobody before, ever! I know I may be young and all but I know how I feel in my heart 'bout you and this ain't no bullshit teenage crush and shit. I love you, Sophia. I really, really do. I mean even if you don't feel the same way 'bout me as I do 'bout you, I'm saying at least give a bitch a chance to take you out and show you a good time. That's all, aiight?"

Taken aback but at the same time strangely aroused by the teen's aggressive display of affection, Sophia Carlin reluctantly agreed.

"Miss Ricks . . . um, I mean, Trina, I really don't know what to say. I had no idea that you felt that strongly about me. Hummm, I tell you what . . . it's 6:00 p.m. right now, and Maurice usually arrives to pick me up around 7:00 p.m. or so. I'll ring him up and tell him that I'll be going out after work with a few of my girlfriends for drinks. He'll buy that. Besides my sorority sisters will vouch for me. But wherever we go, it's gotta be a very discreet location, preferably outside of the city some place far away in either Maryland or Virginia. Because Maurice has eyes and ears everywhere in DC and if one of his snitches rats me out and he finds out that I've lied about my whereabouts . . ." she hesitated suddenly, looking over her shoulder and down at her wrist watch with a look of nervous tension. "Look, it's already way past time for me to grade these tests, clean up, prep for tomorrow and lock the door, so I gotta run. But I'd like for you to leave out and park about three and half blocks down the street at the corner of Village Lane and E Street. When I get finished up here I'll page you and then you can start driving back up the street towards the front gate. I'll meet you right out in front, all right? Because I don't trust these nosey ass folks I work with as far as I can throw them."

"Don't be fakin', Sophia. I ain't come all the way up this joint for nothing, Young. I'm trying to tell you."

"Come on, girl! I'd never do that. I'm truly a woman of my word. You'll see."

"Yeah, okay, I'm gonna be waiting for you too . . . don't lemme down. Holla."

Trina blew a kiss towards the blushing Sophia Carlin before reentering the Crown Vic and cruising through the gates and down the street blasting the latest Go-Go tunes as she left. Down at the corner of Village Lane and E Street, Southwest, she waited patiently tapping her long red-painted fingernails on the glossy black steering wheel, bobbing her head to the pulsating rhythm of the Congo drums coming from the speakers. As Trina became lost in the music of Air Raid, Little Benny and Rare Essence, her pager began buzzing loudly on her side. That caused Trina to squeal away form the curb in the direction of Blue Plains Boys and Girls Village. Once in the front of the gate, Sophia Carlin hurriedly hopped into the passenger's seat and slammed the door shut. Trina turned the music down and turned towards Sophia whispering the words,

"Thank you," all the while gazing affectionately into her eyes. "You're welcome," Sophia whispered back taking the opportunity to plant an amorous smooch on Trina's cheek that brought a sudden erotic feeling of lust to Trina. Sophia gently ran her hand along Trina's dimpled cheek and questioned her about the hardware that protruded from her jeans.

"Oh, don't worry 'bout this joint, Boo. I ain't gonna clap the joint unless some bammas jump out there."

They drove out towards White Flint Mall in Rockville, Maryland. Once there, they entered the Cheesecake Factory, a popular local eatery renown for its delicious assortment of cheesecakes as well as other succulent dishes. Seated in a dimly lit private corner of the restaurant, the women dined on a savory full course Italian meal washed down with a small bottle of Moet. After they finished eating dessert, Trina slid her chair over next to Sophia.

"How'd you manage to escape being carded? You're way too young to drink," Sophia asked, giggling.

"I may be young, but I damn sho' drink and I know how to get fake shit. I mean look at me. Does it look like a seventeen-year-old broad should be havin' titties, hips, and ass like I got? I'm thicker than half o' these grown ass women out here. Ain't nobody gonna question me 'bout no age for real."

Sophia threw her head back laughing heartily. "Well, I can't argue with you about that! You sure do have a lot of junk in your trunk."

"How was dinner, Boo?" asked Trina, downing her third glass of champagne.

"I loved every single minute of it. You really have made my night special. Thank you so much, Trina."

By the time Trina pulled up at her Cleveland Park condo, it was about 2:45 a.m. The two women locked lips with each other moaning and groaning with sexual hunger as they tore at each other's clothing. Soon their voluptuous nude bodies intertwined in a steamy tango of carnal fire. Forty-five minutes and several orgasms later, Sophia Carlin kissed Trina good night and stepped out of the car, looking messy and disheveled, but brightly smiling all the same.

"My God, I can't believe that I actually did that! But I'm sure glad that I did because, damn was it good!" Sophia said winking an eye as she staggered into her upscale Cleveland Park condo. It would be one of several trysts for the two, and Trina inside herself knew that she had Ms. Carlin "sprung".

Trina got home around 4 a.m. and woke up around 2 p.m. later that Saturday afternoon. She ate a light meal, showered, dressed and left out, arriving in downtown Northwest around 5:15 p.m. She needed to do something that would loosen her up. So a fresh hairdo, manicure, pedicure and relaxing Shiatsu massage at a local day spa made her feel much more refreshed and a little less hung over. There was a light, giddy feeling of euphoria and warmth flowing throughout her being. It was subtle but strong, delicate but yet still overwhelming. At long last she had discovered true love and what it felt like to be head over heels in love. She finally had landed someone that she wanted. She no longer needed to be subjected to the unwanted attentions of those who'd seek to prey on her. She felt powerful and proud of herself for taking control of her life's direction. She understood the difficulties that she would have to deal with as an openly bi-sexual young woman, but she was in love and could care less about the challenges ahead.

Once she arrived back home, Trina prepared an evening feeding for little Porsche who bounced up and down giggling and gurgling within her sturdy high chair, banging her little rubber handled utensils on the tray playfully. Trina joined her toddler with a meal of her own, taking quick bites of left over pizza between spoon-feeding Porsche.

"Trina don't eat all of that pizza, girl. I ain't had ne'er bite last night. So just put the rest o' that pizza back up in the 'fidgerator," came the high-pitched, commanding voice of Lucinda Ricks as she strolled down the stairs. Trina shook her head, dejectedly placing the remaining pizza back into the fridge as she returned to feeding Porsche.

Lucinda Ricks was a caramel-complexioned middle-aged woman with a freckled moon-pie face, which showed deep dimples whenever she cracked a smile. She was bottom heavy with wide hips and an overtly plump behind. She, like her daughters, still maintained an undeniable amount of sex appeal for a woman of fifty-one. So much so that she was hit on often by men half her age. Her raven black wavy hair was always done up in an elaborate French roll or up-do. She adored pearls and the luminous, opaque orbs often adorned her neck, wrists and earlobes whenever she stepped out on the town. Her wardrobe was vast and very chic. She usually wore the best at home as well as in public. An intelligent, personable and honest woman, Lucinda Ricks was well liked at work, in her neighborhood and at her church. She only wished that her youngest child could stay out of trouble, even though the reason for her rebellion was well understood by Lucinda, who felt a deep sense of guilt for not preventing the long-standing abuse.

"Where in the hell were you at last night that made you walk up in this house something after four in the morning?" Lucinda inquired of her daughter with arms crossed and toe tapping.

"I was just hangin' out with some o' my girls clubbin' and carryin' on, that's all," Trina answered somewhat confidently.

"I don't give a damn what the hell ya'll was doing. Don't bring your ass up in my house again at that time a morning 'cause I don't know what kind of home training them little skeezers you call friends got, but up in here, you are going to respect me. You understand?" She demanded angrily.

"Aiight, aiight, Ma, my bad, my bad. You got it! I ain't gonna carry you like that no more," Trina responded.

She then finished feeding Porsche before taking the chubby youngster into her loving arms, rocking her to sleep. Once Porsche fell asleep, Trina hopped into the whip and dipped out, heading toward Valley Green projects, blasting a Little Benny Go-Go cassette loudly from the car speakers as she sped away from Barry Farms, distancing herself from her mother's short, but bitter tongue lashing.

Day after day, week after agonizing week, Trina's mother and her Uncle Otis stayed on top of her, complaining about this and bitching about that, working her nerves to no end. To Trina it seemed as though their griping and nagging would last an eternity and she yearned for the day that she'd have enough money to move out. It never occurred to her that all of her mother's and uncle's fussing was simply a strong dose of tough love and nothing more. At that particular time in Trina's young life, she didn't care about following certain rules and regulations, because the bitterness that still rested in her heart and mind prompted her to set her own rules for her life.

While she loved her mother and maternal uncle, she still blamed both of them as well as society as a whole for not coming to her assistance during her darkest hours of pain and sorrow. Also, Trina had witnessed grown women in the hood being beaten and abused by their so-called husbands and boyfriends all too often during her seventeen years; the mere thought of a man raising his hand to her engendered a fury that was uncontrollable and deep seated. Trina didn't intend to be a victim any longer, not for anyone. She would call the shots from now on and no one would stop her. Not even her own peeps. The go-hard, thuggish nature of life in Southeast DC's notorious Barry Farms Dwellings had strengthened her resolve and developed within her the necessary skills to handle her business out on the mean streets of inner city Washington.

Her growing love for Sophia had increased her bold and defiant attitude.

While she waited in line at a McDonald's drive-thru, she was paged three times in fifteen minutes—547-7676 were the seven digits that kept showing up on the narrow glass screen on the pager followed by the emergency code 9-1-1. Trina hurriedly picked up her order and tossed it down unto the passenger's seat beside her, fishtailing the big, white Ford out of the McDonald's parking lot and across the street to a gas station near Alabama Avenue where she phoned Sophia from a payphone.

"Hey, boo, what up whitcha?"

"Trina, I . . . I'm sorry that I blew up your pager . . . but I just had to talk to someone because I'm soooo scared right now, so very scared, baby. Oh, God, help me!" she said through quivering lips. She sounded absolutely terrified.

"Hold up, hold up, young! What the fuck is really goin' on? Somebody fuck with you? Huh? Tell me, Sophia! What happened?"

"Maurice hurt me, Trina! . . . He hit me in the face and then . . . then he fucking pushed me backwards, down the steps!"

"What!" Trina yelled angrily into the rickety pay phone. "You ain't goin' back home tonight. I'm gonna put you up in a nice hotel out in Maryland for as long as needed and as for Lil' Mo's bitch ass, if he even try to call you again, I'm air'n his ass out off the break. No bullshit, young, cuz I ain't trippin' off him nor his weak ass mob. Cuz for real, for real if he tryin' to go like he thorough and shit, I'll holla at a couple o' young'uns from out the Farms and punish all o' them bammas. Watch!"

Soon after, Trina made reservations for Sophia to spend the night at a Silver Spring area Marriott. She spent the rest of the day with several of her gangsta friends back in Barry Farms, cooking up the coke that Shonda had given to her back at Blue Plains. It wasn't a whole lot of powder, but it would serve

Trina well for now. It was enough to make a small profit, flip that and reinvest it in an even larger amount of coke—maybe even a kilo or two next time. So for about eight or nine hours Trina and six of her neighborhood friends worked tirelessly, cooking and bagging the small crack rocks and bagging the quarter ounce of weed that she had stashed away while at the detention center. Trina relaxed against a far wall, with apple martini in hand, watching proudly as her young childhood pals meticulously labored, preparing her narcotic wares for street sale, before she headed out to something to eat for her beloved Sophia.

While picking out choice selections of steamed crabs for her and Sophia to enjoy, Trina was among other customers down at the Wharf when she looked back over her shoulder in anger as a well-groomed, attractive, fair-skinned young man seemingly not much older than herself bumped into her rudely, nearly toppling her over a garbage can that stood nearby.

"What the fuck is your problem, Slim?" Trina snarled angrily.

"Your name Trina ain't it, young?"

"Yeah, my name's Trina. Who the fuck are you?"

"Oh, don't worry 'bout who I am, Cutie. You just bettah slow yo roll wit all o' that dyke-type bullshit, 'specially with Sophia. Cuz Lil' Mo' don't play that shit and he wants yo lil' young ass to stop fuckin' round wit his girl, aiight!"

"O' that nigga Mo', huh? Shiiit! I ain't scared o' no muh-fuckin' body, nigga! Cuz, yo' man Lil' Mo', ain't nothin' but a cold bitch for real, hittin' on females and shit. Tell Lil' Mo' I said kiss my natural black ass. How 'bout that?"

"Baby Girl, don't let yo mouf get ya fucked up, aiight? Cuz, you'se a lil' fine ass, phat to death honey. Know what I'm sayin'? But Lil' Mo' ain't to be fucked wit. I'm tryin' to tell you some good shit."

"Nigga, ain't nobody tryin' to hear all o' that dumb shit you talkin'. Either y'all bammas gonna come wit it or shut the fuck up, for real! Cuz, you bettah believe if you come for me, you bettah come correct! Cuz me and my folks bringin' that drama off the break. So run tell that!"

Trina stood face to face with the older teen, mean-mugging him all the while as a growing crowd of onlookers stood in the distance whispering and pointing toward them. The boy clenched his fist tight and made a slight start as though he was going to rush her, but he quickly abandoned that idea when Trina lifted up her T-shirt, revealing the heavy grip of the Ruger handgun. The teen gangsta nodded his head and smiled as he slowly backed away.

"Aiight, boo, you got this one, but you'd bettah watch ya back. I know that much. Watch ya muthafuckin' back, girl!"

Trina simply sneered at the young man with her hands boldly on her wide hips, showing attitude until he melted into the masses of people walking back and forth along the busy pathways of the Wharf.

It was truly unbelievable how a little bit of money, a fresh ride and a pistol had given her so much confidence and heart. Later on, after dark, she talked one of the neighborhood Barry Farms' hustlers she had known from childhood, into acting as a bodyguard for her. The youngster, Paul "Pooh" Greene III, was a seventeen-year-old high school drop out and neighborhood thug renowned for his brutal mean streak and taste for gun play. During the hazy, summer night, she approached the feared teenaged thug as he sat upon a stoop shooting dice, with several other young hooligans.

"Pooh let me holla at you, young," Trina exclaimed, after greeting the blunt-smoking boys with dap and small talk. Pooh rose from the liquor bottle-covered stoop and followed his old friend a few feet away from his gambling buddies.

"What up witcha?" he asked, exhaling a cloud of pungent smoke into the sweltering night.

"I need for you to watch my back, cuz Lil' Mo and dem on some dumb shit. Comin' at a bitch like they wanna bring some drama, but they got the wrong one, cuz I ain't gonna get caught slippin'. Feel me? I'll pay you 500 a week, all you gotta do is shadow me when I go on my runs, aiight?"

Pooh agreed eagerly as he accepted a thick, rubber band en-circled wad of cash. So whenever she stepped out on the town to party or to handle drug transactions involving bulk ship-ments in other wards of the city, Trina had other means of protection.

Sophia was visibly nervous and jumpy when she emerged from the A2 bus on Good Hope Road at the old Curtis Broth-ers' Furniture Store known for the Big Chair landmark, look-ing around and over her shoulder several times before climbing into the peach-scented interior of the Crown Victo-ria next to Trina.

"Come on, Trina, dear, let's get the hell outta here because I'm like really fuckin' scared right now. You know what I mean?" Sophia said, snapping on her seatbelt and pushing down the door lock. They drove off in silence. Then looking behind her, Sophia gasped loudly as she saw a rust-colored Jeep Cherokee that had been trailing them for the past four traffic lights.

"Trina! Trina! That jeep has been following us. Oh, my God! It ain't nobody but Maurice or one of his boys. Shit! What are we gonna do?"

"C'mon, Sweetie, calm ya nerves. That ain't no Maurice. That's my nigga, Pooh, from round the way. He and his boys got our backs just in case some shit jump off. That's all."

"Whew! Thank, God! Because before I left my place tonight the phone was ringing while I was still in the bathtub, so I waited for the answering machine to pick up the message, right? And lo' and behold, guess who it was? Yep, you guessed right if you said Maurice. Don't you know that Maurice actually threatened my life over the answering machine? He said that if he wanted a dyke bitch, he'd get one, and a whole lot of mean and nasty things about your sister and you. He finished his little tirade by telling me that if he or anyone he knows catches us out in public again that there will be two less pussy-eating bitches in the world. You can count on that shit. That's what Maurice said on my phone tonight. You know a part of me wants to take that recording to the Metropolitan police, but hell, I know as well as anyone else does I'd be signing my own death warrant if I did that . . . so, that's that. I guess I'm fucked for good now—long, hard, and deep. Shit!"

"Girl, don't even sweat that bamma shit, he had one o' his lil' runners come at me with the same type o' shit. So I told the bamma to tell Lil' Mo' to kiss my ass cuz ya see he ain't used to niggas with heart. Know what I'm sayin'? He used to soft ass bammas round his way that be lettin' him punk their asses. He gets none o' that soft shit over here, baby. So you ain't gotta worry 'bout him aiight, Boo?"

Sophia looked over at Trina, smiled weakly and leaned her head gently upon Trina's shoulder and wept.

Once again they dined at the Cheesecake Factory. Afterwards they took in a tour of White Flint Mall's various stores that soon turned into a spur of the moment shopping spree in which Sophia was lavished with a number of expensive gifts just because. Two and half hours later the two women arrived at Sophia's Cleveland Park condo in order to pick up a few of Sophia's belongings before heading back towards Silver Spring for the night. When Sophia flicked on the living room lights, Lil' Mo' Gentry sat nonchalantly smoking a Black & Mild cigar with his legs crossed leaning back on the long leather couch. His dark, bearded face seemed oily and sinister in the dim yellowish lighting of the table lamps. He removed a dark-tinted pair of Gazelle glasses from his eyes that narrowed into evil red slits as he stared with malice upon the two young women standing in the doorway. He blew a series of thick smoke rings into the air before leaning forward and smashing the butt of the Black & Mild into the fabric of the lovely couch.

Leaning forward, he placed a large, powerful forty-five automatic on top of the black lacquer coffee table. Trina's heart felt as thought I would burst through her chest, it was beating so rapidly. She was in a state of shock because she knew that eventually she and Lil' Mo' would cross each other's paths, but this early? She was totally caught off guard and at a loss as to what to do next.

"Maurice! Oh, my God, Baby, please don't hurt us! We didn't . . ."

"Bitch shut the fuck up!" Lil' Mo' barked at Sophia as he slammed a heavy fist hard on the table top. "Ya'll lil' dyke bitches thought I was bullshittin', huh? Stupid bitches! I told ya'll to cut this dumb shit out didn't I? Ya'll muhfuckas got me fucked up if you think you gonna carry me and live to laugh about it!"

"Nigga, you's a bitch! You ain't shit but a punk ass woman beater and shit talker. All o' them bammas who hustle for you out Eastover might be scared o' your dumb ass, but I ain't," snapped Trina suddenly regaining her courage and composure.

"What? What the fuck you say bitch?" yelled Lil' Mo' grasping the forty-five and attempting to rise up from the couch.

Trina, reacted instantly, quickly drawing her trusty Ruger, now equipped with an elongated silencer attached to its deadly muzzle. There was a series of muffled rapid fire gunshots fired at Lil' Mo' from point blank range. Sophia screamed and turned her head away from the horror that unfolded before her. Lil' Mo' Gentry's body did a macabre dance of death as multiple hollow tip shells ripped through his thick-bodied

frame before finally falling lifeless to the parquet wood floor
of the living room.

With immediate follow through and quick thinking, Trina
contacted her runners back in their Barry Farms hood and directed them to Sophia's southwest condo. Pooh had not followed Trina this time, 'cause he had romantic plans in the
works as well—he got there thirty minutes later. Pooh showed
up with five hard looking youths from the "Farms" pushing
two separate vehicles.

Once at Sophia's, the darkly dressed teens shuffled up the
winding stairs of the condo like some menacing procession of
death angels, the muffled cadence of their heavy foot falls
eerily reminiscent of a funeral march. The earlier loud voices
and Sophia's screams had not drawn the attention of the
neighbors; the sight of a group of strange looking black youths
bearing an unusual load, leaving a familiar-looking trail of red
did, and as a result 9-1-1 was dialed by several of the residents.
Once inside the Condo the young thugs quickly went to work
prepping the body of Maurice Gentry for disposal. Strong
fingers applied thick black electrical tape around the limbs
and torso of Gentry's corpse. It was then wrapped up in two
large throw rugs and taken downstairs with great difficulty
due to his heavy build. From there the dead drug lord was
stuffed into the trunk of a '78 Ford Impala and whisked away
to a watery grave in a distant Charles County, Maryland bog
creek.

Pooh and his girlfriend, Nina, stayed behind to help Trina
and the still very shaken Sophia Carlin clean up the bloody
mess that was left behind. Although Sophia was a nervous
wreck after the shooting, Trina knew that by the time the
frightened neighbors could blab their mouths to the cops,
they'd be long gone. She'd worry about details later. She knew
that the cops would come calling soon enough, but they had
no evidence whatsoever. Everything was cleaned up, spic and

span. Even the stylish Bentley owned by the late drug lord was driven away by one of Pooh's crew who excelled at the art of hotwiring. Besides, the neighbors, mostly trendy college yuppies, had not gotten a description of the culprits because fear kept them all holed up in their apartments.

Chapter 4

It's Not a Game

Maurice Lil' Mo' Gentry's disappearance caused major ripples throughout both the local Washington news media as well as its criminal under world. With Gentry dead numerous drug-dealing crews began encroaching on his once solidly guarded drug turf. Soon the city's homicide rate began climbing higher. Nightly shootouts among rival dealers became common, and neighborhoods such as Barry Farms, Sur-Sum Corda, and Trinidad Avenue became notorious killing fields that caused even the most courageous beat cops to avoid them at all costs. Lil' Mo' Gentry had dominated Washington's drug trade for years and now with his strange and sudden disappearance and presumed death, many dealers were left wondering what to do next.

The following week Trina awoke bright and early feeling a bit nervous and sold the hot Ruger to an old guy from McLean, Virginia, for one hundred and fifty dollars. Her troubles were over. It was now another person's problem. She showered, dressed and drove out to Clifton Terrace in order to buy a quarter pound of marijuana and two guns from the feared arms dealer Horatio "Creepy" Fisher. A tall, lean, flashy dressing, thirty-five-year-old ex-con, Creepy had a flourishing business in illegal firearms and narcotics going on in his Clifton Terrace neighborhood and had engaged in turf wars with Lil' Mo' Gentry's crews on several occasions. When Trina had finished paying for the weed and weapons, she asked a special favor of her distributor.

"Creepy, baby, I gotta ask ya to hook a sista up with a big favor, aiight?"

"Aiight then speak on it, baby. That's the only way I'll know what steps to take next."

"You heard 'bout what happened to Lil' Mo'?"

"Yeah, I heard some bammas ran up on his bitch ass and ain't nobody seen 'im since. Why you ask?" Creepy asked curiously, swigging back on a forty ounce malt.

"Cause I'm the one who put them hot balls up in that nigga, and I know your sista, Karen, is one o' the best muhfuckin' lawyers in DC. I know cause she go to the same hairdresser as me. So if the police try comin' at me I'm gonna need some back up, aiight?"

"For real? Naw, girl! You bullshittin! You killed Lil' Mo'? That shit's hard to believe . . . a lil' baby like you? Out here shootin' ballahs like Lil' Mo'? Damn! That's some shit right there for ya ass, Young. Congratulations! Ya done me a muh-fuckin' favor, pretty girl."

"Aiight then, like I was sayin', I'm gonna need your sista to have my back in court if I happen to catch a charge behind this shit, hear, me?"

"Oh fuck yeah! Matter o' fact I'll foot the muhfuckin' court costs for you. That bitch ass Mo' killed my baby brother back in '81 and he shot my man Tony last year . . . he's still para-lyzed from the waist down from that drive-by. So as you can see, I hated that black, greasy, fat, nasty muhfucker more than anything and I stayed up many a night scheming on how to bust his head, Young. So you know I got nothin' but love for anybody who put that bamma to rest."

"Aiight, bet. I'll holla at you later, Creepy."

Trina left Clifton Terrace with her illicit products and the confidence of knowing that her connect would have her best interest in mind from now on. An hour later Trina drove across town into Silver Spring to visit Sophia at the Marriott Court-yards Hotel. She had seemed to have gotten herself together somewhat but still there seemed to be an overwhelming aura of fear and nervousness that Trina could not help but detect. She was not at all pleased by Sophia's extremely skittish behavior because her frayed nerves could cost them dearly if she were to be questioned by the cops.

"Trina, you've committed a murder! And now you've gotten me caught up in the middle of this garbage. What are we going to do now?" Sophia wailed.

"First of all, you need to shut the fuck up with all o' that dumb shit you talkin'," Trina snapped. "You were the one tellin' me 'bout how the nigga was whippin' your ass and now you actin' all brand new. Don't play me for no fool, Sophia, cause I ain't goin' back to juvie and leavin' my daughter again for no muhfuckin' body. Please believe that! All you gotta do is just sit back, calm your nerves, keep ya mouth shut, and lemme handle things from now on, aiight?"

Around noon, Trina went into the huge walk-in closet she shared with Sophia, and withdrew a large cumbersome duffle bag, filled with stacks of hundreds and fifty dollar bills. "Boo, I realize that you jive like blown after all of this bullshit, but its gonna be aiight, you'll see. But I do need for you to bring your fine ass over here and help me count this scrilla . . . please?" Trina asked, pouting playfully.

Sophia sighed as she looked away from the widescreen television above the living room coffee table, on the broad Maplewood lined wall. "Well that depends . . . I do need a couple of new outfits from the Versace outfitters in downtown Miami. Hint, hint." She winked mischievously.

Trina huffed, "Girl you ain't nothing but a pimp? But I love you though. C'mon over here, pretty girl. You know you can have anything you want from me . . . almost," Trina said, as she and her gal pal embraced warmly before getting down to the business of counting the large amount of cash Trina had laid out on the living room carpet.

After a tedious forty-five minutes of counting and recounting, Trina was satisfied with the final tally of the cash and left Sophia's at 1:15 p.m. She drove over to the Farms to pick up some drug money from a few of her young runners. Afterwards, she played a few games of spades with Pooh and a few other Barry Farms Hustlers, collected her winnings and drove away.

Within a three-month span, seventeen-year-old Katrina Ricks had two first degree murders to her name, had organized a small drug ring, involved herself in a full-fledged lesbian relationship and had a dangerous gun smuggler as an ally. Trina knew that in time she'd have to land an apartment of her own since she was involved in so many illegal activities. She didn't want to bring unwanted attention from cops or dope peddlers to her family. Trina was dealing with some dangerous individuals and precarious situations. Trina and Sophia hooked up at least nine times during that time period, spending a great deal of time in Montgomery County, which they enjoyed so much that the lovers agreed to live there one day.

One evening, Trina delivered a briefcase of $3,000 to Creepy Fisher for a shipment of crack cocaine out in Clinton Terrace. Afterwards, she was about to start for Silver Spring when a DC police cruiser pulled up in front of the dope spot creating a chaotic rush for cover from the various dealers and fiends.

"Hey, you! Young lady," barked a heavy voice, "Get your ass over here, now!"

She cursed bitterly under her breath, praying that the policeman would not search her vehicle. Instantly Trina was searched as well as her car where a quarter ounce of marijuana was discovered along with major cocaine residue visible in the ash tray. Trina was told then and there that she was being arrested for illegal possession of narcotics.

"Let's go!" yelled the powerfully built officer. He rudely slammed Trina up against the squad car where she was quickly and roughly handcuffed and driven to the nearest police precinct where she was hastily processed and taken to a basement level interrogation room to be questioned.

"So, Miss Ricks, I guess you know something about a shooting out at the Juniper Condos last night, don't you?" inquired a swarthy Filipino looking detective.

"Nope, I dunno nothin' 'bout no shootin' at no condos," Trina retorted sharply. "I don't even know nobody in Southwest." A second detective leaning against the drab, gray wall chuckled sarcastically while lighting up a cigarette.

"Look, home girl, I've checked your record and you don't want to end up back in juvenile hall because this time you'll be taking a much longer vacation. You'll be eighteen on October 15th. So if I were you, I'd cooperate because spending anywhere from fifteen to twenty years in a hardcore women's prison for murder would really suck, don't you think? "

"Y'all muhfackas is lunchin' like shit, Joe. What kinda shit y'all smokin'? Please let a sista know so I can get some too!"

The Filipino detective pulled up a chair and seated himself right next to Trina staring her directly in the eyes. "You wanna fuckin' play games with me, sweetie? Bad idea, real, real fuckin' bad idea. There were witnesses who heard the gunshots and described a young black female fitting your description. So either you come clean about your relationship with Maurice Gentry and your whereabouts last night or else things are gonna get real ugly real fast for you, got it?"

"No, I don't got it cause you don't get it. I don't know shit 'bout no shootin' I don't even know the bamma you speakin' on for real. I can't give you no information I ain't got. Know what I'm sayin'?" retorted Trina seeming calm, bored even except for an occasional rolling of the eyes.

"You do understand that you're walking on thin ice, don't you?"

"Oh, I'm aiight. I'm gonna be fine cause y'all ain't got shit on me and you know it!"

"Where were you on the night of the murder between the hours of 11:30 pm and 4:00 am in the morning?"

"I dunno. Probably gettin' me some dick. What was you doin'?"

"Listen, you fucking obnoxious little bitch! You're pushing it!"

"Your mama's a bitch! Lemme up out this raggedy muthafucka. I got a baby at home I gotta get to!"

"Oh, really? Okay, mommy dearest, you can go as soon as you tell me where'd you get this?" the detective who smoked the cigarette snapped, slamming down the Ruger Trina had used to kill Lil' Mo', hard upon the metal table top the sound echoed loudly throughout the small, damp room.

Trina's eyes went wide with dismay as she viewed the familiar weapon that she'd handled so often. The teenager fought to restrain the mounting panic which threatened to overwhelm her with hopelessness.

"That shit ain't mines. I don't own no gun. Y'all got me fucked up. I ain't no gangsta. Shit, I ain't even s'pose to be here! Y'all wastin' your time talkin' to a seventeen-year-old girl. I told you I gotta get home to my daughter, damn!"

Trina may have acted hard, but in reality she was terrified. Her freedom would depend on her resilience in the face of this major challenge and she continued to frustrate even the best efforts of the interrogators to break her down.

"I ain't never seen that gun before in my life. Can I please go home now?" Trina repeated. The interrogator nearest to her roughly grasped her cheeks with his heavy hand, squeezing her face so hard it caused her lips to pucker.

"You'd fuckin' better talk now or so help me God, I'll fuckin' make sure you end up behind bars with a cellmate named Big Bertha!"

"Get your fuckin' hands off me muhfucka! I know my rights! You can't fuckin' touch me or none o' that dumb shit y'all doin for real! First of all I'm underage and a female. Y'all muhfuckas two grown ass men with guns and shit on, ain't you s'pose to have a female cop down here with y'all? Y'all could be doin' anything to me down here in this basement and shit. Matter o' fact, if you touch me again, I'm gonna say y'all two was feelin' me up. Watch! My sister, Rita Ann, is a detective just like y'all two. I know a lil' somethin', somethin' 'bout how the police s'pose to run shit. Plus I got peoples who work as lawyers. So if you don't slow ya roll, I'll sue the fuck outta you for police brutality. How 'bout that?"

The detective who smoked shook his head in frustration as he slowly paced back and forth.

"You have some unbelievably big balls for a seventeen-year-old lil' shit. You know that don't you? I heard through the grape-vine that you've been having an ongoing lesbian relationship with Maurice Gentry's fiancée. Is that true?"

Trina looked surprised. "What? Who told you that?"

"Listen, we frankly don't give a flying fuck what your partic-ular sexual orientation is . . . at seventeen you wouldn't know your asshole from a hole in the ground. But we do know that everybody and their mother has seen you hanging out with your old algebra teacher, Sophia Carlin. You know that super sexy Redskin's Cheerleader? God, now she's hot, I've got the Redskinette swimsuit issue. I'd fuck her any day of the week myself. Anyway tell me, I mean tell us more."

"I don't know no Redskin's Cheerleader and I don't fuck with bitches, so tell ya lil' snitches to get their information straight, aiight? Do that for me?"

"People, oh excuse me, I mean scum from several of your east of the river haunts have told us different; according to the dope pushers and crack heads in those areas you and sexy little Ms. Carlin have been quite an item. It's pretty funny that everybody has seen you two out and about, yet you don't seem to know who she is. Imagine that . . . now Gentry's missing. Everybody also knows that Lil' Mo', that crack dealing scumbag, was not too happy about you and his fiancée's little lesbo fling, hmmm. When you put two and two together . . . looks like you know a whole helluva lot more than what you're telling us."

"Well, like I said earlier you ain't got shit on me. You don't know me and none o' your hatin' ass dry snitches know me either. I know a whole rack o' people, male and female, don't nobody know nothing 'bout my sex life cause I don't go around telling people my fuckin' business. Shit, Lil' Mo' was a big ballah making long dollars off crack and killing bammas for a while. You and I both know that he had a whole rack o' jokahs want'n to peel his cap back and you fuckin' with lil' ole me? Fuck that shit! I ain't answering or even sayin' shit else until I speak with a lawyer."

"Well, you've got a point there, Miss Ricks," agreed the detective who paced the floor.

Suddenly, there was a loud buzz at the door and when the detective opened it, a petite smartly dressed woman barely five feet tall came through the heavy metal door, followed by two beefy uniformed cops who stood against the wall with their massive arms folded across their broad chests.

Immediately, the feisty little lady slammed a briefcase that seemed nearly as large as she upon the metal tabletop and snatched some paperwork from the inside.

"Excuse me gentlemen, but I am here to demand the release of my client, Miss Katrina Ricks. I am attorney Karen Fisher, and I have here with me an official writ of habeas corpus for Miss Ricks' release."

She flashed a large beige colored document with a shiny court seal and notarized imprint upon it before the astonished eyes of the detectives. The girl had to have had big time juice out on the streets to have a lawyer come so soon to her aid with a writ, they surmised. As the detectives reluctantly released Trina, honoring the statutes of the writ, they both cursed the fact that although they knew that the teenage girl they were releasing onto the streets of DC was somehow involved in the disappearance of the city's most feared criminal, they had absolutely no concrete evidence, nothing other than hearsay, to charge and book her with. And it did not sit well with them at all.

"Aiight y'all, now you can get back to doin' some real police shit, like hangin' out at Dunkin Donuts or some shit like that . . . smooches!" Trina said sarcastically, blowing a kiss toward the highly upset detectives, swinging her luscious behind seductively as she exited behind attorney Fisher.

Trina had mad respect for Karen Fisher, especially when she learned that all charges were dropped because the arresting officers failed to read her her Miranda rights.

Chapter 5
On The Come-Up

Throughout the remainder of 1985 and on into the first few months of 1986, Trina felt tremendous joy over having landed a permanent partnership with Horatio "Creepy" Fisher and his violent Clifton Terrace mob. At first the drug runners working for Creepy were somewhat skeptical of allowing a teenage girl into the fold. They doubted that a female would have the nerve, know-how, or grimy behavior to be successful in the dope game. However, she proved them wrong through her razor sharp street smarts, iron will, and ride-or-die attitude. In time, news spread that it was she who had offed Lil' Mo' Gentry and her growing street crew was finally solidified amongst the thugged out members of the Clifton Terrace mob. Trina was satisfied that she was finally accepted by the tough talking ex-cons who had originally shown her either indifference or unwanted sexual attention. She had over time, via the hard knock life of the hustler, earned their devotion and respect. Although Trina herself very rarely mentioned Lil' Mo' Gentry or the fateful night on which she murdered him, the street corners and projects of DC were abuzz with tales of Lil' Mo's killing and Trina's involvement therein. This continual gossip kept Trina on high alert, edgy, and at times very irritable from sleepless nights spent worrying about repercussions. She still had her neighborhood homie "Pooh" and his crew from her native Barry Farms shadowing her on pick-ups and deliveries for Creepy.

Unbeknownst to the Clifton Terrace Mob or even Creepy Fisher himself, Trina excelled at working out big money drug deals with major dealers from Richmond, Baltimore and Philadelphia and soon became Creepy Fisher's top earner. Creepy Fisher, like most men who laid eyes on the curvy teenager was strongly attracted to Trina and within no time the two began a steamy sexual relationship with Trina enjoying all the special perks that came with being a drug lord's girl. Trina maintained that her only reason for intimacy with the opposite sex was strictly for financial or other types of personal gain and nothing more. And if a guy happened to show interest in her sexually, he had better be prepared to pay handsomely for her time and carnal favors. Time and time again she'd spurn the advances of several younger members of the Clifton Terrace Mob not because they were unattractive or lacked the game needed to woo her, but because they lacked adequate funds to pique her interest. She stood fast to her motto: "I don't fuck niggas with short money."

Trina had no desire to follow any sort of moral ethics or decency code when it came to making a dollar. She knew that her young nubile physique turned heads wherever she went and she used her powerful sexuality to extract huge sums of cash from those lustful men who were wealthy enough to pay for it. On the darker side, the sexy, deep chocolate femme fatale was not above brandishing a semi-automatic and copping a few hundred dollars by way of early morning armed robberies or late night carjackings. Every now and then an unfortunate corner liquor store or 7-11 would fall prey to Trina and her armed thugs from either Sur-Sum Corda or the Farms. Sometimes she would extort money from neighborhood businesses such as Chinese carry-outs and pizza delivery shops by convincing the owners to dish out anywhere from five hundred to a grand a month to provide protection from armed robberies of both their restaurants and drivers. A cheap price to pay in order to avoid robbery and possible death, Trina would say to the proprietors who always seemed to cooperate, especially when staring down the double barrels of a sawed-off shotgun. The storeowners always paid their protection money on time and without the slightest complaint. She had a young low-ranking crewmember collect the cash from each place on the first Tuesday of each month.

She was an astonishing criminal mastermind, hatching dozens of complex schemes a day, perfecting them over several weeks and netting major profits within the span of a few months of putting them into action.

"If there's one thing I like more than sex, it's gotta be money. 'Cause havin' an orgasm, even the multiple joints, make ya feel good as shit for a minute . . . but that cheese, my nigga, that cheese'll make ya feel good for a lifetime!" she said to her beau Creepy Fisher once during post sex pillow talk.

On both sides of the Anacostia River, she was now given the greatest respect, even by gangstas, thugs, and known felons twice her age. It was now official, she was one of the District's rising stars in the treacherous universe of its underworld. With the knowledge of the Lil' Mo' Gentry slaying, numerous store robberies, carjackings, and the negotiations of untold millions of dollars in drug shipments into Chocolate City, her power on the streets of DC and surrounding areas could no longer be overlooked. Her personal earnings skyrocketed from a few measly hundred dollars per month to around fifteen thousand per week by September of 1986, an enormous amount for the now eighteen-year-old teenage mother.

During her leisure time she and Sophia painted the town

red by partying at all the area's most exclusive nightclubs, dining at expensive Georgetown eateries and going on wild shopping sprees from as far north as Boston to sunny Miami.

Porsche, now a rambunctious two-year-old bundle of energy, enjoyed the very finest of everything money could buy. Toys, clothes and sparkling miniature trinkets crowded the toddler's room and closet by the trunk full often causing Mother Ricks to shake her head in bewilderment over where her young daughter got the money to afford such lavish gifts for her child. Lucinda Ricks had a hunch about Trina's source of income, but prayed that she was wrong about it each time the thought came to her mind, even though the possibility of it was great.

Trina urged Sophia to quit her day job at the Blue Plains Boys and Girls Village.

"You don't need that bull shit no more, Cutie," she explained as she ran her fingers through Sophia's hair. "I'm makin' more money than the fuckin' Mayor right about now. So you ain't gotta punch clocks for nobody."

Having been spoiled rotten by Lil' Mo', Sophia was quite fond of the good life and nice things. She only kept her autumn gig as a Redskinette. This particular occupation of Sophia's, Trina not only accepted but thoroughly encouraged and one afternoon after a passionate hour of lovemaking Trina expressed to Sophia why she enjoyed her cheerleader gig.

"Cause I love watchin' you shakin' that phat ass and makin' niggas drool on game day, starin' at them sexy legs o' yours," Trina said with a smile.

Considering the expensive lifestyle Sophia enjoyed Trina didn't get any complaints from her concerning her teaching gig. Trina still lived at home out in Barry Farms with her mother and daughter Porsche. Sophia permanently left her condo apartment in Cleveland Park taking up residence in a new four-bedroom luxury hi-rise suite in Silver Spring. Trina actually lived out of both her mother's Southeast rowhouse as well as Sophia's suburban condo, though she enjoyed and preferred Sophia's place much more.

Rita Ann tore into Trina soon after hearing about her arrest and interrogation several months earlier. Rita Ann, Mother Ricks, and Uncle Otis ganged up on Trina yelling, fussing and cussing while little Porsche cried and screamed a tearful tantrum in the background. But Trina remained calm, comforting her baby girl within her arms rocking her to sleep as her family continued to grill her into the ground. After Porsche was taken to her bed upstairs, Trina came back downstairs and took her turn at giving her family the third degree. After fifteen minutes of fiercely defending herself and reprimanding her three relatives, she had them not only believing that she was innocent of Maurice Gentry's death, but feeling heavy guilt to boot. It was exactly what Trina was hoping to accomplish with her rebuttal.

Trina drove over to Sophia's place late one Friday evening in early October 1986, after winning several thousand dollars at the Atlantic City Black Jack tables earlier in the day. She had a purse filled with money and she was feeling pretty good about herself.

"Whassup, Cutie on duty? Trying to hit the clubs tonight?" she asked with a smile.

"Oh most definitely. Let's hit the Eastside."

"Eastside? Oh, naw, Young. All o' them niggas from round Lincoln Heights and shit be out Eastside . . . all of Lil' Mo's peoples and a rack o' his ex-bitches stay goin' up that joint."

"C'mon, Tee," said Sophia reassuringly, "nobody's gonna even recognize us, Baby. Stop being paranoid."

"What!" snapped Trina, "how in the fuck do you figure that them bammas ain't gonna recognize us? Specially you. I ain't fuckin' round with Eastside baby girl, that's it and that's all!"

"Ok, Ok, . . . Jesus! Aiight, how about we go to Lea Royal's party out in Fort Washington?"

"Yeah, I guess we can stop past Lea's crib. I almost forget that today was her birthday."

Trina kept a closet full of expensive diva gear at Sophia's place. She also had access to a beauty salon/spa within the luxury hi-rise where she treated both herself and Sophia to a full body massage, a facial and freshly done nails right before their hair was beautifully styled and arranged for the outing. Trina dressed comfortably in a Christian Dior black and white sweat suit that showed off her sultry curves and magnificent booty. But she still packed a small tech-nine assault pistol with a full clip into her Fendi bag for protection. Sophia was drop dead gorgeous in a radiant fuchsia colored Sergio Tacchini pantsuit. Both women dressed for the brisk October night, which was unseasonably chilly, in matching white ermine fur jackets. They made a stunning pair as they entered Trina's new 1986 custom Mercedes Benz. She had it flown into town from a Berlin, Germany dealership. She was the only person in the entire region to own one. It was tricked out with the best auto accessories money could buy . . . JVC stereo system, sparkling chrome rims, custom seating and an awesome metallic silver finish. She'd forked over a cool seventy grand for her imported road toy. And now she could finally floss just like her male peers on the grind.

At Lea Royal's enormous split level home at 2217 Fort Foote Road, they entered a jammed packed living room alive with throbbing Go-Go music, multitudes of well dressed young men and tantalizingly good-looking females of various ages who flaunted their tight young bodies for the attention of the lustful guys eyeing them all around. They went straight towards the well stocked open bar and ordered a round of apple martinis as they mingled with several mutual friends who were seated there also. Even when she seemed nonchalant and at ease, Trina's eyes were constantly darting back and forth taking in the boisterous activities of the revelers around her.

Lea's was a veritable palace of upscale opulence, featuring 3 and a half inch exotic, artic fox fur carpet extending throughout the three levels of the mansion. Antique French inspired furniture accented every one of the 22 spacious rooms, where authentic oil paintings adorned the walls, huge sparkling chandeliers hung from the rafters within the entrance and both the dining and living room areas. The high-tech kitchens covered an extensive area, with state-of-the-art stove and sink fixtures with 24-karat gold inlayed covers, which gave an exceptionally swank feel to the entire room itself. Marble, imported from Rome, covered the six bathrooms, while Jacuzzi tubs were to be found in the bathrooms that occupied the master bedrooms. Within the two sprawling dens were pool tables, fully stocked bars and a miniature movie theatres equipped with reclining chairs to seat at least a dozen viewers.

There was more than enough to eat at the birthday bash and the girls stuffed themselves with the catered delicacies. Extravagant drinks such as Moet, Cristal and Dom Perignon flowed freely. Lea Royal herself spotted them and came running over, embracing both with loving smooches. Lea took them on a tour of her beautiful home which at the time had every single room filled to capacity with intoxicated, giggling teens and young adults. By twelve-thirty five the DJ had the entire house thumping with pulsating music and excitement. Droves of late comers poured through the front door and on into the jumping party. Trina's eyes carefully followed every person as they entered the door. But by the time one o'clock rolled around, Trina hadn't noticed anything out of place and the house had been full of partygoers for quite some time. So she relaxed her guard a bit and decided to get her swerve on with a few of the guys who continually requested her presence on the dance floor. Both Trina and Sophia danced with a number of male guests well into the wee hours of the morning, downing pricey bubbly and munching on what remained of the costly finger food in between sweaty groove sessions.

Every hour or so the DJ would allow a guest come up to the podium that was set up in the huge living room and give Lea a special birthday shout out and present her with a gift or two. At some point during the long drawn-out speech and thunderous applause that followed, Trina suddenly sat up straight and locked eyes with a twenty-something-year-old guy who flirted with her boldly across on the other side of the bar. He looked familiar to her. *Damn was he phine!* she thought to herself. He was a deep chestnut brown with a fresh fade and neatly trimmed goatee. He was obviously older than she, maybe twenty-one or twenty-two. His broad shoulders made him look all the more delectable in his spiffy gray Armani suit. Then she recognized him from several local boxing matches at DC's "House of Champions". He was the local middleweight champion prizefighter. She just couldn't remember his name.

"Damn!! Who is that phat ass young'un right there?" sighed the young boxer in admiration of Trina's beauty.

"Who is you talkin' 'bout?" asked his obviously envious female companion.

"Who am I talking 'bout? I'm talking 'bout that little dark-skinned joint with the big ole' butt in the black and white sweat suit . . . See? Right over there at the end of the bar sitting next to the pretty redbone."

The short sassy girl in the pink and white Fila Sweats stared with jealousy in Trina's direction, her heavily mascara-coated eyes narrowed in growing anger. She took a quick sip of Remy Martin and glared back at her boxer boyfriend, "You think that lil' black hood rat bitch look good? Ya'll triflin' niggas will fuck anything!" she snarled, rolling her eyes scornfully.

"Why is you hatin' and shit? I'm sayin' though, the lil' young'un is phine and phatter than muhfucker. I mean c'mon now, even you know that ya self, shorty."

"Ain't nobody hatin' on that lil' chicken head wench. She ain't nothin' but a lil' ole' welfare recipient from the Farms. She ain't nobody!"

"Well I tell ya what . . . she damn sho' don't look like she on no welfare to me," the prizefighter shot back, still making eye contact with Trina while slurping down the last drops of champagne at the bar.

"I'm pretty sure I seen that broad before, I just don't know where."

"You probably seen that hooker down on 14th Street or on Georgia Avenue working as a stripper in one o' them nudie bars."

"Ya know what? Just for that I'ma find out for myself who she is, whether you like it or not . . . aiight?" announced the young man tapping the bartender on the shoulder.

"Slim, who is that lil' young'un over there talking with the other honies? Lil' dark-skinned, thick young'un."

The bartender looked over towards the end of the bar on the other side of the room, then nodded knowingly, "Oh yeah, you don't know her? That's Trina Ricks right there . . . ya know Southeast Trina from the Farms?"

"Naw, young, I ain't never heard nothing 'bout no Southeast Trina from the Farms," mumbled the muscular prize-fighter.

"Aiight dawg, how 'bout Lil' Mo'? I know you know 'bout Lil' Mo', don't you?"

"Yeah, who don't, but what he gotta do with shorty right there?" questioned the young athlete.

"Slim? You ain't heard? C'mon, Dawg. Where you been? She the young'un who pushed that bamma's wig back. She even fucked around and took my man's girl cause niggas claim she goes both ways and shit. Might be true cause the lil' red young'un she with right over there in the corner, used to be Lil' Mo's fiancée."

"What?" gasped the boxer, "you bullshittin'! Lil' cute Shorty over there go hard like that?"

"Oh, most definitely! Baby ain't to be fucked with. She's one of the only female hustlers I know. She makes plenty of money, too. Shit, man, you should check out that bangin' ass Benz she's pushin'. People say she runs with the Clifton Terrace Mob. So most cats watch what they say around her. Ya know what I mean?"

"Huh, man, I got you, Dawg. I ain't gonna step on no toes cause I ain't trying to have no drama myself. But I just wanna holla at her cause I know I know her from somewhere."

"So you still pressed over knowing who this dope dealin' dyke bitch is?"

"You know what, Chelsea? You gotta stop bein' so goddamned jealous. That shit is blowing me, young. You act like I'm trying to holla at the broad or something. All I did was give the bitch a lil' compliment on the phat ole' booty and to find out if we know each other, aiight? So chill the fuck out with all of that attitude and shit, damn!"

"Fuck you!" Chelsea snapped at her boyfriend sharply. "Go home with that bitch tonight. Let her give you some pussy. Dumb ass!"

Chelsea stormed away from the bar snatching her coat from off an adjoining stool as she stomped off through the dancing crowed in the living room.

The handsome young boxer shook his head slowly and chuckled to himself as he watched his envious girlfriend disappear among the mingling throng of youngsters. He took the opportunity to approach Trina and introduced himself. As he took her hand guiding her to the dance floor, he was fascinated to find that the mahogany skinned beauty was even more stacked and stunning up close than he realized. The two danced seductively to Bobby Brown's "Tenderoni" enjoying each other's closeness before Trina noticed that a short, sweat suit clad, busty girl was angrily yelling at Sophia and getting into her face aggressively. Sophia was trying hard to diffuse the situation by calming the irate teenager down, but to no avail. Chelsea was furious that the tipsy cheerleader had accidentally spilled a glass of strawberry daiquiri all over her pink and white outfit as she breezed past en route to the front door.

"Watch where the fuck you goin' bitch! Look at what you did to my sweat suit! Fuck! Dumb ass bitch! I aughta beat yo' ass."

Trina let go of her dance partner and raced over to the scene of the commotion. She roughly yanked the unsuspecting girl by her silky ponytail and commenced to striking her in the face with a painful series of devastating punches which soon dropped her, bloodied and unconscious, to the floor. The astonished and silent crowd stood around staring as the music continued to thump in the background.

"C'mon, Sophia, let's get the fuck up outta here before I fuck around and catch another case out this bitch," growled Trina, helping Sophia put on her fur coat.

As Trina approached the doorway several teens stood in front watching blankly.

"Get the fuck outta my way before you get ya asses dealt with just like I did that bitch!" Trina yelled at the other kids who quickly made a wide path for the two women who departed the house quickly, traveling down the sidewalk to the waiting Benz.

Just then Lea Royal hurried out the door behind them frantically beckoning them to stop. "Trina, Sophia, I'm really sorry about what just happened back there. I hope it didn't fuck your night up. Chelsea Cooper is always fuckin' with people, talking shit, and picking fights. I didn't really invite that bitch myself, but you know Kevin Easley, the boxer? Well, he's a close friend of the family and they go together. So, now you know . . . but I'm sooo glad that you fucked her up. I can't thank you enough 'cause personally I hate her dumb ass. But be sure to watch your back, aiight, cause she's the daughter of Cowboy."

"Say what?!" Trina glanced down at her now sore right

hand that still had Chelsea's caking blood all over her knuckles. "Aiight, Lee-Lee, good lookin' out, girl. Here's two hundred and fifty dollars. Happy Birthday."

The three females hugged one another and bid each other good night, while Trina and Sophia sped off en route to the Capitol Beltway.

"Who in the hell is Cowboy?" Sophia asked as they cruised down the highway.

"He's a crazy ass undercover DC cop. He's in charge of the drug and gang taskforce. He's from Houston, Texas, originally a big ole' redneck white boy who just happens to love black folks. Shit, I think the muhfucka think he's a nigga himself. He always wears a big ole' ten gallon hat, tight ass nut-huggin' blue jeans, and cowboy boots. But I tell ya what . . . that cracka ain't no joke, young. When that bamma jumps out on your ass he comes with somethin' like a dozen or more rollers. Young'un, they be packin' some heavy duty shit, and won't hesitate to air your ass out."

"You think that he'll retaliate behind your fight with his daughter?"

"Oh no question 'bout that, you know them peoples got it in for me anyway behind Lil' Mo' and shit, so you know they gonna be on my ass for sure now."

For the last past thirty minutes a strange vehicle had been following the Mercedes Benz as it cruised the Beltway towards Silver Spring. Pooh and company had not been called to cover Trina this particular time because going out to Lea Royal's birthday bash was a last minute decision. Trina hadn't noticed the late model brown Monte Carlo following her because she was too busy running her mouth with Sophia about the events of the party, plus both she and Sophia were very tipsy.

Six blocks away from the Flanagan Arms Condominiums, Trina slowed down along Georgia Avenue to pick up some food at an all night McDonald's. Then, as if in slow motion, she saw the silhouette of the long body Monte Carlo pull up along the curb opposite her driver's side. Sophia jumped out of the Benz and sprinted towards the McDonald's. She grabbed the handle to the entrance door, but it was locked. Suddenly two people dressed in dark sweats and wearing ski masks hopped out of the other car and began spraying the drive-thru area with semi-automatic gunfire. Hollow tip slugs whizzed away, shattering the glass window panes of the fast food joint, ricocheting off the pavement of the parking lot and piercing nearby cars therein.

Sophia crouched down low against the unprotected glass door and screamed at the top of her lungs. Amazingly she wasn't hit as stray bullets flew all around her. As soon as it happened, it was over. The two unidentified gunmen quickly hopped back in their big boat of a car and roared off down Georgia Avenue, in the direction of DC.

"Trina, Trina," Sophia cried. "Oh, Trina, baby, are you alright?"

Trina slowly crawled up from the glass-sprinkled floor of her bullet-riddled Benz, where she cautiously looked about with her trusty Tech-nine in hand ready to return fire in defense of herself and Sophia. Luckily she'd thrown herself down the moment she saw the Monte Carlo's single working headlight reflected in her side mirror.

"Yeah, I'm aiight, bitch niggas ain't did shit but fuck my whip up. Glad they didn't bust up my tires and shit. Don't worry though; it's a small world. I'll run across them bammas again somewhere, believe that," she said.

Shaking her outfit free of shattered glass particles, she asked, "How 'bout you? You hauled ass up outta your seat even before them muhfuckas started bustin' off. Seems to me like you already knew in advance that we was 'bout to get got."

"What? Trina you're talking crazy! What do you mean I must've known? Are you fucking crazy? God! I don't believe that you just said that to me!"

"Well, what am I s'posed to think, Sophia? You just up and

ran. You left me, Boo! I mean you didn't just walk out, you bounced like shit, next thing I know niggas was poppin' them thangs."

Sirens wailed in the distance. The cops no doubt were on their way, so the girls sped away from the drive-thru in the now bullet-pierced Mercedes headed to Sophia's.

Chapter 6

Duckin' Them Peoples

Seventh District Police Sergeant Billy Ray Turner aka "Cowboy", chewed vigorously on a bitter, sun-cured wad of Redman chewing tobacco as he and a squad of thirteen heavily armed metropolitan police officers converged suddenly outside of the Penthouse Strip Club on Georgia Avenue, one of Creepy Fisher's favorite hangouts. The pigs singled out Trina, the lone female of the criminal outfit, and slammed her down spread-eagled on the polished floor of the exotic night club.

"Creepy, don't worry, Baby, I know what's up. I'll holla at you 'bout it in a minute," said Trina, wincing in pain from the tightly applied handcuffs as well as the knee of one policeman in the small of her back.

Creepy Fisher and his assorted thugs looked on in confusion and nervous apprehension as the officers hauled the female gangsta off to Seventh District police headquarters.

"Look, I'm gonna need for you to holla at ya sista Karen to come bail me out, aiight?" Trina blurted out to Creepy before her head was shoved back into the rear of the premier squad car.

Once at the Seventh District police precinct, the officers led Trina directly back into Billy Ray's office where they finally relieved her of the tight-fitting handcuffs and slammed her down on an old leather loveseat in front of the massive hickory wood desk in the center of the room. Billy Ray ordered the other cops out and slammed the door shut behind them, turning to face the teen. He was even taller than he looked on T.V. Around six four or six five, he was of lean build, but nonetheless sinewy with especially muscular forearms which bore the tattoos of the Texas State flag, a rattlesnake coiled to strike, nude cowgirls, and a soaring eagle. His face was narrow and drawn, weather beaten, and wrinkled like old rawhide leather. He wore a thick, drooping Fu Manchu mustache which gave his gaunt face an even more intimidating look. He wore a pair of dark glasses and dirty blonde hair flowed from beneath his big ten gallon hat, settling unkempt upon his shoulders. He slowly chewed on his tobacco plug occasionally spitting a disgusting glop of tobacco juice into an old tin can.

"Well, well, well, so I reckon' you're the lil' ornery gal who broke my stepdaughter's nose, huh?" he drawled.

"She started it. She was pickin' a fight with my friend who was tryin' to apologize to her for accidentally spillin' some wine on her."

"Is that a fact? So I guess you're just a regular judge and jury all by yourself huh?"

Suddenly, he reached over, grasped Trina by the back of her collar and slung her across the floor of his office, where she crashed against a large metal file cabinet head first, knocking her silly in the process. The girl felt a dull throbbing pain on the left side of her head that made her feel woozy and disoriented. Instinctively she placed her fingers gingerly on top of the spot where the pain was. She drew back her hand and saw bright crimson dripping from her fingers as she became conscious of the fresh blood which slowly trickled down the left side of her face from the gash in her head. Her lovely eyes filled with tears of pain and anger. She clenched her fists and tried to stand. The tall Texan stuck a snakeskin boot into Trina's abdomen and pushed her hard back down on to the floor, as she struggled to rise to face him.

"Gal, you'd best set a spell, cause this ain't your lil' ghetto hood, nor am I one of them lil' ole crack addicts you routinely beat down the road a ways. I'm the poe-lice, remember? I can beat your lil' pickaninny ass all over this room if'n I saw fit, and ain't nary a soul out there's gonna stop it. Matter of fact, most of my men will probably join me in givin' you a sound, solid, whippin'."

"Yeah, y'all triflin' asses would beat on a female wouldn't you? I hate y'all muhfuckas! Ohhh!" Trina huffed in frustration still holding her bleeding head.

"Good, we hate all of you God awful dope dealers. You ain't worth the breath the good Lord done gave you. You rob, steal, rape and kill, and you hate us? . . . Imagine that. So tell me," Billy Ray asked while tossing a small towel over to Trina to apply to her wound. "What do you do for that piece o'shit Horatio Fisher? You sellin' pot? Snow? Or maybe rocks? . . . yeah that's it. You're a crack dealer right? Tsk, tsk, tsk. You're such a purty lil' thang. Why would you wanna get yourself caught up in that type of bullshit is beyond me. So what is it? What kind o' activities does this Clifton Terrace Crew get into?"

"I dunno what you talkin' 'bout, for real."

"Oh no? Well lemme refresh your memory for you, sweetheart. Horatio Fisher is alleged to have committed twentyseven murders in this city from '83 to the present date. He's alleged to have a crack cocaine ring operating out of Sur-Sum Corda and Clifton Terrace which is bringing in an estimated twenty-six million dollars as we speak. It has been said that you, my dear, serve as his number one business partner. Want to talk about it?"

"I ain't talkin' 'bout shit without my lawyer present, you got me fucked up."

Billy Ray sneered angrily, and he hauled off and bitch slapped Trina across her face, a sharp stinging blow that slumped the girl for a minute and brought tears to her eyes. Trina's face stung painfully and she cried bitterly but still lunged for the Texan's throat. But he slapped her again, which brought her to her knees breathing heavily as her nose bled lightly.

"Don't ever try that stunt again missy or I'll really open up a can o' whup ass for you. Now let's try this again shall we? Are you pullin' drive-bys, knockin' off banks, liquor stores, what?"

"I don't do any of those things man! retorted Trina sniffing and choking back her tears.

"Well ya don't go out and buy an imported German-manufactured Mercedes Benz workin' at Burger King."

"I got parents with money okay, happy now?"

"I'm gonna say that you're a goddamned liar," quipped the police sergeant with biting sarcasm. "Looka here, sweetie, I'm a busy man and I'm only gonna ask you one more time to come clean about your drug dealin' sugar daddy, Horatio Fisher, and those gun totin' punks of his or I'm gonna take you down to the women's holdin' cell downstairs and let them hardcore Eastover broads from Maurice Gentry's old stompin' grounds have a lil' get together with you, what do you say? I'm sure they'd love to see you walk your purty lil' self through the door."

"You know what? You'se a fool, you think because you done punked so many young'uns before that you gonna just punk me, too? I took enough o' you hittin' me today muhfucka! I'm gonna show my lawyer my scalp and my bloodied nose. I'm gonna sue your white ass, sure as my name's Katrina Ricks. You think cause niggas stand on the corner slangin' rocks, you can come here to DC with all o' that bamma ass Texas shit, hittin' on people and shit? Don't you fuckin' touch me no more muthafucka!! I don't give a fuck! If you hit me one more time bitch, you'd better kill me cause I'm gonna damn sure fold your big, tall ass up!"

She oftentimes wished that her relationship with Rita Ann could have been better, then maybe she could've used Rita's police rank to keep Cowboy at bay, but the strained relationship between the two sisters had only grown colder since she had left her Mom's house and Rita Ann showed little if any concern for her afterwards.

A heavy knock at the door came suddenly and when Billy Ray opened it another police officer, a Lieutenant, entered and upon seeing Trina's condition immediately chastised Cowboy harshly, treated the girl's minor injuries with dressing and gauze from a nearby first aid kit and sent her on her way but she did not leave before leaving Billy Ray Turner with a grim warning.

"Your ass is grass muthafucka! You hear me! You ass is grass believe that!"

"Why you smart ass lil' bitch, are you fuckin' threatening me? An officer of the law?! Is that what you're doin'?!" hollered the enraged police sergeant.

He lunged for the teenager but was restrained by the larger cop.

"I'm gonna bring your whole organization to the fuckin' ground. You got that, you fuckin' lil' whore!"

"Fuck you, you cracka muhfucka, see me out the Farms! How 'bout that?"

With that said the girl strode out of Billy Ray's office and back onto the streets of DC, free once more. Trina picked up the Crown Victoria as her beloved Benz was at a Beltsville, Maryland auto shop getting restored. She met up with Creepy Fisher at the "Classics" nightclub angrily displaying the wounds and bruises she'd gotten at the hands of the police Sergeant. Trina described in stark detail the events that unfolded while down at Seventh District. Creepy Fisher who had himself been roughed up by the hard core cop with the vigilante-like method of law enforcement was not at all pleased to hear of Trina's hardship.

"You don't need to be gettin' on that dude's bad side Trina. Cowboy ain't the one to fuck with. I'm tryin' to tell ya . . . that white boy go hard. He ain't scared o'shit and he got big heart. So slow ya roll, lil' girl, slow ya roll."

"Nigga, fuck a Cowboy!! Y'all niggas might be scared o' him but I ain't!"

Trina boldly went about her business of drug dealing, robbery, burglary and other criminal pursuits as she had prior to her run-ins with the law. However, she soon discovered that Creepy Fisher was correct in his assessment of Billy Ray Turner's wrath. For by the beginning of December 1986, the police investigations, harassment and surveillance surrounding her became so intense that she could barely make a single move without the fuzz knowing about it. She was constantly being pulled over, searched and questioned almost every day. Luckily for her, she'd gotten a valid driver's license on her nineteenth birthday. The rollers followed her to the clubs even giving the management at certain nightclubs and cabarets a hard time if they allowed the nineteen-year-old Trina admittance where the minimum age was twenty-one.

She no longer packed a weapon of any kind due to the constant police pressure. Yet rumors swirled on the streets that Lil' Mo's relatives and remnants of his drug empire from Lincoln Heights and Eastover were preparing to stalk and kill her any day now.

The month of December '86 was hardly a merry one for the nineteen-year-old girl from Barry Farms. The cops raided Sophia's Silver Spring condo with the approval of the Montgomery County Police Department and the management of the luxury suite in which she resided. Billy Ray Turner and his DC police squad searched every inch of Sophia's apartment on Christmas Eve with a fine tooth comb, carefully checking the spacious two bedroom condo looking for narcotics and weapons that may have been cached there by Trina.

Once she arrived from an evening of holiday shopping, the

stunned NFL Cheerleader was questioned thoroughly about her whereabouts as well as her relationship to both Lil' Mo' Gentry and Trina. "So this is Sophia Carlin huh? Damn she's fine. How'd you manage to pull a bitch that most men can't get with?" said a young baby-faced cop to Trina nudging her and staring lustfully in Sophia's direction. "Both you and that Redskinette sure are sexy. How 'bout I hook up with the both of you for a little threesome action? Oh I promise I'll be gentle."

"Eat a dick," Trina spat with irritation.

"C'mon, Trina lets cooperate with the police so that they can just get out and leave us the hell alone," Sophia spat angrily.

"Well first of all, if you didn't hang around with hoodlums, male or female, you wouldn't be in this predicament as we speak, right or wrong?" asked the cop. "But hey I guess the love for big cars, big houses and even bigger money can render even the most intelligent of people temporarily insane."

The day after Christmas, Creepy Fisher paged Trina, who upon contacting him, was summoned to meet with him down at the wharf. Trina arrived at Phillip's Seafood House around two o'clock in the afternoon. Reservations had already been made. A tuxedo-attired waiter directed her to a cozy, dimly lit booth seat for two on the upper level beside a window overlooking the mighty Potomac River. A small lamp provided light on the stylish mahogany wood table. Another waiter dropped off a small plate of jumbo shrimp, beer battered fries, and a bottle of White Zinfandel wine.

The Clifton Terrace drug lord was dressed impeccably in a royal blue Versace suit with matching alligator skin shoes. He'd just come from his favorite barbershop and thus sported a neat fade and beard trim which revealed much more of his natural boyish good looks. As he raised his wineglass to his lips, huge six carat diamond cufflinks sparkled radiantly within the warm glow of the light.

He offered her a glass of wine he'd poured earlier and they

both tapped their glasses together in a toast to friendship and the holiday season. Trina gulped the wine down in a hurry, anxious to hear what he'd have to say. Surely it must be of great importance or else he wouldn't have asked her to meet him for lunch, Trina thought as she studied the steely gaze of the man before her.

"Trina, baby," Creepy began, "I couldn't get you off of my mind to save my damned life these past couple o' days. Do you know that? I'm jive worried 'bout you, boo. The poe-poe wants you bad as shit, young, and that's no bullshit. I tried to tell you 'bout fuckin' round with Cowboy's crazy ass, that redneck bastard ain't gonna stop comin' at you, until he locks your ass the fuck up. Tried to tell you some good shit, but you wanna do what you wanna do, right? So I said fuck it, let her learn about them peoples the hard way. Cowboy is one crazy white muhfucka. I outta know cause he used to run up on me and my folks all the time back in the day. We used to have to take an ass-whippin' and get hauled down to D.C. jail on top o' that. Then once we started gettin' long paper, we'd have to come up off that money each time he came around just to keep 'em from fuckin' with us. Now you makin' some good money yourself right now but you just ain't got to the level where you flippin' enough weight out here to keep a jokah like Cowboy from pressin' you. So, you just gotta be on the down low for a minute cause the bamma waitin' for you to fuck up. You see, all he gotta do is catch you slippin' one time and that's your ass. But peep this . . . when you out here fuckin' up an shit, them peoples don't just wanna lock you up . . . they lookin' at all the niggas you fucks with as well. Now I done told you 'bout how that bitch ass Cowboy rolls an shit, I know the muhfucka ain't got no love for me or my peeps an we ain't got none for him either. But I ain't had no trouble with dude for over two an a half years an I ain't tryin' to fuck my hustle up by gettin' this started all over again. So you gonna have to stay from round this part of town for awhile, aiight?

"Oh, so it's like that?" Trina asked with a prickly attitude.

"C'mon now girl don't get all in your feelings, aiight? You know I fucks with you. You know that! Shit, everybody gotcha back, but I for one ain't trying to go back to jail. I did five years down Lorton, five long ass years. So fuck that shit! I ain't never goin' back up in that bitch. So do a nigga that favor, aiight?"

"Aiight baby, I feel you. But what about the keys of coke I got for us and that fifteen pounds of Kine bud I worked out last week from New York? I mean, shit, a bitch gotta eat too, ya know."

"C'mon, Trina! Boo, you blowin' me with these fucked up questions. Don't I always make sure my folks is aiight, 'specially you, cause you my boo? I'm gonna give you a whole key for yourself to flip anyway you want. You can cook it up or sell it as powder out Maryland or VA. You can have three pounds of the Kine bud too. You know I got you! If you need some steel, I got that too; AK's, Mack's, Nine's, whatever. You ain't even gotta pay me. And of course I love the pussy so I'm gonna get with you every now and then. We can rent one o' them fly ass hotel suites and we can get our fuck on all weekend long. But all o' that police fuckin' with a nigga bullshit, I ain't got time for all o' that drama in my life. Know what I mean?"

Trina nodded in agreement. They locked lips in a sultry kiss for several passionate minutes. Trina gathered up her purse and fur coat preparing to leave when her drug dealing boyfriend gently grasped her left arm pulling her back towards him.

"Listen, baby, I forgot to tell you somethin'. One o' my niggas down Lorton told me that a couple o' young'uns from round Lincoln Heights was the ones who tried to get you the other night out on Georgia Avenue."

"Yeah, you right! Them bitch niggas tried, but they failed. Then they bounced like some ole suckas."

"Oh, I know what happened. Don't worry, I got some dudes

finding out some info on them lil' niggas as we speak. Hope-fully they'll get back to me real soon with some good news so I can handle that light work for you. But anyway, them niggas out Lincoln Heights and young'uns from Eastover done promised to hit your head. So be careful pretty girl, aiight? I mean my Clifton Terrace Crew gonna do what we do best to air bammas out who come talkin' that dumb shit, but you gotta get your game face on and keep it on. Feel me?"

"Good lookin' out, baby," Trina said planting a wet one on Creepy's cheek. "Don't worry 'bout' me. I'm gonna be aiight. You just calm ya nerves. I'm a big girl who knows how to han-dle herself out here on these streets. So bammas better not sleep on the kid for real 'cause I will push a nigga's shit back believe that."

Trina paged Pooh before leaving the Southwest DC eatery and in less than twenty minutes a dark green '76 Cadillac Brougham pulled up in front of the restaurant. Pooh lounged behind the steering wheel of the colossal caddy puffing on a Black & Mild cigar while three other sweat suit-wearing toughs grooved to the go-go tunes of Lil Benny in the back-seat. Trina waved goodbye to Creepy Fisher as she entered the passenger side of the Cadillac, and she and her crew disap-peared down the street en route to the Farms. Trina smiled to herself knowing that she would carve out a handsome profit in both Maryland as well as Virginia. Then her thoughts quickly went back to vengeance.

"Pooh, them bammas out Lincoln Heights been talkin' 'bout some . . . they wanna air me out, young. So I want every-body, I'm talkin' 'bout all y'all niggas to get them thangs ready cause we 'bout to show these muhfuckas that just cause I'm a female it ain't hardly sweet out here."

As they crossed over the South Capitol Street Bridge, Trina glanced back towards the three teen boys bobbing their heads in unison with the beat of the music.

"Y'all niggas pay attention aiight? I'm gonna need y'all to be so on point, that on point ain't on point, aiight?!"

"You got that Trina. We ready to rock these niggas, young," a slender dark skinned boy with a wicked scar along the right side of his face retorted as he pulled out a shiny, silver chrome plated Desert Eagle nine millimeter, proudly displaying it for Trina to see.

Trina smiled with approval and leaned her head back on the headrest enjoying the up-tempo rhythm of the Congo drums serenading her from the speakers.

December '86 was coming to a close. It was already past Christmas and most of the citizens of the Nation's Capitol prepared for New Year's celebrations, but not everyone was in a joyous mood. Sophia had long since grown tired of living life like a common fugitive on the run and virtual prisoner in her own home due to nonstop police surveillance under the direct orders of one controversial Police Sergeant Billy Ray Turner. When Trina dropped by to see her around midnight, Sophia was in an ugly mood, which quickly progressed from shared irritability between the two lovers to a full fledged shouting match that ended with Sophia tossing a wine glass at Trina. Trina, enraged beyond words at her partner, left the condo in a huff, slamming the door hard behind her.

Sophia had several issues going on which added to her recent mood swings and irritability. First of all, Sophia had been seeing Kevin "Two Piece" Easley since Lea Royal's birthday bash earlier in the year. Although the middleweight champ originally sought the affections of Trina, he backed away when told by outside sources that Trina was romantically linked to Clifton Terrace drug lord Horatio 'Creepy' Fisher, a name that caused shudders to run down the spines of even the most fearless of the district's thugs. The skirt-chasing boxer decided that pursuing a sexual fling with the older of the two bi-sexual gals would prove both easier as well as safer.

During their phone conversation one evening Easley suggested to Sophia that they meet up somewhere for drinks. They did. And as usual with such secretive hook-ups, one thing led to another and a one-night stand resulted. Yet afterwards Sophia felt none of the guilt or shame that she thought would've come over her due to her unfaithfulness to Trina. Sophia felt herself falling for the brawny, broad shouldered prizefighter. And she was not ashamed.

Everybody knew that Trina had been sleeping with Creepy Fisher on the side, so why couldn't she enjoy the strength, comfort, and satisfaction that only a man could give. After all, Sophia thought to herself, she was bi-sexual as was Trina. Plus, she had missed all three of the Redskins' final regular season contests and she'd made cheerleader practice only once in the past week. When she finally showed up in her burgundy and gold cat suit, she was told to take her pom-poms and return home by the director. She was given a stern reprimand and warned that if she missed practice during the coming week, much less the play-off game at RFK on the first Sunday of the New Year, she'd face termination.

Trina, on the other hand, during those dark winter days of December cared little about anything or anyone but herself, with the exception of her young daughter, Porsche, whom Trina made a point of seeing as often as she could—considering the stressful set of circumstances surrounding her. Trina's child provided her with one of the few sources of joy she felt she had left at the time. Other than the brief peaceful moments spent with her rapidly growing, happy little toddler, Trina stayed looking watchfully over her shoulder. She was always searching for enemies or potential enemies among the residents of the hood going about their daily routines or the multitudes of dope fiends she served while grinding in the heavily trafficked drug spots of Southeast. Squad cars and police sirens, even from a distance, caused her intense paranoia.

So much so, that by the end of January 1987, she'd collected a sizeable group of young runners, supervised by her good friend Pooh, to actually handle the business of hand-to-hand street corner drug sales while she collected the profits each night, bringing her some small sense of comfort. Early one Wednesday morning near Valentine's Day 1987, Trina's Crown Victoria blew out a rear tire along Good Hope Road. It was around 2:45 am and frigid outside. Trina cursed out loud kicking the side of the vehicle before wrapping her thick, triple fat goose down jacket around her and donning her soft, warm fox tail hat. Briskly she hurried towards a solitary gas station, walking quickly more from wanting to get out of the cold than from fear. Yet still she thoroughly inspected the surrounding streets, alleys, buildings, and parked cars with a keen roving eye for any suspicious activity. When she was satisfied that only she and the Ethiopian attendant behind the bullet-proof plexiglass of the cramped little booth were the only people present she began using the pay phone. Then from her right side along the dark deserted side street adjoining Good Hope Road, Trina heard laughter and footfalls upon the pavement accompanied by the heavy smell of marijuana.

Cautiously, Trina turned her head seeing five men in their late teens or early twenties dressed in dark hoodies headed in her direction to the rear. Instinctively, her natural street smarts kicked in and she reached into her coat clutching the handle of her Tech-Nine tightly while still remaining on the phone line. Trina didn't know if these cats were members of Lil' Mo's Lincoln Heights Mob or not, but the young men were almost upon her and she had to act quickly. Hanging up the phone, Trina turned in the opposite direction moving at a rapid pace towards her disabled car. The five hooded men turned immediately following her across Good Hope Road spewing profanities and threats behind her as they pursued her towards the distant vehicle. Trina's heart rate increased dramatically and her breathing became labored for she knew that the event she'd feared was now unfolding. Either she'd find a way to escape her would be killers or she'd become another victim of the nation's murder capitol. Knowing the streets like she did, she knew that the boys who were after her more than likely wanted to kill her in some dark, remote area of the street where there'd be no possible witnesses. They must have trailed her all along. And who knows . . . they may have even shot her tire flat with a silencer.

Trina's first instinct was to take off and run, but she had never been a timid, fearful female in the face of danger. Though she now faced sure death, she'd still maintain her gangsta. Very few people were up at this time in the morning except a wino or two; a couple of homeless persons lay bundled up in filthy sheets along benches at the bus stop, but no one else. Even if there were people around or watching, it wouldn't do Trina any good because in the projects of DC, residents almost always minded their own business and fearing retaliatory action from the neighborhood drug dealers much more than they feared the police. She was happy that she had recently begun packing a gun again despite her earlier misgivings.

Trina had little choice but to stop at some point and bust shots in the direction of her attackers. All that came across Trina's mind at that point was the sweet, smiling face of her two-and-a-half year old daughter whose playful antics she'd never behold again if she were gunned down on this cold February morning. The hood-wearing young men began cussing loudly at her as they crossed the street moving in behind her for the kill. It was now or never. Trina didn't want to be shot in the back, so she quickly ducked behind her Ford and squeezed off a rapid fire series of gunshots from the Tech which rattled violently in her right hand as she took deadly aim at the oncoming gunmen.

The still silence of the morning was broken by thunderous gunshots as the five hoodlums returned gunfire at Trina. Trina winced as hollow tip slugs whizzed, whined, and zipped passed her along the pavement and through the air. She shuddered and crouched in the fetal position as bullets crashed into the side of the big Ford, smashing the windows and puncturing the engine causing a heavy leakage of fuel and water which pooled along the curbside. Then all of a sudden during the wild shoot out, she heard the rumble of a familiar car engine. From her crouching position she could see the silhouette of Pooh's big body Cadillac roar up along Good Hope Road.

From the darkened interior of the caddy, Trina saw twin flashes of flame spit forward, followed simultaneously by the deafening boom of a sawed off shotgun. The shrieks of agony let her know that her attackers were in deep trouble. Trina repositioned herself, firing off yet another multitude of murderous rounds into the group of pistol packing youngsters. She saw two of the gunmen lying dead out on the cold street, bleeding profusely from what seemed like a dozen or more bullet wounds. Another one was blasted in the back by Pooh's sawed off Shottie peppering his entire back side with buckshots. The young boy slumped to the pavement weeping as his back was ripped to shreds by the blast. Yet his pumping adrenaline summoned enough strength for him to scramble to his feet and attempt an escape, right before Pooh's younger brother, Jay, put him to rest with a gunshot to the back of his skull.

Jay and another Barry Farms' youth noticed two of the other hit men fleeing across the street. So they gave chase occasionally squeezing off a shot or two in their direction. However the enemy youths had gained a considerable amount of distance while running and soon disappeared between the neighboring buildings scattered along Good Hope Road, making good on their escape.

Police sirens began wailing in the distance. Either they'd heard the gunshots themselves or someone alerted them to it. Whatever the reason, at that point it mattered little. Five-O was on the way and would be crawling all over the place at any moment now. Trina and her homies hopped into the Cadillac and raced away from the crime scene, recklessly dodging both other cars and red lights along the way.

Once back at the Farms, Trina stayed over at Pooh's place for a few hours before checking in on Porsche and her mother a little later.

"Good lookin' out, sweetie. Damn good lookin'! 'Cause I thought sure as shit that I was gonna get kilt out there," sighed Trina while hugging her friend and slapping a thick roll of rubber band wrapped bills into his palm. "That's all you ai-ight? I haven't even counted the joint. But it should be some-thin' like seven fiddy or eight hundred . . . either way it's close to bein' a grip. We kilt three o' them bamma ass niggas, but two o' the other jokahs got away from us."

"Now we gotta get rid of all this muhfuckin' evidence and shit. I ain't worried 'bout that car cause it ain't mine, it belongs to one o' my peeps' brother and that nigga's locked up down Lorton. We gotta get rid o' these guns so I'm gonna holla at this young'un from Baltimore who stay buyin' and sellin' all kinds of guns. So by the time five-O trace the bullets back to our shit, these hammers gonna be in some other jokahs' hands. And more than likely, knowin' how bammas up B-more roll, it's gonna have not only fresh fingerprints but fresh bod-ies on them joints, too, huh man! That way if we fuck around and get late, them bitch ass polices ain't got shit on us. But my nigga, we ain't tryin' to get locked up. So you, Jay, and every-body else 'cept the lil' runnahs gots to chill the fuck out for a minute cause them peoples gonna be lookin' to put the cuffs on a muhfucka for sure. So for 'bout maybe a month don't buy or do nothin' that's gonna attract attention. I trust you like you was my own lil' brotha, but you gotta let the rest o' these young'uns know that if they get locked up don't tell the police shit. Cause they gon' put the press on you once they hem you up at the precinct."

Pooh agreed to all of Trina's decisions. After a hearty breakfast, at the first hint of dawn, Trina left for her Mom's where she remained until Friday of the following week. During that tense week and a half stay back at home with her daughter and mother she did a lot of thinking.

The local news media covered the shootings in detail for several days afterwards confirming Trina's notion that the murdered men were members of Lil' Mo's Lincoln Heights Mob. The homicide department would soon launch an investigation into the triple slayings and in no time the cops would once again drag her in for questioning. Her stress levels had gone through the roof behind worrying about the DC Police and thugs from both Lincoln Heights and Eastover, who'd definitely be out to shoot her on sight behind the murders of three more of their own.

It got so bad that Trina even lost a few pounds, evident from the slight loose fit of her clothing. DC was becoming too much of a liability for her to remain in the city much longer. She needed a quick change of scenery for a minute or two, just until things calmed down for a while. So she thought hard and long about possible options. She needed a temporary place of residence, and believe it or not, an actual legit job if only for a while. Then as she flipped through her phone book Trina came across her Cousin Alonzo Bundy's number.

Alonzo had left the Washington, DC, area long ago to settle in Greensboro, North Carolina. He had moved right after high school in 1971, and had been there ever since. An ex-cop himself, Alonzo had invested his hard earned savings into contract security and over the years his investment had reaped handsome benefits for the slender built, distinguished forty-nine-year-old former Greensboro beat cop. He owned Tarheel Protective Services Incorporated, a security company which held several commercial contracts in some of Greensboro's most violent and drug-infested housing projects. He had always inquired about Trina moving down to the country, offering her a job as well as room and board if she relocated there.

She always turned his offers down stating that country life was too slow and boring for her city tastes. Besides, everything about the country and country folk screamed BAMMA.

But now North Carolina seemed more and more like a refreshing oasis. Moving there for a few months would certainly have its advantages. Surely the DC cops wouldn't have a clue as to her whereabouts. Nor would she have to worry about harm coming to herself or loved ones from enemies in some payback shit. *Doing security couldn't be that bad*, she thought. And even though she only turned nineteen on October 22nd and was devoid of any work skills, or even a high school diploma, her cousin would hire her just because she was family.

In the meantime she knew that time was of the essence with all of the publicity the triple murder generated throughout town. The cops, especially homicide detectives, would be hot on her trail in a matter of days. They would also surely question or even harass anyone caught carousing with Trina. So she purposely avoided her mother's home, Creepy Fishers' dope spot, and Sophia's luxury hi-rise condo in order to spare her loved ones grief.

She telephoned Creepy via a cell phone she'd bought recently so that the call would not be traced back to her mother's.

"Whassup, Creepy? This Tee," she said in a somewhat nervous tone. "You heard 'bout them three bammas that got kilt out on Good Hope Road last week? Well, it was me and a couple o' my folks from round the way that got them niggas! Two of 'em got away though. But that shit's all over the news, TV, radio, the papers, everything. So I'm 'bout to bounce, young. It's too muhfuckin' hot in the city for me right now. But I wanna see you and Sophia before I roll out. So where you tryin' to hook up at?"

"Aiight, just meet me out Maryland at my baby mama's apartment. She stay in the Princess Triangle Apartments on Dodge Park Road off of Route 202. That's PG County, so you ain't gotta worry 'bout no cops from DC fuckin' with you out there. Meet me there in two hours. I gotta go see 'bout some money somebody owe me first, aiight?"

Trina got on the metro rail and rung Sophia's phone as she exited the Orange Line at Landover Metro Station. Then she caught a cab to the address Creepy had given her. She arrived about a half-hour early, but it was all good because Creepy was there when she arrived.

The apartment was a large run down looking rats' nest with dirty, snotty-nosed brats running and playing all over the grounds. Welfare mothers dressed in house robes, slippers, and wearing rollers in their hair, stood along the dirty walkway leading towards the unit gossiping nonstop about various he say-she say happenings within the complex.

Climbing the flight of steps to the third floor Trina was simultaneously met with flirtatious wolf whistles and catcalls from a group of loitering teen boys as well as several sarcastic remarks and envious stares from a group of big haired, eye rolling hoochie mamas. Trina continued on, ignoring the verbal and visual distractions along the stairwell and knocked gently on the door marked T-3. Creepy Fisher opened the door with a smile and admitted her inside. He then introduced her to a big-breasted, full figured Amazon of a woman who constantly yelled at three hard headed little boys who ran about the house fighting and creating chaos. Her name was Bernadette.

Bernadette had lots of weave in her hair, and it hadn't been done for quite some time. It looked awfully old. She wore way too much make-up and her eyes were glazed over and blood-shot from smoking weed that was smelling up the place something awful. She looked to be in her late thirties. Bernadette was a big girl, but even at her hefty size she was still shapely. She wore a sheer red satin negligee that left little to the imagination. She was a good-natured lady who laughed at her own dirty jokes and always had a bit of juicy gossip to tell. Bernadette offered drinks from a cabinet filled with hard liquor and refused to take no for an answer. The apartment was a sizable three-bedroom unit that bore a seventies style. Outdated psychedelic paintings hung all over the drab off white walls, and Mary Kay products so littered the table tops and floor that one had to step over piles of pink colored boxes the whole time.

Trina smoked a blunt with Creepy and Bernadette while explaining to them the reasons for her leaving the area for a few months and where she'd be living during that time. Creepy Fisher was more than understanding of Trina's decision to leave the DC area and assured her that he'd take care of both Little Porsche and Sophia financially until Trina returned. Then Sophia arrived, and Creepy winked at Bernadette who took the hint and led the boys into the master bedroom as Creepy trailed slowly behind them leaving Trina and Sophia alone in the living room to talk in private with each other. Slowly Trina took her time in explaining her plans of relocating briefly and why. Plus she related that while away in North Carolina she'd have a legit job lined up.

"Working security in the projects? C'mon baby, are you sure that you wanna go all the way down South just to do that?" Sophia responded.

Trina gently kissed her lover on the lips.

"Baby, I'm not just goin' to North Carolina to work as no rental cop. I'm goin' down there cause I gotta get the fuck away from DC before I end up in jail or dead."

"Trina, Boo . . . what am I gonna do without you being here with me?" Sophia said tearfully.

"Don't worry yourself, sweetheart. Creepy done promised me that he's gonna take care o' you and my daughter until I get back up here," answered the teen confidently. "Creepy's trustworthy . . . a real man of his word. So you gonna be ai-ight. I'll only be gone for a lil' while. I promise you. There's no way in hell that I can possibly stay away from you or my daughter for long. Believe that . . . okay?"

Sophia threw her slender, bracelet-covered arms around Trina's neck, kissing her with intense zeal and bawling bitterly.

"I love you so much. Please, please, don't go! I don't want you to go! Trina, I don't know what I'll do without you!"

Trina embraced her lover warmly, caressing Sophia with all of the amorous fire that caused the teenager to take a man's life for her. With tears of sorrow welling up in her own eyes, Trina got up and quickly left with Creepy Fisher who had been standing next to the front door for the past several minutes awaiting her. As she exited the apartment she herself broke down in tears thinking about Porsche's bright smile and playful antics, along with Sophia's mournful pleas for her quick return to the area.

Creepy drove Trina to Dulles National Airport, traveling along the Beltway in silence except for the muffled sounds of Trina's gentle sobbing and sniffling in the backseat as she lay curled up behind him. There was a connector flight to Savannah, Georgia, that would have a brief layover in Greensboro at around 2:30am. Trina took it.

The very next day on March 3, 1987, Trina was in Greensboro, North Carolina. She was welcomed with open arms by her first cousin Alonzo Ricks and his family of five. She was finally free from all of the drama of DC. Now she could start over again.

Chapter 7

It's Like A Jungle Sometimes . . .

For once in her life, Trina actually worked at a legitimate gig and ended up being a model employee. Her cousin assigned her to Squirrel Brooke Terrace Apartments, a low-income housing project located in the northeastern section of the city. Squirrel Brooke Terrace was a squalid, twenty-five unit complex that was an infamous breeding ground for drugs and violence. Even local authorities attempted to avoid, at all costs, the crime infested area known simply as "The Jungle." Alonzo Ricks could hardly keep quality guards employed at Squirrel Brooke for that very reason.

The intimidation of the security guards by resident drug dealers had caused a high turnover rate among his officers, which threatened to cause him to lose the contract with the apartment complex. He had to find someone qualified or not, male or female, who had the balls to work the post without fear. That person was his cousin, Trina. Trina was actually a pretty good security guard. She especially liked shooting on the gun range in order to qualify for her license. Everything else concerning her employment was handled by Cousin Alonzo.

The other guards felt safe being in Trina's presence because of her fearless attitude and easy communication with the criminals of the neighborhood. They had no idea of knowing how at home she was in the harsh surroundings of the ghetto. Only this time she was the one with the badge. Trina, unaccustomed and uncomfortable with the idea of wearing anything resembling a police uniform at first, soon begun to accept and even enjoy her newfound authority. She took delight in forcibly taking contraband such as narcotics, guns, and money from both the dealers and their startled customers. Occasionally, Trina and her fellow officers would use the confiscated marijuana and money for themselves, turning in the weapons and hard drugs like crack, heroin, and PCP to the cops. However, more often than not, Trina, realizing the seriousness of her recent legal troubles as well as the possibility of jeopardizing the contract of her cousin's security company, turned most of the illicit products of her weekly drug busts over to the fuzz. Trina did care about a few other folks, especially family and close friends, and after all, this man was her cousin.

Within the first two weeks of April, '87, she was promoted to night supervisor. The other guards, mostly local men and women many years her senior, didn't like the fact that the nineteen-year-old, inexperienced out-of-towner had been placed and promoted so quickly. Yet few of the long-term guards desired the rigors and pressures of late night supervision of the rugged complex. Trina's bravery in the face of danger was remarkable to watch.

It was this same spunk that endeared the others on her shift to her. Such as the rainy night on the 17th of April when a group of five resident girls refusing to leave the front of the building where they'd been loitering for hours loud talking, smoking weed, and drinking well into the wee hours of the morning, attacked and badly beat a fifty-six year old female officer leaving her bloodied and bruised on the cold, damp floor of the lobby. Trina directed two of her officers to stabilize and treat the injured guard until the paramedics arrived. Another was told to write the report. Trina herself went in search of the assailants. A little more than two hours after the incident, Alonzo Ricks arrived at the site, after first visiting the officer who was recovering from her injuries in a downtown medical ward. He was amazed to discover Trina in the company of the police laughing and joking together as they hauled five female residents away in handcuffs. Three of the girls bore black eyes, bloody noses and other facial bruises—evidence of a street fight. Trina was a sight to behold with a nasty purplish shiner under her left eye and three long scratches along her neck, which she dabbed at continuously with a handkerchief to stop the bleeding. After the police took the women from the property, Alonzo sent over to Trina as she was treated for her wounds by guard carrying a first-aid kit.

"Trina, don't you ever take on a group of people in this complex by yourself. Never again girl! You could have gotten yourself killed. Follow the procedures of the security handbook next time, please," argued the owner of the company, smoking a cigarette to calm his nerves.

"Mrs. Harris just got beat down by five young'uns just cause she asked them hoes to leave the front. I'm sorry cuz, but I ain't lettin' some shit like that go. Mrs. Harris is jive like my mother's age and shit. Matter o' fact, she even remind me of Ma. So when somethin' like this bullshit happens I ain't thinkin' 'bout no security handbook and shit. I'm gonna go straight gangsta on a muhfucka off the break. And that's what happened. I straight punished them country bitches."

"What?!" exclaimed Alonzo in confusion. "Trina come with me to the command center please," he said angrily as he briskly stomped toward the command center with a nonchalant Trina in tow.

Once inside the office, Alonzo slammed the door shut and locked it. Even though the heavy door was closed, the staff could hear the owner's voice booming from within.

"Listen up Trina, you're my first cousin and I love you dearly. But I won't let you get out here and put you life in unnecessary danger. That could also cause me to lose this contract I've worked for almost six years to land. I know that you've done a hell of a job here at the site. That's why I decided to promote you to night supervisor. You've got more heart than any of my officers . . . even the men! But still Trina, darling, I'm running a business here. So I have to ask you never to do something like that again. Okay?"

"Aiight, aiight, whatever," Trina answered sharply.

Alonzo, noticing Trina's irritation wrapped his arms around her affectionately, kissing her on the forehead.

"Alright Sergeant, I guess that I'll let you get back to having your wounds dressed by Officer Bryd, and I'll see you when you get home this morning, okay?"

Trina nodded silently in agreement and unlocked the door, returning to her nightly patrol duties.

By the end of the month, Alonzo Ricks held a luncheon in his cousin's honor at his annual "Employee of the Year" celebration. Trina had worked diligently to bring the drug dealers of the apartment complex to justice and ironically she'd busted over twenty-two dealers and recovered a colossal amount of narcotics and guns to boot. Greensboro's police department even awarded Trina a handsome plaque for her work in ridding one of Greensboro's most notoriously violent projects of crime. She accepted it reluctantly, not wanting to get too chummy with Five-O, regardless of what department they might be from. To Trina the boys in blue were still eternal enemies of the hood.

Eventually Trina's combative personality and stubbornness caused more grief than good on the job. She got into still more confrontations with other female bad asses of the complex which often led to wild, hair pulling cat fights. Male residents were not exempt from her harassments and on several occasions she'd threatened dealers with her service revolver.

Trina began drinking and getting high on post. She'd invite one particular drug dealer whom she'd taken a liking to, to spend time for an entire duty shift alone in the command center with the door locked and all radio communication silenced. She openly and aggressively flirted with certain female officers and abandoned her post often for hours at a time before arriving right before she was due to sign out.

Alonzo Ricks seethed silently for weeks before finally getting the nerve to discipline his young relative. Though she was not fired she was immediately removed from the Squirrel Brooke Terrace apartment complex, demoted, and placed at another post altogether. The new post that she was assigned to was located out in the boondocks, far outside of the Greensboro city limits. She was bored beyond words sitting in her little rinky-dink one room shack. She had no television, radio, or human company within the largely abandoned construction site surrounded by the forest of tall Pine and Juniper trees, which brought wildlife of all types onto the property raiding the garbage dump in search of food. The daily isolation and extreme boredom drove Trina up a wall. She'd even begun shooting at the raccoons, opossums, and other woodland creatures just to kill the boredom. Eventually Trina just couldn't it take anymore and resigned from Tarheel Protective Services completely. She worked briefly in the front office with her cousin Alonzo for about two months, but clashed over the company's decisions and policies with both Alonzo and his wife Helen.

So by mid July '87, Trina found herself back on a plane returning to the nation's Capital. She was home sick. North Carolina was much too rustic and slow for her. Trina's heart seemed to skip a beat in anticipation of reuniting with her beloved Sophia and Porsche once the plane passed across the majestic Washington Monument and U.S. Capitol building.

Always a hustler at heart, Trina had saved over seven thousand dollars from the drug money she'd taken from dealers she'd busted while at Squirrel Brooke Terrace. Plus she still sold some drugs on the side herself once the other competition had been removed from the premises. She smiled to herself knowing how much of a good time she'd show Sophia and how she'd spoil both her daughter and lover once she'd settled herself.

Having learned much about law enforcement techniques and the law in general gave Trina newfound leverage in dealing with the cops. And this knowledge gave her an overwhelming sense of confidence. So her time spent in Greensboro as a rental cop had paid off after all. As always she had learned several new schemes while working with her cousin in the front office of Tarheel Protective Services, Inc. She'd devised a plan to invest in a legitimate business so she could launder drug money without drawing unwanted police or IRS scrutiny to herself. Uncle Sam had nabbed many criminals, past and present, for tax evasion. But Trina was determined not to end up like Al Capone and others. She was now armed with the knowledge to avoid such legal pitfalls.

She sauntered through the Dulles Airport, looking sexy and chic in her braided side-strap sandals and pin tucked denim dress, drawing stares and whistles from dozens of flirtatious men of all ages. Her brief stay in North Carolina had done wonders for her previously frazzled nerves and she'd quickly added the pounds she'd lost to her amply developed body. She carried a thick stack of greenbacks in a black leather Prada purse, which she'd taken from the hustlers down in Greensboro. The uninspired ragtag airport security paid little attention to the monitors or the buzzing passengers passing through the magnetometers, in their haste to hurry the long line of luggage bearing customers onto the awaiting plane which, benefited Trina, greatly.

The first thing that she wanted to do was to see her darling Porsche. She'd brought a few items of clothes and several toys for her baby down South. Then she'd visit Sophia in Silver Spring. Trina hadn't seen her lovely sweetheart for a while now and yearned to hold Sophia in her arms again, to taste her sweet full lips, and to make love all night throughout the apartment until they fell asleep exhausted and sweat soaked from passion in each other's arms.

She called Pooh as usual from the airport, where he picked her up a half hour later as she stood outside waiting with her one small suitcase. Trina spent the better of four hours hanging out with her mother, daughter and neighborhood homies laughing, catching up on neighborhood gossip, and playing several hands of Bid Whist and Poker.

The neighborhood blabbermouth, Theresa "Tee-Tee" Parsons, related to a shocked Trina that in her absence, Sophia had been seen around town bunned up with local boxing champ Kevin Easley. And rumor had it that Sophia was more than three months pregnant with his child. Tee-Tee Parsons worked at the Motel 6 along New York Avenue.

"That's where they always come almost every Saturday night. I know cause I'm the manager out there. He always brings girls up there to smash off with his ole cheap ass. All o' that fuckin' cake that nigga got. Shit, he'd be takin' me to a five star hotel if he wanted to get some ass. But anyway girl, he brings Sophia up to the Motel 6 every Saturday night around eight or nine o'clock faithfully. I know cause they book the room for the weekend and leave out early Monday morning around six or seven."

Trina's eyes watered up and spilled tears of frustration, anger, and pain down her lovely dimpled cheeks. She gathered up Pooh and five of his thugged-out friends to drive her to the Motel 6 at seven o'clock. Once there, she'd hide inside the motel room that Tee-Tee would assign to the couple when they arrived at the Motel 6. Trina gave Tee-Tee $350 for her tip-off and for granting her access to room #725.

Trina entered the cheap motel room with its cheesy, late sixties furniture and a roach or two crawling along the loud, plaid wallpapered surroundings. She snuck into the wide closet and shut the door, waiting for the opportune moment when she'd spring out of her hiding place. She had dozed off while sitting on the floor of the dark closet when she heard the flesh-on-flesh smacking of intercourse joined by guttural groans and whimpering. Opening the door slightly Trina's jaw clenched tightly and her eyes flashed fire as she watched in disbelief as the muscular young boxer took Sophia in his powerful arms mounting her from behind, thrusting himself into her with the raw passion of an aroused stallion while Sophia arched her back rotating her luscious hips to meet her man's thrusts with equal fervor. She dug her nails into the mattress, wailing with delight like a bitch in heat as Kevin Easley shot his load hard and deep within her moist love canal.

Without further waiting, Trina flung the closet door wide open over turning a small rickety end table in her haste to exit the closet. Flicking on the overhead lights, she lunged into the room. "You skank ass bitch you," Trina snarled furiously.

The naked sweaty lovers scrambled all across the bed in shock at being confronted by some crazy person in their motel room.

"Bitch, who the fuck are you," the champ demanded defiantly. "And what the fuck is you doin' up in here?"

Trina gritted her teeth and breathed a sigh of rage.

"Nigga shut the fuck up before I smack fire outta yo' dumb ass. Sophia! Bitch! Don't act like you don't know me, trick!"

"Trina, what the hell are you doing? Have you lost you fucking mind? I thought that you were in North Carolina?"

"Well, I ain't in no fuckin' North Carolina, ho. I'm right here, right now 'bout to tear yo' ass the fuck up!"

"Trina, baby c'mon. You just can't do things like this, you gotta think about what you're doing. I need a man! I'm tired of the gay lifestyle Trina. I just can't lie to myself or you anymore, baby. I'm sorry!"

Trina stared at the stark nude couple hugging each other before her and felt a tinge of nausea overcome her for a split second before she regrouped.

"You'se nothin' but a tired ass skeezah! That's all you are . . . you run to the highest bidder, don't you? First Lil' Mo', then me, and now this fake ass Sugar Ray right here, you just straight triflin' . . . ughhh man! I fuckin' hate you!"

Hearing the anger in Trina's voice made Sophia cringe within the strong embrace of her new boyfriend for she knew what Trina was capable of doing and she was terrified.

"I bet you the whole time that I was down South you was laid up with this bamma nigga livin' off the loot Creepy was givin' yo stupid ass, huh? Shit, I coulda had that money sent to my daughter and mother for real," Trina said, her hands trembling with emotion.

The boxer hopped up from the bed and stood his ground in front of Trina, his muscular body glistening with post sex perspiration.

"Lookahere, Trina, you had your chance but I guess it wasn't meant to be. Me and Sophia love each other and it ain't shit that you or anybody else can do about it. You're a phine ass woman yourself. You can have any man you want out here. But comin' up in here talkin' shit and threatnin people like you doin' is gonna get you fucked up. I don't hit females, but tonight I'll make an exception. If you think you gonna fuck around and do somethin' to my girl with me standing here, you got me fucked up. This woman's carryin' my seed up in her. So you better just get the fuck on before you gets dealt with!"

Suddenly Trina felt her blood boil within her. She'd reached the limit of her composure. Instinctively, she reached her hand into the loose pocket of a gray Georgetown Hoya hoodie she had changed into at her mother's. She drew the Sig Sauer handgun and squeezed the trigger striking Kevin Easley in the head, blowing his brains out as he flopped backwards onto the bed soiling the dingy brown and white bed sheets crimson with his lifeblood that poured from the gaping exit wound at the rear of his skull.

Sophia stared wide-eyed in horror at the dead man beside her as his cold eyes gazed upward toward the ceiling. She screamed at the top of her lungs before Trina smacked her hard across the side of her face with the pistol, opening up a terrible gash along the left side of Sophia's face that bled profusely.

"You ain't never had no love for me. I thought that you was different, special, but no . . . you just like all the rest . . . you used me, too. So for that, I got no love for you neither, bitch!"

With that said, Trina snatched a pillow, put it over Sophia's head and shot her four times through the pillow causing feathers, flecked with blood and bits of brain matter, to flutter about the room. Trina then left immediately after wiping down doorknobs, handles, and various other items that could allow the murders to be traced back to her as best she could before leaving.

Trina was met by Pooh and his crew out in the parking lot of the low budget motel. The teens drove off down New York Avenue on into the night, Trina discarded the murder weapon in the Anacostia River.

For a long time afterwards Trina sat alone in the dark interior of a borrowed '77 Cobra Mustang, parked in the lot of Haines Point Park. Looking out across the dark, choppy waters of the Potomac. Pounding back shot after powerful shot of Remy Martin, wincing from the initial bite of the robust cognac as it warmly made its way down, spreading its vaporous wings within her chest, as Trina viewed the numerous drops of gently falling rain cascading down the windshield she tearfully broke down. Sobbing mournfully for her now departed lover whom she would never again hold close to her bosom. Oh how she did love that woman. However, she would now hold only bittersweet lost memories of the smiling cheerleader, who had won her heart. With no one to comfort her, she had only the company of the falling rain.

Chapter 8

Gutter Ass Tales of Southeast

It was well after one in the morning when Trina and her crew left the scene of the Motel 6 murders. She hadn't noticed anybody in the hallways or parking lot on her way out. Nor had Pooh or his cronies seen anyone either. Tee-Tee Parsons had left the premises early that night around ten o'clock complaining of stomach cramps. Truthfully speaking, the Barry Farms native knew that something potentially criminal was about to go down. And though she'd never snitch on her neighborhood friends, she'd have nothing to do with the intensive police presence and questionings that were sure to come once the murder victims were discovered. So Tee-Tee left a twenty-something Venezuelan woman with relatively poor English in charge during her absence.

Two hours after the shootings, Trina had Pooh drop her off at the Presidential Towers Apartments in Hyattsville, Maryland, where she would stay with a coke client of hers, Nancy Marie Gomez. Ms. Gomez was an ex-gal pal of Creepy Fisher's and one of Trina's best cocaine customers, many times purchasing over a thousand dollars worth of flake in a week. Even if D.C.'s finest were hot on her trail, they would not be able to pursue Trina across state lines. She was warmly welcomed into the spacious, lovely home of the single mother of two, who registered her in as a guest on the apartment's sign-in registry in the lobby.

There were well-tailored doormen in spiffy blue and red uniforms outside the entrance and armed security guards patrolling the property in small squad cars as well. The foyer of the hi-rise building was huge and beautifully furnished. Pretty brass and leather sofas sat within the cobalt marble splendor of the lobby, while the gentle gurgling of porcelain water fountains mingled with the beauty of tropical ferns and sweet smelling azaleas to further please the senses.

After registering, Trina was taken up to the ninth floor where she followed Nancy Gomez into her handsome two-bedroom suite. Nancy showed great hospitality to Trina, giving up her bedroom and choosing the sofa bed in the living room for herself. Trina removed her clothes and slid into a warm, cozy bubble bath that Nancy had drawn for her. As she stretched herself out beneath the tepid water of the tub, she took a few sips from a glass goblet of sparkling champagne and sighed with exhaustion as she begun to think long and hard about her next move.

She'd just killed a popular Redskins cheerleader and Kevin Easley, by now the middleweight boxing champion of the world. There was no way around major local as well as national news coverage concerning these latest homicides. Yet, now after her initial sorrow over what she had done Trina didn't feel any remaining remorse for taking Sophia Carlin out. Sophia turned out to be just as doggish and untrustworthy as any man would have been. Who knows what type of dirt she might have been capable of? In a fit of anger she might have dry snitched to the police about the Lil' Mo' Gentry murder or any number of things she'd known about Trina's entire criminal lifestyle, from dope dealing to carjacking sprees. She would've had the evidence to send Trina away for the long haul. So with that in mind, Trina felt something of a relief that a potential dry snitch was now silenced forever.

As the two women sat around laughing and reminiscing about past events, Trina was shocked by the news of 'Creepy' Fisher's recent murder.

Pausing, after a long laugh, Nancy hung her head in silence before clearing her throat and revealing to Trina the details of her ex-boyfriend's bloody slaying.

"Ya know Creepy got killed right?"

"What?! You gotta be shittin' me!" Trina exclaimed, recoiling with shock.

"Nah, for real though, he got shot like 30 times off of 44TH street, Northeast. Some niggas caught him sleepin' right outside the Shrimp Boat," retorted Nancy, slowly shaking her head in pity.

It was easy for females to alter their looks with a simple trip to the beauty salon. Plus she was somewhat thin when she left to go down South compared to the thick, luscious shape she boasted now since she'd returned home. The old Trina was nonexistent and she would work hard to keep it that way. Her family would have to be hipped to what was going on except for Rita who had just recently returned to the Washington area herself after receiving a years' worth of training as a FBI agent in an undisclosed location outside the area.

Trina awoke the next day and treated Nancy Gomez and her two young daughters to breakfast and a matinee movie of their choice. Later the four traveled to Potomac Mills, where Trina bought several dozen outfits for herself and got a two-hour makeover done on herself that left her looking ever more radiant than before.

For the entire following week the local television news programs, as well as the headlines for the Washington Post and Times, featured the slayings of Sophia Carlin and Kevin Easley. The local newspapers played up the killings as drug related, while the evening news programs ran segments featuring a local Southwest drug dealer sought in connection with the murder case named "Niko" Kirkland owner of the South Dakota Avenue Ford Dealership. The reputed cocaine dealer was said to have had an ongoing feud with Kevin Easley over a woman. This bad blood between the prizefighter and coke dealer had resulted in a February '86 free-for-all between entourages of the two men at the Metro Club in Northeast. No murder weapon had been found to place blame on anyone suspected of the gory crime.

The FBI had taken over the investigation because of the high profile victims as well as the prominence of the suspect. Agent Rita Ann Ricks was assigned to the case. Trina's jaws dropped open in major surprise as she read the article in the Washington Post's Metro section.

"What? Let me find out Rita's with the feds now," Trina thought out loud to herself. *It would definitely be a trip if they ran across each other in the street one day* she thought smiling. But then Trina's smile vanished, replaced by an evil scowl. *Naw it wouldn't be a trip. I wouldn't be anything nice, if that day became reality.*

When the weekend came around Trina donned a sexy hot pink spandex cat suit with matching Reebok Classics, her hair and nails were flawlessly done. She'd learned to ride a motorcycle while in Greensboro and had bought a slick black Kawasaki, which she rode down to Anacostia Park in order to enjoy a cookout with Pooh and several other friends. Afterwards everybody begged her to follow them back towards Barry Farms where they planned a huge block party where bands such as Air Raid, Trouble Funk, and Little Benny would perform until late in the evening. It was an irresistible temptation to hear the cranking sounds of the Congo drums, bongos, and bass guitars, the camaraderie of niggas from round the way . . . it would be surely missed because she would not be there today or any other day for quite some time.

So far her elaborate makeover had worked well. Even kids she knew since childhood walked passed her looking on intently, the girls with curiosity as to her identity, while the boys lusted after her with testosterone driven angst, yet still not recognizing who she was. Trina spent the remainder of the evening at a Langley Park crack spot that she'd taken an interest in since she moved to Hyattsville. Trina singled out two Jamaican dealers who seemed to be the bosses of the block and began to talk business with them. At first all she got from the two dreadlocked ballers was a hard time and lots of sexual harassment. That is until Trina broke out the knot. As the eyes of the foreign dealers went wide with excitement and interest, she smiled slowly knowing that she'd taken control of the situation and that the dreds would act accordingly from this point on.

The crack traffic coming in from New York and Philadelphia was much better quality than the rocks from DC and as a result the demand for the New York/Philadelphia buttah scuttah was making the transplanted hustlers rich. Native dealers from DC and PG County, Maryland, became very resentful that these imported shot callers were gaining wealth in the beltway region, resulting in daily gun battles erupting all over the region between DC and New York dealers for control of choice drug turf.

A once big time Brooklyn-born drug dealer held complete control over much of Edgewood Apartment complex for over two years before being gunned down while he sat in his Lincoln Continental along Rhode Island Avenue. Many of his fellow Brooklyn area hustlers tried to succeed him, but by that time many native Washington drug crews had grown in size and gained sufficient firepower to repel the New Yorkers' foothold on the city. After the New Yorkers and Jamaicans were ousted, dozens upon dozens of violent homegrown drug crews spread throughout the city, settling in various sections and exerting the same deadly violence on each other that they'd previously visited upon the New Yorkers.

Trina could pinpoint accurately that the largest drug profits would most likely go to the hustler who would run his or her organization with the same business-like efficiency as the mafia, instead of the foolish and unnecessary gunplay displayed by the immature nickel and dime dealers standing on these streets currently. These small time hustlers knew little, if anything, about organization and proper planning, which would prove to be their undoing when faced with competition by such an advanced operation.

Trina's research revealed to her that the most business-like baller of the bunch was a quiet former banker named Trey Wills, who hailed from Valley Green, Southeast, a notoriously violent neighborhood which had drugs a plenty. Valley Green's very name intimidated most residents of the District, who knew the deadly reputation of the locale. It impressed Trina also that several of her Barry Farms' friends such as Pooh, Tyrone Shell, Alvin Skilcraft and others considered Trey Wills a friend and often did brisk business with the Valley Green dope dealer. Valley Green was very similar to her own Barry Farms Dwellings and it would make an ideal place in which to operate a bustling drug operation. Early the following morning she hopped on her motorcycle and sped off towards Valley Green.

Trina located the thirty-something hustler sitting on the upper tier of some old bleachers overlooking an even older-looking basketball court featuring a group of bare-chested sweaty teenage hoopsters who yelled and argued more than they balled. Trey Wills was a fair skinned, handsome older man with curly hair and a neatly trimmed beard. He was perhaps thirty-five or thirty-six with a medium build and proportionate height. He dressed in fine tailored suits and wore tasteful diamond jewelry which was not too flashy but just right. With soft gray gentle eyes and a ready smile on his good looking face, Trey seemed more like an understanding father than a powerful and dominant drug lord. The distinguished gentleman who constantly drunk from a liter bottle of fresh spring water had been dealing drugs out the Valley Green projects for several years drawing very little attention to himself while younger members of his crew engaged in the majority of shoot outs with rival crews.

Since the seventies Trey had sold marijuana, PCP and heroin. He had made a decent amount of money. But the crack era of the 1980's had placed within his hands another tool with which he'd build enormous wealth, the likes of which the District had never seen. Trina was attracted to this studious entrepreneur at once. Here was a man who reminded her of what she'd always wanted in a man—an older fatherly type who could plan properly, give orders, and maintain an orderly outfit.

Since she'd been gone, the crooked cops of the city, Cowboy in particular, as well as the numerous rival dealers had decimated the carefully organized operation she'd put together during her stint as a drug runner, now she was in desperate need to get things back on track and she could think of no opportunity better than what she was now presented with.

"I just got back in town a lil' while ago," Trina explained with excitement, and I need some extra cake now that I'm back home to stay. So I was wonderin' if I could hook up with you and ya crew for a minute, make a few moves here and there. You know . . . until I got enough to move weight on my own. Whassup?"

"Well, you seem to have your priorities straight young lady.

"I've heard a great deal about you. You're damn near more popular than Chuck Brown in the city right about now. Matter of fact, I'm quite impressed by your brain as well as your beauty. But I don't think that we've ever formally met before, so let me introduce myself—I'm Treyville Luther Wills. How should I address you Ma'am?"

"Katrina—but people who know me call me Trina," she answered without bothering to reveal her last name.

"You may have hustled before, making moves here and there earning a lil' bit o' money, getting your feet wet, making a name for yourself out on the streets, basically getting your weight up, but now if you plan on doin' business with me and my organization you gotta think even bigger. Be prepared to climb even higher up the ladder of success—but I do advise you, it's going to be difficult. Are you willing to put in the time and effort to prove yourself worthy of joining this organization, lil' lady?" Trey Will's steel gaze fell upon the teenager with penetrating depth and intensity.

"I been servin' fiends out here on the grind ever since my sixteenth birthday. I ain't got much by the way of schoolin' and shit. But hustlin'? Shit, you show me a broad that can get out here on the corner with $500 worth o' rocks and come home two hours later after my mob finish flippin' that shit with over $2,500. You can't! You know why? 'Cause ain't another hustler out this muthafucka, male or female, that can put in work like me. I'm tryin' to tell you some good shit!"

"Is that right? Well, I know Pooh had said that you worked for Creepy before he got killed a while back. Shit, Creepy wasn't bringin' in much dope money. I mean he made more loot off of his arms deals than anything else. So you must've been bringin' in some straight chicken change huh?"

"You a lie!" Trina snapped back quickly. "I always kept a knot on me. I used to walk around with somethin' like three grand a week on a regular."

"Yeah?" Trey Wills was eyeing her with intensity fueled more by business interest than by eroticism. "Well, Miss Lady, seems like you know a lil' somethin' somethin' about the hustle game. That's good . . . real good."

"Yeah I know a lil' somethin' somethin' 'bout it, I guess," Trina admitted smiling proudly. She then continued, "I helped set up plenty of big time deals for Creepy too with hustlers from New York and Philly. I did a whole lot o' shit for Creepy when I was slangin' them thangs for him cause I'm a businesswoman like that."

"Oh, I can see that," grinned Wills.

He had already determined within his quick mind that Trina was more advanced in her business skills than most others her age.

"You already got me sold on you, dear. But because this is business and I've got a whole lot of runners who've been on the grind for me for a minute now, I gotta start you off small for now, okay? I've gotta put you on probation for the first month or two. I'll give you a quarter pound of bud, a little bit of smack here, some snow there, see how you flip it for myself. And we'll go from there. Tell you what we'll do . . . I need somebody to run this ice cream route for a few weeks until the kids go back to school late next month. So I want you to drive the ice cream truck. You serve the children their goodies from the front, while your fiends will be served their products from the rear. That'll be your gig for now."

Trina's enthusiasm disappeared immediately. She wasn't trying to drive anybody's ice cream truck. Driving an ice cream truck from block to block—that was some bamma shit. But she understood that Trey Wills was the biggest player in the Beltway region's drug game, so patience and humble appreciation would have its benefits in time.

"Aiight then," she assented. "But I hope this ain't no permanent thing cause I'm much more important to you on the front lines than behind the wheels of some dumb ass ice cream truck."

"It's a well known fact that you are no stranger to bustin' guns and what not, as a matter of fact word on the street is that you're one of the very best in the murder game. Is that right"? Trey inquired bluntly.

"Please, I got a couple o' bodies to my name."

"Recently or back in the day?"

"Both."

"Damn! You a bad girl. I see right now that you aren't going to be pushing that ice cream truck for too long. You holding any hardware right now?"

"Yep, I got a Tech right now."

"Solid, solid. You alright money wise?"

"I got like four grand on me right now."

"Very good, just keep it to yourself cause you just can't trust everybody, know what I mean? Open up a savings account tomorrow at the Chevy Chase Bank on 722 Constitution Avenue, that's my personal bank. Go to teller number three, Ms. Lorraine. She'll take care of you for me, okay? Lemme tell you some good shit. If you hang around with me, you're gonna learn not to carry around all of that money on you all the time like the rest of these ignorant young'uns out here. All that's gonna do is cause you to get yourself robbed or worse . . . and for what? Who are you tryin' to impress? Trust me, its unnecessary bullshit. Aiight, pretty girl? I'll holla at you at two thirty tomorrow afternoon. Don't be late either. This is business."

Thus Katrina Ricks entered into the next level of her rising criminal career as a member of the Valley Green Cartel, the largest, wealthiest, and most widely-feared organized drug ring in the Washington, DC area, a powerful criminal organization that boasted an unbelievable profit margin of 35 million dollars in two years. The VGC had cocaine shipped inside the interiors of hollowed television sets throughout the region and masterminded an operation that laundered money through used car dealerships to accounts in Bahamian banks.

Trina spent the remainder of July '87 delivering crack cocaine from the numerous neighborhood crack houses to the plentiful addicts who rushed to meet the ice cream truck along its many routes around Southeast. She never had to worry about Five-O because most of the local beat cops were already paid off by Wills. Her one major worry came from the various stick-up boys who had become bold of late and made a killing off of the robbery of unwary hustlers. But she was well prepared for jackers, packing two loaded assault weapons, an AK-47 and a Ruger nine millimeter in the glove compartment and along the back seat of the truck. She always stayed strapped while on her daily ice cream routes.

Ever since Lil' Mo's murder the surviving members of his crew began new loyalties with a number of his former dealers fighting amongst themselves for control, thus losing interest in exacting vengeance on Trina.

By the time August came around, more than fifteen drug spots had gotten robbed, three in broad daylight. Four of Will's young dealers had also gotten shot during the robbery spree of summer '87. So Trina suggested to the Valley Green gangsta that he should equip all of his vehicles, including her ice cream truck, with bullet proof windshields and steel exteriors, as well as providing the members of VGC with body armor whenever they were out on the grind.

"Damn good idea, boo. Good lookin' out," Wills agreed with enthusiasm. "I'm gonna jump on it first thing tomorrow morning. Take the rest of the day off and go shopping or what not, aiight?" Trey Wills pulled out a checkbook and signed a check for two thousand dollars and gave it to her with a warm fatherly smile. "Have a good time today. I'll see you bright and early tomorrow morning at nine a.m. I got somethin' for you to take care of for me aiight?"

Trina arrived at Trey Will's row house at approximately nine o'clock, feeling anxious about what task she'd be given. She felt honored at the idea of Wills singling her out for a special operation.

"The H Street Crew is working their way onto our turf slowly but surely. Fuckin' with our profits. You know I ain't having that bullshit," explained Wills, his usual gentle, smiling face giving way to one of burning rage and homicidal intent.

Trina looked upon the man who had earned the infamous reputation as one of the most brutal gangstas in the city's history.

"I'm gonna give these young'uns a stiff warning this go round, just to get their minds right, and let them know whose boss out this bitch. So lemme let you in on the caper."

Listening carefully to her instructions, Trina bailed out from Will's living room with yet another two grand stuffed into her Gucci purse, this time in a thick rubber band wrapped stack of bills. Thirty-five minutes later she drove up to a large open-air drug spot near Alabama Avenue, Southeast. Relaxing behind the wheel of a plain looking blue Toyota Corolla she bought a dime bag of weed from a ratty looking dealer no older than maybe twelve or thirteen. She nonchalantly rolled herself a blunt and began smoking at her leisure as she sat staring out at the bustling activity going on along the dope strip. She quickly observed a small group of dingy-looking teenaged runners selling their narcotics to the dozens of customers who'd drive up to the corner to be greeted by two or three of the youngsters before quickly speeding off down the street and merging into the traffic beyond.

Trina puffed on the blunt for several minutes as the brisk business of drug/money transactions continued nonstop across the street from her. Noticing a bald, forty-something

year old man, seated on the hood of a brown Blazer chattering on a cell phone and counting countless stacks of hundred dollar bills, Trina determined that he must be the shot
caller of the block. She quickly stepped out of the car, crushing what remained of the blunt under foot as she exited.
With fluid motion, she pulled out the AK-47 assault rifle
from the back seat and slung its loose strap across her shoulder. After inserting the curved banana clip into the powerful
weapon she proceeded across the street towards the rival
dealers.

"All y'all muhfuckas get the fuck down on the ground . . .
right the fuck now!" She commanded with authority. "Drop
yo asses down! I ain't playin' no games out here with y'all niggas!"

Buyers and dealers alike stared at her in wide-eyed terror.
The shocked individuals taken aback by the entire event began
prostrating themselves along the garbage-strewn sidewalk.
The leader of the dealers nervously sank down onto the hot
pavement glancing at the AK pointed menacingly at everyone
lying upon the sidewalk. Trina removed many valuables from
the prostrate men and women before leaving from the strip.
She took jewelry, drugs, cash, and guns. Trina lit up a bob as
she kept the robbery victims at bay with her AK-47. Then she
moved over to the boss and pressed the muzzle of the AK to
his temple.

"Stay the fuck from 'round here in Southeast . . . you bitch
ass nigga. This town belongs to Trey and the Valley Green
Cartel, aiight? If you and yo weak ass mob keep fuckin' wit us
y'all gon' get yo shit pushed back. Please believe that. Now get
the fuck on!"

She made everybody strip naked and commanded them to
run or drive away from the drug spot totally nude. Laughing
heartily, she walked across the street towards her car counting
the thick stack of bills as she entered the Toyota. She backed

away from the curb, drove around the corner about a half block and sped down the side street towards the busy intersection where she dodged in and out of traffic before disappearing into the sea of cars zipping back and forth along the beltway.

Chapter 9
DC (Dodge City)

"**N**ow that's what the fuck I'm talkin' 'bout! Don't give the competition a chance to set up shop in your territory. You gotta let them know right away that they're not welcomed in your neck of the woods. Know what I mean? Damn good job, baby girl. Damn good job!" Wills said, jubilantly praising the girl later that evening. "It was also a nice lil' slap in the face to the cats from H Street with you robbing them and making them strip butt naked. Nice."

He grinned as he swigged down a drink of spring water from his ever-present water bottle.

Trina immediately folded her arms across her ample breasts and began tapping her right foot irritably. "How'd you know about all o' that?"

The drug lord laughed out loud and took another long drink of water.

"I had to post a couple of my gun men. Cats from round the way, you know. In a van not far from the dope spot where you were earlier as back up just in case things got ugly for you, ya know? I can't have my soldiers, especially one as pretty as you, getting their wigs split, got it?"

"Yeah okay, whatever," Trina answered with a cool air of indifference.

For she knew the real reason as to why Wills had armed
sentries posted up on the corner of the strip. He needed to
know without a doubt if she had the heart and street smarts to
run up on rival drug dealers and force them from the neighborhood. Though Trina was a little agitated by Trey Wills undercover method, she fully understood why he did it and left it
alone after that.

"You handled yourself better than most dealers I've ever
had working the streets for me. You may be a pretty, young
thang on the outside, but you're all gangsta on the inside and
that's gonna take you far in the dope game we play out here on
the grind. You've just earned yourself five grand a week just for
being so go hard."

By the beginning of September 1987, Trina no longer drove
the ice cream route, but instead she was promoted by Wills to
begin setting up new open-air drug markets throughout various neighborhoods in both Southeast and Northeast. She also
set up several crack houses in the very same neighborhoods as
distribution centers, with a large five room row house located
on 37th Street, Southeast, serving as the premier center for
the production of both crack cocaine and PCP-laced marijuana known locally as "loveboat" or "lovely".

The task that she was assigned was time consuming and
very dangerous, but Trina enjoyed proving that a female could
be as thorough as any male dealer if not even better at turning
change into chips if given a fair chance. She was a master of
the many rules of the hustle game and doubled the Cartel's
profits handsomely as a result. Around eleven thirty late one
Sunday night as she supervised a group of runners at a 15th
Street dope spot, a dark Range Rover roared around the corner screeching to an abrupt stop across the street from the
dope spot. Customers and skittish dealers alike fled for their
lives before the heavy vehicle.

"Shit!" Trina grumbled raising her hands above her head slowly as six other thugs jumped from the SUV pointing the assorted muzzles of Barettas and Mac-10s in her direction.

For a split second she felt the sickening sense of fear fall over her like a thick blanket of fog, as a lump entered her throat and events of her young life raced through her mind *"please don't let me die like this,"* she pleaded to God silently within as thoughts of her young daughter and mother flashed across her mind's eye. What a horrible thing it would be to die on a cracked sidewalk at the hands of some punk ass youngsters. She yearned to draw the Tech-Nine from her waist and spray the men surrounding her, but that would be suicidal to attempt, considering the odds against her. There was nothing to do but wait for what she thought would be certain death.

"Aiight Muhfuckas, if y'all gonna shoot me then handle yo Goddamned business!" she said boldly without showing any signs of fear.

"Shut the fuck up, bitch!" snapped the ringleader of the crew, an unattractive high yellow thug with heavy ape-like features and a sinister looking blind left eye that brought chills to Trina's spine when she gazed at it.

"If left up to me you'd of been kilt as soon as we got outta the whip. But the "big" man told us not to kill you, at least not this time around. But I'm gonna tell you this much, if we ever catch you fuckin' wit our dope spots or runnin' up on anybody from the 8th & H Street Crew you gonna get yo lil' phine ass fucked up. So I suggest that you keep that dumb shit over in the Farms and Valley Green, aiight? Now gimme all yo' shit! Hurry the fuck up bitch! I ain't playin'!"

Trina handed over all of her money, drugs, and her weapon to the threatening gunman. The thugs hopped back up into the truck and raced away across 15th Street towards the distant intersection, leaving Trina alone to fume.

When the three young runners cautiously emerged from around some abandoned buildings, they were quickly greeted by boisterously loud profanity and flying fists delivered by an enraged Trina who rushed upon them like a wild lioness furious at her dealers for abandoning her when she needed them most. After the brutal reprimand of her drug runners, Trina telephoned Trey Wills informing him of her unpleasant run-in with the H Street Crew which also led to her being robbed by them as well.

Hustling in DC was even more perilous than it was in other cities due to the almost daily acts of senseless violence that always ended in cold-blooded murder of the worst kind. Bullet riddled corpses littered the city. Retaliation was the norm and many times the relatives and friends of targeted drug dealers would end up paying the ultimate price as a result. Widespread killings were used by district dope pushers as a means of warning rivals as well as punishing a particular offender.

Never one to back down from danger, Trina was back on the grind two days after her confrontation with the rival H Street Crew. Only now she added snipers to the rooftops of her drug spots and gave them walkie talkies to communicate with each other and with crew members hustling below. She kept a handgun on her person at all times even when she wasn't hustling and began having Pooh and his gun slinging pals follow her in a second vehicle wherever she went, once again.

Early in the morning around seven thirty on September 24, 1987, Trina received an emergency phone call from Trey Wills to ride out to Valley Green immediately. Once there, she found Trey pacing back and forth along his living room floor nervously, stroking his neat beard and stopping just long enough to take a sip of cold spring water. His handsome face was contorted in a tight ball of rage and his fair skin flushed red. His soft, grey eyes gleamed with an ominous look seen only in the eyes of a killer when contemplating homicide.

"Hey Trina, have a seat," instructed Wills.

The drug lord wasn't his usual jovial self. He didn't smile, nor was there any small talk or wise cracks as was the norm.

Trina knew already that something pretty bad went down or was about to go down.

"You know my man Houston got shot late last night, around two in the morning. He died of his wounds about a half hour ago at DC General."

Trina sighed and hung her head sadly. Todd Houston had been Trey Will's chauffeur and was a fun-loving, well-liked member of the Valley Green Cartel who brought a feeling of lightheartedness, humor, and joy to the group of otherwise rugged, tough-talking thugs.

"Houston was shot five times in the chest while he and his family slept in their Southwest row house," Wills continued angrily. "His wife, his three children, even his German Shepherd was killed right along with him. Houston's wife and three young daughters were all found shot to death with their hands and feet bound with black electrical tape. The dog was shot four times and left dead on the hallway floor. Only some stupid ass, trigger-happy young'uns would take out a whole family like that, Tsk, tsk, tsk . . . that's some bull shit right there, I'll tell you."

"You know it ain't nobody but them niggas from 8th and H who did that shit," Trina said in a gruff and angry tone, "we gotta put a stop to this shit here and now Trey. I'm sick and tired o' these bitch ass niggas, young! We can't keep lettin' these muhfuckas carry us like we soft, Slim! It's time to pull them hammers out and straight bust these niggas heads," Trina vented loudly.

"Oh no doubt, I'm most definitely with you on that one," agreed Wills wholeheartedly.

"You ain't said nothin' but a word, my dear, as we speak I got plans for some good ole' fashioned get back, Valley Green style, feel me?"

"First off, these little nickel and dime hustlers ain't never dealt with the type o' drama I'm gonna unleash on their asses. 'Cause if they only knew who they was fuckin' with, they'd have never pulled no bullshit like this. Know what I'm sayin'?" Trey Wills stated sternly. "Anyway we 'bout to pull a caper on them clowns and we gonna pop the shit off tonight, OK?"

"Whatever, Slim, I'm with you. You know that."

"Solid. Like always I pay my folks for services rendered. So I'm gonna break you off somethin' proper after you put in this work aiight? So I need you to go home, get yourself all prettied up, get the good hair and nails did. Throw on some sexy, clubbin' gear cause that's where you're goin' . . . clubbin' tonight. Be back at my place round 'bout say . . . ten thirty. And remember I want you lookin' straight vicious, aiight? Ten thirty here at the house 'cause I got somebody I want you to meet tonight also. Enough o' this chitter chatter let's go. We got a lot o' shit to do tonight."

Trina highballed it on her motorcycle back towards Maryland felling giddy with excitement and anxiety as she dipped in between and roared past vehicles along the busy beltway. She was no stranger to murder by now and actually looked forward to the sinister thrill that comes in the act of taking a human life, especially in order to avenge the death of a home. And what about this person who Wills wanted to introduce her to. Who could it be? Could it be someone she knew? Was this individual good looking? Male? Female? The night would bring interesting possibilities, a new potentially charming acquaintance, an opportunity to bust shots at the H Street crew and some time to show off one of her many expensive designer outfits. She hadn't been so charged about going out to the club for a long time; she was looking forward to it with great anticipation.

Later that night Trina arrived at Will's home at ten fifteen, fifteen minutes ahead of the appointed time. Her anxiety levels reached maximum proportions as she parked the bike in Will's driveway and walked up the stairs. She was looking sublime and sultry in her plum colored Wilson's leather two-piece outfit. The two carat diamonds twinkled brilliantly within her wrist watch, bracelet, earrings and heart-shaped pendant which dangled from a thick herringbone chain that adorned Trina's slender neck with a golden luster. She rung the door-bell and greeted Trey Wills with a kiss on the cheek as she crossed the threshold of the drug lord's row house. Trey smiled broadly as he took in the beauty of his gorgeous drug runner. She looked ravishing in her sexy apparel and jewels. The form-fitting low cut top accented her shapely figure and bulging cleavage. She wore her thick curly locks in a fashion-able coiffed do that draped down across her lovely cocoa brown shoulders and down her back.

As Trina stood in the living room joking around with Wills, a young caramel complexioned stud of a man entered the room from the kitchen. He stood around six foot two or three with a sculpted body and clean-shaven babyish face. He was in the process of getting dressed for the club and appeared wear-ing a pair of checkered boxers and tank top.

"Oh, yeah, lemme introduce you to Kofi. This is Trina." Trey Wills announced in short order. "Have a seat, sweet-heart, Kofi is about to hop in the shower. He'll be out in a minute."

Before Kofi went to take a shower, he quickly came over to the sultry young lady and took her hand into his own, "Hello sweetheart, my name is Kofi D. Whitman. Now that we know each others' names, I'm gonna look forward to working with you later on tonight, aiight . . . I'll holla at you in a minute."

As Trina eased onto a couch near the stairwell, she eyed the well-built young man as he climbed the stairs appraising his strong back, sturdy legs, and tight butt.

"Hey!" Wills laughed, snapping Trina out her lust-filled dreamin. "Get yo' mind off of Kofi's ass and worry about this job you gotta handle later on tonight," Wills said in a serious tone.

"What you about to get into tonight is some serious shit. So, you gonna have to get your mind right in order to be on point with this joint. Ain't nobody got time for bullshittin' or fuckin' round. That's why I hollered at you before anybody else in my whole mob. Cause' you've proven that you got heart and you got what it takes to get shit done the right way. But if you think I'm gonna let you go up in the joint with your nose wide open behind my man, Kofi, then maybe I got it wrong. Maybe you're not as mature as I thought. And in that case I'll put somebody else on the job. But you and I both know that you're the one for this job and no one else. I need for you to kill Carl Wormsley. Some cats call 'im 'Nutt'."

"Oh, snap! You mean black ass Nutt from Clay Terrace? His lil' sista Kisha was locked up with me out in Blue Plains. He graduated from Spingarn. I know the nigga," exclaimed Trina.

"I see. But did you know that he's the leader of the 8th and H Street crew, and right now he got a whole lot o' spots in Northeast locked down? He's got a couple o' heroin connects out B-more and he's got access to a mid-western supplier of PCP, so he and his mob's makin' a good little piece of change. He got a couple o' go hard niggas in his crew willin' to go to war for him if he gives the word on it. But far too many of his crew members are young-minded and unskilled in the day-to-day operations of a dope enterprise. So if anything were to happen to Nutt, and it will . . . them lil' hardheads will be lost and turned out."

"Aiight, aiight! My bad. I did get a lil' bit carried away lookin' at dude cause he is phine as shit though. But you know that I wanna punish these bamma niggas as much as you do, if not more so. Cause if you ain't forgotten, them jokahs ran up on me off the late night creep. So I owe them bammas one. You feelin' me?"

"Without a doubt I'm feelin' you, baby girl. Anyway a reliable outside source informed me that Nutt is throwin' a big time birthday bash for himself later on tonight at the Ibex Night Club."

"Ibex? I thought you said the nigga was gonna be clubbin'

out Maryland?" exclaimed the handsome young man as he emerged from the shower nude except for the thick white towel encircling his lower body.

"Naw. What I said to you earlier was that they're gonna take some strippers out to a house in Maryland where they're gonna lay up with 'em all night long. Tonight at the Ibex my man Nutt's doin' it big for his birthday. I heard he's gonna have two live Go-Go bands performing there, a couple o' local comedians, the Georgetown Hoyas, strippers, and a whole rack o' other muhfuckas gonna be skinnin' and grinnin' up in his face. So it's gonna be easier than a muhfucka to peel his cap back right in the middle o' the festivities and roll the fuck out cause it's gonna be so many muhfuckas up in the joint all at once. So you two are gonna have access to the party cause I know the doorman personally and he already knows what to do for me concernin' that 'cause it's an invitation only affair. So if you don't have a special pass or if your name's not on the guest list you just short. Trina . . . Boo, you tot'n', right?"

"Think I ain't?"

"That's my girl. Kofi gonna walk with the forty four caliber. I already know you got ya lil' Tech joint hidden up in the purse. So now that you both are ready, let's handle this light work and get the fuck up outta there. The same driver that's gonna drop y'all off is gonna be waitin' in the getaway car right outside on the corner of Georgia Avenue and Military Road. So once again, get in, kill that bitch nigga and get out . . . that's it and that's all."

Trina and Kofi loaded their weapons for the deadly task which awaited them. Kofi listened to a brief review of instructions from Wills before escorting Trina out to the ornate Lincoln Town car that Wills had provided for the hit.

The Ibex Night Club was jumping with lively Go-Go music, hip hop, and R&B and a sweaty partying crowd of young adults mostly in their early and mid twenties. Dozens more waited outside the entrance in a long line that trailed down the steps and out near Military Road. Each time the heavy door was opened to admit a couple or group into the vociferously loud interior of the establishment, thumping bass would escape leaving the eardrums of passersby ringing from the beat.

The doorman, a large beefy fellow with a mean looking scowl permanently frozen upon his pug-ugly face noticed the young couple waiting impatiently in the slow moving line and waved them to the front where he quickly took their tickets and directed them toward the bar.

The assassins noticed a magnificently set table near the bar in which a large number of special guests were seated. The two or three dozen assorted men and women sat among a vast multitude of colorful balloons, birthday cards, and champagne bottles laughing and chatting inaudibly as the deafening music masked their conversations. From the distance of the doorway, Trina and her escort worked their way through the tangled maze of dancing revelers to the bar next to the birthday table and ordered two rounds of rum and coke. They were right next to the empty chair where Nutt Wormsley would sit once he arrived.

The doorman had to have been paid nicely by Wills for the position of the party table was set up directly across from the exit door in which an unidentified man nodded and flashed a thumbs up sign when Trina and Kofi looked over in his direction. Though her trigger finger was getting itchier by the minute, she still felt the same type of nervousness and butterflies that she felt right before shooting Lil' Mo' Gentry. So Trina gulped down a mouthful of rum and coke and took in a deep breath to regain her composure. She had never tag teamed with another shooter before and she was trying hard not to show how uncomfortable she'd suddenly become with the entire set up.

Glancing over at Kofi, she found he looked completely calm and cool as can be. He even flirted with a few women seated next to them at the bar, acting as though he was at the club to pick up honeys, not to kill someone.

Damn! *Was he fine*, Trina thought, looking on as Kofi conversed with a busty girl with big hair and gaudy make-up. It was very rare for the mostly lesbian Trina to show a marked romantic interest in the opposite sex, save for monetary gain. However this time it was different, strange even. She could not deny her attraction to the suave, clean cut twenty two year old hunk sitting next to her. Occasionally he'd turn to her and chit chat briefly about mostly trivial matters or offer to buy her another round once her first drink neared the bottom of the ice-filled glass. But she'd cooly decline his offer and in general showed him an outward lack of interest the entire time they were there.

She still harbored an inbred distrust of men, planted deep within her psyche by the brutal violation of her body visited upon her nightly by a depraved stepfather not so long ago. Trina had only felt like this for one other person, and that individual was a female. Never had she felt her heart go pitter-pat for any male . . . that is until now. There wasn't anything or anyone that Trina wanted that she couldn't eventually have. She now had her sights set firmly on Kofi Dwayne Whitman.

Immediately the D.J. announced over the air that Carl Wormsley had arrived and a thunderous chorus of "Surprise!" went up from the crowd of partygoers as the shocked drug lord entered the room followed by his thugged out entourage. After the D.J. and crowd delivered a raucous rendition of "Happy Birthday", Nutt Wormsley and his H Street crew were all seated by waitresses and cordially greeted by the owner himself.

Nutt had only been seated but for a few short minutes before club staff, his henchmen, and desirable young women all began fawning over him as though he was a living god. It always amazed Trina To see how power, prestige, and money would 'cause anyone to kiss ass.

Trina got up from the barstool on which she sat and straightened her hip-hugging, leather skirt and pounded back the final sip of rum and coke before gently placing the ice-filled glass back onto the countertop. Her soft hazel brown eyes narrowed as she zeroed in on the arrogant leader of the 8th & H Street crew, who sat amidst the joyous applause, laughter, and ribbing of his many admirers as he observed two topless, thong wearing strippers emerge from the top of a huge birthday cake which had been rolled out to the middle of the dance floor. Trina carefully looked over every single person, male and female, seated at the long table along with Nutt and his crew. Everyone was caught up in the moment as Nutt Wormsley enjoyed the erotic gyrations of the sex kittens before him. They were all oblivious to anything else going on in the immediate area, which was just perfect for Trina and Kofi.

Trina was ready to open fire but still both she and Kofi knew better than to blow it by ruining the element of surprise through any abrupt action. They'd have to bide their time until the right time presented itself and eventually it would.

Trina took Kofi up on his original offer and had yet another glass of rum and coke placed in front of her by the waiter who was almost too enthralled by the risqué strip tease going on to properly serve his customers. Kofi lit up a Black & Mild cigar and joked with the waiter and a few other guys at the bar as they all lusted over the exotic dancers.

Trina realized that Kofi was no rookie to the dark world of crime. He handled himself like a pro. No outward signs of jittery nerves could be seen as he casually puffed on the cigar and drank down several shot glasses filled with rum, occasionally grimacing from the bite of the strong amber liquid. Even during this time of serious concentration on the matter at hand she couldn't keep her eyes off Kofi Whitman.

With everyone's attention focused on the raunchy strip tease, Trina nudged Kofi and nodded toward the laughing wolf-whistling crowd at the table cheering on the sexy dancers whose movements became all the more racy as bills were tossed toward them by the aroused men. Now was the perfect time to strike. Trina slowly reached inside her leather purse fishing around for a second before her fingers felt the cold steel of the Tech Nine. She grasped the weapon and clutched it tightly within her, right hand. Kofi, who carried the powerful forty-four magnum in his loose fitting slacks, removed the weapon and held it on his lap as he sat on a barstool near the edge of the counter.

Applause erupted among the partygoers as the exotic dancers sashayed from the dance floor toward the dressing room in the rear. Several local comedians roasted the drug lord humorously bringing hearty laughter from everyone present including his two enemies. Afterwards an amateur Go-Go band took center stage bringing the crowd to their collective feet stepping in time with the beat of the Congos while the energetic band worked up a sweat under the luminous glow of the spotlight shining down on them in the center of the dance floor.

Trina held the assault weapon steady as her partner moved away from the barstool and made his way over to where Carl Wormsley was sitting. Nutt was laughing with a few of his boys when his killer approached the table from his blind side. Trina watched in amazement as the new object of her affection took aim at the H Street leader with both hands wrapped firmly around the grip of the massive pistol. The barrel of the forty four spewed forth bright red orange flashes of flame as the young hit man squeezed off three murderous rounds into Wormsley.

The thunderous report of the gunshots reverberated throughout the club as everything suddenly came to a shocking halt. Several women screamed out in wide-eyed horror as they watched the mortally wounded Nutt jerk about violently as hollow tip shells ripped into his chest, shoulder, and abdomen. Nutt with the final embers of life, clutched at the massive bullet wound in the center of his chest with his right hand and grasped the table cloth with his left pulling it along with the contents of the table top to the floor as he fell from his seat.

As the one time violent drug dealer lay dead upon the floor, the club itself became a chaotic scene of pandemonium and disorder as scores of terrified and screaming guests bolted toward the front door in a mad dash to escape the gunshots, trampling to death several unfortunates during the ensuing stampede. Trina covered Kofi as he beat a hasty retreat towards the side exit door with a steady spray of gunfire from the Tech Nine mowing down four of Nutt's henchmen in the process.

During their successful escape, the couple left a madhouse of screaming women and yelling men, to which was soon added the loud wails of police and ambulance sirens. Once Trina and Kofi left the frenzied panic-stricken atmosphere of the Ibex Night Club through the side exit door they were picked up within a two-minute span of time by the driver of the Lincoln Town car on the corner of Military Road directly behind the club itself. Seconds later as the two assassins lounged back comfortably on the plush velvet upholstery, they both breathed a long sigh of relief as the long luxury vehicle drove away rapidly down the side streets and back roads of the District's most notorious hoods.

"Aired his bitch ass out," Kofi said bluntly.

The excitement of living dangerously in combination with the alcohol made him feel bold and he began putting his mack down.

"Thanks for coverin' me back at the club. Cause if it hadn't been for you I'd o' gotten shot up on that joint. You know we 'bout to get paid like a muhfucka off this hit for sure. Damn girl, you straight go hard, don't you?"

"Gotta go hard if you tryin' to survive in the game, you feel me?" answered Trina calmly.

He moved over closer to her and wrapped his beefy arm

around her shoulder playing in her hair as he pulled her in closer to him. Trina was inflamed with desire and made no attempt to push him away.

"Since we're gonna see each other almost every day why don't we start seeing each other outside o' hustlin' and shit? Cause I seen the way you been starin' at me and I feel the same way 'bout you, Boo. So, whassup? You tryin' to make this thing of ours official or what?"

"C'mon now. What do you think? Of course!" Trina said smiling broadly. Without a moments notice, he took her in his arms and placed his lips upon hers in a steamy, tongue tangling kiss, Trina's heart rate increased and she felt the unmistakable moisture of feminine arousal saturating the sheer fabric of her panties. As the two youngsters engaged in a heated display of hormone-driven affection on the back seat, Trina once again made no effort to resist his advances.

Chapter 10
Guns & Roses

The brutal murder of Carl "Nutt" Wormsley at the Ibex Night Club caused a sensational fervor within the local news media and for weeks the airwaves, papers, and barbershops were replete with suppositions as to the identity of the killers. Though the media may have been stumped as to who could've carried out the hit, DC Police as well as most of the hood knew better than most who had the clout and motive to pull off such a daring contract killing. Cops apprehended Trey Wills at his Valley Green home and dragged him down to the 7th District Police Precinct for an intense questioning and interrogation process that lasted for over ten straight hours. But he held fast to telling them absolutely nothing in addition to giving them the run around. After ten hours of hard line questioning, the 7th District Police had come up just as empty as when they first nabbed their prime suspect. They reluctantly released the Valley Green drug lord and went back to the tedious task of gathering vital evidence in the elusive murder case.

It seemed to everyone in the hood that Trey Wills would escape the clutches of the law yet again. But the infuriated sur-

viving members of Nutt Wormsley's H Street Crew were determined to destroy Wills and his cartel for the murders of
their leader and the four crew members who'd accompanied
him to the club on that fateful night. Trina and Kofi were
never mentioned in connection with the murders, and Trey
Wills showed them both appreciation for a job well done by
paying out a hefty sum of fifteen grand a piece as well as two
new vehicles straight off of the showroom floor. A Mercedes
Benz for Trina—she'd lost hers a while back by never returning to get it from the repair shop. She simply had chalked it up
as a loss. Kofi was treated to a Cadillac. Wills was more than a
little pleased about the hit and assured them that because of
the efficiency of the job, they'd be considered for future operations.

In a bold and blatantly disrespectful move, Wills mailed off
sympathy cards to the parents and baby mamas of Nutt
Wormsley. In the meantime, Trina was asked to secretly monitor the activities of the 8th and H Street Crew reporting their
weekly movements back to Wills. But he didn't send Trina
back on the strip to oversee the day-to-day operation of his
various Southeast area Crack spots. The drug kingpin understood that the girl was now far too valuable to his cartel to ex-
pose to unnecessary danger on the streets of the projects.
Trina had now been promoted to a high-ranking level in the
Valley Green Cartel. Her duties now consisted of handling
Will's business operations whenever he was out of town on
business or pleasure trips. She ordered the dope men to carry
out their jobs as usual and received the bulk of Trey Will's cut
at the end of each day or week that he was absent, never skimming a single dime off the top for herself, but always delivering his full earnings to him upon his arrival. And woe to the
baller who attempted any such thievery himself on her watch
for her punishment could be fatal.

In her own leisure time she could be found in the company
of Kofi Whitman. And the more the two thug lovebirds got

with each other the more they wanted to be closer. Their love affair blossomed more and more with each candle light dinner, movie, and of course hotel visit. By October 23rd, 1987, Kofi suggested to Trina that they move into their very own apartment together.

"I dunno about that, Baby . . . I ain't never lived with no man before and I told you before that this is a first for me," she answered with blunt honesty.

"Look, I know all about that bullshit your stepfather did. You've told me like a dozen times. You gotta get that negativity outta ya head, Trina! This is me you talkin' to, Kofi . . . K-Dawg. I ain't yo' punk ass stepfather. All men ain't a bunch of child molesters and shit. You gotta give a nigga a chance to show you how a woman's s'pose to be treated. Can I get that much? . . . Damn! I mean fuck it! If it don't work out I'll leave the apartment to you. We can get a month-to-month lease if you want."

"Well . . . I dunno. It could work out. I do jive like fuck with you like that," she admitted giggling lightly, staring at him seductively with those hazel bedroom eyes of hers. "But then again, I'm still not too comfortable with ya'll niggas—specially pretty boys like yourself. Y'all just got too much shit with you. That's all. I know you got plenty bitches that wanna get with you so don't even go there with no 'you're the only one I'm fuckin' with' bullshit cause it'll only piss me off that you're lyin' to me."

So you're tellin' me that I'd cheat on you? Is that what you're sayin' . . . huh?"

C'mon, young, stop playin' with me and shit. Every nigga I know fucks around at some point. I ain't met a male yet that ain't a dawg. Some o' y'all just cheat a lil' bit more than others. That's the only difference."

"Oh, is that right? How you figure that?" Kofi questioned persistently.

She shook her head lightly chuckling to herself at the audacity of the question.

"You know good and damn well what the fuck I'm talkin' 'bout, nigga. Don't act dumb or better yet, don't treat me like I'm one o' them lil' dizzy broads you used to fuckin' wit' . . . I don't give a fuck how phat a bitch is or how good her pussy is, y'all muhfuckas just never satisfied with one woman for too long. I mean I'm not sayin' that y'all can't love your woman and all. I'm just sayin' that it's in a man's nature to chase pussy . . . that's all. I mean, I ain't mad at ya for real though cause if most females would recognize that simple fact of life they'd save themselves a whole lotta grief. That's something I'm gonna teach my daughter cause I'll be damned if I'm gonna let her be one o' these naïve chicks who don't know shit 'bout niggas."

"Girl, you just too go hard for you own good. I know what yo need to calm you down some," he said placing her hand on the rock hard bulge which protruded visibly along the front of his sweatpants.

"See what I'm talkin' 'bout? Y'all ain't nothing but walkin' hard-ons. Look at you!" she smiled pulling her hand away and playfully smacking him sharply on his broad shoulder.

"Girl, don't even act like you don't like ridin' this big muhfucka, shit! You better act like you know!"

"Yeah nigga, but you the one that be curling up sleep after I throw this tight young pussy on yo' big bubbled up ass and what?"

With that said Trina knew that she'd won the verbal sparring contest and the couple embraced each other warmly. Trina felt safe and protected in Kofi's strong arms though she could handle herself more than adequately against any foe. It felt good to leave that concern to someone else for a change.

Kofi was extremely handsome, suave and debonair in his style of dress and behavior, and yet still . . . he was a straight gangsta, thorough, tough and fearful of no one, regardless of who they were or their reputation. He reminded her of a sort of male version of herself. It was for all these reasons that she was so intensely in love with him. But as always in the life of a hustler the euphoria of a young love affair couldn't overshadow the harsh, oftentimes unpleasant reality of the dope game. Contrary to the belief of Trey Wills that the H Street Crew would soon disband due to the lack of mature business-like leadership, instead the drug crew had been taken over by Nutt's thirty-five-year-old Uncle Roland Carter.

Carter had been home from serving an ten-year prison sentence at the Lorton Reformatory Facility in Virginia for about two weeks now and vowed to avenge his nephew's murder at the gravesite. A short, thin balding man with a narrow rat-like face and tiny stony gray eyes, Roland Carter was a formidable and wily adversary who was more than able to reorganize business in the direction which his late nephew would've wanted it to go. Some in the dope game even had Roland Carter going to heights yet uncharted by his murdered nephew.

Roland Carter at one point and time was a member of the notorious "A Team", a violent youth gang that ruled the streets of inner city Washington, DC, especially during the early '70s. Carter had a most unsavory reputation of being willing to murder anyone who angered him or stood in his way. He was rumored to have choked to death a stripper who refused to give him oral sex when he was only eighteen and was named as a suspect in dozens of murders and attempted murders throughout the city as well as Maryland's P.G. County.

Dubbed "Killer Carter" by cops and dealers alike, Carter was a blood thirsty man who'd even ordered three hits from his Lorton, VA, prison cell through letters and phone calls. It didn't take long for the grim command given by Killer Carter to be carried out.

On Halloween night, two of Trey Wills' crack dealers were found shot dead inside a red Ford Bronco parked in a wooded area of P.G. County's Fort Washington Park. When Park

Rangers discovered the vehicle the engine was still running as the two men, both twenty years old, lay dead in the blood soaked back seat. They had been tied up and shot execution style. One of Trey Wills limousines was then firebombed a day after the P.G. murders, killing Wills' favorite aunt, her husband, and Wills' personal driver who had spirited Trina and Kofi away from the scene of the Ibex shooting. And as one final calling card, Trey Wills' two beloved rottweilers, "Kurupt" and "Cashmere" were killed and dismembered with a handwritten note that gave a chilling warning. It read . . .

November 3, 1987,
   You are the biggest bitch in DC. You a punk and a sucker. I'm going to keep killing your folks just like I killed your dogs. If you a real man like people claim you are, see me on these streets. I dare you to 'cause you can't see me—you too scared. So stay your little bitch ass right where you belong in Valley Green 'cause when I see you I'm going to kill you and until that time I'm going to kill everybody and anything that you love. Believe that! You gump ass nigga.

                                        Sincerely,
                                        Roland Carter

   P.S. (Watch your back)

"I don't believe this muthafucka had the nerve to even come near this house much less leave some dumb shit like this! Fuck! I don't like shit like this!" said Wills crumpling up the handwritten note and tossing it into a nearby wastebasket.

"Well? Let's put this cat to sleep just like we did his nephew. Work ain't hard for real," suggested Trina, speaking from the level of a top lieutenant in Wills' army of thugs.

"Hold up, hold up . . . I've been in this type of situation before, Trina and believe me, you can't just go tit for tat all the time just cause some hothead bamma poppin' off at the mouth and bustin' guns to make a statement. I'm just as pissed off as you or anybody else around here because of everybody who lost their lives because of that lil' bastard including my dogs I loved dearly, but hey that's the nature of the beast. You've got to take the good with the bad out here, baby. The game comes with lots of heartaches, headaches, and losses as well as money, power, and riches. That's just how it is. Been that way since the old days of Al Capone and Bugsy Siegal and shit ain't 'bout to change now."

"Trey, I don't mean no harm or disrespect, but that's bullshit, Slim . . . niggas gonna think you soft if you don't bring that drama to them jokahs. I know 'bout all o' that philosophy shit you talkin' but fuck all that mystical Zen shit right about now. This nigga just kilt yo' boys, yo' auntie, yo' uncle . . . and even yo' dawgs, young Nigga, Fuck THAT!! If you don't take care o' this nigga, I will. Trust me!"

"Trina, Boo . . . listen to me . . . you gotta learn to relax, think things over with a clear head, and not raw emotions. You see, going off of your emotions will get you locked up or even killed. You see there's more than one way to skin a cat. You gotta use all of your resources, all of the time. Never become one dimensional because then you'll invite disaster. Besides, I'd rather concentrate most of my energies into makin' a dollar rather than havin' shootouts with a muthafucka every other day. That type of shit makes you hot, and when the block is hot you can't make no money, and if we can't make money, we don't eat or live lovely like we doin' right now. You want that? Of course not! Now go home and calm down. You'll see. I got this."

After receiving her usual father-like hug and kiss from Wills, Trina left Valley Green feeling very angry and confused by her boss. For the first time Trina questioned the manhood and courage of Trey Wills. She did not realize that although they both were hustlers to their very core, Wills, having been a college educated banker before his entry into the illicit world of drug trafficking, had a working knowledge of how to operate a successful business and had studied with interest and open-minded enthusiasm the business philosophies of Mafia families such as the Gambinos, Genoveses and Gottis of New York and New Jersey. The quick-tempered Trina knew or cared little of such things.

Growing up in the rough neighborhood of Barry Farms Dwellings had instilled a sense of kill or be killed type attitude within Trina and anything opposite to that would receive very little respect. However the "old man" as Trina called him affectionately, never failed to amaze her with his many connections and clout within the Capitol City.

On the 16th of November, Wills was ordered to see the D.A. down at the DC Courthouse. He asked Trina to accompany him as he went downtown dressed in a formal gray business suit and tie. District Attorney Francine Gonzalez was a Mexican-born raven-haired beauty by way of Los Angeles. She possessed delicate golden brown skin, sexy full lips and a body that wouldn't quit.

"What are you are doing, Will? Do you think that these murders bode well for you or something? I need for you to put a stop to the gunplay now. Do you understand, Mr. Wills?" She angrily yelled at Wills, "It better stop and I mean NOW!"

"Look, you'd better back up off me. Don't forget that you're on my payroll, aiight?"

"Absolutely. That's exactly why I've summoned you down here today. I do business with you, Sir, because you are a businessman, not a thug. Now I'm from L.A. so I know a thing or two about gang warfare and battles over turf. And I know that it causes a domino effect of terrible things, which affects everyone involved. Now this city already owns the title of Murder Capitol of the nation, but the real problem begins with our local media. This is Washington, DC, for christ's sake, Mr. Wills. Do you realize how many people read *The Washington Post* as well as *The Times*? Now every single T.V. news program and radio talk show is focusing on the alarming murder rate and the crack epidemic that fuels it. As expected the city's government is taking major heat which means my office is in the media's crosshairs. If something's not done soon about the turf war between your guys and whoever you've got a beef with, heads are going to roll and trust me when I say to you, Mr. Wills, I'll be damned if mine will!"

"True that. But you've got the wrong person. I've been doing business with you for a while now with no problem whatsoever. The reason for both of our headaches is coming from 8th and H Street and an ex-con named Roland Carter."

"Hmmm, that's funny because just yesterday around noon I spoke to that little guy you're talking about and he went on and on about you killing his nephew at that nightclub on Georgia Avenue, and how you and your crew were the aggressors, not him. Said he was fresh out of the can down in VA and wouldn't dare violate his probation. I don't know . . . he sounded really sincere, you know. I'll just say to you as I said to Mr. Carter—stop the fucking killing today, not tomorrow, not next week Tuesday—today! Alrighty then, have yourselves a nice day . . . and oh yeah, please close my door on your way out. Thank you for your time, Mr. Wills."

For the remainder of 1987 and for four months into 1988, drug-related violence and murder subsided considerably with an increase in police presence and widespread arrests and crackdowns. However with the bitterness and verbal threats boiling over between 8th & H Street and Valley Green, many people in the inner city knew that it was but a matter of time before one of the young thugs from either side squeezed off on somebody and that would start the ball rolling again. On top of it all, other upstart drug crews from around the city's projects had sprung up during the citywide police crackdown. Two other 7th District drug crews began to stir up trouble by setting up drug spots in neighborhoods not their own. Good Hope Road spawned a crew dubbed "Money Makin' Young'unz" and Langston Lane gave rise to a bold group of crack dealers, and armed robbers who went by the name "Soufeast Soldierz".

6th District also bred an extremely violent crew of fifty-five young ex-cons who hailed from Mayfair Mansions and called themselves "Fifty-Five Killer Mob" specializing in both narcotic trafficking and black market gun smuggling. They were well organized and savagely aggressive, immediately dealing a brutal death to anyone seeking to take over their turf. They ruled Mayfair Mansions with an iron fist and few crews if any dared challenge them.

Trina hadn't seen gunplay of any type for several months now since the crackdown and was growing very irritable and uneasy by the day. She was ticked off about the murders of Valley Green Cartel members, which still had not been avenged nor even talked about further. And now all of these other newly formed drug crews were strong-arming their way into Valley Green territory, without so much as a single peep out of Trey Wills. She'd had enough of her boss' timid approach to the disrespect of the various rival crews moving in or their territory especially the hated H Street crew.

Trina decided to gather up Pooh and a group of Barry Farms youth and take matters into her own hands when finally shit hit the fan. She, Wills, and two other Valley Green Cartel members were enjoying a Mike Tyson heavy-weight prize fight on pay-per-view down in the basement of Wills' rowhouse. Suddenly there was clatter of semi-automatic gunfire and the shrill crash and tinkling of shattered glass. Bullets could be heard hissing back and forth throughout the kitchen and living room. Though they were safe down in the basement, Trina and company still took cover down on the carpeted floor of the basement as they waited out the thirty seconds of hell going on upstairs.

No doubt this latest attack was supposed to be a direct attempt on the life of Trey Wills. Surely this latest assault could not go unchallenged. Though Wills went unscathed, another of his crew, Courtney Niles, had just come from the kitchen with a bowl of popcorn, and attempted to descend the stairs when the shooting began. She was lucky to have escaped with only a minor flesh wound from shattered glass debris. The girl was not badly hurt, but after she was treated and released from D.C. General, she gave up drug dealing forever.

Trina noticed that afterwards Trey Wills was a nervous wreck and never really recovered fully. He was as he said a businessman not a thug and now it truly showed. He wasn't built for the grimy parts of the drug game and now that segment of the hustle had taken its toll on him. The failed hit, which had been prepared to take out Wills, had Trina thinking about little else than revenge, she felt as the second in command to Wills himself, she would finally be able to give the 8th & H Street Crew a taste of their own medicine.

Trina traveled to Baltimore and brought a dozen or so assault rifles from a connect who was a well-known arms dealer and good personal friend of Trina's. She brought back AK's, street sweepers, and AR-15's. Then she went on a late night trip to Northeast, DC.

The crew usually hung out on the stoop of a red brick rowhouse along 8th street. Many times until the wee hours of the morning smoking weed, drinking, and playing the dozens. The home that they hung out at was Nutt Wormsley's parents' home and Nutt's younger brothers Donald and Frank still hung out with the older crewmembers each day.

The house, which was located directly across the street from a Rite-Aid Drugstore, was on a dark quiet street after nightfall. Sitting along with her reliable homeboy, Pooh, and a few other Barry Farms hoodlums in Pooh's big Cadillac, smoking a blunt or two, Trina zeroed in on a group of five or six young men laughing and joking on the stoop of the red brick building, oblivious to the fate that awaited them.

Trina took one last drag on the potent roach of the blunt

before plucking it out the window and into the dark. She exhaled a heavy plume of marijuana smoke and nodded to Pooh.

"Aiight, Dawg, let's go air these niggas out!" Trina said placing the last of the hollow-tipped Black Talon shells into the magazine.

She slammed the clip into the AK-47 and pointed out the targets. Pooh started the engine of the long Caddy and drove slowly pass the stoop. As the car passed the neighboring houses just before the red brick house, everyone inside the Cadillac begun locking and loading their weapons. The Caddy finally stopped in front of the stoop and turned the headlights off. The teens on the stoop had been smoking marijuana and drinking heavily so their senses were slightly impaired. They peered suspiciously at the strange vehicle before finally realizing the danger they were in.

Trina pointed her AK-47 out the passenger's side window and sprayed the steps with a furious volley of gunfire which was accompanied by the machine gunfire of her partners in the backseat, who leaned out the windows on both sides mowing down the teenagers who could do little to save themselves during the late night sneak attack. Everybody on the stoop lay dead or dying as their blood leaked out onto the steps and trailed down the sidewalk. Dogs began barking, car alarms sounded loudly, and lights came on all over the narrow street on both sides.

The car raced away from the murder scene as terrified residents screamed and wept as they looked on at the bullet-riddled bodies sprawled out on the bloody steps. Trina rolled up another blunt as a victory smoke. She had finally meted out the same measure of vengeance and now the rivals of Valley Green would know that to challenge them would mean immediate and harsh consequences.

Chapter 11
Top Bitch in Charge

A t first Trina dealt with the idea of not seeing her daughter or mother pretty well. After all it was for their own good. She was deep in the game and with cops as well as rival gangsters hunting her down, she couldn't risk bringing any harm their way. She hadn't seen or held her daughter in her arms for such a long time, it began to wear on her mind.

The hustle game had blessed her with material riches, power, and the fear of her enemies. Yet, sadly it had cursed her with constant watchfulness, mistrust of others, and a desire to protect her loved ones which left her with no choice but to limit the time she'd spend in their lives to the point of being almost non-existent.

Already she had a crazy cop after her, numerous crews from various hoods in the city, and God only knows who else considered her an enemy. So she had to live with the fact that she might never have a chance to see her beloved family again. During these painful times of soul-searching, Trina preferred to keep to herself going on long lonely walks along the Anacostia River or on desolate bike trails beside the babbling brooks of Rock Creek Park.

Kofi noticed her somber moods and tried his best to cheer her up, but to no avail. Even though she was a thug, tough as nails and many times ruthless, she was nonetheless still a young woman and most importantly a mother. She desperately missed her mother and child and fretted over them for the remainder of May 1988.

During the early weeks of June 1988, Kofi decided that Trina needed a change of scenery in order to take her mind off of things for a while. So he and Trina spent almost the entire month of June traveling to such exotic locales as Miami Beach, Cancun, Mexico, The Virgin Islands, Las Vegas, Hawaii and Jamaica. Kofi spent thousands of dollars in round-trip airfare, hotels, shopping sprees, and leisure activities, all to please his 'ride or die' chick.

On the last leg of their exotic month long vacation, Kofi saved the final week for Hawaii. As Trina slept soundly within their Montego Bay ocean front resort room, Kofi placed a pair of roundtrip airline tickets on the nearby night stand beside a large vase of fragrant long stem roses. When she finally arose from her drunken slumber, she was pleased to find the roses and tickets. She met Kofi as he walked into their resort room from outside, on the sun drenched deck, with a passionate open-mouthed kiss and warm embrace.

"Kofi, thank you sooooooo much for being such a sweet heart! I love you. You know that right?" Trina cooed as she draped her arms around her man's big, broad shoulders.

"Anything for my lady. Anything to make you happy, gorgeous," Kofi replied.

The young couple rode first class aboard 'Air Hawaii' for several hours, over the gulf of Mexico. They cuddled closely in their reclining chairs eating a delicious continental meal, while crossing the beautiful, vast stretches of water across the Pacific viewing Prince's box office hit "Purple Rain" on the cabin's movie screen. After landing in Oahu, the couple had their luggage delivered ahead of them toward their luxurious hotel suite. They enjoyed the lush, tropical scenery surrounding them, from the back seat of an elegant whit limousine. When the lovebird finally reached their destination Trina was blown away by the sheer size and splendor of the vacation suite, in which Kofi had booked a magnificent, saltwater aquarium complete with various tropical fish and colorful coral reefs, that took up the entire wall above the king size bed. Miniature palm trees were fashioned as canopy poles while large tiki masks decorated the wall opposite the bed. Twin tiki torches stood on both sides of the back door, leading to the outside veranda. Trina could do little but fall into Kofi's waiting arms, holding him tightly for, what seemed to her, an eternity.

One night as they strolled hand in hand, clad in a bikini and swim trunks across the beautiful white sands and gentle surf of Waikiki Beach in Honolulu, Kofi and Trina made passionate love beneath a drooping palm tree which added to the romantic ambience of the moonlit beach. After the conclusion of the sweaty erotic interlude, they huddled wet and naked in each other's arms looking out across the moon bathed sea and dark shadowy volcanic mountains beyond.

"You know I love you, Tee. You mean everything to me . . . everything. I'd die for you, girl. I truly mean everything I just said. So please, Baby, let's just move in together like I suggested earlier. I wanna be there to love you. I wanna be everything that a man should be for his woman. Know what I mean? And don't come telling me no bullshit 'bout some you ain't ready and you scared or none o' that shit. Cause I ain't havin' it. Aiight?"

"Stop bein' pressed! We can look for some place to stay when we get back to DC on Friday. Okay? You happy now? Damn!"

"Don't be playin' and shit, Tee. I'm serious now. As soon as we get back home we're gonna go apartment huntin'.."

"Didn't I tell you that we'd look around for a place? Boy,

you worrisome as shit, ain't you? Keep fuckin' with me and I'm gonna tell you hell to the no. So that's it my nigga."

"Girl, I'm tired of you carryin' a nigga. I'm gonna put his dick in yo' mouth if you don't shut the fuck up."

"Boy, shut yo' mouth and hold me tight with yo' phine ass. But for real though, I'm gonna really like livin' with you, Kofi. You know how much I love you . . . even though you get on my muthafuckin' nerves sometimes. You're my man and I love you, boo."

Later that night in their beachside bungalow, Kofi couldn't sleep. He was too excited. He and the woman whom he loved were about to begin their life together under the same roof. He poured himself a late night shot of rum before turning in. He took this time to admire the one person who had gotten close to his heart. As he looked on Trina's gloriously stunning beauty, as she slept peacefully across the King-sized bed, the moonlight-dappled shades of horizontal shadows came through the Venetian blinds falling across her curvaceous nakedness. He felt blessed to be able to call this most lovely dime piece his own.

When the love struck couple returned to the Nation's Capitol, it was the second week of July '88. Though she wished that she stayed longer in the beach front paradise Hawaii had provided, she knew that play time had come to an end and there was now work to be done. Trina's first order of business was to meet with Wills as soon as they returned home from the airport. Trina met him at an IHOP in Crystal City, VA. When she arrived, Wills was already present sipping on a tall glass of apple juice and reading the Metro Section of *The Washington Post*.

Trina approached the lonely booth where he sat and kissed him on the cheek before sitting down across from him. Wills folded the paper neatly placing it beside him on the seat and fixed his gaze upon her. He seemed a little agitated about something, so she inquired.

"Whassup, Trey? Why you lookin' all mad and shit? You got woman problems again, Boo? Tell me who she is and I'll go straight to her chin, aiight?" Trina announced playfully trying to lighten the heavy mood that hung over the table.

Wills smiled weakly, looked up towards the waitress who'd approached him and ordered another apple juice for himself while Trina refused any food or drink. When they were again alone Wills spoke candidly.

"Do you know anything about the murders of five kids on 8th Street, Northwest a couple of weeks ago? It's been on the news almost every night. Word on the street is young'uns from out Barry Farms were responsible. Did you have anything to do with those shootings?"

"You damn Skippy, I did! Shit, I'm the one who made the phone call to my mob to go get them bastards," Trina said boldly almost forgetting that they were in a public place.

"Goddamn it, girl! I've told you more than once not to bring unnecessary drama on yourself out here. You got a dozen muthafuckin' cops just waiting for you to make a mistake and here you go fuckin' up again! You're gonna . . . Trina, I'm tryin' to tell you, you're gonna learn!"

"Well, I don't give a fuck! You see I ain't like you, Trey. I ain't lettin' muthafuckas strong arm us and not bust their muthafuckin' heads open. I'm gonna keep on air'n bammas out 'til they get it through their thick skulls not to fuck with VGC."

"Well, it's on you now. I ain't got shit else to do with what you pulled out here on these streets no more because I got my own problems that I've gotta deal with. You see, while you've been doing your thing for the past couple of weeks, I've been fighting a federal prison sentence that I've basically lost. Me, my brother Richard, my man Louis Knight, and my boy Jeremy Giles were all indicted on a fourteen count racketeering charge to include counts for drug-related murders, conspiracy to sell dope, prostitution, and dope dealing. So sweetheart,

I'm looking at thirty years to life. My baby brother, Ricky, poor guy . . . he got hit with three life sentences for the twenty-five murders he was indicted on. Louis was hit with nineteen years and Jeremy got life. I have been buying my time. I got a dream team of the best lawyers money can buy, so I've been assured that I can beat almost every single murder count except maybe two. "Ever since the a dry snitch dropped dime on us back in '85, the Feds have been fucking with us ninety goin' north. I've been in and out of court more times than I've cared to remember. So far I've managed to prolong the trials and stay outta prison, but I pretty much think that my luck, as well as my folk's, has run out". But my attorneys have assured me that I'll probably do only about fifteen of the thirty-year sentence . . . hell that's still one long ass vacation. Know what I mean?"

"Goddamn! Trey . . . Baby, I'm . . . I . . . I dunno what to say. I'm so sorry. That's fucked up. Damn, that just ruined my day. Damn."

"Yeah, I'm gonna be gone for a good lil' while down Lorton. So I'm preparing myself for the long haul. If the Feds get enough dirt on me from their stinkin' ass snitches, who knows, I could end up in prison for life."

"Trey, I'm real fucked up 'bout what's happened to you and all. I'm talkin' 'bout fucked up more than anything. But life gotta go on and business is business. Somebody gotta handle the day-to-day operations of the Cartel. Know what I'm sayin'? So have you thought about who'd be runnin' shit in your absence?"

"Already two steps ahead of you, baby girl," he said knowing exactly what pretty partner in crime was hinting at. The individual is sharp, very business-like and most importantly old school in thought and action just like me. I thought that that one quality would keep all of the drama that's poppin' off under wraps. I think you'll approve of my decision."

Trina did not even trying to conceal her disappointment behind the slight of having to partner up with somebody. Hadn't she more than proven herself to him time and time again? She loudly reminded her boss of the tens of thousands of dollars in illicit drugs that could possibly be lost under the wrong guidance.

"Calm your nerves, Trina, everything's gonna be taken care of. You'll see for yourself. Don't nobody care about my money more than I do. Believe that! Even a Lorton prison cell won't be able to keep me from running my business the way I wanna run it. Feel me? I've always been more than fair and generous to every last one of my people. Everybody from the gardener to my personal accountant got broke off proper like. And you of all people know that better than almost anybody else round this joint. Now you know I fucks with you. I love you more than some o' my own blood family members. So you gonna be aiight. I'm gonna put you in charge of all drug profits coming from the streets. You're to place fifty percent of my earnings in Wayne and Burrison's Funeral Home in Capitol Heights. My nephew Wayne knows what's up and he'll hold on to it for me. The other half you're gonna learn to break down aiight? Two-thirds is gonna go in your pocket and I want you to give the rest which should roughly be about another whole third to Bridgette Cruise cause she's gonna be your second-in-command. So there you have it . . . you are in charge now. But being in charge comes with big responsibilities, young lady. Both of you gals are full of fire but I need for the both of you to get along together, because with your skills at negotiating large scale drug deals, along with Bridgette's financial expertise, my organization won't skip a beat. But I gotta say this: You can't be out here lunchin' just because some lil' bamma got on your bad side or because you're P.M.S'n and every muthafucka and his brotha's piss'n you the fuck off. Naw. We can't have no more fuckin' up . . . period. I need you to run this shit the same way I would if I was home, got it? I know that you're more than capable of handlin' your business on a top executive level cause now you ain't got a choice. You asked for it, well now you got it. But don't fuck my money up with no dumb shit, Trina . . . I'm serious as a heart attack girl cause I ain't got no problem with demoting you back down to ice cream route runner if you cause trouble . . . no bullshit."

"You know I gotchya back, Trey. Have I ever let you down before? Huh? You already know the answer to that question, don't you? But I'm gonna tell you what I don't like the fact that you got me partnered up with that old simple ass Bridgette. You know good and well I can't stand that bitch. Uhhh!" snorted Trina in disgust.

"Look Trina, you're a good earner and all. You've been more than loyal to me and the Valley Green Cartel, but you're only twenty-years old. I know that you're much more mature than most young'uns your age but you've still got a lot to learn. And Bridgette has been in the game for a long time. Way back in '79 when the both of us used to sell nickel bags of weed in high school . . .

"Well that broad don't care too much for me either. So I'm quite certain that she's gonna be just as pissed as me once you tell her 'bout our lil' partnership thing."

"No, she ain't and even if she feels a lil' bit uneasy 'bout joining forces with you at first, she'll get over it real quick. You see, she's a thirty-six year old mother of three, so she's got the maturity needed to handle shit like this . . . besides she and I go way back. She won't want to disappoint a nigga."

For four days the Valley Green drug lord and his number one earner talked over all of the important business aspects of the Valley Green drug activities that he'd want not only to continue, but also to flourish even greater in his absence. During the four day criminal conference, Trina outlined with extreme attention to detail the various blueprints she had developed for the further advancement of the Valley Green Cartel. The three day meeting between Wills and Trina, which began on June 26th, was joined by Bridgette Cruise on the 30th who sat in on the business discussions, listening, debating, and adding her two cents worth as well.

A thirty-six year old, divorced mother of three teenaged daughters, Mrs. Cruise was an ungainly looking, coal black woman with short nappy hair, slight facial hair small beady black eyes and a hefty, potato sack like body that drew laughter and jokes of all types, behind her back of course. For though the homely older woman was an easy target for jokes and put downs, she was a fierce adversary to anyone whom she deemed an enemy. She often carried a switchblade concealed on her person and had been known to slice and dice those who'd made the mistake of disrespecting her to her face. She had little, if any, fashion sense at all and wore cheap poor fitting dresses on her dumpy frame and her feminine hygiene was questionable at best. She drank hard liquor mostly scotch from an old fashioned flask within her tattered handbag. Her breath and pores stank of it, often offending other members of the Cartel. Most people disliked the overweight lady for one reason or another. Only Trey Wills himself had love for Cruise. But of all the people who disliked Bridgette, none disliked her more than Trina.

Trina hated the elder woman with a passion and Bridgette equally felt nothing but contempt for the young Barry Farms native as well. Trina despised the older woman's poor hygiene and slipshod habit of dressing herself, yet she envied Cruise's undying loyalty and friendship with Wills, which transcended the test of time, and to Trina's chagrin showed no signs of being compromised. On the other hand Bridgette Cruise, a heavyset, ungainly looking female felt both intense envy and disdain for the lovely, young dime piece who'd so quickly moved up through the ranks of their organization, damn near overnight. Even with the smooth, peace-making attempt of Wills to patch bad feelings up between his two lieutenants, it would be a tremendously difficult task for even him to work out. But Wills had people skills that were at times uncanny and after a two hour sit down with both women, Wills had them shake hands and promise him that they'd work together for the good of the Cartel regardless of their personal feelings toward one another.

"Now then ever since we've straightened that bullshit out, once and for all I'm gonna need you two sistahs to make this money. That's it and that's all! Make this money, Shorty and keep makin' more and more until you stop fuckin' breathin; that's all I care 'bout . . . don't ever forget that shit!"

The two women stared each other in the eyes as they nodded in agreement with their leader. Trina's intuition picked up on the animosity that the older woman felt for her even though Bridgette smiled broadly in Trina's face a few feet across from her. Trina's temper instantly rose sizzling within her. Right then she decided within herself that if Bridgette Cruise ever crossed her it would be the last time she'd ever cross anyone again.

"I'm 'bout to dip, Trey. Holla at you tomorrow. Aiight?" Trina said cutting her eyes at Bridgette Cruise as she left.

Ever since Trina had joined their drug ring, cruise made little to no attempt to hide her dislike and distrust of the younger woman. Even, at one time, suggesting that Trey banish her from the crew altogether. This as well as other tales of Bridgette Cruise's animosity toward Trina reached her on her ice cream route via other members of the crew, who had taken a liking to the brash Barry Farms native.

Trina drove home towards Hyattsville feeling very much satisfied that for once she'd have a shot to run things the way she saw fit. That meant that she'd pocket more money than ever before and she'd bring down swift and brutal justice on enemies of the Cartel both far and near. Her only regret was having to work beside her arch rival Bridgette, much less sharing profits with her. To Trina that arrangement was a blower, the worst possible decision ever made by drug lord Trey Wills. She wondered *what possible business skills could Cruise have? Hell, she only halfway washed her ass for goodness sake!* Trina vented to herself, never being able to come up with satisfactory reasons for Wills' trust and devotion to the pug-ugly woman other than the fact that they were old high school buddies who sold weed in between classes. But that indeed was none of her business and she left it alone after that.

Right after the 4th of July celebration, Trina and Kofi begun the process of finding themselves an apartment that they'd both agree on. She told him all about her top ranking position in the Cartel and he showered her with praise and wished her well.

"Trey damned sure picked the right one to run things while he's on lockdown! Shit's 'bout to get hectic for other crews out here. Niggas better recognize," Kofi exclaimed filled with pride over Trina's achievement. "You just pace yourself and use caution before you make major decisions and business deals. Aiight, Boo?"

"Use caution? Pace myself? What? Boy, you sound dumb right about now. Fuck you mean use caution? I'm the one who hooked Trey up with hustlers from New York, Jersey and Philly. I'm the one who boosted this cat's income to where it is right now! Me! All by myself! So, I pretty much carried the load the whole time for real. Shit, if you don't know, you betta ask somebody!"

On July 9, 1988, the couple moved into a luxurious, fully furnished Georgetown Cottage apartment. The handsome love nest featured a hilltop view overlooking the Potomac River, three bedrooms, four bathrooms, mahogany and marble floors, marble foyer, gourmet kitchen, den, family room, a Jacuzzi, and built-in surround sound. The rent was $1,950 per month, but it was a lovely place in an exclusive Georgetown neighborhood where once JFK and Jackie had lived during the 1950's.

Trina loved the high-end crib and insisted that they keep it. Kofi had part ownership in his father's trucking company and used his father as a co-signer in order to pass the thorough credit check of the owners, who demanded proof of the income of a young Black man attempting to move into such an elite and predominately White neighborhood. Kofi rented the cottage on a month-to-month basis being unable to sway the fifty-seven-year-old stockbroker to allow him a year's lease. Nevertheless, both Kofi and Trina adored their new home. They threw a house warming celebration the following week after moving in.

Decorating their new home in both textures and colors to give an authentic, old Georgetown feel, Trina had Kofi buy two large PB square slip-covered sofas in natural twill; honey-colored sea grass wingback chairs accented the living room area. In the spacious dining room sat a teak dining table and two benches colored in warm mahogany. Bamboo table lamps with paper shades were mounted on the walls at each end of the sofa. The surround wallpaper was a white on beige Brock Hampton star pattern by Farrow & Ball. The windows were adorned with persimmon-colored Dupioni silk curtains, which flowed delicately in the late evening breeze coming in through the open panels. Exotic ivory mottled granite countertops covered the kitchen and bathrooms. The enormous backyard was handsomely manicured with brilliantly colored snap dragons, primroses and English daisies, while the flowering cherry trees and quince dogwoods provided comforting shade for both company and the couple themselves, out back.

Most of Trina and Kofi's childhood buddies and relatives attended the house-warming party bearing gifts and partying well in to the night, before slowly departing.

By the middle of July, on the 18th to be exact, Trina took Wills for the long drive to the Lorton Reformatory Correctional Center down in Lorton, Virginia. Trey Wills wanted to travel down to his awaiting prison home via private transportation instead of being all packed together in a hot, stuffy prison bus. And being the man he was, his street rep, along with a little bit of bribe money was more than enough for him to secure such personal perks. After they got to the facility, Trina and her leader hugged each other tightly, exchanging mutual words of encouragement and kisses on the cheek. Trina looked on sadly as the Valley Green drug lord was escorted in handcuffs by four burly Lorton prison guards into the facility with which he'd become quite familiar for a long time to come. Trina loved Trey Wills like the father she never had. He had been good to her. His wise words had taught her much and on occasion she would continue to send him cards for his birthday and holidays. And when time permitted, she and a crew of his old drug runners would travel down to the Lorton Prison to surprise the debonair old drug lord with a visit.

Later in the evening, Trina stopped off at Will's house to pick up a few of her personal items to take to her new digs in Georgetown. When she arrived she encountered Bridgette and her oldest daughter, Cassandra Lee, lounging in the living room gorging their fat faces on Domino's pizza.

"Hey, girl!" giggled Cassandra, steadily stuffing herself with slice after greasy slice of sausage and pepperoni pizza. "You want some?" she asked before letting go a loud disgusting belch.

"I don't want none o' that shit. Can you please move your legs so I can sit down, huh?" Trina snapped angrily.

"C'mon and move over here, Cassandra. Okay? Jesus!" Bridgette said irritably, clearing a space on the wide couch beside her for her daughter.

Cassandra reluctantly gathered up her food and drink which were scattered all over the coffee table and sat down next to her mother. Trina plopped down on Will's leather recliner and took up the T.V. remote and began channel surfing. Bridgette's eyes shifted from her daughter over to the girl nonchalantly leaning back in the big, soft leather recliner watching music videos and chatting on the phone. Bridgette cleared her throat and spoke up.

"Look, Trina . . . you need to get off the phone cause we gotta have a talk, for real."

"Lemme hit you back, okay? Trina said to her friend on the other line right before hanging up. "We gotta talk about what?" Trina asked in a cold tone barely looking in her elder's direction as she continued to flip through T.V. channels. Bridgette inquired about the day-to-day plans of the Cartel when Trina interrupted her.

"Ain't no plans 'bout to be given out to nobody yet. Everything is all good as far as I can see right now. Cats gonna basically get out here and sell this dope just like they been doin'. Ain't gonna be nothin' no different 'lest I tell you so, aiight?"

Bridgette and her daughter both stared at Trina with an unmistakable look of resentment. Trina boldly stared back at them, spinning around in the recliner in order to face the mother and daughter duo. She cracked her knuckles and clenched her fists expecting a fight. She was ready, even yearning for a chance to lock horns with Bridgette and her daughter both of whom Trina was sure would jump her at any minute. But this time she was wrong, nothing happened. Bridgette Cruise's eyes had narrowed into mean looking slits and she twirled a tiny toothpick back and forth between her thick red lips as she closely studied the youngster sitting across from her. She wanted to react to Trina's disrespect, but decided against it at the last minute.

"You know what? I ain't even gonna argue with you, Boo. You got this . . . holla. Let's go Cassandra, baby. I gotta get the fuck up outta here."

The Cruises cleaned up their mess, gathered their belongings and left Wills' house feeling pissed. Trina had let Bridgette Cruise know in no uncertain terms that it was now her show and all others would have to answer accordingly. Yet she realized that it was only a matter of time before she and the older Cruise would come to blows . . . or worse.

Trina stayed busy for the remainder of July '88, putting new plans into action, setting up new dope spots, crack houses and organizing new drug connections with outside dealers from as far away as Miami and Los Angeles. Several hundred dollars worth of monetary profits and drugs had come up short around the last week of the month which prompted an infuriated Trina to gather her troops together in order to hear an especially grim warning. A slow, torturous death would befall any Valley Green Cartel members who were caught skimming money or drugs. The stolen narcotics and cash were never recovered nor were the perpetrators ever found, however, Trina's warning had the desired affect on her crew because nothing of the sort ever happened afterwards. Trina also demanded that the 7th District, all of Southeast, be taken over by force from the other upstart drug crews that sprung up all over just before Trey Wills' imprisonment. Subsequently this order led to a series of bloody drive-by shootings that targeted several drug crews in and around Southeast Washington. These brutal attacks, many of them occurring in broad daylight, resulted in over two dozen or more killings . . . bringing the City's murder rate to epidemic levels.

By the second week of August, most of the Cartel's rivals were reduced to nothing and once more Valley Green dominated the Southeast's drug trade. Trina boldly moved the crew's headquarters to Condon Terrace, for a time joining the forces of the Valley Green Cartel with her thug homies from Barry Farms. She adopted a new name for the Cartel—'Go Hard Soldierz'. With the combined might of two of 7th District's most lethal crews from two of its most notoriously dangerous hoods, dope profits began skyrocketing beyond anything that Trey Wills' leadership had gained.

Once again Katrina Ricks had gained both the envy and fear of her enemies as well as the interest of the hated police. Early one Friday morning around 8:30 am, Trina's longtime friend Pooh interrupted her as she ate breakfast at his home.

"Hey Trina, guess who at the door? . . . That crazy ass Cowboy!"

Trina nearly choked on her apple juice as she looked up from her plate with a startled expression.

"You bullshittin', Joe? . . . Cowboy?

"I ain't bullshittin', that redneck muhfucka is right outside this door."

Trina's jaw tightened and her eyes narrowed as she recalled with in herself how the Texan had manhandled her in his office, harassed her to no end, and pretty much stressed her out to the point of her having to skip town altogether for a while. She had nothing but contempt for the cop and for him to dare approach her again brought her anger to the boiling point. She reached down on the chair beside her and grabbed a nickel-plated Desert Eagle, slammed a nearby clip into the bottom grip and cocked back on the handgun placing it within a partially opened drawer in the desk on which she ate.

"Open the fuckin' door," she snarled menacingly.

Chapter 12
Gotta Go Grimy Sometimes

Billy Ray Turner waltzed into Pooh's living room with arrogance and brazen disrespect of the drug dealer's den, knowing full well that he had very little to fear from any of the thugs in the room. Trina sat leaning forward on the desk twirling her finger around the rim of the glass in front of her as she glared angrily at the 7th District detective behind a dark pair of sexy Dolce & Gabbana sunshades occasionally glancing down at the burnished chrome of the powerful semi-automatic lying within the darkened drawer. She almost wished that the Texan would make a wrong move, giving her a reason to put a few choice hollow tips into his chest. But more importantly she wished that the overly curious detective wouldn't recognize her. Maybe it was because she had matured a little more or maybe it was the smart charcoal gray business suit that she rocked. Or maybe it was the sunshades, but whatever it was, it obviously worked because the hated Billy Ray Turner looked at her briefly and walked right passed her without so much as raising an eyebrow. Later Trina, would boast among her subordinate drug dealers that it was the sassy, raven black extensions she'd recently attached, that threw Turner off. The tall, sturdy Texan tipped his broad ten-gallon hat backwards a bit just enough to show his intense ice blue eyes covered over with bushy masses of eyebrow fur. He chewed slowly on a plug of tobacco as he walked over to a nearby couch and plopped down next to Pooh, spitting a nasty brown tobacco boogie into an ugly stained tin can.

"So now that your pathetic loser of a leader has gone bye-bye down in the Virginia sticks for a spell, I reckon y'all lil' dope runnin' darkies is sho nuff 'bout to behave ya selves a bit. Ain't that right, now?" drawled Cowboy sarcastically while blowing a kiss in Trina's direction.

Trina smirked and fingered the trigger of the loaded pistol.

"What the fuck you want, Cowboy? Huh? Why is you fuckin' with us? Damn!" Pooh was evidently upset as the tone of his voice suggested.

""Ha, ha, ha, HA! Don't act dumb with me, boy! You know damned well why I'm here. Now either you pay me my weekly cut that you niggers owe me or I'm gonna take every last one of your Black asses down to the DC jail. Okay, now . . . I'll just set for a spell and let y'all kinda digest that lil' ultimatum and get back at me with the RIGHT answer in a minute or two. I'll wait right here."

Pooh consulted with Trina and two other crewmembers that were present at the time. Trina directed one of the low ranking crew members to bring her a chair. Once the chair was placed next to her, Pooh sat down and began typing away at a keyboard in front of a computer monitor. Within minutes Pooh pulled up on the screen dozens of City government officials who had their names and positions added to a complex list of 'special' friends who Trey Wills secretly paid off for favors rendered. Wills, always the strict businessman had each individual's name alphabetically arranged along with the amount of weekly or month pay each official would receive.

Trina and Pooh quickly found the crooked cop's name and weekly fee. She ordered Pooh to satisfy the crew's weekly debt to the Texan. Reluctantly Pooh reached into his pocket pulling out a huge wad of cash from which he peeled off twelve one hundred dollar bills, tossing them before Cowboy spitefully.

"Aiight muhfucka . . . here's ya shit. Now get the fuck up outta here!"

Cowboy chuckled as he bent down to gather up the money that lay scattered all across the floor. After placing each Benjamin neatly into his worn leather wallet, he stuffed the billfold into the back pocket of his tight fitting denims and arose facing Pooh, as he placed another plug of chewing tobacco inside of his upper lip and gums.

"You dope niggers is powerfully dumb. Ya know that? Ya see if I chose to I coulda busted a bunch o' you good-for nothin' jungle bunnies a long time ago. But I thought long and hard about it and said *Billy Ray why work yourself into a lather just to stop a couple of stupid porch monkeys from killin' one another with guns and dope?* Hell, you're doin' the Government of the United States a powerful big favor by thinnin' the herd down a little. Saves us taxpayers money from havin' to support your lazy, shiftless, welfare beggin' asses."

Trina who was furious from the start could take no more of the redneck's racist comments and rose up abruptly from her chair removing her sunshades and laying them on the desk.

"Yeah, you can talk that shit if you want, but your hands is just as dirty as ours, partnah. Looks to me like if some shit was to go down all of us, yo' white ass included, would go down together. Now I don't think that the brothas up in the pen would treat you too nice, Detective Cowboy and you know this! So don't even come up in here with all o' that ole' bamma ass KKK bullshit. Aiight? Before somebody fuck around and drop a dime on yo' bitch ass. How about that?"

Trina saw that her bold warning had shocked everyone in the room including her enemy. She now had dirt on her hated enemy and could've cared less whether the detective recognized her or not now. She had him by the balls and he knew it as he finally begun to recognize her face and voice from before.

"So lil' darlin', I guess you're back to stay, huh? . . . Sorry but I can't say that I was all broke up when you were gone. What brings you back here?"

"That ain't none o' yo muhfuckin' business, Joe. You just worry 'bout doin' what Trey was payin' for you to do for us out here on the streets and it's all gravy. But as soon as you get to fuckin' with us, I'm gonna make sure the Mayor, the media, and everybody else know what's really goin' on down at 7th District. Feel me? Yeah, I thought so! Ya see I'm a hustla bitch so I don't give a fuck 'bout you or the oath you took to serve and protect. So you got a whole lot more to lose than a twenty-year-old Black "hood rat" like me. I'm gonna be aiight regardless."

"You're talkin' like you're in charge now or something. Are you?"

"You goddamn Skippy I'm in charge and I'm gonna be in charge until Trey gets outta prison. As you know that ain't gonna be no time soon. So anything that you want brought to his attention, you gonna now refer it to me. Got it?"

"This is a pretty tough way to make a living for any poor bastard least of all a young woman. I've been knowin' Trey for a long time and trust me when I tell you that most of them dealers working the little corner streets, back alleys, and crack houses round here are some real mean hombres . . . ornery as a nest of sidewinders. And I doubt if those rascals will take kindly to a twenty-year-old female tellin' them what to do."

"Them same dudes you talkin' 'bout already seen my work. They know what time it is. They seen me punish bitches and they seen me punish bitch ass niggas. I ain't trippin' cause don't nobody want that drama for real." Trina remarked as she pulled the heavy Desert Eagle from the drawer and carefully uncocked it, ejecting the clip into her free hand where she placed both magazine and weapon back into the drawer sliding it shut.

"I see . . . It's gonna take a hell of an effort to cut down on the competition threatening to come in here from Northeast. And I heard that a couple o' P.G. County dealers have been planning on extending their business towards the District, namely Southeast."

"Yeah? But see Trey let that bullshit happen when he was runnin' the show. Young'uns thought he was soft so they jumped out there. But I'm about to put the brakes on all o' that dumb shit. Watch!"

"Plus you've got those spics over in Northern Virginia calling themselves Mara Salvatrucha or MS-13. They're multiplying like fuckin' rabbits and movin' into DC, specifically Columbia Heights. They're mighty dangerous and there's too many of 'em to arrest. Not to mention the dope boys right around here in Condon Terrace. Rumor has it that these Condon Terrace dealers are kinda bent outta shape over your Barry Farms' posse setting up shop here. Word on the street is that they're setting up to force you and your buddies outta here."

"You co-signin' like shit, ain't you? But Hey, I guess 'cause you the police you know everything that's goin' on in the hood. Huh? Well run tell this . . . I don't give a fuck 'bout no MS-13 nor these niggas round here in Condon Terrace. If niggas wanna see us then tell 'em to bring it then, cause all that talkin' ain't shit to me for real. Trust me, muhfuckas will find out sooner or later that it's not a game out here. Now go and deliver that message, muhfucka!"

Trina had a young thug with long braided hair slam the door shut behind Cowboy as he departed in the direction of his unmarked police cruiser that was parked out front. Trina soon afterwards, along with Pooh, lectured seven of the teenaged dealers about what they had just witnessed. They had been exposed to the type of corruption that comes with great

wealth. Here was an example of a decorated and highly regarded police detective who had served in the Vietnam War
and was a Texas Ranger before traveling east to Washington,
DC, to join the Metropolitan Police Force, and for twelve
hundred dollars per week, he could be pimped as easily as any
prostitute strolling along the sidewalks of 14th & U Street,
Northwest. City officials of all positions were on Trey Wills'
payroll and with the crack cocaine epidemic at full tilt throughout the Beltway region, the crew had too much money to
make and too many political allies in their back pockets to fear
anyone now. Not even a Chief of Police or for that matter a
sitting Mayor was exempt from a hefty bribe. Everyone had a
price and for the right amount of money you could have anything or anyone that you wanted . . . no questions asked. Only
the public, taxpayers, and the uppity but totally brain-dead
middleclass working stiffs believed wholeheartedly in that
American pie bullshit. Anyone making a salary of forty grand,
if offered the same salary per month or even per week, they'd
be your personal slave. Trina knew it, as did most everyone in
the projects.

While Trina and Pooh hipped their young drug runners to
the rules of the hustling game their lecture was interrupted by
a phone call. Trina pointed to the young thug nearest the
phone and signaled for him to answer it. The teen answered
the ringing phone, spoke for a brief minute, placed the receiver down onto its cradle and turned slowly to face his two
leaders with a grave look upon his face.

"That was Ali and them. They said a couple o' stick up boys
ran up on the Langston Lane spot about a hour ago and
roughed our young'uns off for all their rocks and money and
shit. My man said they bust off at them niggas, but they rolled
out. Plus Choo and Spook got shot. Both of them young'uns
laid up in DC General Hospital right now. Ali said they're in
the E.R."

"Fuck! Where in the fuck was the muthfuckin' lookouts? I

told y'all niggas that I wanted no less than four lookouts on the spot at all times! Two on the roof, two on the ground with walkie-talkies. Why didn't that shit happen, Pooh? Huh? Why?" Trina screamed out in anger.

"Trina, you know ever since March, Allan, Chucky, Pete, and that nigga Brock all got locked up out 37th Street. You know this! Ain't no more lookouts right now or did you forget? We been doing what we can to cover that spot," retorted Pooh as he threw up his hands in frustration.

"Aiight! Whatever!! Fuck that!! We gotta concentrate on this shit right about now. Ain't nobody but that punk ass Roland tryin' to get back at us for shootin' up his spot on 8th & H. Don't worry though, we gonna break that bamma nigga off proper like and that's off the no bullshit."

Trina downloaded from Trey Wills' computerized files the entire roll call sheet of the fifty-seven Valley Green Cartel membership and carefully decided on who she'd round up to go on the retaliatory mission. So thorough were the computer files of the business-minded Wills that it produced a detailed bio on each dealer that included their earning abilities, level of street smarts, loyalty, courage, and various other personal details of their past dealings with the Cartel over the past five years. This info helped Trina to easily place the best people for the job at hand.

On Langston Lane there sat a large weather-beaten row house that served as a crack manufacturing plant of sorts for the Go Hard Soldierz. The three level house was used to cook crack on the first level, make sales on the bottom level and provide prostitution on the very top. This particular building provided the VGC with their most profits, serving the entirety of Southeast Washington with the addictive drug. And now the masked bandits had robbed the Valley Green Cartel of more than fifty grand worth of crack and an unestimated amount of cold cash. To top it off, two of their own now were hospitalized in critical condition with gunshot wounds to the head and torso. Trina wanted to answer her enemies with speed and brutality so she acted quickly.

"Pooh, I want you to holla at all my peoples up in the Farms. I already got seven carloads of young'uns from Valley Green on the way over. They'll be here in a minute or two. Ali, you know all o' them young'uns from Congress Heights, right? Holla at 'em. Tell 'em to get them hammers ready and meet up with us here at the crib cuz that nigga Roland done fucked up for real. He don't know it yet but his bitch ass 'bout to get got!" yelled Trina, her hazel brown eyes flashing with fury as she ordered her crew with the leadership of a seasoned Kingpin.

"I'm 'bout to go check on Choo and Spook real quick," Trina barked out orders over the phone to the dealers stationed at Wills' house.

Trina called down to DC General Hospital and got in contact with Trey Wills' personal physician, Dr. Lloyd Racine, M.D. Dr. Racine was a white, Yale-educated surgeon who served as the head doctor of the hospital's trauma unit. He specialized in gunshot wounds and rarely lost a patient. He, too, was on Trey Wills' long list of well-paid professionals who served him well by fixing up written reports so that there'd be nothing for the cops to follow up on. However this was usually unnecessary due to Wills' control over the police themselves.

Trina grabbed her Desert Eagle and raced out the door. Outside on the curb was lined over a dozen vehicles of all sizes in all of their tricked-out glory, blaring the tunes of Rare Essence, Chuck Brown, and Trouble Funk from their assorted speakers. All along the sidewalks beside the cars, teen and young adult males from all across Washington's most violent district danced, smoked weed, drank, and loaded shells into clips that were then placed into a wide variety of assault weapons.

"Yeah! That's what the fuck I'm talkin' 'bout!" Trina yelled gleefully, "Y'all niggas ready to ride?"

She as always jumped into the passenger side of Pooh's Classic Cadillac. Dozens of heavily armed young thugs piled into the cars behind her, in front, to the right, and left. And five youngsters hopped into the back of Pooh's Caddy. Engines roared to life as one by one SUVs, Benz's, and Beamers squealed off in clouds of smoke taking their cargo of cold-blooded killers to do their murderous deed. As they rode down the streets of the City, Trina heard the clank of metal clips entering the interior of pistols. She smiled wickedly.

Trina spoke to the crew one last time from her cell phone before they disappeared down the highway in the direction of 8th & H Street.

"Handle yo' business!" she snapped before hanging up.

As Trina looked up into the rearview mirror, she could make out the gleaming chrome of the nickel-plated Nine-Millimeters clutched in the hands of her crewmembers seated in the back. She pulled out her own gun and put it up in the air for the young men to behold.

"Y'all see this? I call her Lil' Trina cause like me, she's beautiful, but deadly."

As the bid Caddy pulled up into the visitors' parking lot of DC General Hospital, Trina cautioned the youngsters to behave themselves accordingly by turning down the loud music and concealing the hardware while she and Pooh went to visit their wounded comrades. As soon as they entered the doorway a petite Asian nurse approached them with a clipboard in hand. Trina shook hands with the nurse, as did Pooh.

"Ms. Ricks, Dr. Racine has been expecting you. So could you and this young man please follow me into the E.R.?"

"Yes, Ma'am. Uh, how are the two young men doing? Are they conscious?"

"Well, both gentlemen are now undergoing surgery as we

speak. Their injuries, though serious, should be able to be operated on successfully by Doctor Racine's team of surgeons."

The three walked down what seemed to be a perpetually winding bland white tiled hallway, which went passed numerous rooms filled with bedridden patients and clustered groups of white jacketed doctors and R.N.'s checking notes and administering meds. Visitors stood around sign-in desks or watched T.V. from lounge areas. A strong, antiseptic smell stung Trina and Pooh's nostrils as they traveled behind the rapidly walking little nurse toward the emergency room. Lights blinked on and off while strange buzzing and bleeping sounds came from numbered rooms covered by nothing more than thin curtains. Finally the three individuals came to the entrance of the operating room that was bustling with activity and chatter between busy doctors.

From the group of masked, glove-wearing surgeons, Dr. Racine looked up from the operating table, whispered to his second in command to take over the surgery in his place, and quickly ushered both gangsters outside the room. Shutting the door behind him, the doctor removed his surgical mask and took them aside. Dr. Racine was a tall, slender distinguished looking yuppie, around thirty-one or thirty-two. He had a neatly trimmed black beard and was slightly balding up top. His deep tanned complexion suggested a Mediterranean heritage, such as Spanish, Portuguese, or Greek. He was highly regarded by Trey Wills and for damn good reason. In the seven years he'd provided medical services for the Cartel, only two of Trey Wills' men ever died on Racine's operating table.

"I gotta tell you, both kids are in pretty bad shape," Dr. Racine admitted looking over his shoulder at the closed door of the operating room where his staff worked feverishly to save the lives of the critically wounded teenagers. "Both of them have lost a great deal of blood from the bullet wounds.

They both have been shot multiple times in the upper body as well as in the neck and head area. So it's going to be touch and go for a while here, but I work with probably the best group of doctors in the City. So rest assured they will put through. Now due to the severe nature of the injuries, there might be a twenty percent chance of paralysis, especially for the kid, Sammy or 'Spook'. But hey . . . he will live."

"How long do you expect for them to be up under the knife, Doc?" asked Trina.

"Well, I guess it could take over an hour or two from now—maybe more, maybe less. The important thing is we have to get them stabilized and keep their vitals up. That's about it for now."

"Aiight, Dr. Racine. Good lookin' out. Anything my boys might need or want while they recoup put it on my tab. I'll be up here to pay it weekly. Okay? And I want you to see me this week. Let's say Friday at Tony & Joe's Seafood House over in Georgetown. I wanna treat you and your whole staff out to dinner. So come ready to pig out. Aiight, Cutie?"

"You're lucky . . . if I was ten years younger and not married, you would be in a whole lot of trouble right now, Miss Thang! But, yeah, sure I'd love to and those guys back there . . . they'll eat you out of house and home. So dig deep in that Fendi bag of yours, okay?"

Trina laughed and hugged the doctor around the neck.

"The phrase 'It's not whatcha know but's who you know'— young, true once again."

With doctors, lawyers, cops, and God knows who else on their side, Trina felt as though there was nothing that she could not accomplish. Trina, Pooh, and their young lynch mob headed toward their headquarters at Trey Wills' Valley Green home, while they left the doctors to operate on their partners. Trina and her Barry Farms homies ordered Chinese food and retired to the basement to watch cable T.V. Trina made a phone call to Bridgette Cruise to come over immediately. She knew how much the older lady hated her. But this time she needed to test Bridgette's loyalty to the Cartel, and see for herself the know-how and skills that Trey Wills had boasted about.

Chapter 13

Hood Wars

Bridgette Cruise arrived approximately fifteen minutes after receiving Trina's phone call. The hefty woman lumbered in out of the late summer shower damp looking solemn as she shook her umbrella free of moisture and hung up her wet coat. Bridgette wore a tasteless moss green frock pulled over a black denim dress. Though she kept a purse filled with money and drove a brand new Bentley, she still never cared much for dressing herself in the elegant, chic, fly, or modern apparel that Trina often rocked. She preferred to wear her same old, frumpy bargain basement type gear for both work and play. As Bridgette descended down the staircase, it creaked beneath her great weight all the way to the bottom.

"You know that Roland and them bamma ass niggas from out 8th & H are off that dumb shit again, right?" Trina said getting straight to the point as Bridgette Cruise stepped into the basement. "A bunch o' lil' fake gangstas robbed our crack house out Langston Lane early this mornin'. Bastards got us good! I ain't even gon' lie. Cats got us for our rocks and got that cheese up off us, off the early mornin' creep. Choo and Spook got hit tryin' to stop them niggas from roughin' us off, but they got ghost on a nigga. My dawg, Dr. Racine, is over at DC General right now operatin' on them lil' niggas, cause they got fucked up real bad. Northeast niggas don't usually fuck with Southeast. This bamma think he can come over here and run up on Langston Lane and not get dealt with? Naw, Joe! We gonna split that nigga's shit wide the fuck open cause his bitch ass done violated one time too many!"

"Trina. Boo, that lil' muthafucka is crazy as shit. I know him. You gotta be careful fuckin' with that simple ass Roland Carter. You think we can take 'em?" asked Cruise cautiously taking a swig of gin from a small pint glass bottle stuffed deep within her handbag.

"Think? I don't think shit! I know we gon' take 'em. That nigga ain't nobody for real. He might scare you or them niggas down Lorton, but he ain't nothin' but a cold bitch to me. Believe that shit! I'm tryin' to tell you," Trina added emphasis to her statement by snapping her fingers and weaving her neck with a classic Sista attitude. "I'll kill that muthafucka's whole family if left up to me cause that's just how I go. Muthafuckas can sleep on me just cause I'm a female and I'm young if they want to. They gonna fuck around and come up missin' just like Lil' Mo' and that's off the no bullshit! You see for some strange reason Trey started actin' like an ole bitch right before the Feds got to him. And that's a simple fact punk niggas like Roland and them think it's sweet out here in Southeast. So I'm here to let niggas know that ain't nothing hardly sweet east of the river, young. All they gon' get is that muthafuckin' drama. Feel me? Trey figured if we kilt Nutt and shit, the H Street Crew would break up, 'cause them young'uns ain't know shit 'bout runnin' business without no leader. But nobody expected for Roland to get outta Lorton and come home runnin' shit like he did either. This dude came outta Lorton strong armin' niggas off the break out Northeast. Then he brought that bamma shit out here to Southeast and started carryin' Trey like a muhfucka, and Trey let 'im do the shit. Hollerin' 'bout some he wanna chill for a minute. That tactic ain't work cause that bamma started killin' niggas all over the fuckin' place. I tried to tell Trey to deal with Roland right away cause I already knew this dude was gon' be a whole lotta trouble . . . especially after Trey let 'im get away with punkin' him the first time. Niggas say Roland done hooked up with the 21st Street Mob from around Little Vietnam and Lil' Mo's old Lincoln Heights Crew. So them jokahs jive deep right about now. So I ain't trippin' off none o' them other lil' crews and shit. Now Bridgette, I fucks with them lil' niggas Choo and Spook. But even if they get kilt, it won't damage the Go Hard Soldiers cause lil' hustlers like Spook and them come a dime a dozen. Sorry to say . . . but they don't mean shit to nobody but their peoples. If a muthafucka wanna do some real damage to a crew, he, or in my case, she gotta hit the one who runs shit . . . the nigga that calls the shots. Now the way that this nigga Roland is goin' out here, ain't but a matter o' time before he comes to get me . . . or singles you out. But I ain't gonna sit on my ass and wait for a carload of dudes to run down on me and shit. Oh no, I gon' bust his head before he even get a chance to run up on me . . . or you. So I want you to get that bamma, and I mean I want his bitch ass dead before this week is out!"

Bridgette's eyes widened and she begun shaking her head slowly as everything that Trina had said was processing.

"I dunno 'bout that, Babes. I ain't never had to do nothin' like that for Trey before. Besides, you got plenty o' lil' trigger happy young'uns workin' for you. Go holla at one o' them."

"You heard 'bout what happened to Choo and Spook, right? Well, I ain't got time to use young'uns to go after nobody like Roland. He's too well seasoned. He'll punish a couple o' teenagers and shit. I need an old head who knows a lil' some-thin' 'bout slow walkin' a nigga. Feel me?"

"Look Trina, I don't mean no harm, but I take care of the books and make sure that our dope spots are well stocked with products. I don't do no disposal jobs! If you that pressed to ice this dude you might wanna do the job by ya damn self."

Trina closed her eyes and slowly stroked her temples in frustration for about five minutes before she laid eyes on Bridgette Cruise again. When Trina did look at the woman that she despised, she scowled with fury in those hazel eyes at her accountant's failure to comply. Yet she swallowed her pride and forced herself to relax.

"I used to put in work back in the day all the time. I've paid the cost to be the boss round here. Trey put me in charge and told me to run things while he did his time down Lorton. And that's what I'm gonna do."

Cruise rolled her eyes and snickered mockingly. Trina at that point almost lost it.

"Obviously you don't know me very well. I coulda been kilt that nigga Roland, but Trey told me to chill cause he didn't want no heat to fall on him from the Feds. That's the only reason why that dude's still livin'. If I wanted to I'd hop in the whip myself and go up to 8th & H and spray the whole fuckin' neighborhood. It wouldn't make a difference to me one way or the other. But I figured that since Trey was sweatin' you so much, talkin' 'bout how thorough you were on the streets, I wanted to see some o' that for myself so I can brag on your skills too. I've put in work. Most of these young'uns done got their hands dirty. You the only one who ain't shown that you got heart and shit. So now you got a chance to show me . . . show us . . . what you all about."

Cruise grumbled something to herself as she glared angrily at the young boss. Bridgett's hand instinctively reached down into her handbag searching for her trusty blade. But as much she hated and wanted to cut her twenty-year-old nemesis, Bridgette knew enough about the Barry Farms-bred bad girl to know that had she pulled a stunt like that, it would've been sure death for her. And she had her daughters to live for.

"Last time I checked Trey left both of us in charge of things for him in his absence . . . not just you. He told me that himself. Ain't that right?"

"No doubt, girlfriend. Trey did say that. But you swellin' up and shit, and hatin' on me so much that you ain't hearin' me out. Now if you just calm the fuck down you'll find out some good shit. I never said that you had to be the one to pull the trigger or nothin' like that. I just asked you to go out and get that suckah ass nigga. I don't give a fuck HOW you get his ass. I just want him got! You can order a couple o' cats to run up on him. You can hire a professional hitman if you want. You can have one o' Trey's bomb experts go and rig his ride or his house, or whatever's clever. I don't care. Just as long as Roland end up dead just like his nephew Nutt. Now do you see where I'm comin' from?"

"What if I tell you to go fuck yourself?" Bridgette asked foolishly.

"Then you gon' get yo monkey ass the fuck from around here. That's how that's gon' go down right there," replied Trina straight forwardly.

"Oh! So I guess you gonna just say fuck what Trey told you to do, huh?"

"Pretty much. Cause as it stands right now I'm your boss not Trey. And yes, you are one of the leaders here, but you're number two and don't you fuckin' forget! Ever!"

Trina drew her big Desert Eagle, cocked it and allowed it to dangle loosely in her left hand while she stared fixedly at Bridgette Cruise through those lovely but wicked hazel-hued eyes of hers.

"I'm so tired of fussin' with you, girl. I'll do it if it'll make you happy. I guess you've made ya point." Bridgette said as she walked back up the stairs and out the door.

Trina got praise and laughter at Bridgette Cruise's expense from her rowdy young comrades as Cruise slammed the front door. The teens marveled over how Trina had once again won

a face off with the ill-tempered Bridgette Cruise without resorting to violence. Surprisingly, Trina began feeling as
though she could benefit from the old lady's know-how and financial accounting skills, if she could just break her stubbornness somehow. One thing was for certain; the two of them
could not go on beefing for very much longer.

For the remainder of the night, Trina and her crew smoked
an ounce of potent hydro and played Bid Whist as they for-
mulated the plans for eliminating Roland Carter. Killer Carter,
as he was known, had been attacking several other drug crews
throughout the city besides Trina's. He had murdered seventeen people since he'd gotten out. He'd joined up with Lincoln Heights, and 21st and O Street, Southwest known locally
as the "Wild, Wild West". He was now much more than simply a worthy foe. He now could be considered one of the most
dangerous criminals in the District of Columbia. His unified
drug crews could rival anything that Trina's crew could muster
up. But Simple City, Mayfair Mansions, Potomac Gardens,
58th Street and Clay Terrace had equally ruthless and oppor-
tunistic street crews bullying their way into the neighborhood
turfs of older more established crews bringing the ominous
threat of a violent and bloody autumn in the hood. Only the
most well organized and heavily armed crews would remain
standing once the drama started. Trina knew this and begun to
prepare for the oncoming turf wars that would take place.
Turning towards Pooh, Trina began to belt out orders.

"I gotta get some work done for me today and no later.
Who over at your house back in the Farms?"

Pooh told Trina the names of everyone present at his home
playing videogames and getting high. After hearing the names
of the gangsters recited, she decided on one in particular.

"Call up there and tell Grogan's brotha, Lil' Ghetto to get
at me right now. And I mean with the quickness!"

Less than thirty minutes later, Lil' Ghetto bounced through
the doorway. The sixteen-year-old thug was a fair skinned,

freckled-face teen of smallish size and height, who wore over-sized gold chains and expensive Timberland boots whereever he went. He also sported a high-top fade haircut known locally as a "Box Philly" which became his signature style. He wore his designer jeans in the typical baggy style that hung below his waist exposing his boxers. He was obnoxious and irritating with a painfully obvious "Short Man's Complex". Yet Trina respected the boy's courage and fiery temperament and had witnessed several people in the past fall at the end of a smoking gun handled by the youth.

"S'up, Lil Ghetto? I need you to take care o' somethin' for me real quick, Slim."

Mike eased over next to Trina and Pooh in order to get the scoop while constantly pulling up his oversized jeans that drooped down past his behind. While listening he took several big swallows from a forty ounce bottle of Private Stock Malt Liquor, letting go a disgusting belch or two at times.

"You know any o' them bammas out 8th & H?"

"I used to fuck with a couple bitches out that joint," answered Lil' Ghetto frankly, his voice slurring slightly from intoxication.

"Well, anyway I need you to go up that joint and bring one o' them niggas back here to me, aiight? "

"What you talkin' 'bout?"

"C'mon, Man. Don't act all brand new on a bitch. Go up on H Street or 8th Street wherever Roland Carter and his mob be hangin' and kidnap one o' them muthafuckas. Put that thang in his face, make 'em get in the whip right quick and haul ass outta there. Anybody jump out there, put them hotballs up in 'em. That's it and that's all. You understand that, don't you?"

"Whatcha gonna do with 'im once I bring 'im here? Why don't I just shoot them muthafuckas instead a some bringin' a nigga back here and shit . . . for what?"

"First of all, don't ever question me 'bout what I'm doin', aiight? When I want your opinion on some shit, I'll ask you.

Other than that, you need to just mind ya business and do what the hell I tell you to do. Your monkey ass 'bout to get paid ten thousand dollars! Five grand just to take the job and five grand once you drop one o' them suck ass niggas off at this crib. Now either you in or you out cause I'll get somebody else if you ain't interested for real."

"Naw, Trina. Ain't like that. I'll take the job . . . I ain't gotta problem 'specially if you 'bout to break a nigga off with ten G's and shit. I'm on it, young!"

The diminutive little thug left the house both drunk as well as overjoyed at the thought of pulling in ten thousand bucks for a single gig.

After sitting most of the night drinking and smoking bud with Pooh and the rest of her peeps, Trina, now weary from over indulgence and dwelling on the 8th & H Street Crew, had Pooh drop her off at her home in Georgetown. Her boyfriend Kofi had downed over a dozen glasses of Remy Martin on the rocks as he watched Al Pacino's Scarface over and over again until he became sleepy and bleary-eyed at around four in the morning.

When Trina entered the foyer of the extravagant home, she followed the delicious aroma of the mouthwatering Canadian bacon and scrambled eggs sizzling upon the stove in the large opulent kitchen. She smiled with delight as she saw her man preparing an early morning breakfast for two. When she walked in, the triangular outline of his powerful back and wide built shoulders looked virile and sexy within the white cotton of the tank top that fit him two sizes too small. He pulled out a chair at the table and bid her sit. She obliged happily as she sat before a delectable spread of breakfast delights. Steaming aromatic piles of fried apples, grits, pancakes, and other mouth-watering morsels filled numerous plates on the expensive ma-hogany kitchen table.

"You look tired as shit, Baby. You've been workin' so hard lately that I haven't had a chance to just be jive lovely dovey with you, you know? But I know you been all busy since Trey got locked up. All of this work and no play ain't got you burnt out, Boo?" Kofi asked, as he passed her a huge helping of syrup-covered pancakes.

"Yeah . . . jive like. You know cause I'm the boss right now I gotta do every goddamned thing. You know . . . and yeah it's hard sometimes."

"Yeah, I know it's hard, Sweetie. That's why I've been worried about you, Trina, 'cause you big time now. You just ain't no lil' runner no more, Boo. You the main shot-caller now. So what does that mean? That means a whole lotta jealous bammas gonna want to take what you got by any means necessary. So you gotta stay strapped at all times and you gonna need armed guards travelin' with you at all times."

"I'm feelin' you on that, Baby. I'll get on it as soon as I can."

"I've already took extra precautions and went out and bought two extra Mac-10's. And my lil' brother, Andre, raises, trains, and sells guard dogs of all breeds. So I'm gonna go out to P.G. County bright and early tomorrow morning and bring back two big ass Japanese Akitas. They're basically still puppies 'cept these muthafuckas is huge. You hear me? There's a white and gray female and a solid black male. They got all their shots, papers, and everything. Andre done took 'em through obedience trainin' and house trainin'. So we ain't gotta do nothin', but feed 'em and love 'em. Bein' as though we all the way here up in Georgetown don't nobody 'cept a select few people know our address anyway. And with the dogs up in here anybody who even thought 'bout breakin' in is sure to get a rude awakenin'. Trust me."

"You think I got it so bad that we gotta go get mo' guns and dogs too? Damn! I thought that's why we moved out here round these rich white folks to get away from the haters and shit."

"C'mon, Trina! Boo, you can't trust these hatin' ass niggas as far as you can throw 'em! You got to carry it like you ain't trustin' a soul out here. Shit, even niggas close to you can set you up, you don't know?"

"Kofi, baby, you jive like takin' this shit a lil' bit too far, I think. Ain't nobody gon' do shit to us out here in Georgetown. C'mon, now."

"You see . . . that's the shit I'm talkin' 'bout!" Kofi snapped back angrily, pounding his thick fist on the table.

"You just way too lax when it comes to your personal safety and shit. Everybody in the hood knows you go hard and we all know how thorough you are with the hands and 'specially with that steel. But, baby girl, you know better than anybody that bullets ain't got no names on 'em. And you can catch hotballs just like anybody else. You ain't soft just cause you steppin' up your personal protection program. The president does it, the mafia does it, and entertainers do it too. You big time now, Trina, so you gotta come correct like everybody else does who's in the spot light. Protect ya neck, girl. protect ya neck."

Kofi went over to Trina taking her hand into his as he knelt beside her gazing up affectionately into her hazel honey eyes.

"Baby, I love you more than anything and I don't want anything bad to ever happen to you. That's why I do everything in my power to protect you, Boo . . . I love you so much girl it ain't even funny."

Trina bent down and placed her moist lips upon that of her man's and together their tongues entangled in a tender yet torrid caress of raw passion.

Chapter 14
Puttin' In Work

Francine Gonzolez had been concerned with the possibility of not receiving her monthly cash pay out from the Valley Green Cartel. She was now sending out Norman Shriver to meet with Trina at an exclusive Silver Spring eatery. He'd serve as the D.A.'s lackey, picking up her money each month, so he'd have to first get acquainted with the new leader of the crew, thus the purpose of the dinner. It would be a business meeting of sorts.

Norman Shriver was a sub-par young attorney, twenty-nine years old and fresh out of the Georgetown University School of Law. There, he had a hard time passing the DC bar exam. He disliked being a part of Francine Gonzolez's illicit activities, but he was being paid well for his services and was given the opportunity to litigate several high profile cases that rookie lawyers such as himself could only dream of presiding over. So the fringe benefits kept the young lawyer both loyal and quiet.

Trina begun to attract the unwanted attention of the local news media which hounded her relentlessly whenever she attempted to wine and dine or party in public, anywhere in the

city. She often had to shrug off or flee from the prying microphones, flashing cameras and mile-a-minute questions of local
paparazzi, who normally reserved such attention for the City's
political elite such as the powers within the White House,
Pentagon and Capitol Hill. Trina hated the sudden and
tremendous local celebrity that had been thrust upon her, but
she took it all in stride.

On September 3rd at six o'clock in the evening, Trina received a message on Pooh's answering machine. A woman's
voice—crisp, seductive and sweet—came through the speakers.

"Hello, Katrina. My name is Asia Lynn. I know that you
don't know me, but . . . well, I'd like to really talk to you about
something if possible. You can call me at 501-0110. So I guess
that's all. Thank you and have a wonderful day. Bye."

Trina looked up at Pooh totally baffled by the unfamiliar
voice.

"Who in the fuck was that bitch?"

"Don't ask me, young. But the broad was phat than a muhfucka! She's a little cute red bone joint. I'm tryin' to put my bid
in like shit the next time Shorty show up, for real."

"For real?" Trina said with growing interest. "You sure she
wasn't an undercover cop or somethin'? You can't be too careful out here. Know what I'm sayin'?"

"I'm sayin' though . . . when the broad came up here around
'bout four o'clock, I had my lil' young'uns pat her down off
the break, even before she got a chance to step up in the crib.
She was clean, no wires, no tape recording devices, none o'
that shit was on her. No bullshit."

"Aiight, I got it from here, Dawg. Thanks."

Trina dialed the seven digits she'd written down from the
answering machine. She made contact with the mysterious
young woman and invited her over. At eight thirty-three A.M.,
a hunter green colored 1987 Nissan Maxima pulled up on the
curb in front of Pooh's busy little rowhouse. A sharply dressed,

professional woman got out and walked briskly with briefcase in hand up the walkway towards the front door. Pooh welcomed the young woman and thoroughly patted her down, keeping a watchful eye out for hidden wires or concealed weapons. He also went through her briefcase, carefully fingering through the neatly arranged paperwork, magazines and personal toiletries within—once more, finding nothing out of the ordinary. Satisfied that the lovely visitor was clean he then escorted her back to the den as the numerous teens laying around the living room busying themselves with marijuana smoking and videogames became momentarily preoccupied by her beauty and sweet-smelling perfume.

Pooh introduced the two women once they were all inside the den and Trina slowly began to take in the beauty of the other woman shaking her hand. A very fair-skinned woman, the lady had class and chic style that went hand in hand with her beauty pageant looks. As they shook hands Trina enjoyed the light/dark contrast their two complexions made when blended. Miss Asia Lynn was in her early twenties like Trina. She was very tall—almost six feet with a slender model-like figure, yet still she was shapely with long, graceful legs accented by a pleasingly plump ass and nice round hips. She had almost no breasts, but a wonderful bright smile, big pretty eyes, and a strong well-shaped nose which completed a genuinely gorgeous profile. Her brief small talk was both charming and witty making Trina chuckle often and showing that she was a very self-confident and lively girl with a strong personality. Trina admired her attractive Calvin Klein green and black hound's tooth suit and black leather Fendi briefcase.

"Well, now that we've broken the ice, Miss Ricks, I'd like to discuss with you the reason why I'm here today."

Trina sat back comfortably in the big Lazy Boy recliner, sipping on a glass of Moet that she offered to her lovely guest. Asia Lynn accepted her offer and Trina poured her a glass of the costly champagne and sat back down giving Asia Lynn her undivided attention.

"I'm a co-editor and founder of a new street magazine which covers every area of the inner city experience from Hip Hop, Reggae, and your very own Go-Go music to interviews with famous inmates, as well as hustlers out on the streets of America's projects. We are relatively new with only two issues so far. We're out of Brooklyn, New York, but I'm operating a new office we just opened on Georgia Avenue, right across the street from Howard University. I know you're wondering what's in it for you? Well, I can also answer that for you. We also know how much the cops and Federal agents harass and unfairly profile us as Black people. We don't necessarily condone what goes on in the streets. But hey, it is what it is and everybody's gotta eat. Plus we give you guys a chance to speak for yourselves and believe you me, you do have an audience. I believe that our magazine called T.H.U.G.Z, Totally Hardcore, Urban, Gangsta Zones, will really pop off big time and make a statement becoming a sort of Time Magazine for the hood. Who knows, in time there may be spin offs in the very near future."

"Well, since you put it out there like that, I guess I just gotta hook a sista up. Now don't I?" Trina said nonchalantly swishing around her Moet.

"Good, because I've been here in DC for a little over a month and I've interviewed five Go-Go bands, a couple of small time crack dealers in P.G. County, Maryland, and three Lorton inmates including Mr. Treyville Wills, who at one time owned this town. But what our magazine really needs is a story on the current kingpin or should I say queen of the DC underworld and that individual's name is Katrina Ricks."

Trina swallowed down the remainder of the champagne in her glass and poured herself another glass full of the bubbly nectar.

"You know what? I might have to take a rain check on that cause shit's kinda hot for me right now in the city. I just now thought 'bout that and . . . to tell you the God's honest truth, you just jive like caught me at a bad time right now," Trina answered sighing as she took another sip of Moet.

"Please reconsider, Miss Ricks! My magazine needs this interview in order to stay in print. One simple article featuring you speaking on anything you'd like will not get you in any trouble with the Law. I assure you. It's your constitutional right to speak your mind freely on paper as well as in public. The first amendment guarantees you this right. So don't worry! Besides, I really, really need this interview, Miss Ricks. Please don't make me beg you . . . but of course I know that I'm doing a pretty good job of begging you already. Aren't I?"

Asia Lynn looked sadly into Trina's eyes hoping against hope for a positive response to her desperate plea for help. Trina quickly gulped down the entire contents of the wine glass and drummed her long painted nails along the arm of the recliner.

"Aiight then, I got you, but I ain't gon' be talkin' 'bout what I do to make it out here or nothin' like that. So let's get that straight off the jump. This interview is gonna be my way or no way! Got it?"

"No doubt about it, Miss Ricks. I'm not a snitch and neither is T.H.U.G.Z. Magazine. We don't roll like that . . . never have, never will. We're on your side, remember? So you just relax, take a deep breath and when you're good and ready, we'll begin your interview, O.K.?"

Trina took out a large bag of hydroponic marijuana and poured it all carefully into the emptied husk of a cigar. She added a white dusting of Peruvian cocaine on top of the strong smelling weed and rolled it all into a tightly wound blunt, licking it shut with her seductive tongue. She lit the end of the swollen blunt and began speaking to her interviewer at length for the next half hour.

True to her word, Asia Lynn asked mostly basic and easy to answer questions that never touched on anything personal or incriminating. Trina was asked about life in the Barry Farms neighborhood and to discuss the villainous reputation that Southeast Washington as a whole had received over the years.

"I'm sure that you're one hell of a mommy to your daughter Porsche," Asia Lynn said towards the end of the interview, giving Trina a moment of bitter sweet reflection before she snapped out of it.

"Black women have always been strong and resilient against all odds and young single mothers such as yourself have been continuing this proud tradition for decades now."

Trina's eyes narrowed as she shifted uneasily in her high back recliner. "How the fuck did you know 'bout me having a child, huh?" Trina demanded angrily.

Asia Lynn quickly realized that she'd have to tread carefully, considering the violent reputation of her host. An unwise response could very well prove fatal. "Well Miss Ricks, I assure you that my information came by way of local citizens, who fondly look up to you and your organization as Robin Hood-like saviors, not criminals. Look Miss Ricks—I am not the enemy here. I'm a young black woman trying to make it out here on these streets just like you . . . Trust me, Please."

Trina calmed down somewhat, enough to allow her attractive guest to continue with her interview. Asia Lynn during her entertaining discussion with Trina stayed with topics of interest to those dwelling in the projects such as racial profiling, police harassment, poverty, and poor health care. The conversation between the two women continued for over an hour and an half more before the interview at last came to a conclusion.

"Well before wrapping up here today—it has been said that you were once friends with Sophia Carlin, the beautiful Washington Redskins Cheerleader and local celebrity who was brutally murdered a while back. Can you elaborate on your friendship with her?"

The sudden shock of Asia Lynn's question brought an immediate lump in Trina's throat. Her heart raced within her chest as Trina swallowed hard and took in another gulp of Moet in order to regain her composure. *How in the hell could this be happening?* She'd been promised that no inappropriate questions would be asked of her and so far the interview had gone well . . . smooth, comfortable, fun even—until this that is. The young magazine editor was recording the interview as she questioned Trina, so she'd have to be very careful about answering the Sophia Carlin question, knowing full well that any mistake on her part might land her behind bars for first degree murder. She gently placed her empty wine glass down and leaned forward on the recliner; her stare was penetrating and intense as Trina looked the reporter directly in the eye.

"I ain't never been friends with no Sophia Carlin. Who told you that lie?"

"During my interviews with several of the Lorton inmates as well as two or three of the fellows in the local Go-Go bands, every last one of them said that you and Miss Carlin were quite an item at one time."

Trina was livid. Fuming inside, she knew that someone had told much too much of her business to the magazine editor and now such information could be disastrous for her.

"It is too bad that I could never interview Miss Carlin before her untimely death. Oh, yes! I almost forgot . . . I'd also like to know a little something about that gorgeous stud of a man that was seen with you at the time the 8th & H Street crew leader, Carl Wormsley aka 'Nutt' was murdered. You were at the nightclub called the Ibex, I believe, right?"

Trina's temper began bubbling over with rage at this point. This interview had to be a set up. She wished that she would have followed her first instinct and refused the sit down with Asia Lynn. But the woman's good looks combined with Trina's own lesbian desires had caused her to make a rare mistake in judgment. And now she felt as though she was being interrogated rather than interviewed.

"What the fuck is you talkin' 'bout!?"

"Well, during my DC interviews, I was informed by the bouncer who worked the night of Wormsley's birthday party that you were there and he gave me these pictures of both of you also. See, aren't these photos of you and your man? Oh and by the way, girl, he is sooo phine! You're a lucky lady to have a hunk like that!"

One by one Asia Lynn flashed a series of glossy Kodak pictures featuring both Trina and her live-in boyfriend, Kofi, at the bar and standing together in various locations inside the club.

"Lemme see them muhfuckin' pictures!" Trina barked reaching out her hand abruptly.

"I don't believe that that will be possible, Miss Ricks. These are for me and T.H.U.G.Z. Magazine production staff," Asia Lynn said, smoothly rising and placing her photos and tape recorder back into the briefcase after shutting the recording device off.

Asia Lynn drank down the glass of Moet in one swift gulp, dabbed her mouth dry with a delicate handkerchief, and placed a small blue business card on the coffee table.

"Our interview is now over and I do say that it has been most interesting and informative to have had the pleasure of speaking with you tonight, Miss Ricks. This interview will be in next month's edition of T.H.U.G.Z. Magazine. I will personally mail you a free copy at this address and if you have any questions, please don't hesitate to reach either me or my associate, Sandy Bergman, at the phone numbers indicated on the card, O.K.? Well sorry but I have run. Toodles!"

As Trina watched the sexy magazine editor waltz pass Pooh and the roomful of horny teenagers to her Maxima, she screamed out obscenities while angrily smashing her wine glass against the wall of the far end of the room and paced the floor nervously back and forth quickly mulling over what move she'd make in order to avert a possible disaster. No one, not even Pooh, attempted to calm Trina down as she began trashing the den in an explosive fit of rage. She hadn't felt this violated since her stepfather had raped her during the early '80's. No one ever did such a thing to her and lived to talk about it except for maybe a cop or two. But Trina couldn't just beat down or shoot the popular editor of a national up and coming magazine. She was now under the microscope and would have to behave much more wisely just as Trey had told her.

This young woman had walked into a house full of violent trigger-happy gangstas and walked out unscathed. She knew something more than what she'd let on and Trina was determined to get to the bottom of it all and with the quickness.

Trina was a nervous wreck, and even lost sleep for two days, following the interview. Finally, she could no longer take the anxiety of not knowing the mysterious editor's m.o., and she called the numbers on the card that Asia Lynn had left for her, none of the numbers worked, all had been disconnected. Trina's frustration and anger deepened. When she found Trina contacted Francine Gonzolez and asked her to find some proof of Asia Lynn's employment at the Brooklyn-based urban magazine T.H.U.G.Z. The District Attorney put her assistant, Norman Shriver, on the trail of Asia Lynn. After a quick web search and series of long distance calls to the T.H.U.G.Z. Magazine headquarters in Flatbush, Brooklyn, Attorney Shriver reported that the CEO & Chief Editor of T.H.U.G.Z. said that Asia Lynn Madison had not worked with the company since the Spring of 1986. Trina was now truly puzzled. Who in the hell was this so-called Asia Lynn and what in the fuck was going on?

Chapter 15

Getting the Dope

On September 10, 1988, Donny "Spook" Berklee died of injuries suffered in the crack house robbery in August. Upon hearing the news, Trina and a large group of Barry Farms and Valley Green teenagers hurried to DC General Hospital. Trina joined the loudly wailing relatives of the unfortunate boy as they crowded around his death bed. Trina wiped a tear from her eye as she looked down on Spook's cold form which had now started to stiffened with rigor mortis. When Trina left the gloomy hospital room, Pooh and the rest of the boys went in three or four at a time to pay their respects to one of their own.

While waiting for her crew, Trina visited Sammy "Choo" Jarvis who lay only three doors away. He was recovering but just as Dr. Racine had warned, Choo would never walk again and he'd suffer severe epileptic seizures for the remainder of his life. He'd require heavy medication and constant supervision.

Spook was buried in P.G. County's Harmony Memorial Cemetery on September 17th. Trina paid for all the expenses of the funeral and burial, which turned out to be an elaborate and costly send off. It was attended by hundreds of mourners from all around the District especially Southeast. Trina chose not to attend, not wanting to take attention off of the memorial to Spook, which she knew her presence there would, and to respect the teenager's family who'd given her a chilly reception at the hospital. She, however, understood their anger with her and kept her distance.

Trina would use the time to plot revenge against Roland Carter and the 8th & H Street Crew.

A day after Spook's funeral, Trina's plans begun to come together. Trina had just arrived back in DC from a business trip to Harlem, New York, to establish a deal with a well connected cocaine supplier. She was tired and a little irritable from the long road trip to and from the Big Apple and had dropped past Trey's house just to check on things when the house phone rang in the kitchen. When she realized from the caller id, that it was Lil' Ghetto she remembered the D.A.'s warning about speaking on the house phone and made a short trip a block and a half around the corner to a local pay phone and quickly dialed her young drug runner back. Trina waited for an answer. It came after only two short rings. The voice of Lil' Ghetto greeted her on the other end.

"Trina! Oh, my God! Young! Guess what? We got a couple o' them punk ass H Street bammas, just like you ask for and peep this . . . we got their trigger man Smitty Blue and his lil' cousin Alonzo and shit!" Lil' Ghetto announced proudly knowing that such a deed would most likely promote him to a higher position in the crew.

"Well, that's damn good news to hear! After all I've had to deal with here lately. Shit, I need to hear some positive shit for a change. Where ya'll at?"

"We got 'em over here in the Farms, tied up in Pooh's basement waitin' on you."

"Aiight, good. But I want y'all to bring them jokahs over this joint. Aiight? 'Cause I got somethin' for they ass!"

"Bet! We on the way over!" answered Lil' Ghetto hardly able to hide his excitement. "Oh, yeah, me and my man Jason got them niggas for their rides, drugs, and we got 'bout five grand up off 'em."

"Y'all can keep all o' that shit for ya selves. I just want them two bitch niggas over here with the quickness. You hear me? With the quickness!"

Within thirty minutes, the two bound and gagged thugs stood before Trina in Trey Wills' living room as she sat mean mugging them from the couch. Lil' Ghetto and three of his hard looking homies surrounded the two men leveling the ugly barrels of nine millimeters at their heads as the stood motionless before Trina. The one known as Smitty Blue was the older of the pair looking somewhere between thirty five or forty. He was about six foot two or three and carried a well-muscled frame that looked to be about two hundred and thirty or forty pounds. His cousin Alonzo seemed about seventeen or eighteen. He was a dark brown fairly attractive teen with wavy hair and stood slightly bow-legged. Alonzo was medium height and proportionate weight. He looked calm, but Trina could detect a sense of uneasiness and fear in his dark handsome eyes.

Now on the other hand, Smitty Blue stood before her defiantly scowling right back at her with a hard, evil look upon his repulsive pimple marked face. Trina whistled loudly and from the rear a large pit bull terrier came lumbering from the back its heavy spiked chain rattling with each plodding bound it took towards Trina's side. The stocky built canine leaped up on the couch near her and lovingly licked her hands and face before she commanded it to stop by gently forcing its massive head unto the couch. The pit bull looked up on the two strangers and a low, but ominous growl rumbled deep within its throat as Trina held onto its collar tightly.

"Lil' Ghetto, take 'Phonso and step down stairs right quick cause I wanna have a lil' one-on-one with Mr. Blue right here, aiight?"

The boy nodded and summoned his hoodlum friends down stairs with him as they took their bound prisoner with them to the basement. Trina took a nine millimeter from off the couch beside her and pointed it at the enemy gangsta staring menacingly at her.

""Sit yo monkey ass down and you better quit mean muggin' before I fuck around an' unload this clip on you, ya bitch nigga!" Trina stroked the muscle bound neck and back of the fierce-looking dog at her side while placing the pistol down gently on the coffee table. The pit bull terrier drew its lips back in a threatening snarl revealing a wicked set of fangs lining its bone crushing jaws.

For a split second the H Street thug lost his nerve and Trina saw it.

"You know you in some deep shit, right?" Trina asked the captive sarcastically.

"Whatever, bitch!"

"Bitch!? . . . Bitch? Huh? Nigga, I betcha I'll fuck you up out here. So if you know what's good for you, you'll kill all that hard actin' shit cause I ain't the one to be fuckin' with, Slim! Lemme tell you some good shit . . . I ain't no soft muhfucka by a long shot, aiight? Ya see, Trey might o' let y'all niggas carry 'im, but I ain't him. I goes hard—just ask anybody round this bitch and they'll tell you. I put in work like a muhfucka, so you can sit here in my face and swell up if you want to. I'll let my young'uns downstairs whip yo' ass 'til you shit on yourself, for real. So don't even play with me, muhfucka!"

The rival gangsta said nothing as his jaws clenched in silent anger and he stared at Trina.

"You gon' tell me what the fuck I wanna know today or else you gon' come up missin' and that ain't no bullshit. You understand me, muthafucka?"

"Huh! Well, you gonna have to kill me then cause I ain't tellin' you a goddamn thing. How 'bout that?"

"Oh, yeah? Sic 'em!" yelled Trina and instantly the huge fighting dog leaped from off the couch clearing the coffee table in an effortless bound, landing squarely on top of the tied captive as he fell backwards beneath the weight of the stout pit bull. The pit bull terrier's stinking drool and acrid breath covered the man's face as the dog's mighty jaws loomed inches away from his face.

Trina whistled seconds before the dog's fangs snapped down on the man's wincing face. The dog heeled and rested obediently upon the captive's broad chest, growling steadily.

"Now either you gonna act like you got some sense or I'm gonna let 'Kurupt' here lock down on yo fuckin' face and shit. So what you gonna do, Slim?"

"Aiight! You got it! Just get the pit up off me!"

Trina whistled twice and the pit bull terrier returned to the exact spot on the couch where it sat before resting as if nothing ever happened.

"I know shit, but it's jive cruddy out here. So I know that it's no guarantee that I'll walk up outta here alive even if I do tell you what you wanna know."

"True that, but I'll put some money in your pocket and I'll let you and you lil' cousin downstairs live, if you cooperate, no bullshit. 'Cause I want that bitch ass Roland Carter, not you, Slim. And that's for real!"

"How much we talkin' 'bout?"

"It don't matter to me, Baby Boy, cause money ain't no object right here."

"How 'bout thirteen thousand?"

"If that's what it takes for me to get at Roland then so be it! I don't give a fuck. I got that and more downstairs in the safe right now."

"Lemme see that cheese and then we can talk some more, aiight?"

"Say what? Nigga, you done bumped your head if you think I'm 'bout to go get my shit just so you can talk. You the one all tied up and shit. You the one whose fate is in my muthafuckin' hands! Now you lucky I didn't just let Kurupt punish yo ass. Now I done told you that I'm an honest broad. So please, don't push shit too far aiight? Tell me what I need to know 'bout the 8th and H Street crew and not only will I let you and ya man 'Phonso go free. But I'm gon' break you off with the thirteen G's for yourself and I'll even sweeten the pot a lil' for ya boy. That's it and that's all."

Smitty Blue thought briefly about the bribe that he'd just worked out and he cleared his throat to speak.

"You tryin' to know some shit 'bout Roland and them H Street niggas, huh?"

"That's why you up in this joint, don't you think?" Trina snapped sarcastically. "I wanna know it all. I wanna know who y'all connections are. I wanna know what hoods is down with y'all niggas. I wanna know what spots y'all hustlin' at, where Roland stay, where his baby mama stay, his barbershop, where his lil' side bitches stay at. I want it all! So c'mon and tell me what I wanna know. I'm tired o' wastin' time here!"

"If I told you all o' that shit, them cats would bust my head for sure!"

"Nigga, you betta stop playin' with me before I bust your fuckin' head!"

"Either way, I'ma get fucked up. So what the fuck?"

Trina got up off of the couch and smacked the man sharply across the side of his face angrily, while the pit bull barked ferociously at the frightened prey.

"See you gon' make me catch a case fucking with you cause you insist on playin' and shit when for real your life is at stake! I already promised you money and your life as well as that of your cousin. And you just stay playin' these lil' stupid games. You must wanna die or somethin'.

"Naw, I'm just caught up in a whole lotta shit that's all and I don't know what the fuck to do!"

"Once you getcha hands on this money I'm 'bout to give you, you can flip it and double or even triple your profits and step out on your own. Or even invest in some kinda legit business and get up outta the game for good. Know what I'm sayin? You knew the consequences of hustlin' when you decided to sell your first bag o' weed or vial o' rocks. So don't go actin' all brand new and shit now. The game don't wait, my nigga. You gotta get yours while you can get it 'cause tomorrow ain't promised to nobody out here, Slim. So do you want this money or not?"

"Of course I'll take the cheese, but don't nobody fucks with a dry snitch. Plus them cats I fucks with . . . shiiit, you just don't know . . . I'll be dead in a day. No bullshit!"

"You know what? I'm through fuckin' around with you muthafucka! You done wasted enough time here today. Now for the last time either you gon' speak on it or I'm gonna clap this muthafucka. What's it gon' be?" Trina asked threateningly, placing the barrel of the nine millimeter between Smitty's eyes.

Smitty although terrified, again tried to show indifference and a devil-may-care attitude in the face of death, making Trina even angrier.

"I told you to do what you do! Shit! I ain't gonna tell you shit! Fuck you, Bitch! You don't put no fear in my heart. If you all big and bad like you say you is . . . handle yo' business then, bitch!"

Trina nearly knocked the captive drug dealer unconscious after striking him hard upside the head with the heavy chrome handgun. Smitty collapsed backwards on the floor bleeding copiously from a nasty gash along the left side of his head. Trina's form standing over him looked blurry for a few seconds as his eyes adjusted after the blow. Trina grabbed the captive by the scruff of his neck and dragged him with some difficulty to the entrance of the outside deck. It was there that she placed the muzzle of the semi-automatic to Smitty's bleeding head. Trina yelled out to Lil' Ghetto and the other three guys and they all came storming up the stairs from the basement.

"This bitch nigga think I'm playin' with his dumb ass. Strip his ass naked. I got somethin' for 'im," she announced bluntly.

Smitty Blue struggled, kicked, and cussed bitterly as the four teen thugs ripped his clothes off leaving him totally nude. He squirmed around trying to free his twine bound wrists, but all efforts were fruitless. As he glowered at his captors standing around him laughing and taunting, his ears rung from the constant barking, growling, and snarling of the pit bull terrier jumping up and down beside Trina on its thick leather leash.

"Open up this door and take his ass out on the balcony and Ghetto, you go downstairs and bring Phonso out here on the deck. I want him to check this shit out too."

In a mere matter of a few minutes, Lil' Ghetto had forced the other quickly up the stairs and onto the deck with everyone else.

"Fuck all y'all muhfuckas!" Smitty barked rebelliously as he was pushed roughly through the open glass doorway leading to the spacious red cedar wood sundeck out back.

Down below about ten feet down, the wide muddied backyard was home to over a dozen or more ferocious looking pit bull terriers, barking, growling, fighting briefly among themselves, and looking upward toward their handlers above for a treat. Trey Wills was an avid fan of fighting dog breeds and bred pit bulls, Rottweilers, Akitas and Bull Mastiffs for the illegal and bloody art of pit fighting and always kept no less than twelve powerful and highly aggressive dogs on his property at all times. So Trina decided to test her captive's mettle one final time. While the older man continued to blurt out profanities and threats, he was immediately hoisted high into the air by the four teenagers who grasped him by the waist, arms, and legs then leaned him half way across the side of the deck as the pit bulls snarled fiercely and leaped up, snapping their jaws menacingly in an attempt to get after the screaming man hanging over the railing.

"Look, Smitty, stop hollerin' like an ole bitch cause you'se a hard muthafucka, remember? Huh? Fuck all y'all! Ain't that what you said? You called me out my name and all kinds o' shit after everything I told yo bitch ass I'd do for you and Phonso . . . right here. Well, guess what nigga? You 'bout to get ate the fuck up by them pits down there in the yard. We got a rack o' them joints runnin' round down there. You don't hear 'em barkin' and wild'n out down that joint? They can't wait to dig in yo ass if we happen to throw you down there. So c'mon, Slim . . . you gon' talk now or still fake like you hard?"

"I said fuck you and fuck your whole punk ass mob. That's why my niggas gon' air y'all the fuck out . . . again!"

"Aiight, that's it! Toss his ass over the fuckin' rail y'all. I'm tired of his mouth now."

The four young men heaved the muscle bound enforcer over the side of the sundeck and down below into the muddied backyard where he was instantly set upon by scores of savage pit bulls. His blood curdling cries of agony were drowned out by the bestial sounds of the vicious dogs at the height of their feeding frenzy. Alphonso was forced to look on at the grisly sight of his cousin Smitty Blue being torn apart. Trina ordered the four young drug dealers to bring Alphonso over to her as she leaned next to a bench near the steps of the sundeck.

"Look atcha boy, 'Phonso, them pits straight eatin' his ass up ain't they? Now I don't think you got much of a choice baby. I sure as shit don't wanna kill you 'cause for real, for real, you'se a phine ass muhfucka young. But business is business and if I don't get my information today, I'm talkin' 'bout right now, then I'm gon' have to throw you down to them pits, too."

The boy winced and tried to divert his eyes from the disgusting carnage of the blood stained jaws of demonic looking hungry dogs crunching down on the mangled bones and disemboweled organs of his cousin's half eaten body.

"You gonna tell me every thing 'bout the H Street Crew I wanna know and I'll let you walk up outta here and live, go back home to your folks and what not. Plus like I told your dumb ass cousin, a lil' while ago, I would break you off a lil' somethin' somethin' just for the favor, aiight? But if you piss me off like ya boy just did, you gonna be one ate up ass. You understand me?"

The four thugs leaned a terrified Alphonso further over the railing causing several of the feeding dogs to come bolting over in expectation of another meal of warm flesh.

"You can holler all the fuck you want to. You know how we go out here on the Southside. Ain't nobody gon' tell five-o shit," Trina taunted the boy as he shrieked in fear.

Fear-stricken, nauseous, and horrified beyond human measure, the youngster pleaded for his life.

"Lemme up please . . . please lemme up! I don't wanna die! Please! Oh God! Lemme up," he screamed as two particularly violent looking animals leaped upwards, snapping in the air with a loud crunch of their powerful jaws as they jumped to meet what they thought would be another victim falling to them from the deck above.

Alphonso wasted little time revealing every single shred of information about the day-to-day activities, whereabouts and hangout areas of his crew, their family members, girlfriends, and many others who were said to be close to the H-Street Crew. No detail of Alphonso's story was left unchecked for the five hoodlums demanded that the boy repeat his story nearly ten times just to insure its truthfulness, before finally lowering the weapons from his face. This was an effective tactic Trina had learned from her interrogations down at the 7th District Police Station only she'd do it her way.

After nearly two hours, Trina was confidently pleased that

she had the information which she needed to rid the city of her biggest competitor and most hated enemy thus taking the Go Hard Soldierz to the top of Washington's underworld hierarchy.

"I'm gon' give you this fifteen thousand right here. I offered Smitty Blue thirteen, but you get an extra two G's just cause you so cute and shit too. But you gonna wear these wires just cause I don't trust no fuckin body for real. If you try to take this shit off, my man out Northwest got the trigger box to blow you up, slim. I'll have somebody meet you down at the basketball court at Anacostia Park three times a day for the next week or so. You'll be able to wash ya ass, but that's 'bout all you'll do with your clothes off. You'll be able to handle yo' business doin' everything else you need to do, aiight . . . 'cept try to take them joints off. Feel me? I'm gonna turn the volume on high so I can hear everything said or done in any place you go. You can fart and I'll hear it. So don't get to actin' stupid with ya folks cause I'll give you away. Your boys'll know you got a wire and guess what? I won't let 'em kill you . . . I'll blow all your asses up. So just remember that. I'll pay you each time I have one o' my folks hook up with you. Fifteen thousand each time, okay?"

Alphonso agreed trembling terribly as he accepted the handful of bribe money that Trina forked over after her grim warning had been given.

Her knowledge of high tech security surveillance equipment from her time spent in North Carolina working for her cousin's company allowed Trina to immediately make contact with a loyal coke client of hers from Largo, Maryland who owned a private detective agency. She met with her drug customer at his office near P.G. Community College, and discussed the matter at hand for at least an hour, poring over the details with a fine tooth comb, until both parties were satisfied that everything was covered. Before leaving, Trina handed over an extra five grand and within two days the homes, vehicles, and hangout spots of the H Street Crew were all bugged with state-of-the art audio devices, which, in tandem with the wires on Alphonso revealed to Trina the most intricate details of the H Street Crew's secret world.

Two whole weeks worth of information via wiretaps gave Trina all the knowledge of Roland Carter and company she needed in order to exact her revenge. Trina ordered a dozen of her most savvy hustlers to drive down to Miami and buy several thousand dollars worth of smuggled assault weapons including plastic explosives and C-4. Trina had worked out a high priced deal with an ex-Navy Seal gone bad, to attach such murderous weapons to whatever or whomever she wanted destroyed. And when her weapons were brought to her from Florida, Trina relished the knowledge that no other street crew in the entire city could boast the type of firepower that she and her mob had at their disposal.

In the early morning hours of September 25th, Bridget Cruise came lumbering into Trey's living room while Trina was there, as she often was, giving out orders to underlings and working out non-stop deals with other prominent ballers from New York, Miami, and Philadelphia. The older crewmember greeted Trina respectfully as she entered the living room and seated herself on the couch across from her young leader.

"I see you been real busy lately with the H Street Crew with all the guns and shit you done bought up from down south. We should be just about ready to strike at 'em any day now— am I right?"

"Still gotta work a few things out before we do them niggas. But I'll holla at you when we get ready to put in work though," Trina answered nonchalantly.

"What about this boy Alphonso or whatever his name is? He runnin' round the city with wires on and snitchin' on damn near all of Northwest. I personally think we outta cut his ass loose 'cause he just too damn hot right about now. Don't you think?"

"I told Alphonso that if he did right by me I'd keep him alive and make him richer. So far he been a real nigga, so I ain't gonna hurt 'im, for what? He got 'bout two more weeks to wear that C4 attached wire before he's done with that lil' bit o' work. After it's over I'ma bless him with 'bout two grand extra and I'll send 'em on his merry way, that's it."

"Shit, I don't trust that lil muthafucka. He ain't no different from the rest o' his crew. I sure as hell wouldn't give him shit. I'd put a bullet in his fuckin' brain and call it a day. He's the enemy remember?"

Trina, once again agitated by Bridget's presence and sarcastic remarks bristled, then shot back with a venomous retort of her own.

"Haven't I told you before that if I want you opinion, bitch, I'll ask yo stupid ass? I do what the fuck I wanna do. You understand? You just handle yours, aiight? Thank you. Now get the fuck out my face!"

Chapter 16
Get-Back Justice

On September 28, 1988, at 11:35 p.m., Trina and Kofi spent an enjoyable time partying at an all-night cabaret held at Byrne Manor. She was pleased to have her man back with her after so long a period. For nearly a month he had been away establishing new sites in the Midwest for his and his dad's trucking company, "Whitman & Son's." The huge crowd danced well into the wee hours of the morning. A lively, experienced DJ and a flowing, diverse multitude of party goers made for a very exciting and energy charged atmosphere, where gold jewelry laden hustlers flossed their expensive fashions and high end drinks flowed freely amongst the revelers. Many of the area's more prosperous dealers and their crews had showed up to get their swerve on this particular night and each tried to upstage the others with flashy displays of their ill-gotten street wealth.

Trina, rocking a black satin evening ensemble, stepped into the party with a two-carat three-piece diamond set which shimmered with flawless luster from her neck, earlobes and wrists. Kofi proudly walked beside his gangsta girl looking equally impressive in a custom tailored Gucci suit and matching snakeskin slip-ons. As the two pistol-packing lovers joined the throng of swaying figures grooving out on the strobe light speckled dance floor, Kofi observed the strongly noticeable looks of lust that his lady got from the various men in the cabaret at the time and he felt his ego growing by the second. Trina was not only one of the city's most successful, as well as ruthless criminals, but was also one of DC's most desired women. Many a man filled his imagination with naked Trina poised for action on top of his bed. Kofi knew this as well as anyone and flaunted his bountifully thick gal pal before the wandering eyes of his ghetto peers. However, he was unusually uptight towards the end of the night just before the cabaret let out at 4:00 AM He took to the comfort of Trina's Mercedes that they'd parked at the far end of the lot.

Earlier Kofi had acted strange, as though he was waiting for something or someone because he nervously peered down at his ice cluttered wristwatch on more than a few occasions and swallowed five straight whiskey shots back to back. After Trina danced with three different guys who had pressed her for a dance, she went looking for Kofi out in the partially lit parking lot. When she walked up to him, he was leaning back in the driver's seat listening to Luther Vandross' ballads. She took a seat beside him on the passenger side.

"Why you out here, baby? You actin' jive strange. What's wrong witcha?"

"Needed some air . . . I been drinkin' a lil bit too much, ya know? The room started spinning round and shit. You know how that go. Ain't nobody tryin' to fall on the dance floor, feel me?"

"You're lucky that you my man, cause nigga you full o' shit. You know that? I saw you lookin' at the watch like a dozen times and shit. C'mon I ain't blind but it's all good. C'mon they 'bout to switch it over to slow jams and I wanna feel your big arms around me."

Kofi agreed and followed his infamous girlfriend back into

the cabaret. Once there, the couple enjoyed themselves for the final thirty minutes dancing with vigor and grace as they joined other dancers on the floor performing the Electric Slide. Everyone knew that the handsome couple dancing among them on the crowded floor were two of the District's most feared criminals who had murdered a number of people whom they considered enemies. Even other fellow drug dealers, who knew of the legendary temper of the Barry Farms native went out of their way to avoid any unnecessary conflict with her, giving Trina a wide berth wherever she traveled in the place.

Though she could be ruthless to anyone who crossed her, she also had the undying love and loyalty of entire neighborhoods throughout Southeast. Many a poor family was given a monthly stipend of money, groceries, and clothing by Trina and her crew. She saw to it that the entirety of Barry Farms Dwellings was well taken care of financially funding the local boys and girls club and facilities for the enjoyment of neighborhood youth such as playgrounds, basketball courts, and summer barbecues down at Anacostia Park. Single mothers were especially close to her heart and she demanded that every male member of their crew with a child or children financially support their offspring or face dire consequences.

As Trina giggled and gossiped with a number of girls she knew from her old neighborhood, she spotted the tall, statuesque figure of Asia Lynn Madison elegantly dressed in a beautiful paisley Versace evening gown with a plunging neck line which revealed a dazzling diamond studded choker sparkling around her long slender neck. She was accompanied by a well-dressed, debonair looking Hispanic youth that draped his arms around her in an affectionate embrace as they sat together at a private table in a dimly lit corner away from the dance floor. Trina's smile and carefree attitude gave way to immediate animosity and sullen silence. She had thoughts of vengeance racing through her head a mile a minute. She wanted to walk right over to Asia Lynn and demand that she explain the purpose of her interview and why she'd lied about her supposed employment with T.H.U.G.Z. Magazine. She however simply observed the object of her malice from the densely packed dance floor. She noticed that Kofi had seen her too and once again began to act strangely and insisted that they leave.

"The cabaret is to let out in a minute, but lemme ask you this . . . do you know that tall broad over there in the corner bunned up with that Spanish young'un?" Kofi asked, without really waiting for a reply.

Kofi stared over at the sexy woman chatting with her equally attractive Latino lover across the room for a second then took Trina firmly by the hand and pulled her forcibly toward the exit door behind him.

"Naw, I ain't never seen that bitch before. Why would you ask me that anyway? Does it look like I'd know her or some-thin'?"

The two argued over the subject of Asia Lynn and Kofi's strange behavior after seeing the fake magazine editor. Later, after they arrived at their Georgetown Cottage, they slept apart from each for the first time in their relationship. The next day around noon, Pooh called Trina with some disturbing news. At approximately nine fifteen that morning, Bridgett Cruise had three of her nephews stalk Roland Carter from his H Street row house towards P.G. County, Maryland. There the three inexperienced gunmen made an attempt on the gang leader's life that failed miserably. Disaster followed the botched shooting in the Iverson Mall parking lot that resulted in several non-fatal, but serious injuries including the wounding of a four-year- old girl and her teen mother. Roland Carter suffered a minor flesh wound to his left thigh. He was treated for it and released from PG Community Hospital the same day, while Cruise's bumbling nephews were nabbed by P.G. County cops on Suitland Parkway en route back to the District.

With the boys now in Prince George's County Police custody, there was a major concern whether either of the three culprits would crack under police questioning or not. And to make matters much worse, the shooting incident made breaking headlines on the local TV news programs.

"FUCK!" Trina exclaimed angrily as she flipped channels, seeing the hyped up coverage of the day's events presented on the screen.

Kofi, who'd just come in from walking the Akitas around the block noticed her emotional trauma as she stared at the screen as though in a trance.

"What's goin' on now?" he asked from the kitchen.

"I'm fuckin' tired of that ugly, old hag Bridgette! That's what. Kofi, I gotta do somethin' 'bout her dumb ass," spat Trina waving her boyfriend over to the big screen television in the living room. "Baby, tell me why this bitch tried to kill Roland this morning by gettin' some niggas I don't know from Adam to do the job. Pooh just called me a lil' while ago tellin' me this and how the shit's all over the fuckin' news. The lil' dudes got locked up by PG out on Suitland Parkway and get this shit . . . they ain't even kill Roland. He's back on the streets as we speak right now and shit."

Kofi sat down on the couch beside Trina and shook his head slowly in disbelief as he listened to the umbrella-toting reporter describe details of the shooting in the mall's parking lot as a gentle early autumn rain fell steadily. It was almost uncanny the way Roland Carter escaped the drive-by with his life. His new 1988 Jaguar Coupe was bullet riddled beyond measure and eight innocent bystanders had received gunshot wounds to various parts of their bodies. Yet Carter, with the exception of the thigh wound which proved to be nothing more than slight graze, walked away virtually unscathed. He was given the customary battery of questions by PG's finest, but staying true to the game, admitted little, if any, plausible information to the cops regarding the motive for the shooting or the identities of the suspects being held in police custody.

Vexed with the ex con's lack of cooperation, the policemen abandoned the hospital room interrogation and chalked the incident up as a "gang related" situation occurring between two rival DC drug crews. Not wanting gang violence from the mean streets of Washington to spill over into their jurisdiction, the PG County Police let Carter know in no uncertain terms that neither he, nor any other District drug dealers, would be welcomed into the county in the future. With their reputation as the region's most aggressive police department, Roland Carter knew that the PG Police meant business, and he took their stern warning to heart.

"That bitch just fucks up off G.P. Now it's really gonna be some shit out here. Cause everybody and their mama know that we all beefin' right about now. So now Roland's gon' be watchin' his back like shit, young. Which means the element of surprise we was putting together is all fucked up. And on top o' that, them bammas that fucked with Roland gonna be out to get us for damn sure now. All behind some dumb shit that bitch done did."

"Trina, you gon' have to be real careful, much more that before. As a matter of fact, I want you to call me every hour on the hour from now on."

She and Kofi ate a hearty Italian meal of delicious shrimp scampi and filet mignon en Brochette at a classy Italian eatery not far from their place. The meal itself was splendid as was the rich ambiance of the five star restaurant, but nothing could truly take Trina's mind off of the inevitable street war that would soon ensue between her crew and Roland Carter's.

After leaving the restaurant, Trina entered the cottage took a quick shower, dressed in her biker gear, and prepared to take her motorcycle out for a late night ride.

"I gotta go pick up some money from my peoples out the Farms. I'll be back in about an hour or two, sweetie," Trina said covering Kofi's mouth with a deep, passionate kiss before revving up her sleek, polished Kawasaki street toy.

Away she roared down the quiet Georgetown street popping a wheelie or two as she darted into the busy intersection, speeding past cars as if they were standing still. As she raced towards her neighborhood at a speed of nearly a hundred miles an hour, she noticed a large dark-colored truck following her close from behind. The truck had to be traveling at a rate of over ninety miles an hour, as its blinding headlights drew closer and closer in Trina's rearview mirrors. Trina's street smarts kicked in and she accelerated plunging the red marker on the speedometer all the way down to the right pulling away quickly from the pursuing vehicle. In the distance she could see a green light so she raced darting past other motorists in order to race through it. However, as she neared, the traffic lights went from green to yellow to red in what seemed like a matter of mere seconds.

Trina cursed to herself as she pulled up behind an Oldsmobile waiting in traffic. The big truck was nowhere to be seen but three other cars—a late model Trans AM, a Ford Mustang, and a slick looking Corvette pulled up on both sides of her. She immediately felt uneasy and soon her uneasiness turned to terror as several young masked men began firing handguns in her direction, peppering other vehicles with slugs as they sprayed the immediate area with heavy gunfire. Ducking, Trina kicked her street bike into high gear as she fishtailed through the waiting cars and past the light that had just turned green. All three sports cars were moving at unbelievable speeds to her rear, her left as well as her right, firing at her furiously as she crouched down as low as she could on top of her motorcycle.

Bullets zipped passed her shattering the rear windshield of a vehicle just in front of her causing it to swerve into the next lane wildly crashing into a passing van and flipping over onto its side near a left guard rail. Slugs shattered against the pavement also as the relentless hit men kept coming fast after the speeding Kawasaki. As she cleared the Jefferson Bridge, two more cars crashed against each other in a failed effort to dodge the reckless vehicles racing along in pursuit of the speeding bike. Trina swung a sharp right heading towards the Farms when she noticed two big body cars blocking the path up ahead. She cussed out loudly as she spun the bike around in the direction of the Anacostia Metro stop, hoping to lose the growing caravan of death cars hot on her heels.

This was her neck of the woods and she knew that if she could elude her would-be-killers down the dark back alleys and lonely side streets of her old stomping grounds, it would be highly unlikely, even as deep as they were rolling, they'd dare enter into the threshold of the Farms. For there was always a sizable group of Trina's cohorts hanging around making late night drug sales, shooting dice, or simply loitering about drinking, joking, and getting high. These youngsters were all heavily armed and would not hesitate to open fire on any outsider bold or foolish enough to intrude.

Like a flashing blur of silvery chrome lightning, the Kawasaki jetted past the Anacostia Metro Station with no less than three sports cars bearing down from behind. It was now nearly four AM and the streets were fortunately free of heavy traffic that made for a hair-raising game of cat and mouse between Trina and her attackers along the dark streets of Southeast Washington. Trina continued to keep a comfortable distance ahead of the following cars, yet they chased her along the main thoroughfare and side streets, relentlessly. Before long she was in the vicinity of Eastover and Indian Head Highway and in Lil Mo' Gentry's old hood—not a good move. So once more she decided quickly to make a U-turn back in the direction of either Barry Farms or Valley Green, knowing she'd have a fighting chance against her enemies in either neighborhood.

Pressing the accelerator down upon the handlebar, the black and chrome street machine popped an abrupt wheelie and roared through more than one red light back towards deep Southeast. The corvette was the nearest vehicle giving chase and about the only one who could somewhat keep up. She'd heard police sirens miles back and believed that five-o may have caused a few of the other cars to give up the chase. By the time she raced by St. Elizabeth's Mental Hospital, the corvette had closed the gap to within about twenty yards and the rapid stiletto clatter of semi-automatic gunfire rat-a-tat-tatted all around her once again. This time, however, slugs penetrated her bike's exhaust pipe, shattered the left mirror, and twice grazed her smooth biker helmet, causing her to take her eyes off the road for a split second. The bike careened forward into one of the city's monstrous potholes spinning wildly out of control and crashing up against a parked Ford Festiva along a dimly lit side street corner. Trina went airborne right after the terrific collision with the parked car and landed awkwardly up against a row of plastic garbage cans, a blow whose impact rendered her unconscious.

Slowly Trina came back around. Her head throbbed painfully and she felt agonizingly achy all over. Shaking the final bits of cobwebs from her unsteady head, she came to the sobering realization that she was stuck in the back of a car's trunk. Her helmet had been removed and now she was being shaken and tossed about among the tools, oil cans and other miscellaneous items in the trunk. Trina banged on the trunk furiously with her clenched fists and kicked against it with both feet, which drew laughter from inside the cabin of the cruising vehicle.

Trina's heart began to race as she was driven to God only knows where for what she knew would end in her murder. Finally, the big navy blue '71 Chevy Impala came to a halt and she heard all four doors slam shut one after the other. Inaudible male voices drew louder as her captors approached the rear of the vehicle. The heavy hood trunk was flung open and Trina welcomed the refreshing night air into her lungs after having been cooped up in the stuffy, gasoline and oil smelling stench of the truck. Five tough looking kids of various sized and shapes looked down upon her from outside the car.

"Damn she phat to death, young! Too bad we gotta bust her head open," said a squat, bearded youth obviously older than the others.

"Who in the fuck is y'all lil' gump as niggas?" snarled Trina.

"Bitch, you best to keep ya mouth shut before you get your simple ass pimp slapped!"

"By who? You? Nigga, you better get your boys right here to jump me cause I betcha I'll stomp the livin' shit out of your half pint ass!"

The short stubby kid angrily jerked Trina up by her collar and was instantly felled by a heavy blow from Trina that landed squarely on the left side of his jaw. Highly embarrassed to have been dropped by a single punch from a female, the young man tried to rise up from the dusty pavement where he fell. But the surprising impact of the punch had knocked him silly and his wobbly legs gave way beneath him, causing him to topple over backwards a second time bringing riotous laughter from his boys who rode him without mercy for ten minutes afterwards.

"Look we gon' take you out Maryland cause that's where you gonna die tonight. But before we kill you, we gon' all fuck you," threatened a dark, bald man tantalizingly whispering in Trina's ear as he held the Baretta nine millimeter to her temple and fondled her ample breasts.

Trina's blood ran cold as the cold hollow muzzle of the Baretta pressed hard against her head, and grimy fingers squeezed hard on the soft flesh of her tits. Boldly she shoved the man's hands away from off her chest and turned to face the deadly snout of the pistol.

"You'd better just shoot me right here and now muthafucka, cause I sure as hell ain't 'bout to let you or your weak lil' crew rape me, slim. So do what you gotta do now 'cause you ain't gettin' no pussy from me ever," she said with hostility.

The gunman cocked back on the handgun and pressed the gun even harder against her head all the while laughing like a crazed maniac.

"You must not've recognized me, huh? You see, that night back in the Ibex . . . remember? That night Nutt got kilt . . . I was sittin' at the table right there with 'im. I was sittin' at the table bullshittin' with the rest o' my niggas from round the way, drinkin' and checkin' out all the phine lil' honeys comin' up in the joint and shit. And then, lo and behold, I checks out this bad ass, dark skin joint, you know? Tall, sexy, thicker than a muhfucka, I eyed her the whole time . . . yeah, I eyed her even up until the time she and her lil' pretty ass boyfriend shot the shit outta my man Nutt. That lil' bun-bun was you and now I gotta even up the score that I promised Nutt's baby mama, Keisha, that I would . . . kill you."

Chapter 17

Escaping the Jaws of Death

Trina knew the drill all too well. Mostly because she herself had either participated in coordinated hits or directed others to carry them out for her. She was sandwiched between two lanky teenagers who filled her ears with vulgar talk of impending gang rape and slow agonizing death as she sat uncomfortably in the backseat of the smoke filled Impala.

It was now well past five AM and the long dark stretch of highway seemed deserted except for the occasional passing car and lonely traffic lights along the way. Trina could tell from the passing landmarks that they were somewhere in St. Charles County, Maryland, a suburban area that offered more than enough dense forests, overgrown thickets, and marsh-like bogs in which to dump a corpse or two. No one would be around to hear you scream for mercy and by the time some hunter or hiking crew happened upon your remains, the woodland scavengers and the elements would've long reduced you to a scattered jumble of bones. No one ever wanted to die like that—alone, surrounded by your enemies, tortured brutally and finally left lying dead in some tangled forest as turkey vultures circled overhead awaiting their chance at a gruesome meal.

Trina had seen men, who considered themselves brave and fearless, reduced to an unmanly and embarrassing spell of bawling and bitterly pleading for their lives to be spared once they realized that the threat of a violent end was apparent. Yet Trina learned from some of the dope game's sharpest minds how to prepare for anything from enemy drive-bys and police raids to cop interrogation and rival kidnapping. So instead of giving way to a panic attack, she calmly sat still while the intoxicated young men continued to degrade her with filthy sex talk as they cruised down the dark streets and dusty dirt roads of St. Charles County.

Trina was now fully aware that if she would bide her time, she'd be able to put her crucial plan into action thus preventing her murder. She had to pinpoint a particular plan of action and act upon it with the quickness. It would be extremely risky considering the overwhelming odds she faced. Yet only two choices were left to her—one, suffer a brutal gang rape and death at the hands of this vile group of perverted teens or, two, escape or die trying her best to. She had long made up her mind to attempt the latter.

On and on they drove for what seemed like hours, the boys picked at her nonstop as they passed a blunt around choking and laughing from its psychedelic affects. Trina patiently glanced down at the illuminated time on her pager. They had driven now for over an hour and a half. Southern Maryland is a very long, sometimes lonely stretch of land covered over with lush woodlands and golden marshes and the highways and dirt roads seem to go on forever. A gentle rain had begun to fall steadily as they continued down the dark country road of St. Charles. Trina couldn't believe that they didn't pat her down! These stick up kids were young and dumb. They were too occupied with ridiculing their victim, instead of taking care of precautionary measures. The kidnapper in the passenger seat had been drinking heavily since the time they placed Trina into the trunk and now the affects of over-indulgence and the bumpy ride down the pebble-strewn, dirt road caused the youth to become ill. The nauseous boy quickly slapped his hand over his mouth and fumbled for the door frantically. The driver swerved off the road to the shoulder allowing his partner to throw open the door and vomit in the weeds.

As the drunken young man power-puked along the side of the road, Trina sprung into action elbowing the boy on her left hard in the face, breaking his nose in the process. As the wounded kid slumped over to the side, holding his bloody nose as he groaned in agony, Trina turned just as the kidnapper on her right drew his pistol. But before he could aim and fire on her, she had plunged a switchblade with violent force into his neck and upper torso splattering her victim, herself and the back seat with gore. The mortally wounded thug dropped his gun to the floor and clutched his throat that was now spouting blood everywhere. While Trina fought to shove the dying teen's body off of her, she was punched hard on the side of the face and back of the head by the driver who'd leaned over across the seat and was grabbing a hold to her at he drew his clenched fist back to deliver yet another blow.

The driver of the vehicle was a lean and wiry youth giving up about twenty pounds to the sturdier built Trina and therefore struggled to overcome her during the roadside tussle. Nonetheless, the raw masculine strength exhibited by her rival proved to be too much, even for a female thug such as herself. And as the fist fight spilled out onto the dark road, Trina got the worse of the confrontation and her lovely face was soon a swollen mass of cuts and bruises. Yet the ruggedness of life in the Farms had instilled pit bull-like tenacity within her and she continued to grapple and swing on her adversary with growing ferocity. Back and forth they fought clawing, punching, kicking and wrestling, banging into the side of the parked car and wallowing around in the weeds, each one seeking a strangle hold on the throat of the other.

Finally Trina caught the break she needed to overcome the

young H Street gangster. During the struggle, the boy lost his footing and fell awkwardly against the hood of his Impala injuring his back severely as a result. As he laid on the ground wincing in pain, Trina slowly walked over to his prostrate form and slowly leveled the point of the man's own gun at his chest. Four thunderous blasts shattered the silence of the lonely dirt road. The boy's bullet-riddled body twitched around in a brief and ghastly manner before finally relaxing in eternal stillness.

Trina thought to herself, *Rookies . . . one down and two to go.* She walked over to both the injured boy and the drunkard who laid face down and unconscious where he'd thrown up, and executed them both with two bullets to the back of the head. After killing her enemies, she cleared the car of bodies and drug paraphernalia then sped off in the opposite direction as fast as the big-bodied Impala could travel down the road.

She traveled fifteen miles before stopping at a rural Maryland gas station to fill the nearly empty tank. Trina's left wrist was visibly swollen and throbbed with agonizing pain that shot up and down her arm whenever she tried to raise it. She knew that during the fight with the H Street hoodlums, she'd broken it. She needed medical attention but she dared not check herself into Southern Maryland Hospital Center for fear of the questioning she'd have to endure from both hospital staff and police.

As Trina considered her options while trying to ignore the excruciating pain in her left wrist, another car pulled up to the right, on the opposite side of the pump. A young, spry White couple emerged from a red Ford FL50 pickup truck and went into the late night quick mart. Trina seized the moment and quickly left the Impala on the side of the gas station with the engine still running. Trina was both surprised and pleased to see that the truck's doors were left unlocked. So she quickly hopped into the passenger's seat and settled herself down on the huge seats. Trina removed the nine-millimeter she'd used to dispatch the H-Street boys a short time earlier and laid it in her lap while awaiting what she deemed would be a free ride back into the city. The truck's interior was wide and spacious and the electric guitar laced songs of Bon Jovi pulsated from the speakers. Trina marveled at how anyone could be so careless as to leave their vehicle unlocked with the keys still in the ignition, but she'd need someone to drive her home. In her condition she wouldn't be able to make such a commute without extreme pain and difficulty.

When the man and his girlfriend approached the truck, the girl, a slender strawberry blonde hopped up into truck and turned to face the menacing muzzle of the rubber grip nine-millimeter. A scream stopped within her throat as Trina placed the weapon between her terrified green eyes.

"Shhh!!!" she snapped, moving in closer to the frightened girl. "Look ain't nothing gonna happen if you just do what the fuck I tell you to do, aiight?"

The White girl nodded as tears streaked down her rosy cheeks ruining her make up in the process. By the time her boyfriend entered in the truck, Trina had the gun aimed still at the head of his girl who related Trina's demands to him in full detail and warned him of the consequences that would befall them if the orders were not followed to the letter.

"Lady, I'll do anything you want. Just please don't hurt us, okay? Anything you want!"

The man, a ruggedly handsome California surfer-type with a tousled mane of auburn, which fell wild and unkempt across his forehead and down upon his broad shoulders, cautiously offered Trina medical attention upon seeing her battered face and swollen left wrist.

"Don't try nothin' stupid cause I'll blow ya girl's brains out all over the inside of this fuckin' pickup if you pull some dumb shit. Got it? So don't even go there," Trina growled moving the semi-automatic from between the girl's eyes to the very top of her head.

The girl cupped her face in her hands and sobbed pitifully as the snout of the pistol pressed down on her scalp.

"Please, trust me. I'm a registered lifeguard for St. Charles County and I have a first aid kit out back on the flatbed. If it's okay with you I'll go and get it and properly dress your wounds and put a sling on that wrist for you until we can get you to your doctor."

Trina stared at the driver for a brief while then she allowed him to get the first aid kit from the back. When he returned with the first aid kit, Trina first had them drive down the road a ways until they were hidden under the shadows of some nearby trees. There under the bright glow of the ceiling light of the truck, Trina allowed the white boy to carefully dress her facial cuts and bruises. Then he stabilized her fractured left wrist with the use of a sturdy make-shift splint. Though the injured wrist was now stabilized Trina had to be given a small handful of Advil tablets in order to ease her suffering some-what.

"Good lookin' out, white boy. Now let's get the hell up outta this camp."

Trina lowered the gun from the head of the girl who still hadn't stopped crying since having it thrust in between her eyes earlier. The stranger put the heavy duty pickup in gear and sped away down the road in the direction of the Capitol Beltway. Trina gave directions to DC General Hospital where she'd already paged the trusty Dr. Racine and he'd already paged her back letting her know that he was on site and read-ily available to her. With quick thinking she also paged Kofi, who, like the doctor, paged back within a few minutes. Though she had no phone available, she left Dr. Racine's of-fice phone number in the following page, thus alerting her boyfriend to either call or come to the hospital. The trio trav-eled in edgy silence across the long stretch of the beltway and freeway headed to DC General Hospital. The white boy glanced over at Trina occasionally while switching lanes, anxiously looking forward to unloading this most unwelcome passenger at the hospital. Trina had begun an actual round of small talk with the girl who had since stopped crying and was now conversing with her carjacker, to the wide-eyed astonishment of her boyfriend. The boy pressed along the highway at a rate far exceeding the fifty-five mile per hour speed limit. Traveling at such breakneck speed got them across the DC line and in front of DC General in less than thirty minutes.

"See, you still breathin' ain't you, baby girl," said the thug diva softly stroking the girl's curly blonde locks and smiling face with her right hand.

Redirecting her attention to the driver, Trina dug down into the side pocket of her jeans and removed an enormous wad of benjamins before the surprised couple who looked at each other then back down at the cash with a wide-eyed look of utter disbelief.

"Lemme see . . . this right here's 'bout twenty five hundred bones, ya know what I'm talkin' 'bout? It's y'all's now cause I really appreciate you patchin' me up and shit. So take this cheese and get y'all's lil' white asses up outta here," she said, winking an eye as she placed the pistol down into the back of her pants.

Then as she exited the pickup truck slamming the door behind her, Trina turned and leaned on the window staring the suburban kids down with a suddenly evil look.

"I better not get in any trouble cause o' y'all two, aiight? 'Cause I'll find you or somebody I know will find you. Don't even think that your lil' lily white neighborhood will save your asses from a crazy Black bitch like me. So take this money, keep ya mouth shut, and I'll see you when I see you . . . holla."

Trina watched as the big pickup disappeared down the street as the dawn brightened the horizon of the nation's Capitol with its golden sunrays washed against a powder blue sky. As Trina registered herself into the emergency room, several patients recognized her and greeted her warm heartedly wishing her a speedy recovery as she left them en route to Dr. Racine's workspace. Trina didn't volunteer any information about her injury to the others. And though a lot of them were itching with eager curiosity as to the nature of Trina's injured wrist and bruised up face, no one was bold or stupid enough to press the gangsta girl for an explanation. Kofi arrived at last, looking worried and distraught, racing down the hospital's corridor until he came to the E.R. where his battered lover was patched up.

"Trina, baby, I got here as soon as I could. How are you? Are you okay?" he asked frantically looking his girlfriend up and down with startled disbelief.

"Just a little bit sore, that's all. Dr. Racine got me all drugged up with pain killers and shit. So I ain't hurtin all that bad," she explained with growing grogginess.

Trina left DC General around 7:50 AM with all of her cuts and contusions re-dressed and her fractured left wrist professionally set with a soft cast which Dr. Racine estimated would be removed in about two months. Kofi drove his injured lover back to Northwest to their Georgetown home, where Trina collapsed upon the couch in a deep, much needed slumber. By the time she awakened, it was around 8:00 PM and darkness had again settled on the Chocolate City. It was a difficult task for her trying to dress, shower, and prepare her hair and make-up with only one good hand. However, her boyfriend Kofi took time away from his day job out in Hyattsville, so he could be of some assistance to her. She, as always, could rely on Kofi.

Kofi was the perfect boyfriend, attentive to her every need—from cooking and cleaning to helping her in and out of the shower. Sexually she received a great amount of personal attention, mostly of the oral variety, which of course she never refused. When she recovered somewhat, Kofi drove her over to one of her favorite beauty salons, KiKi's, on Rhode Island Avenue where she got a sassy looking cut with honey blonde highlights. Her facial swelling still had not gone down completely and her stylist applied tasteful make-up to her face, which masked the few cuts that remained clearly visible. All in all, her natural beauty had returned to her with vibrant radiance. She then treated herself and Kofi to dinner and a comedy show at the BET Soundstage before wrapping up her night at Trey Will's house in Valley Green.

After going over the month's finances with Pooh, she rung Bridgette Cruise's phone and demanded that she arrive at Trey's place as soon as possible. Pooh smiled and shook his head as Trina slammed the phone down furiously on its cradle. Knowing Trina as well as he did, Pooh knew that nothing good would come from this late night summons.

Chapter 18
The Big Pay Back

Trina's second-in-command pulled up in Trey's driveway around 1:17 p.m. The heavyset woman stepped out of her old Bentley with some difficulty before slamming the door and making the long laborious trek up the winding sidewalk and up the red brick steps. By the time she entered the living room, Bridgette was nearly out of breath. She tossed her shawl over on a nearby chair then dropped her 285 pound frame down on the leather sofa with such a heavy impact it caused the seat to sink deeply beneath her massive girth. Her beady, little, evil eyes shifted back and forth between both Trina and Pooh as she downed a miniature bottle of Gordon's Gin, grimacing from its pungent taste before at last addressing them.

"Hey, y'all . . . you know Metropolitan done found ya bike out on Martin Luther King Avenue right? It's kinda fucked up, but not too much though. They got it down at the police impound yard waitin' for you. Plus Channel 4, Channel 7, and 9 News been here twice since yesterday looking to get the scoop on you. But I made sure nobody said a word to 'em, feel me?"

"Bitch please! I don't wanna hear that shit," Trina retorted sharply. "I wanna know why in the fuck you sent them stupid ass lil' nephews of yours out to get Roland, when you coulda got Pooh right here, Lil Ghetto out the Farms, Kofi, or anybody else out this bitch instead o' them clown ass niggas you fucks with," she snarled.

Bridgette pounded back another gulp of straight gin and smirked, "Ain't my fault they fucked it up . . . shit they the ones you need to be bitchin' at, not me."

"They your muthafucking peoples, bitch. You the one who sent them fuck-ups on the mission and shit. So I'm straight holdin' yo' monkey ass responsible for their actions."

Bridgette sighed with an air of obvious frustration and explained as best she could about how she'd grilled the boys herself about their errors in judgment regarding the Roland Carter hit. She knew how the boys had laid in wait outside of Roland's H Street row house for over two hours waiting for him to come out. When he did emerge from the house, two metropolitan police cruisers drove slowly pass them totally ruining what would've been a near perfect sniper-like headshot from point blank range. It was then that they pursued the H Street Crew leader towards Maryland where they were thwarted in their assassination attempt once more, this time in the parking lot of PG County's Iverson Mall, due to the fact that the gang leader took advantage of the high number of shoppers traveling back and forth throughout the parking lot en route to and from the mall. Roland Carter avoided death by intermingling with the dense crowd of people in the lot who were oblivious to the presence of the car filled with gunmen cruising the lot with drawn weapons protruding from the windows.

"That just don't make no kinda sense at all. You mean to tell me everybody up in the hooptie was tote'n and not a one o'em popped this cat?" Trina asked. "Shit, I guess not, the nigga still breathin,' ain't he? What I'm not understandin' is how a rack o' muhfuckas in a whip can't drop one lil nappy head ass bamma and get the fuck up outta there? Naw . . . I just don't understand some shit like that."

"I dunno what to tell you . . . I gave 'em the job . . . they fucked it up, it ain't my fault."

"Humph! I s'pose being a fuckup just runs in your family, huh? Seems to me like all y'all Cruises is jive like slow or somethin' . . . borderline retarded for real. I coulda gotten my four-year-old daughter to bust Roland's head and your nephews rollin' as deep as they were couldn't even graze dude! C'mon, now! That shit right there is just straight garbage!" Trina yelled at Bridgette with fury.

"Like I said to you just now, that ain't got shit to do with me . . . not a goddamn thing! I wasn't the one who pulled the trigger."

"Yeah, what the fuck ever! You hand-picked them punk ass nephews of yours, knowing that you coulda hollered at a rack o' young'uns from out the Farms or right here in Valley Green who would've jumped at the chance to take Roland's bitch ass out for a lil' piece o' change. Some of 'em would've done his ass for nothin' and you could've bet he wouldn't have walked out of the parking lot alive. But no, you purposely went and picked a bunch o' sorry ass, no 'count jokahs to go after Roland, knowing that the possibility of him surviving the hit was pretty good. Which means what? . . . Roland and his mob would be gunnin' for me off the break . . . Yeah, me and my folks done peeped your card for sure. And now your days of runnin' around here with ya face all broke up like you smellin' shit and comin' out ya mouth all fucked up to people is over with and that's off the no bullshit!"

Bridgette Cruise's jaw line tightened and her shifty black eyes narrowed into slits as she raised her gargantuan frame up off of the couch and leaned in forward with her meaty hands on her hips.

"What in the fuck do you mean my days are over with?"

"First of all you better get that muthafuckin' bass out ya mouth before you get your big ass knocked out. Secondly, you and ya whole family's some shit and don't nobody want y'all stinkin' asses round here no more. That's what I mean, . . . you fat bitch. Now get ya shit and get the fuck on!"

"You dirty lil' dyke you!" snorted Bridgette Cruise rumbling over towards Trina while quickly withdrawing a sinister looking straight razor from her handbag as she drew near.

Trina reached for her Desert Eagle but had no need for it, because Cruise was already staring down the empty, black hollow of a .44 caliber handgun that Pooh had drawn as soon as Cruise rose up from the couch to confront Trina. Trina smiled slowly and wickedly as the obese woman stopped instantly in her tracks as Pooh held the powerful pistol squarely against the left side of Bridgette's head.

"You'se a stupid ass broad if you think my boy Pooh gon' just sit here and let you rush me. Then you a whole lot dumber than you look!" Trina snickered. "Now I'm gonna let that one slide and you'll walk up outta here alive . . . but if you ever, ever, swell up on me like that again I'm straight stretchin' your fat nasty ass out. Believe that shit! Don't think that just cause I got this cast on that I won't fuck you up," Trina concluded cold-heartedly.

Bridgette slowly and very carefully backed away from her young leader with arms raised high in a gesture of submission and surrender hoping that she wouldn't be shot dead by the gun-wielding thug to her left. Pooh continued to keep the .44 trained on the old lady's head until she again seated herself on the couch. Then Pooh lowered the gun, safely putting it away, as he sat down between the two women.

Nervous and highly stressed by the events of the past few minutes, Bridgette returned the razorblade to her handbag and removed another miniature bottle of booze in its stead. Turning it to her lips with a shaky hand, she downed nearly the entire contents in one huge gulp, her face wrinkled in a hideous grimace as the liquor burned her throat and soothed her nerves.

"Let's keep it real from now on, aiight? You ain't got no love for me and I damn sure ain't got none for you. As a matter of fact, I can't stand your ugly fat ass. I know you want things around here to be just like it was back in the day when you and Trey used to hustle in high school and shit, but that was then and this is now. You ain't really wanna kill Roland cause you figured that sooner or later that nigga would get me and then all o' your problems would be over. You could then run this crew the way you saw fit. But where you fucked up at is under-estimatin' a bitch like me. You see, I ain't ya everyday type broad. I keep it gangsta all day everyday. Please believe it. And a muthafucka gon' have to get up off the early mornin' to ever have a chance to catch me slippin'. I know you see me talkin', but you don't hear me though. So like I said to you earlier, you gonna have to get to steppin' cause even though you a bitch, a fat nasty one at that, I ain't tryin' to kill you for real though . . . cause you'se a mother . . . just like me."

For a moment Trina's tone took on a quality of caring consideration for the older woman sitting across from her.

"I'll see to it that you get the money that's rightfully yours, but after that I want you and your nephews to kick rocks. I mean what I say. Leave and don't, I mean don't ever, show up around her again."

"What the hell is you talkin' 'bout, this is Trey's house, girl, not yours! I've known Trey longer than you've been alive and you gonna just kick me out the door? That's funny . . . real funny."

"I don't give a fuck how long you and Trey done known each other. Trey's dumb ass is locked the fuck up right about now. He can't help you. Shit, he can barely help himself at this point. Now we can do this one or two ways . . . either you can get up off o' yo' fat, greasy elephant ass and walk away peace-fully or sit up here talkin' a whole lotta bullshit and end up gettin' them hotballs put up in you. Make a choice cause it don't matter one way or the other to me." Trina responded winking at a stern-looking Pooh who was stroking the handle of the massive .44 whose smooth chrome finish gave off a sil-very metallic sheen up under the overhead chandelier.

For the second time Bridgette Cruise rose from her seat as did Pooh with his loaded handgun at the ready. Bridgett Cruise stared long and hard at her young rival, her deadly, black eyes burning with unspoken hatred and anger. Trina stared back at the hefty woman standing before her fuming and put up the middle finger on her right hand all the while smiling sarcasti-cally, hoping to provoke the old woman into doing something foolish. Though a confrontation seemed only seconds away be-tween the two bitter enemies, the older criminal decided it best to back down for the final time.

"Fuck you, Trina! I hope you burn in hell where you be-long!" were the parting words that Bridgette Cruise fired at the seated thug diva who was joined by her pal Pooh in rudely cracking jokes about Cruise's obesity and homely appearance, as she gathered up her belongings and exited the door towards her car for the last and final time.

By the Friday of the first week of October 1988, Trina had begun wearing a bullet proof vest. She ordered vests for her top earners, like Pooh and Lil' Ghetto. Trina also insisted that Pooh and Lil' Ghetto accompanied her when she conducted drug transactions with her underworld connects. She had high tech security systems installed at all of her hangout spots in-cluding Pooh's house. Also close circuit cameras, electroni-cally-activated doors requiring special access cards replaced the original bolt and lock doors at Trina's home and office. She was always heavily armed even when in the presence of her posse. She was determined not to be caught off guard ever again by anyone, and she paid a hefty sum for all of the state-of-the art security equipment she had introduced in each of her residences.

On the 13th of October, Trina arrived at her swank cottage to find her boyfriend, Kofi Whitman, nonchalantly engaged in a friendly game of chess with one of the neighbors. Trina stopped in the entrance of the living room looking on in silent fury. She was still taking medication for her injuries and the constant pain often caused her to become short-tempered and irritable and the sight of Kofi enjoying a trivial game of chess with a next door neighbor, instead of tending to her needs, simply infuriated her.

Trina stood at the threshold glaring at the two chess players while they methodically moved the wooden pieces across the checkered board. Sensing the growing tension in the room, the neighbor wisely excused himself from the drug dealer's home bidding goodbye to Trina on his way out the door.

"You're a sorry ass excuse for a man, slim!" she yelled bitterly "How in the hell are you gonna sit up here and play some fuckin' board game, when you should be lookin' after your woman who is hurt. Nigga you got me fucked up fo' real!"

"C'mon, Trina . . . boo, don't even go there, girl. I've been helping you out for the last week or so. Cooking, cleaning, and waiting on you hand and foot . . . You got some nerve comin' at me like I ain't been there for you. All I've done is been good to you, and you come at me with this bullshit? I can't believe how ungrateful you are!"

"Aiight, I give you that one. You was there for me during my recovery and all, but where was yo' ass when them H Street bammas was tryna kill me. That shit just don't sound right to me. If you was there to protect me in the beginning, nobody would have had to help me recover."

"Say what? What the fuck is you sayin'? You tryin' to say that I had somethin' to do with you gettin' got by the H Street Crew? Huh? Is that what you sayin?"

"You been actin' real shady since we been to that cabaret at Byrne Manor last week after you saw that female up in the joint. Matter of fact, who is that bitch? You know . . . the pretty one that was all bunned up with that Spanish lookin' dude."

"I dunno what you talkin' 'bout, girl. You lunchin' and shit."

"Look here, boy, don't fuckin' play with me. You know that bitch cause you started trippin' as soon as I pointed her out to you. You been fuckin' her or what? Trina snapped pulling out a Tech 9 with her one free hand and training it on her boy-friend as she walked over towards him.

Tina rudely swept the chess board and pieces off the table and onto the floor as she pulled up a chair next to Kofi and placed the weapon inches from his face.

"Who the fuck is that bitch? I wanna know now! Have you been smashin' her off or what?"

"No, I'm not. I ain't fuckin' that broad, aiight! She's Nutt's baby's mama," Kofi replied dryly.

"Oh for real?" she lowered the weapon from out of Kofi's face and rose up out of the chair placing her hands on her shapely hips and snapping her fingers in front of him with sass. "So who was the muthafucka with her?"

"That's her new boyfriend I guess. I don't know."

"I wish the fuck I would've known that shit that night," Trina said with malice in her voice. "Why the hell didn't you let me know all of this shit, young? Why did you keep all of this from me, Kofi?"

" 'Cause I know how bad your temper is, young. You would've ran up on the broad ready to start wreckin' and fuck around and got shot. Or you would've shot one o' them up in the joint, and then five-o would've been all over you like white on rice. I was lookin' out for you the whole time."

"Whatever, Slim! The police works for me remember? You got the game fucked up, young."

"No, Trina, you got it fucked up this time around, sweetheart. You see, you might have metropolitan on your payroll, but PG County is a whole other story. Trust me, I know."

"Aiight then, why'd you wanna dip all of a sudden after seein' the two o' them in the cabaret?"

"I didn't feel like havin' to deal with no unnecessary drama that's all."

"Don't tell me you got bitch in you all of a sudden? You scared o' them muthafuckas?"

"I ain't no bitch, aiight? I just know that there's a time and place for everything. Them cats was somethin' like ten or fifteen deep in the party that night. Only a fool would've jumped out there. I mean, why would you even try to tempt fate? I don't know 'bout you, but I like breathin'," the young man said bluntly. "Besides I was the one who told you about protecting yourself better out here on the streets; I went out and got the two guard dogs for us and everything. And now you questioning me about my loyalty to you and this crew? Now that's what I call fucked up, young!"

Trina's threatening, screw-face demeanor softened a bit as she took into consideration the validity of Kofi's words. He had preached constantly to her about the need for armed henchmen around her at all times and he had brought the two large Japanese Akitas to their home for added security. But still she felt that her boyfriend hadn't been 100 percent truthful with her. He knew much more than what he had told her and she just knew that somehow he was not to be trusted any more.

"Baby, you mean everything to me," he said taking the gun from her and taking her hands into his as he stood gazing into her soft, hazel brown eyes. "After all we've been through, after all I've done for you, how could you possible say such a thing about me, baby? I love you, Trina, boo. Can't you see that?"

"That's what your mouth says, but if I'm your bun-bun for real then you'll get rid of Roland Carter for me, won't you?"

He released her hands and stepped back looking at her dumbfounded that he had just been asked such a thing.

Trina smirked sarcastically, "Like I said, you a bitch ain't you?"

Kofi sprung forward angrily getting up into his lover's face.

"I've told you about callin' me a bitch, girl! I've killed plenty of muthafuckas long before I knew you existed, so I ain't scared o' nobody for real, for real."

"Oh yeah? Then how come you gettin' all in your feelins' behind that comment? I'm your boss now, just like your Uncle Trey was before me. So just like he would've given you an order to carry out, I'm givin' you one—kill Roland Carter! That's it and that's all."

"Oh, so you carryin' it like that, huh?" he growled angrily, "you want me to go out and pop the second most dangerous criminal in DC just like that, right? You must be crazy to think that anybody can pull off a hit like that without long and careful planning, Trina. You talk about being a leader like my Uncle Trey . . . well if you remember, my Uncle Trey introduced us on the night of the Nutt Wormsley's hit. He'd planned that hit for over a month and a half, going over with the club's lead bouncer and me the details of the hit twice a week. Now if you can get down with details to that intricate level, I'm down. But if not, I can't do it cause I'm a professional hit man, not a fool like ya girl Bridgette Cruise, aiight?"

"You right . . . I'll to do my homework on it," she responded.

She liked Kofi's approach to the premeditated murder of her rival Roland Carter. She realized that he was in fact a part-time killer-for-hire and it was this reason that attracted her to him. He took her into his powerful arms and planted a long sensual kiss on her waiting lips. She still quivered with passion whenever she embraced the handsome black Adonis—the one and only Kofi Whitman.

She still loved him greatly, but love had not been kind to her in the past and she refused to allow her heart to win over her ambitions. She looked her man straight in the eyes and let him know just how serious she was about her objective.

"I do love you, Kofi. I love you more that any man I've ever been with, but you had better realize that if I ever catch you shit'n on me in any way . . . I'll kill you. And I mean it, Kofi. I'll put your ass to sleep no bullshit."

Kofi knew just how serious his ruthless gal pal was and he said nothing in response to her deadly threat. So for the remainder of October '88, the couple went about the task of preparing to rid Washington, DC, of Roland Carter and his 8th and H Street Crew.

However, Trina and Kofi's bitter arguments continued on, at times nearly becoming physical. Trina's mistrust, along with the other major issues, soured their once solid relationship, setting the stage for a future confrontation that would prove to be catastrophic.

Chapter 19
The Backstabbers

By November of 1988, Trina was scheming on a major plot to destroy Roland Carter and the H Street Crew with an intensity that bordered on obsession. She had not dealt with an enemy such as Roland Carter before. He was a savvy business-man who had carved out a prosperous drug and prostitution industry from his Northeast, Washington headquarters. He had joined forces with Lincoln Heights, Eastover, and Orleans Place. Word on the street was Carter was close to brokering a major deal with hustlers from Condon Terrace, the hated ene-mies of Barry Farms Dwellings. Carter was an obnoxious and bold rival whose heartless gunmen had disrupted several fu-nerals of enemy drug dealers with violent gunfire creating chaos and causing entire church congregations to stampede out of the services screaming in terror into the surrounding streets. He'd robbed two armored cars in Montgomery County, Maryland and was always a threat to rob and shoot up enemy drug spots in broad daylight as often as during nightfall.

Carter had become that latest scourge to hit the streets of the Chocolate City. And he dared anyone to challenge his au-thority. No other criminal had the balls to stand up to the

ruthless power of Roland Carter and his dangerous crew ...
no one except Trina.

By the end of the Thanksgiving holiday, Trina had several
of Carter's open air drug markets and crack houses shot up and
robbed. His leaders were carjacked or had their homes in-
vaded by ski mask wearing gunmen who both robbed and shot
them to death. Drug customers of Carter were intimidated
into changing over to Trina's dope spots. Most of Carter's out
of town drug connects were negotiated into doing business exclusively with the Go Hard Soldierz to the tune of $20,000
more than what Roland Carter had paid them for their bulk
drug deliveries.

By early December over twenty or more H Street crew
members had gotten killed by thugs loyal to Trina. Funerals
for fallen drug dealers were being held weekly, many times
three or four in a single day. Crack houses along East Capitol
Street and Trinidad Avenue were fire bombed. The spate of
drug-related murders from November 28th to December
20th was one of the most bloody in the city's history claiming
over forty-five victims in all. Law enforcement was under
major pressure to bring an end to the carnage, but the police
chief and district attorney claimed that the city was much too
understaffed and ill-equipped to combat the heavily armed
drug crews.

On Christmas Day 1988, Trina summoned Alphonso, the
H Street gangsta informant who Trina had spared from a cruel
death after he was kidnapped by her Southeast goon squad.
She had put together a lavish holiday get together inviting
scores of her gang members, neighborhood friends, and business associates to receive and exchange costly gifts at the posh
Washington Grand Hyatt Hotel. The tall lean youngster was
driven in style to the lively holiday celebration in an elegant
limousine. The turncoat looked very handsome and dapper in
a blue wool and cashmere Zegna three button suit and black

oxford shoes. He strolled into the grand ballroom accompanied by two beautiful women who snuggled affectionately against him as he wrapped his long slender arms around them Seeing Trina approach, he removed his dark Versace glasses and warmly embraced the thug diva who placed a small metallic gold embroidered gift into his hands.

"Merry Christmas, 'Phonso. Here's a lil' somethin' somethin' to bring you some holiday cheer, huh man," said a smiling and quite tipsy Trina.

Urging the informant to open the beautifully wrapped box, Trina stood smiling with satisfaction as the young man's jaw dropped open in shock as he removed over $50,000.00 in cash along with a Christmas card and a diamond studded Rolex watch.

"I told you that I'd give you the hook up if you did what I asked of you, right? Well you did and I have. Now what you gonna have to do is get up outta the city all together cause shit's 'bout to get even uglier out here on the streets o' DC. I worked out a sweet deal with a connect I fucks with down South named Snookey Lake. I got a bangin' ass condo on Sea Pines Plantation on Hilton Head Island. Ain't none o' them bamma ass H Street clowns gonna know where the fuck you went to, ya know? You ain't gotta worry 'bout payin' no rent for a year. I took care o' that for you. Now all you gotta do is hook up with Snookey Lake and keep ya money flowin', feel me?"

The boy counted the money along with his sexy escorts who giggled with glee as their drug dealing boyfriend thumbed through what seemed like an endless supply of $100 bills. He once again hugged his former kidnapper thanking her nonstop for everything she'd done for him.

"Thank you so much, Trina! I ain't never gonna forget what you done for me. If you ever need me for anything just holla at me cause I got that okay?"

"Don't worry 'bout me, 'Phonso. You just enjoy livin' in the lap of luxury with all them rich white folk down there on Hilton Head, aiight? And don't worry 'bout nobody hurtin' ya peoples up here cause I'm gonna have my mob look out for ya mama and sisters. And I know where ya baby mama stay out Maryland, so I'm gonna have a couple o' young'uns look out for her, aiight?" Trina said feeling the holiday spirit as she watched the young man positively beam with excitement and appreciation.

Trina had Pooh drop Alphonso and his two dimes off at his Temple Hills, Maryland apartment after the joyous celebration ended around 3:35 AM The next day Trina had just stepped out of the jacuzzi when her phone rang in the bedroom at 9:52 AM It was Pooh on the line and he had some unpleasant news.

"Trina, guess what? Alphonso's dead!" he said frantically. "A broad I fuck with in Marlow Heights called me this morning around 'bout an hour ago and said the police found that nigga and his two bitches shot multiple times up in his apartment and shit. Somebody dry snitched on 'em, young, and Roland put 'em to sleep. Ain't nobody but him and shit."

"Goddamned it! Trina snapped with frustration, "that's just what I need—PG County cops gettin' in my business! Now they gonna show this shit on the evenin' news and tomorrow morning it's gonna be all in the *Washington Post*, probably on the front page at that. Besides all o' that comin' drama, I jive liked that lil young'un too, he was alright with me."

Trina read the front page headlines in the *Post* as well as the steady news coverage on TV. She began to slowly put two and two together concerning Alphonso's murder. She knew well the grimy nature of the business she was a part of and how even the most trustworthy of associates would take advantage of an opportunity to gain leverage if presented to them. And she felt in her heart and soul that her two most trusted allies, Pooh and Lil' Ghetto, had been responsible for the triple homicide at Alphonso's place in Temple Hill's Skoal Manor Apartments. Fifty thousand dollars was enough money to get nearly anyone killed. She wanted to believe that this time maybe she was wrong, but she would know for sure in time.

By the Saturday following Christmas day, Trina noticed both Pooh and Lil' Ghetto flossing new pieces of gold jewelry around their necks and wrists, and both youngsters had their individual cars detailed and tricked out with expensive customized spoiler kits. She had been right all along and now it was confirmed. Pooh and Lil' Ghetto had killed Alphonso and his women. She wasn't angry though, just disappointed somewhat that they'd risk getting themselves and her burnt for a few extra dollars which they'd earn anyway. She liked Alphonso but he still was a member of the H Street Crew even if he did sell them out. He was a snitch and a snitch has no love on the streets. She was content to believe that Pooh and Lil Ghetto actually did the boy a favor for if he happened to have been found out by Roland Carter, he would no doubt have endured slow and agonizing torture before finally being dispatched.

On New Year's Eve, Trina was once again plotting to resume a new series of attacks against the H Street Crew and their interests throughout the city with drug crews. She had formed allegiances with crews from 37th Street, Langston Lane, Shipley Terrace, Potomac Gardens, and 10th Place, all of them her Southeast brethren who looked to her to double their drug profits and to get back at Roland Carter for the murders of their loved ones. Roland Carter had not backed down since the bloody street war began in November. Instead the H Street drug lord met the challenge with a round of brazen daylight gun battles and drug spot robberies of his own.

Several Southeast dealers were blown to bits by booby-trapped vehicles and others were found mutilated after being kidnapped and subjected to hours of inhumane torture which

Carter had developed a sick fetish for administering. As the death toll began mounting to record numbers, the national media began focusing in on the gang violence which had now surpassed that of Los Angeles, New York, Chicago, Detroit, and New Orleans combined, landing a major black eye on the city itself and the local government in particular.

During the midnight celebration at the classics night club, Trina sat at the bar fuming with anger as the intoxicated revelers around her counted down the waning seconds of 1988, as the gigantic sphere descended downward on the televised screening of Times Square, New York. The thunderous roar of Happy New Year erupted from the crowd along with the blare of party horns, noise makers and sizzling sparklers. Multi- colored confetti fluttered about the club as party goers joined together in singing a Go-Go rendition of Auld Lang Syne.

"I'm 'bout to dip, young," said Trina to Kofi as she stared blankly at the television screen above the bar featuring a smiling Dick Clark surrounded by scores of kissing couples and flashing neon numbers circa 1989, constantly being scrolled across the bottom of the screen.

"I just can't get into this New Year's party like I want to 'cause I got way too much shit on my mind right now behind all o' this news coverage. I know any day now the D.A.'s gonna be ringin' our phone off the hook, houndin' me 'bout all this bullshit. Every time I look around I'm in the middle of some drama even if I didn't cause the shit. Sometimes it makes me wanna get the fuck away from the city for good I tell you. Aight, sweetheart I'm out, I'll feed the dogs when I get home and I'll see you in the morning cause I'm tired as shit."

But as soon as Trina got home there was an urgent message awaiting her on the answering machine. It was District Attorney Francine Gonzolez demanding that Trina contact her immediately at her home, regardless of the time she received the message.

"Fuck! I knew it, I just knew that bitch was gonna call sooner or later," Trina said to her self as she impatiently pressed the redial button on her phone.

"Katrina," retorted the feminine voice heavily laced a with Mexican accent, "I need to have a talk with you ASAP young lady. I'll be at my home out in Merryville. That's a neighborhood of Fairfax, Virginia. I expect to see you there at 3:00 PM sharp. My address is 2033 Hyannis Port Lane."

"What?! You want me to come over to your place? Oh, naw. Why can't we meet at the restaurant or at a park or some place like that 'cause that's jive like a hike for me. You know what I mean?"

"Listen up, Miss Thang, when I want your goddamn opinion, I'll fucking ask you for it okay? I'll see you at 3:00 PM Goodbye."

"Fuckin' bitch!" Trina said slamming the receiver down from her ear.

Trina stayed awake for most of the night pondering whether or not she'd take that ride out to Virginia. The D.A. was as crooked as they come, taking hush money from the city's most infamous hoodlums in exchange for the freedom to indulge in all manner of illegal pursuits without the threat of prosecution or police harassment. She had been especially gracious to Trey Wills and the dope crews of the greater Southeast area of the District. So Trina, on the one hand, felt secure in the fact that this would be a typical business meeting with D.A. Gonzolez and nothing more than maybe a tongue lashing concerning the recent spike in homicides. Yet on the other hand ever since her abduction and near murder at the hands of Carter's H Street Crew and the secretive slaying of H Street informant Alphonso by her very own thugs, Trina was overly cautious and untrusting of everything and everyone. And for the D.A. to want her over to her personal residence rather than her downtown office at the DC Courthouse, struck Trina as very unusual and unsettling as well. She felt somewhat comfortable having Pooh,

Lil' Ghetto, Rico, and Sandman rolling to VA with her as they cruised across the busy Woodrow Wilson Bridge en route to Francine Gonzolez's Fairfax home.

At Gonzolez's stately looking luxury town house, Trina and her small entourage parked in the visitors' parking area and was about seven deep with a few more young ruffians tagging along for the ride and free marijuana. The mean looking group of youngsters proceeded up the steps leading to the entrance of Gonzolez's seldom seen home, wise cracking and loud talking all the way to the top. Upon ringing the doorbell, a casually dressed D.A Gonzolez opened the door, welcoming the starter jacket wearing youths who filed past her and into the cozy fireplace-lit living room where they were immediately set upon by uniformed Fairfax County officers, who roughly took down a few of the youths who attempted to flee the area on foot or physically fight back. The rest were taken into custody without much resistance as all were shocked by the unbelievable turn of events that had just befallen them.

"What the fuck is this all about!" Trina demanded loudly, as she was forced up against the living room wall and frisked thoroughly.

"Shut up right now, you. You'll be read your rights and given the customary single phone call once we take you and your pals down to the station for processing. Now I'll take that pretty lil' nine millimeter you got there, little lady."

"Hey guys, check 'em all for weapons. I think we've got one of those big bad DC posses right here."

Trina hung her head pitifully. She felt tears welling up in her eyes and though she didn't want to cry, her tears streamed down her cheek freely. She felt like such a fool for not taking heed to her inner voice, and now she'd been betrayed by someone whom she trusted as a loyal business associate. She felt raped all over again, only this time it had nothing to do with sex. Trina quickly got a hold of her emotions, wiped the tears from her reddened eyes, and calmly surrendered to the law men who read her Miranda rights, and placed a single shiny metal handcuff on her outstretched right wrist. The rest of her crew mumbled angrily amongst themselves and eyed the sarcastically grinning cops with animosity. But other than that, they were relatively cooperative while being read their rights and placed in handcuffs.

After the group of thugs were arrested and stripped of their hardware, they were led downstairs by police escort to an unmarked minivan which whisked them across town to the Fairfax Police Department. There they were all directed into a large empty interrogation room with a single bright ceiling lamp whose 200 watt bulb brightened the entire area with overwhelming brilliance that irritated the eyes.

"Remain here until you maggots are seen . . . get comfy cause you're gonna be here for a while," said a burly cop with a Marine style buzz cut and powerfully built arms, "Start any trouble in here and I promise you, you're all are gonna fucking regret it. This isn't your scumbag DC Government guys you're dealing with, okay? This is Fairfax County here buds, the Commonwealth of Virginia and we don't tolerate none of your stupid nigger bullshit down here. So behave yourselves like good little drug dealers and we'll be right back. But I need you little Miss Ghetto America . . . get over here. You're coming with me."

The officer locked the heavy steel door of the interrogation room behind him as two equally massive uniformed white boys took their positions outside of the door. The lead officer walked Trina down a long hall to another room at the end marked Fairfax County's District Attorney. He took a long key from his dangling key chain, opened the door and nudged Trina inside. The cop winked at her before easing outside the room and closing the door gently behind him as he left. Trina no longer had the handcuff on her one free hand as the cop had removed it during their travel down the hallway. Trina rolled her eyes in disgust as she turned to go further into the room. Before her was a large rectangular oak table in which over fifteen assorted men and women all well dressed sat all around silently staring at her as she stood staring back.

DC District Attorney Francine Gonzolez had switched from casual sweats and bedroom slippers to a snazzy, navy blue fully lined skirt suit and matching lizard skin ankle-strap pumps. She pulled out an empty chair halfway from under the table and patted the seat while looking towards Trina. Right next to Gonzolez sat Gordon Lesko, Fairfax County's D.A. and close friend of the beautiful DC District Attorney. But more shocking than that was the number of local felons who sat around the table in business suits and tasteful dresses. The room seemed to be a 'Who's Who' of Beltway region ballers and local drug lords from various parts of DC, Maryland, and Virginia. And leaning back arrogantly in his chair with arms folded next to the bearded, gaunt faced Lesko, was the infamous Roland Carter, who snickered silently to himself as Trina looked over the assembled gangstas.

After whispering with her Fairfax counterpart, Gonzolez stood up and took her place behind a tall podium and spoke into the curved microphone behind it.

"All right, Katrina, have a seat now, because it's time to start the meeting."

Trina waltzed over to the empty seat, gritting on Roland Carter as she strolled around him. A round of laughter escaped Carter's lips as he observed Trina's cast enclosed left wrist; three of his fellow henchmen joined him in the cackling laughter.

"What the fuck happened to you, baby girl? Ya man and you been goin' through some kinda domestic violence type shit or somethin'?" Carter asked drawing even more laughter and mirth from his trio of thugs, even a few other drug dealers seated at the table snickered lightly at Carter's bold and sarcastic question.

Trina felt her composure disappear as fury swept over her,

causing her to leap up out of her seat and, pointing at the four H Street hoodlums, deliver a few choice words of her own.

"Oh naw, boo, you see I got jumped a lil' while back by a bunch o' bitch type niggas, like you. I got my shit jive twisted up as a result, but you best believe them jokers ain't gonna be fuckin' with nobody else. Know what I mean, Roland? You punk bitch you!"

Trina had hit a nerve and she knew it too, for she smiled wickedly as the laughter of Roland Carter and his crew quickly morphed into ugly scowls of hatred for the sexy, young female gang leader. If it hadn't been for the cops disarming the hoods before bringing them together, there would have been gunplay for sure.

"Listen you two, cut the crap right now," yelled District Attorney Gonzolez, "you two love birds can get on with your pillow talk later on your own time. But as for here and now, you all are going to shut the hell up and listen to what we have to say!"

The area's most notorious drug dealers did just as they were commanded. They sat up straight in their seats and focused on the District Attorney of the Nation's Capitol. A formidable litigator in her early years, Francine Gonzolez now managed the law enforcement agency of the most powerful city in the world and had established numerous connections among movers and shakers both legal as well as criminal. She maintained a wholesome, trustworthy image of a sharp politician and successful crime fighter for the local media hounds and fellow lawmakers. But on the flip side, she had her hand in the cookie jar of every major player in the District's treacherous underworld. She was a shrewd and highly aggressive business woman who would not hesitate to use the powers of her office to get what ever she wished. For this reason, she was both despised and respected by each of the violent kingpins seated at the table.

"You scumbags are going to bring this beef of yours to an end, and I mean today! It ends right fucking now! Not only are the local news programs and papers reporting all of the murders, but now major news programs such as CBS, NBC, ABC, and even international media such as the U.K.'s BBC and Saudi Arabia's Al Jazeera Television have featured the high crime and murder rate of the District. Capitol Hill is beginning to complain about the problem on the Senate floor and in the House of Representatives. The Mayor has been tearing my ears up with each and every bit of bad press in the papers or on television. It has come to my attention that President George Bush is considering the development of a special FBI-approved task force to investigate both the rampant drug related violence in the city, as well as reported corruption within the District Government! Guess what? If you think that I'm going to crash and burn because of the utter stupidity of you cocksuckers, you've got another thing coming! You better believe that before I allow something like that to happen, I'll have no choice but to resort to some unpleasantly drastic measures to get my point across to all of you! Now we can continue to make money and do business together for years to come with absolutely no problems. However you guys have not seen me as a true bitch. Trust me, you don't want to make me go there!"

The gangstas and hard core drug lords whispered amongst each other showing obvious sighs of growing concern over the veiled threats of the D.A.

"Now Katrina, we all know how much you and Mr. Carter here truly dislike each other, and all of us present here today realize that in reality this meeting here today is all about the street war that's been going on between your respective crews. You guys have done a whole lot of damage not only to each other, but to this city, this tri-state region, and to all of us . . . your associates. Now there's a lot of young guys and gals here today who are in the game and looking up to you two for guidance and what type of role models do you think you make to them, huh? This is supposed to be operated like a modern day fortune 500 business, not some Jesse James Wild West shoot'em up review. You know why the New York and New Jersey crime families such as the Gambino's, Genovese, and Gotti's thrive? Because they know how to come to terms with the business aspect of this thing of ours. Everyone can have a piece of the pie without all of the unnecessary gunplay, because that stupidity hurts everyone financially as well as otherwise, don't you all agree?"

"The one here causin' all of this drama ain't nobody but that stupid ass bitch right there!" snarled Roland Carter, pointing a diamond ring encircled finger at Trina.

"What? What, the fuck you say nigga?" Trina blurted out angrily as she pushed her chair to the floor rising up abruptly.

"Bitch, you heard me. I ain't stutter. You better sit yo ass down before you get smacked and shit!"

"Go ahead. Smack me, you lil' punk ass nigga. Betcha I'll be the last muthafucka you ever smack."

"Listen up you two, shut your fucking mouths this instant, before I have my friend Mr. Lesko do with you as he and his Fairfax County Police chief see fit," District Attorney Gonzolez snapped back.

"Whatever Joe, send me to jail, and bet you won't see your fuckin' cut every month. I know that much!" Trina answered back sarcastically as she seated herself once again at the table.

"You know what your problem is Katrina? Your attitude really stinks and your smart aleck mouth is unbecoming of a young lady as attractive and intelligent as you are. Now I know that you're upset and all with Mr. Carter here. And yes, I agree he's an incomparable asshole, but if you speak to me again in that manner I'll have your ass in the slammer faster than you can say Barry Farms!"

Trina felt herself losing control of her already boiling temper. She wanted desperately to strike out physically against both Francine Gonzolez and the grinning Roland Carter, but she knew better than to do anything so utterly stupid. So she sat at the table silent, stone faced, and tight-lipped, taking a detailed mental inventory of the H Street Crew's mocking laughter of her as well as the D.A.'s blatant threats regarding her freedom. One by one she vowed that she would get even with them all.

When all was calm again, and the talk subsided among the drug dealers sitting around the table, DA Gonzolez had an officer assist her in setting up a digital film projector, which then focused towards the far end of the wall where a large pull-down screen covered a black board. The lights were turned off and the light stream issuing from the whirring movie projector illuminated the screen beyond. The screen featured a map of Washington, DC, which had various sections of the city color coded with greens, blues, reds, and purples signifying assigned territories in which each drug crew would operate. The shadowy form of D.A. Gonzolez rose from the table and moved over to the brightly lit screen which bathed her in its light, highlighting her swarthy, Mexican features. Her audience watched curiously as she took center stage with a yardstick in hand.

"As you can see here on the map my colleagues and I have appropriated certain sections of DC in which each of you shall carry on your drug business free from the threat of rival gang attacks or police intervention. I assure you that this exclusive design, which took hours of preparation, will by all means be fair to all of you, and greatly discourage, if not altogether eliminate, violence between you. Earning ability, size, and wealth shall determine which crews will command the largest territories. Yet, you guys with modest numbers and short money will be allowed to maintain territories suited to your size and earning power . . . so we all will be making a profit and a pretty damn good one I should say."

The assorted hoodlums mumbled among themselves for a few minutes as the District Attorney stood before them smiling broadly. The thought of hustling out on the street corners of the Nation's Capitol without the natural violence and bloodshed that went hand-in-hand with the ill-gotten prosperity of the dope game took most of the tattoo-covered thugs for a loop. They'd welcome the chance to make money without having to battle neighborhood competitors or elude police officers, but for how long would this urban tranquility last before gunshots once again rang out within the projects of the District?

The overhead lights were turned back on, the screen pulled up into the wall, and the projector put away into an office closet. As Francine Gonzolez thanked each and every criminal with a firm handshake, a complimentary bottle of champagne, and a small blue booklet outlining each crew's home turf and the preordained rules and regulations which each crew would obey were dispensed.

"Thank you guys for coming out. I hope that you'll find our new rules to your liking and please remember that violence and reckless behavior will no longer be tolerated under any circumstances whatsoever. Any individual or crew found in violation of the rules that we've provided for you all to abide by will be dealt with immediately and decisively. So break the rules at your own risk. I will be holding all of you leaders responsible for the actions of your crew. Any leader who does not discipline rowdy members within their crew will answer to me personally. A minimum of five years in Lorton will be given out to anyone found engaging in gang warfare, ten to twenty shall be tacked on for any death that occurs as a result of such violence. It's not a game people . . . wake up! Alright Katrina, you're free to go . . . you and your crew. All of you other guys will have to wait your turn. Everyone will be going home tonight so don't be alarmed. Now Katrina, I see how you're looking at Carter and I'm telling you right here and now, you and your gang are off the hook. So please don't try anything stupid, okay? Because if you do, I know without a shadow of a doubt, that your ass will belong to Fairfax County

Police at that point, and trust me, you don't want to end up in the Fairfax Prison system."

Trina gave her enemy Roland Carter one last threatening stare before turning and sashaying out the door followed by a Fairfax County policeman. No matter what demands District Attorney Francine Gonzolez had voiced at the meeting, Trina had made up within her mind that the shit-talking Roland Carter would die, just as soon as she caught him slipping, preferably after hours at one of his favorite hangouts.

Chapter 20
Hit 'em Up!

For seven months after the Fairfax Gangsta Summit, the drug dealing crews of Washington, DC's inner city behaved just as the D.A. had instructed them to. No one dared risk upsetting the temperamental Francine Gonzolez, who'd promised lengthy prison sentences for any disobedience. Besides, the money was rolling in steadily to crews, both large and small, making many an upstart baller richer than they'd ever imagined possible. However, by the dreadfully hot dog days of mid-August '89, petty jealousy and back biting between a few of the younger, more inexperienced crews from 14th & Clifton Terrace, Northwest and hot-headed youth gangs from 58th in Northeast, began escalating slowly, from a mere war of words to a few bloody brawls at area nightclubs to a full fledged turf war with several teens getting seriously injured by gunfire on both sides.

By August 26, 1989, youths from the Tyler House projects had joined forces with 14th & Clifton Terrace in their battle against the 58th Mob, who in turn enlisted the help of their Northeast neighbors such as Paradise/Mayfair Mansions, Edgewood Terrace and Clay Terrace to name a few. Though unsettling and bloody, the two weeks of bad blood and turf wars between these small, loosely knit groups of teenaged thugs resulted in only one death and received very little of the local or national news coverage which the Go Hard Soldierz or the H Street Crew had gotten.

Trina, as well as everyone else in the hood, knew about the beefs raging between the youth gangs of Northwest and Northeast and she could've cared less if they all wiped each other from the face of the earth. It would mean more territory for the Go Hard Soldierz to conquer and set up shop. She only wondered why the H Street Crew was so low-key all of a sudden. Surely it could not have been all because of Francine Gonzolez's warning alone. She knew better knowing the blood thirsty mentality that Roland Carter possessed. She knew that he too was carefully plotting an intricate plan of attack on her and the Go Hard Soldierz. The crew who struck first and struck hardest would most likely gain total control of the District's drug trade.

During the period between January and June, Trina had established no less than eight businesses, both legitimate and illegal within DC and across the border in Prince George's County Maryland. One of her most lucrative investments was a strip club located in Palmer Park dubbed 'The Ho House' which featured both male and female dancers, lap dancing, and gambling on the first floor, prostitution on the third and an in-house crack cocaine den in the black light lit basement. Despite its location with a moderately populated middle class neighborhood and a mere 15 blocks away from the PG County Police Precinct, the split level house on the corner of Galaxy and Warner Drive was left alone by neighborhood residents, despite the heavy traffic which surrounded the location every night. The neighbors who'd become weary over the years from violent attacks by prior criminals within their community had learned wisely to leave well enough alone.

Trina visited The Ho House every Saturday night to pick

up her weekly earnings from the three sections of the establishment and enjoyed the lively atmosphere of the strip tease before leaving out on other business. Each time she visited the place she'd pull up in a different vehicle, a Benz one week, a BMW the next. Occasionally she'd swing by in a Cadillac or on a motorcycle with a crew of her fellow drug dealing homies roaring up behind her on beautifully painted street bikes themselves.

One Saturday night around 10:15 PM, Trina and Pooh pulled up in front of one of their crack houses on Langston Lane to drop off a kilo of powdered cocaine before heading out to Palmer Park for the weekly cash pick-up. Trina's crew numbering six armed hoodlums, not counting herself and Pooh, all hopped out of a large olive green '89 Chevy Suburban laughing and clowning around with one another as they waited for their leader to emerge from the passenger side of the SUV. Trina added the finishing touches of make-up to her eyes and face and swabbed a thick coat of lilac-colored gloss onto her succulent lips before flipping up the sun visor and stepping out of the truck. No sooner than her Timberland boots hit the pavement below, did a gray Thunderbird squeal around the corner coming to a halt about twenty feet away opening fire from its dark interior.

Three members of her crew collapsed instantly to the ground as hollow tip slugs tore through their young bodies. Everyone else including Trina crouched against the Suburban for protection, as the enemy continually sprayed the immediate area with heavy gun fire. Trina felt the stinging bites of several slugs slamming into her back as she raced into a narrow alley beside the crack house. Luckily she had the good sense to have been wearing the light-weight bulletproof vest Kofi had suggested; otherwise she'd have been dead for sure.

Even though the Teflon vest spared her from death, the bullets had pelted her pretty good and her back burned with pain as she crouched down behind a row of filthy, stinking, garbage cans in the rat infested alley way. With extreme caution, Trina peered around and above the rotting trash to get a look at the identity of her attackers. With a nickel plated Baretta drawn and cocked back for discharge, she positioned herself against the wall and once again slowly looked around the garbage bag-topped cans squinting to catch a view of someone, anyone who could be responsible for the sneak attack that had just taken out three of her boys.

As she huddled behind the shelter of the garbage cans, Trina breathed heavily and felt her heart pounding in her chest like a pair of Congo drums. She was happy that she no longer had the cumbersome cast on her left wrist to worry about because it would've been awfully difficult to aim and fire with it on. The commotion outside the crack house raged on as she heard the profanity laced chatter of her own crew as they returned fire in the direction of the Thunderbird, as its tires screamed away from the crime scene and down the street around the ad-joining corner beyond Langston Lane.

Trina hopped up off the ground and sprinted towards her crew knowing that the penalties for gun violence would be more than she cared to deal with. Other than a few curious onlookers who peeped cautiously from in between their Venetian blinds and the barking chorus of neighborhood mutts, the coast was pretty much clear.

"C'mon, let's get the fuck up outta here," Trina snatched open the passenger's door and jumped in as did the surviving three Go Hard Soldierz crew members.

Pooh had driven only about three blocks from the spot of the shooting when a metropolitan squad car parked outside of a nearby steamed crab truck came up suddenly as he breezed passed. He'd already raced through two red lights and was well over the 25 mile per hour speed limit. The cop, who at the time was busy flirting with the cute girl within the crab truck, turned only to notice the speeding truck squeal away around the corner at a dizzying clip.

Trina's eyes burned with a fury not seen since her deadly night of vengeance against her stepfather, Maynard, long ago. She knew it could be none other than Roland Carter's H Street goons who were responsible for this latest strike and she was determined to strike back.

"Them bammas was pushin' a grayish lookin' Thunderbird, look jive like a '78 or '79 model joint. But the jokers was tote'n street sweepers and shit, young! We lucky to get up outta there alive, Joe. Too bad May, Lil' John, and Kenny were got though."

One of Trina's thugs announced through labored breaths, that Roland Carter had connections with an arms dealer from Baltimore who smuggled the latest in para-military weaponry in through the harbor via New York. The street sweeper was one weapon which Trina had long wanted to get her hands on for the deadly power and rapid fire capabilities it held, but had yet to find a reputable source from which to purchase it.

A half hour after the shooting, Trina and her crew arrived at Pooh's Valley Green rowhouse. Once inside, she contacted Francine Gonzolez by phone.

"Mrs. G., Roland and them just tried to kill me out Langston Lane 'bout thirty minutes ago," she said, sounding upset.

"Yes, yes . . . I've been given heads up on the incident from the 7thDistrict Police Precinct. Mr. Carter is more trouble-some than I realized."

"See, that's the type shit I'm talkin' 'bout. That muthafucka don't know when to stop! I hope you don't think I'm supposed to just sit back and let this cat bust off at me and my peeps every chance he gets without tryin' to protect myself and shit?"

"Calm down, Katrina. I have the situation fully under con-trol . . . like I said to everyone at the Fairfax meeting, anyone breaking the code of ethics that we've proposed will be pun-ished immediately and severely. There is an "all points bul-letin" in effect for the H Street Crew as we speak. We'll have most, if not all, of the culprits in custody within the next 24 hours, okay? So relax. We know that you guys weren't at fault. Get some rest. I'll talk to you tomorrow."

When Trina hung the phone up, she felt only slightly relieved after speaking with the D.A. It was comforting to know that neither she nor her homies would have to face police harassment. However, Trina was not pleased that she had not gotten a chance to pop one of Roland's thugs because even though Francine Gonzolez promised to bring the gunmen who'd attacked them to justice, still she knew that in order to charge them she'd have to have solid evidence. Sure three of her own crew had met a swift and bloody end on Langston Lane, but not one from that neighborhood would dare speak to the cops, as was the norm in the hood.

Other than pestering Roland's boys down at 7th D about their whereabouts during the time of the shooting and other bullshit harassments, the H Street assassins would probably walk out of the precinct with nothing more than a petty concealed gun charge. District Attorney Gonzolez would use the arrests to give the appearance of an aggressive city-wide police crack down on crime. This smoke screen would keep the media hounds off of her back and get her closer to the DC Mayoral office. Like everyone else in the game, District Attorney Gonzolez cared little about anyone else except herself and Trina knew it, so she'd planned ahead how she'd handle the drive-by shooters without the D.A.'s lukewarm assistance.

She had Pooh round up nearly two dozen of Southeast's most violent hoodlums from the neighborhoods of Benning Heights, Potomac Gardens, Congress Park, and her own beloved Barry Farms. The large group of hard-looking criminals met with Trina at Pooh's place, where she went over the details of her plan for vengeance. The eleven o'clock news programs highlighted the Langston Lane shootings which killed the three teenagers associated with Trina and the Go Hard Soldierz. The next day, Good Morning America and CNN broadcast

the shooting as the latest in the District's uncontrollable summer crime wave. The *Washington Post's* Metro Section covered
the shooting with a two page article which disclosed to Trina
information which was unbelievably shocking.

District police had found the 1979 Ford Thunderbird used
in the shooting abandoned burning outside of the Forest
Ridge apartment complex. When the raging flames were finally extinguished by DC fire fighters, the charred, smoking
frame of the vehicle revealed the badly burned remains of a
human being along with a smoldering Sig Saver handgun.
The body was taken to the District Morgue where the present
medical examiner, upon completing the autopsy, declared the
Jane Doe as one Bridgette Celia Cruise of 2213 Galveston
Place, Southeast. Dental records had identified her clearly.

"That snitch'n ass fat bitch," Trina snapped furiously reading over the *Washington Post* article a second time. "That's
what the bitch gets for fuckin' around with Roland and them—
good for her dumb ass!"

Now an entire slew of new possibilities came into Trina's
mind. Knowing how much animosity existed between she and
Bridgette Cruise there was no doubt that the erstwhile Go
Hard Soliderz member had joined forces with the enemy to
murder her. But instead, she'd signed her very own death warrant by seeking out the help of the vicious Northeast drug
lord.

By the 30th of August, District Attorney Francine Gonzolez's
task force apprehended over thirty members of Roland Carter's
H Street Crew and held them in custody at the DC Jail on D
Street, Southeast. The city's news stations swarmed down to
the DC Jail in droves of microphone-carrying, camera-flashing, videocam-recording reporters jockeying for position to
get the juiciest interview with the notorious Roland Carter
himself.

At 10:05 AM on September 5, 1989, Trina drove up to the
District of Columbia Courthouse on Indiana Avenue. She was

followed by twenty three ex-cons loaded in five S.U.V.'s, who then parked across from the massive court building from which Roland Carter and company would emerge right after their morning arraignment. After parking, Trina ordered the hoodlums to remain in the vehicles with the engines idling in order to instantly trail the H Street Crew to wherever their destination might be. Because once there, the Go Hard Soldierz would all exit their trucks and pump their enemies full of hollow tip slugs. They'd be caught by surprise and due to the fact that they'd just left a court arraignment, none of them would be packing steel. Trina smiled devilishly in the anticipation of the coming slaughter of the hated H Street Crew. Then without warning the entire area around them was alive with bright flashing lights of red and blue along with the incessant chirping of police sirens.

"Fuck," quipped Trina leaning her head back in annoyance at the latest failure of her deadly plans for Roland Carter. "Gimme all of them hammers," Trina snarled at the five, armed youths in the Chevy Suburban with her.

One by one, the gunmen gave up their semi-automatic weapons to Trina who quickly placed the chrome hardware into a huge lockbox containing two kilograms of cocaine on the floor of the passenger's seat. She calmly placed her own small Tech-9 into the metal box along with the other guns and coke. She then instructed the cornrow-wearing thug beside her to secure the lid before the police approached her vehicle. Other members of the Go Hard Soldierz were already being frisked up against their trucks when three metropolitan cops came up to the driver's side window.

"Why is y'all fuckin with us? We ain't done nothin' . . . we just sittin' out here chillin', that's all," she said blankly as the policemen stood outside of her window.

"Yeah, right! You must think I'm a fool, don't ya? You just chillin' huh? Right outside of the courthouse just before your boy Roland Carter steps out with his entourage? Plus, you've got hmmm, I'd say around about twenty some guys out here right now. Officer Bill Ray Turner got wind of your little get-together this morning and alerted us at 2nd District to be on the look out for this pre-arranged gangsta party of yours. I gotta give it to Billy Ray's whistle blower, Detective Tom Kelly, for givin' us heads up or else there would have been a whole lotta blood shed out here today."

"Detective Tom Kelly, huh? Oh, alright, I got you . . . trust me, it's all good."

"Whatever that means, honey, doesn't matter right now cause you're goin' to DC jail . . . you and your boys. So please step outta the truck!"

"I ain't doin' shit without seein' a muhfuckin' search warrant!"

"Oh, so you wanna be a smart ass, right?"

"Call it what you want. But I done been there and done that. I know my rights, officer. You gotta have a search warrant to check my personal belongings unless you have proof beyond a reasonable doubt that there's something illegal going on inside my vehicle. Plus, you ain't even charged me with nothin' . . . hollerin' 'bout some step outta the truck and shit!"

"I see, you got a little bit of brains to go with all of that beauty and ghetto booty, huh? Well check it . . . your boys got steel on them and I know there's weapons on y'all too. Don't even play like you don't know what I'm talkin' 'bout either. So you're looking at a weapons charge as you know it's illegal to possess a fire arm in the District of Columbia unless you're a federal or metropolitan police officer." The cop was being sarcastic and blunt, rubbing this information in Trina's face. After all, what was she going to do about it?

"Well I guess you gon' be shit outta luck cause ain't nobody in here got no weapons on 'em, how 'bout that!"

"You wanna play games and shit right," gritted the distinguished forty-something looking cop snatching the driver's side door of the suburban open glaring at Trina while doing so. "Get your ass up against the truck and assume the position right now! I'm tired of playing around with your smart mouthed ass! Hey, Frank, get the rest of these kids outta the car while I pat baby girl down for any concealed weapons."

Trina was given a rapid but very thorough frisk job that to officer's disappointment revealed nothing but a small dime bag of weed which he poured out onto the sidewalk grinding it under his foot spitefully. His partner also came up empty in his search of the other occupants of the S.U.V.

"Well, I'm gonna check your vehicle and each and every one of your lil' ballers in the other whips had guns on them. So that alone gonna cause you to catch a case anyway. So today just ain't your day, boo."

With a sense of urgency, Trina put both her powers of seduction as well as bribery into action in order to avoid arrest for herself and her gun-wielding crew.

"Look here, officer, I know that if I promised you some o' this booty you'd say yes. No man ever turned me down before. Give us a break, baby. Trust me, you won't be disappointed either. I don't fuck niggas who can't do shit for me. And right now let's just say, I need you to do me this one big favor and I'm willin' to pay for it any way you want me to, aiight," Trina whispered in the policeman's ear as they stood over to the rear of the Suburban away from the prying eyes and ears of the other cops.

She ran her fingers across his chest, downward until she felt the thick bulge between his thighs. She gazed up into his eyes, smiling with pleasure at his instant arousal in her presence. She placed ten $100 bills along with her pager number into his hand.

"Page me around 7:30 P.M. tonight, I'll meet you at the Washington Vista Hotel. Maybe I can thank you for this favor you done for us today.

Fifteen minutes later Trina, along with the rest of the Go

Hard Soldierz, was traveling back uptown toward Valley Green.

"You don't be fuckin' around girl. I thought we was gonna get locked up for sure this mornin'. How'd you get over on the police this time around?" asked Pooh inquisitively.

"What's the old sayin'? Ya gotta use what ya got, to get what ya want . . . well whoever coined that phrase ain't never lied. Cause money and sex makes the world go round, Pooh and I'll use 'em both to my advantage. You feel me?" Trina responded with frank truthfulness.

Once they had all arrived at Pooh's house, Trina angrily called Officer Billy Ray Turner aka Cowboy at his 7th District Police Precinct demanding an explanation for the early morning police interference.

"Cowboy," she barked into the receiver, "tell me why you got the 2nd District fuckin' with me and my peeps off the early mornin' and shit?"

"I sure did have 'em fuck with you, you who somehow managed to weasel your way outta the slammer I see. Anyway, you can't be everywhere, that's why I've managed to organize a raid on your crack house out on Langston Lane about an hour ago. There's a dozen of your crack dealers and about twenty or so customers down here being processed at the precinct as we speak. They'll all be down at the DC Jail in about a half hour."

"C'mon man! What the fuck? Why the hell am I payin' you all of this muhfuckin' money each and every week if you gon' keep on back'n down on your part of the bargain and shit? See, you got the game fucked up, playa!"

"Look here, lil' Miss Murder Inc! You and I may have a deal goin' but that don't mean that I ain't gonna do my job to keep the city's image clean, and negative press out the news, understand? There was just a triple homicide right outside of your dope den, which drew the unwanted attention of every fuckin' news station in town or didn't you notice? You may not have

ordered the shooting. We know who did that, but it occurred
right in front of a notorious crack house that you just happen
to run. Now I wouldn't care if the dope spot belonged to my
dear old dad, I'd shut it down as sure as my name's Bill Ray.
But you got lots o' money being the big shot drug dealer that
you are . . . bail their asses out. That should be a piece o' cake
for the likes o' you."

Trina slammed the phone down in disgust and got in contact with a local Northeast Washington bail bonds man who
served as one of her biggest sex clients at The Ho House,
many times paying for the services of Trina's in-house prosti-
tutes three to four times a week. The boys' bail came out to
$25,000, which Trina bartered for a month of free prostitute
services, as well as a quarter pound of potent hydrophonic
marijuana. Afterwards she hired an expensive dream team of
highly sought Washington lawyers who worked hard to free
the drug dealing crew of their charges during the three weeks
of court hearings. The law firm of Liebowitz and Kraft was
successful in clearing the twelve crack dealers of the major
felonies they had faced except for a handful of minor ones that
stuck. Yet still Trina felt little vindication over the legal victory
of her attorneys and for the remainder of the month of September she went into a deep and dark depression, one which
caused her to isolate herself from even her closest friends.

Trina spent a week in Cancun, Mexico, all alone where she
wrote several long letters to her estranged mother and daughter Porsche now five years old. She mailed postcards and exotic Mexican souvenirs to them as well. She tried to pamper
herself while vacationing in the tropical paradise of Mexico's
travel oasis, but other than brooding over her failures and
longing for the opportunity to see her mother and child, again
Trina dwelled on the grim subject of vengeance. She promised
herself that when she arrived back home in the states, Roland
Carter would die.

Chapter 21
The Wait is Now Over

Trina arrived back in DC on October 10th. She took care of most of her illegal affairs earlier during the day. That same night she wanted to have a little fun, so she invited some of the neighborhood girls from the Farms to party with her at the Republic Garden Nightclub. She and her hoodrat girlfriends enjoyed themselves well into the wee hours of the morning with much celebratory dancing, drinking, laughter, and the constant attention of many male admirers. Before leaving the club, Trina was approached by a prominent Hip Hop mogul who presented her with two tickets to the annual Hip Hop/Go-Go Octoberfest at the Capital Center in Landover, Maryland.

All of the area Go-Go bands would be performing along with some of the day's hottest rap stars such as Big Daddy Kane, Eric B & Rakim, Doug E. Fresh, and Slick Rick to name but a few. Local youth from DC, Maryland, and Virginia would converge on the Capitol Center by the hundreds. Trina loved concerts and the celebrities the really large ones drew. She considered herself a local celebrity in her own right and enjoyed flossing her hood wealth before both her admirers as well as the many haters who wished her harm. She knew that she'd get special VIP treatment from the concert sponsors so that she could mingle with the performers back stage and she'd party with them at the after party.

The Octoberfest would begin with Howard University's Homecoming football game festivities. There'd be fraternity step shows, comedy, dance, and talent shows held at the university, all peaking with the football game between the Howard Bisons vs. the FAMU Rattlers. Trina would enjoy every minute of every show leading up to the grand finale concert at Landover's Capitol Center. She was having so much fun that she nearly forgot about who she was and the objective that she promised herself she'd see carried out.

Trina then had her suspicions about the tickets that were given so freely to her by the record producer at the club. She'd been tricked into making unwise decisions before that had cost her dearly in more ways than one. Her small inner voice was once again warning her as she toyed with the pair of tickets as she sat behind the wheel of her Suburban. One Friday evening as the crisp autumn breeze kissed her face through the half lowered window of the SUV, Trina knew that she'd never again disregard her powerful intuition again. With the concert of that magnitude, and star power the region's big ballers and shot callers were sure to show their face in the place. This wasn't a place that a drug lord in the midst of a street war would want to be caught dead at. She took the cigarette lighter she'd just used to fire up a blunt and touched the flame to the tickets, which caught fire slowly then blazed a brief, bright orange just before she tossed them out the window onto the sidewalk.

Fifteen minutes later, as she waited while her truck was undergoing a tune-up and tire job at a local auto repair shop, she was paged by Kofi. She contacted him on her cell phone a few minutes afterwards.

"Whassup, baby? I ordered us dinner from that new Japanese steakhouse down the street from us. So bring that ass home before it arrives cause you know I ain't eatin' until you get here. Oh yeah! Guess what? I got some good news for you," he said sounding excited on the other end, "you gonna like this shit I'm 'bout to tell you."

"What? Tell me, boo."

"Nope . . . I ain't tellin' you nothin' until you come home for dinner. Besides I'm horny as shit and I need for you to break me off some tonight, know what I mean?"

"Boy, you ain't nothin' but a freak, you know that? Anyway, I'll be there in about thirty minutes. I'm gettin' my truck detailed and shit."

Pooh and Trina drove over to her Georgetown digs, where Pooh took the truck to fill it up with gas for the week while Trina entered her home to have dinner with Kofi. As she entered the gorgeous living room she was pleased by the romantic setting of candle light, romantic smooth jazz melodies, and a mouth watering spread upon the kitchen table awaiting her. Kofi greeted her with a lovingly warm hug and passionate kiss before leading her over to the dinner table and pulling out a chair for her to sit. As they dined by candle light, serenaded by the mesmerizing love songs of Sade, her boyfriend at last revealed his information.

"Trina, my love, you ain't gonna believe this," he exclaimed while leaning over his half-eaten meal of Teriyaki steak and Japanese style steamed vegetables, "tell me why the nigga Roland's gonna be at the Octoberfest after party out Maryland at Crystal Skates! You know how many muthafuckas gonna be at that joint? It's gonna be packed like shit . . . he ain't gonna be expectin' nothin' with so many folks around, and all we gotta do is get in, do his ass, and hit Branch Avenue back across the DC line, and that's that. You feel me? This is your chance to finally get rid of this bitch ass nigga!"

"You ain't lyin' 'bout that shit! How you happen to find out where he was gonna be at," Trina asked inquisitively as she sipped on a glass of Cristal.

"Don't worry 'bout that. You got your connections and I got mine. Only thing you need to worry 'bout is bustin' that muhfucka's head and shit . . . that's it. There's gonna be a whole lotta young'uns there tryin' to get autographs with Chuck, E.U. and all them rappers like Big Daddy Kane and Rakim and them. So ain't nobody gon' be thinkin' 'bout getting shot at."

"That's all well and good and everything, but with all o' them people all over the place, how in the fuck we gon' be able to pop Roland and then get up outta the joint without causin' a stampede?"

"Again, all that's been taken care of, boo. Just calm down and rest your nerves . . . I got this!"

"You'd better!" she said pulling her handsome lover over to her seductively as she arose from her seat.

Instantly they locked lips lustfully tangling their tongues together in a torrid caress of unbridled desire, Kofi lifted the curvaceous form of his gangsta bun-bun and carried her over to the plush leather couch in their luxurious living room. Like dogs in heat, the two lovers tore at each other's clothing in a mad effort to feed their sexual hunger. Trina nibbled on Kofi's left earlobe and neck as he mounted her missionary style. Trina's dark nipples stiffened on her firm 38DD breasts as Kofi's wet tongue encircled them between his moist lips. She groaned with earthy pleasure as Kofi sunk his thick, hard manhood deep within her dripping walls, pumping her slow and steady as she encircled her shapely legs around the small of his muscular back.

With the flames of carnal fire burning bright within her now, Trina gyrated in unison with her lover squealing with delight each time the huge head of his dick stimulated her G-spot. The couple was going at it with such gusto, their two Akita guard dogs came romping over to the double glass French doors leading to the broad backyard to investigate. Kofi turned Trina around on the couch and entered her doggy style, her plump ass cheeks rippled like jello each time he slammed his 8 ½ inches into her gaping, pink slit. Kofi's sinewy body shuddered as he neared ejaculation then he pulled his woman closer to him as he moaned loud and guttural as his thick, veined penis spurted a heavy stream of semen deep within Trina's womb, the warm rushing sensation bringing about her very own series of explosive climaxes. Spent by the intense love making interlude, the sweat-drenched couple fell asleep together in a nude embrace upon the living room couch while the candles flickered down and died into trickling wax and the amorous melodies of Sade continued to play on in the background.

On the Friday before the Howard University's Homecoming events were to unfold, Trina again threw caution to the wind and purchased two tickets to the Octoberfest After party. Even though her better judgment warned that she not go, Trina could not pass up a prime opportunity to get rid of her biggest competitor and most despised enemy in the entire city. The very next day she spent several hours shopping and visiting her hairstylist in order to prepare for the festive events of the day that would hopefully end with Carter's murder. Trina had Pooh's older sister, Kathy, drop off several shopping bags filled with clothes, shoes, and toys for her daughter, Porsche and $1,500 cash for her mother. Trina missed them both terribly, but decided that until the danger of Roland Carter and his 8th and H Street Crew had been erased, she still could or would not come into contact with them except for mail correspondence via cards and letters, and the occasional phone conversation, which lasted for several hours between her and her mother whenever Trina did call.

By 1:30 pm Trina and Kofi attended the football game between Howard and FAMU. They were joined by Pooh, Lil' Ghetto, Black Rick and Big Stinka, four extremely violent youths from Barry Farms Dwellings, each with a long rap sheet of past felonies. Bored by the lackluster play of the Bison as Florida A&M went up 24-3 by halftime, Trina and company left Howard University Football Stadium along with scores of other disappointed Howard supporters to involve themselves with other more enjoyable activities of the Homecoming weekend. The five partners in crime kept themselves busy along the colorful and crowded Georgia Avenue for several hours awaiting the time of the after party. So by 12:30 AM, the group hopped into Pooh's Caddy and headed toward Temple Hills. Once there, Trina had Pooh park outside the Branch Avenue Motel Inn. He and his three partners would wait out in the motor inn's parking lot with walkie talkies in hand awaiting word form their leader to pick them up right after the hit.

After giving Pooh the orders of the night, Trina placed the second of the walkie talkies in her boyfriend's hand and the two finely-attired assassins proceeded across Branch Avenue toward the lively, music filled after party jumping off within the huge Crystal's Skating Rink. At the entrance was a flowing red carpet spread out towards the sidewalk and at the doorway stood two hulking bouncers who seemed threatening even though they wore nicely tailored silk suits. Although Trina and Kofi were behind several other couples, they were given the celebrity treatment, the bouncers ushered them into the party ahead other patrons stamping "VIP" on the back of their hands. This gesture was somewhat strange and surprising to Trina. Usually one had to have broken someone off some love in the form of a monetary, drug, or sexual favor in order to have received such high class benefits . . . Trina had done nothing to have deserved this blessing. She felt flattered. A broadly smiling Trina, sashayed with ass bouncing strides past the bouncers and through the broad doors silently assuming that Kofi had arranged this A-list treatment.

When the couple stepped into the party, the throbbing music of local Go-Go band Rare Essence cranked out from the vibrating speakers surrounding the skating rink turned dance floor. While the multitudes danced and crowded around the gold laden rap stars, Trina and Kofi took two seats near a pair of wall-sized airbrush paintings of champagne bottles and glasses and a Jaguar sitting on sparkling rims, which drew dozens of smiling youths who posed before them for $10 photos.

Trina looked about and noticed more than a few of Roland Carter's hooligans lurking amongst the other partygoers. She'd catch a nasty look from one of them occasionally before they'd disappear among the dancing throng. There were also several kids from the late Maurice Lil' Mo' Gentry's Lincoln Heights neighborhood who were keeping a close watch on both Trina and Kofi as they sat eating finger food and sipping on Long Island Iced Teas. Trina stared back at these haters and nudged her unknowing boyfriend to move on toward the smaller VIP room next to the thumping dance floor.

In the velvet room, the lighting was much dimmer with a mini chandelier hanging from the ceiling and several tables bearing metallic gold tablecloths dotted the modest room with lava lamps sitting on top of them. The walls, which were sound-proof, blocked out much of the excessive bass and noise coming from next door. While sitting there comfortably talking with Kofi, a handsome couple came over smiling and laughing as they embraced the two drug dealers with glee. It was Nancy Dardin and her fiancé Christopher Heath.

Nancy Dardin, a tall fair-skinned beauty, was a rising star in the Washington area's legal community having just graduated from Georgetown University's Law School. Both the lovely young attorney and her well paid engineer lover were frequent cocaine customers of Trina's and tonight they were elated to have run across her for more reasons than one. Trina secured a $1,500 drug transaction with her coke clients less than 15 minutes into their conversation. She took a personal check from Nancy Dardin and instructed her to meet up with her at the McDonald's on Georgia Avenue at 12:30 PM the following day in order to pick up her coke.

The two couples sat together for a half hour sharing laughs, drinking, and planning future vacations together before bidding each other adieu. Trina took Kofi by the hand and led him onto the dance floor that had grown even more crowded by the time 1:45 AM rolled around. After they worked up a sweat dancing to the music of Go-Go Godfather, Chuck Brown & the Soul Searchers, Trina stepped into the ladies' room and contacted Pooh and company to enter the skating rink at once. She'd spotted a number of enemy crews skulking about inside the after party mean-mugging on her and growing bolder in their intimidation tactics.

At approximately 1:52 AM, Pooh, Lil' Ghetto, Black Rick, and Big Stinka came strutting through the doors after paying the $13 person cover charge. They quickly joined up with Trina and Kofi. Together they sat near the photo shoot area where Trina had been earlier in the night, and discussed the murderous plans which they'd set forth originally.

Pooh and his three road dawgs mingled amongst the guests where they immediately took to the dance floor after selecting a choice wallflower or two to accompany them. Yet still they kept a constant vigil on each others' whereabouts especially those of their attractive leader and her boyfriend. Trina excused herself while sitting with Kofi to use the ladies' room a second time. Then upon returning to his side ten minutes later, Trina leaned in close and whispered into his ear.

"Go and get your swerve on with one or two o' them lil' hoochies leanin' on the wall over there . . . it's all good. I don't care. Shit, two of 'em over there starin' you down anyway. That'll give me a chance to peep this cat out wherever he might be in this joint. I know good and damn well he's up in here cause his mob is all over the place. I'll find his ass sooner or later. Aiight, boo? Go ahead and enjoy ya self. I'll holla back in a few."

Trina and Kofi kissed each other softly and then he headed over towards the two giggling cuties on the far end of the dance floor who blushed with modesty as he got closer. Trina bought another glass of Long Island Iced Tea and walked back and forth through the lively, chitter-chattering crowd carefully scrutinizing everyone she could as she passed by couples, groups, and singles, moving through the dense crowd. A watchful Pooh broke away from the dance floor shadowing his boss step for step, but a few feet away. Several times Trina was hit on for her digits or asked to dance by flirtatious male party guest whose advances and requests she'd respectfully decline while moving on with her unwavering search for Roland Carter. Then as she walked through the adjoining VIP area, Trina at once recognized the tall, statuesque form of Asia Lynn as she stood beside the doorway, drink in hand, laughing it up with several other women.

As always, the stunning beauty was impeccably dressed from head to toe in an elegant Christian Dior ensemble with a sexy pair of stiletto-heeled pumps that added flair to her regal attire. Completing the diva's gear was an expensive two and half carat diamond jewelry set which shimmered with bling brilliance around her slender neck and wrists. A short, bearded dark-skinned man dressed in a bright red and black suit with matching derby hart and alligator shoes came strutting over to her playfully smacking her on the behind, prompting Asia Lynn to slap him on the shoulder in response drawing giggles from both her and her lovely friends. It was none other than the dreaded Roland Carter himself posturing arrogantly in the presence of the admiring women as three of his tough acting gorillas looked on. He whispered something in Asia Lynn's ear which caused her to chuckle lightly as he turned to leave.

Asia Lynn hugged each of her girlfriends and skipped daintily behind Carter in an effort to catch up. As the striking dime piece passed Trina, she stopped suddenly and turned back towards her. Trina's fists clenched preparing to strike out at the girl if she tried anything foolish. Instead, Asia Lynn spoke quickly while checking around for unwanted ears.

"Trina, hurry and follow us out into the parking lot. I'm

going with him to his car. It's the blue Jeep Grand Cherokee parked to the right next to the Octoberfest's tour bus. C'mon."

Trina hesitated instinctively then followed immediately behind Asia Lynn. Surely this woman who'd tricked her into believing that she was an editor for a popular Urban magazine had bumped her head if she thought that Trina would again fall for another of her bold-faced lies, Trina thought to herself as she rushed behind the couple towards the front door. It had to be a set up. There was absolutely no way that Roland Carter would not be packing a gun at this event. Who knows? There might even be others laying in wait for her when she emerged ready to pump her full of lead once the front doors closed behind her. That may have been a possibility, but this time she would be more than ready for any surprises.

Trina stopped just short of exiting the skating rink when six hard looking members of Carter's entourage filed out the door one after the other into the parking lot. Yeah, it was no doubt in her mind to the intentions of the little welcoming committee who'd gathered outside for her. She calmly backed away from the door and proceeded back into the area of the dance floor where she rounded up her crew, letting them in on the situation which had unfolded within the past few minutes.

"Trina, boo, you stay here. I'll go outside with Pooh and them and air these cats out for you!" said Kofi pulling a loaded clip from the left pocket of his dress slacks.

"Oh, hell no!" retorted Trina, "I don't mean no harm or nothin' sweetheart, but I been waitin' too muhfuckin' long to finally get at these jokers, 'specially that ass Roland. Uh, uh, I gotta do this bitch nigga my damn self. You slip out the side door and go get the whip down the street. And make sure you get back up here with the quickness, aiight? C'mon, Pooh. We 'bout to give these niggas what they want."

Trina watched as Kofi slipped unnoticed through a emergency exit which had the alarm deactivated by one of the building engineers shortly after she'd bribed him with a mere

$150 in cash. With Kofi safely out the building and on the opposite side of the parking lot, Trina nodded towards her four gunmen and headed out the same exit. Quickly the five pistol-packing thugs disappeared through the emergency door and out into the brisk cool of the autumn night beyond.

Five shadowy figures skulked around the far side of the skating rink sizing up the small group of hoodlums standing around in the middle of the parking lot up ahead. They were passing around a blunt and laughing amongst themselves as they stood next to a black tricked-out Audi. Not far away Roland Carter's blue Jeep Grand Cherokee sat silent and still. He'd taken Asia Lynn into his vehicle and asked of his partners that he not be disturbed.

"Them jokers think they got shit all worked out, thinkin' we gonna just walk up outta the joint not knowin' what's up . . . well them muhfuckas 'bout to get it just for sleepin' us," Trina exclaimed in a low voice as she pointed towards the six roughnecks.

Trina attached a dark-colored silencer onto the barrel of a Smith & Wesson nine millimeter which prompted her four friends to do the same. Then slowly they began sneaking toward their unsuspecting victims using the parking lot's multitude of vehicles as makeshift shields in close proximity of their adversaries. Together they raised their pistols and simultaneously broke from the cover of the shadows firing off round after deadly muffled round into the six suddenly startled youths. Like dominoes, the boys dropped to the ground. Felled by the hail of bullets, the wounded and dying teens could do little to protect themselves as they lay bleeding and groaning in agony on the cold pavement of the parking lot.

Trina headed off towards the Jeep Grand Cherokee while Pooh and the other Southeast thugs finished off their fallen rivals by emptying their clips on the prostrate forms lying at their feet. Trina ejected the one empty clip she'd just used on Carter's crew and inserted a fresh fully loaded one just for him.

When she was outside of his driver's side window, she could see him laid back on his reclined seat placing his right hand upon Asia Lynn's head as she took the length of his rock hard erection into her warm moist mouth. Oblivious to his surroundings as he savored the delightful pleasure of Asia Lynn's erotic oral skills, Roland Carter's very last sight of anything was the figure of Trina hovering outside his window taking aim on him with a huge nine millimeter. Asia Lynn screamed and recoiled as several powerful shots slammed into Carter's chest, shoulder, and neck.

Blood spatter splashed across the windshield, steering wheel, and top of the ceiling as well as sprinkling Asia Lyn with crimson dots of gore as she covered her mouth in terror. She knew that Trina was going to kill Carter, but the sudden attack had taken her by surprise. Trina hated Carter passionately, but the idea of him getting a blow job from his dead nephew's baby's mama disgusted her all the more and she placed the end of the silencer-covered barrel directly on his blood soaked chest and pulled the trigger three more times causing the drug lord's body to jerk and heave violently with each gunshot.

Trina looked over at the frightened Asia Lynn who huddled in a fetal position in the passenger seat, trembling as she looked Washington's most lethal enforcer in the eye. With Carter's semen still trickling from her bottom lip and chin, and flecks of his blood all over her face and dress, the gorgeous Asia Lynn now appeared soiled and less than pristine causing Trina to walk away while shaking her head pitifully. She could've very well killed Asia Lynn right there and then, but instead Trina realized that Asia Lynn essentially had worked to set Carter up for her to murder. So she thought better of it and spared the life of the woman who'd lied to her before. Three times now Asia Lynn had come into contact with Trina and had walked away unharmed.

Trina joined the rest of her fleeing posse as they all dashed away from the scene of the crime and bolted toward the huge Cadillac, which had screeched to a halt just in time outside of the skating rink's front doors.

"C'mon, Kofi, get up outta here!" Trina screamed at the top of her lungs.

Several people made their way out into the parking lot seconds after the shootings and had begun. They were horrified beyond belief at the gory scene that unfolded before them. Trina realized the magnitude of what she and her cohorts had just carried out. There were quite a few followers of Roland Carter within the building who would surely retaliate with gunfire once they found out what had just happened to their leader and homeboys.

As Kofi squealed away from the parking lot, the screams of anguished women, as well as shouts of enraged young men, echoed in the background as the late model Caddy raced away from the Crystal Skating Rink and on across the Maryland state line back into the safe borders of their native Washington, DC.

"Whew, Wee! That shit was close than a muthfucka, young!" Pooh blurted out excitedly.

"Think it wasn't?" returned Trina looking back for any signs of cops or enemy gunmen as they sped along Suitland Parkway en route to the Farms.

"I'm glad that I recognized ole' girl inside the joint, or else we woulda been the ones stretched out on the pavement right about now! Matter o' fact," she said turning to stare fiercely at her boyfriend as he drove rapidly along the dark highway. "What the fuck's up with that bitch, huh, Kofi? Will y'all in here right now tell me what the fuck happened with ya girl Asia Lynn?"

"Fuck you mean what happened and shit? I done told you 'bout comin' at me like that, young!"

"Nigga fuck all that dumb shit you talkin' cause I'll steal the fuck outta yo bitch ass right here in this car, muhfucka! So don't even try to break bad with me cause I ain't one o' them lil' soft ass bitches you used to fuckin' wit'! You better open up you muhfuckin' mouth 'bout what that bitch was doin' in the party tonight or you gon' have some drama on yo hands, Slim!"

"Trina! I told you who the fuck she was before, didn't I?"

"Boy, you better stop playin' with me! I wanna know how you knew Roland was gon' be at the after party tonight. Did she tell you or somethin'?"

"Aiight! Aiight! Yeah, she told me. Aiight, you fuckin' happy now? Shit!"

"Oh, really? Why you and that ho so buddy-buddy and shit? You must be fuckin' that bitch!"

"She ain't no bitch! She's my first cousin, aiight? She was lookin' out for us."

"She is, huh? Well that's all gravy and everything, but your cousin still fucks with them H Street cats, so I don't trust her as far as I can throw her."

"Last week I met with Asia Lynn at Jasper's. She said that even though it would be dangerous and that she'd have to do some things with Roland that she didn't necessarily want to do in order to draw his attention away from y' all, because they'd planned to kill you at the Octoberfest after party ever since August. Roland had been pressin' her for some ass since he'd gotten outta Lorton and shit. So she promised him some on the night of the after party. She told him she wanted to fuck him in the parking lot cause the idea of bein' caught in public turned her on. That of course was a set up . . . a set up designed for you to kill him."

"Aiight then, I guess I was wrong . . . sorry, but it did jive like look suspicious as shit though. I'm gonna have to thank her personally for helpin' us get that jokah. When you see her again tell her I said good lookin' out."

The multiple homicide outside of Crystal Skating Rink caused a major power shift once more on the streets of inner city Washington. Not since the murder of Carl "Nutt" Wormsley had a gangland killing generated such local news coverage, far more than a week and a half. The slaying of 8th & H Street drug lord, Roland Carter, and his six thugs dominated the front page stories of the local newspapers of DC, Maryland, and Virginia. Not to mention the day-to-day details of the crime, as well as bios of the major players involved including Trina, shown on area television news programs.

Roland Carter's memorial service drew even more mourners than his nephew, Nutt Wormsley's had earlier. Along with over 1,300 mourners, Carter's elaborate funeral featured several Go-Go band personalities, at least four rap stars, athletes from area sports teams both collegiate and professional, and numerous drug Kingpins from as far away as Boston and Atlanta. Ironically, Francine Gonzolez spoke at Roland Carter's service, which was held at the Ebenezer Baptist Church.

She used the solemn occasion as a chance to build up her flagging public relations with the local media by criticizing violence and discouraging drug use amongst area citizens in general and youth in particular. Many saw the DA's parting words for the deceased as a part of her mayoral campaign speech.

Trina sent a bereavement card to Pope's Funeral home where Roland Carter's body laid in state for public viewing prior to the memorial service. This rude and callous gesture drew fury from the loved ones of the deceased drug lord, causing rumors of a retaliatory strike against her from the surviving members of the H Street Crew to abound on the streets for days after Carter had been laid to rest. Trina, however, could've cared less about the salty feelings of Carter's young henchmen. With Carter now dead and no other legitimate heir to take over his position within the 8th & H Street drug crew, she realized that she now truly stood alone as the top hustler in DC.

Chapter 22

The Queen Bee Reigns Supreme

The remaining months of 1989 gave way to the new decade of the 1990's with very little violence in inner-city Washington. With the absence of Roland Carter, the H Street crew slowly but surely disbanded. The inexperienced youth and constant bickering among the remaining dealers made them vulnerable to police stings and attacks from rival crews particularly Trina's own Go Hard Soldierz.

By March 1990, the once feared H Street Crew was but a memory. Other DC crews who'd once opposed Trina's authority, such as the Lincoln Heights Mob and others, reluctantly but wisely joined ranks with the larger, more organized Go Hard Soldierz. After witnessing the slow yet steady destruction of the remaining H Street Crew at the hands of Trina's well-organized and heavily armed team of hooligans, all other drug dealing crews in the ghettos of the Nation's Capitol bowed to the iron will of the gangsta diva rather than face her awful wrath.

As a result of the riddance of her toughest competitors Trina began taking over 80% of the region's illegal drug money to include that of P.G. County, Maryland and Fairfax

County, Virginia. Early on April 19, 1990, Trina's uncle, Otis Ricks, succumbed to complications following a massive stroke he'd suffered in January. By May, she learned that her sister, Rita Ann, had become head of the Atlantic Coast Division of the FBI.

Trina paid for her uncle's funeral and all prior unpaid hospital expenses, which had accumulated after he'd exhausted all of his Medicare benefits. She also saved his Forestville home from foreclosure and refinanced the four bedroom split-level house at 6336 Waterford Drive. After remodeling the house to the tune of $34,000, she suggested to her mother, Lucinda that both she and her daughter Porsche move from the little run-down rowhouse in Barry Farms to the much more spacious accommodations out in P.G. County. Her mother gladly accepted the offer of her younger daughter. Lucinda Ricks and her six year old granddaughter moved in on July 5, 1990.

As for the information concerning her older sister Rita Ann, Trina simply smiled with quiet amusement. Gossip going around on the streets on Washington's projects painted a drastically different picture of the proud FBI leading lady of the Washington area chapter. Rita Ann Ricks had given birth to two illegitimate children since she and Trina had seen each other last. One of her children, the most recent baby, supposedly had been fathered by a married Saudi Arabian diplomat. Trina grinned at the memory of how her sister had been so full of upright qualities and spotless morality in which she stressed to Trina that she should follow. Yet she'd gotten knocked up by a married man. Trina wished that she could somehow rub it in her face, but the very thought of a possible scandal made her pleased all the same.

Trina's own relationship continued to waver in between highs and lows. Enjoying romantic outings and engagements on the one hand and having fierce knockdown, drag out arguments on the other. Due to the high profile news coverage of her illegal drug business and alleged participation in a number of the area's murders, she and Kofi's lease was terminated by the original owners of the Georgetown Cottage. The neighbors had become uneasy with the idea of a couple of dangerous dope dealing felons among them. And the constant traffic and at times loud Go-Go and rap music coming from the residence did nothing to help matters any, as they were the only young black couple living in the affluent Old Georgetown neighborhood.

As a result, the criminal power couple changed addresses almost every six months or so, living out of exclusive hotels and luxurious gated community homes in various parts of the District and P.G. County. However with the tens of thousands of dollars at their disposal locally as well as safely secured in offshore bank accounts, neither Trina nor Kofi ever ran into a problem acquiring anything or anyone they wanted. It was nothing for the two of them to enter establishments such as restaurants, car dealerships, and retailers which catered to a privileged clientele and intermingle amongst Washington's elite, such as Supreme Court judges and media personalities.

Trina loved the unsettling effect on the rich mostly White patrons whenever she stepped foot in the room. Yet her own wealth, albeit ill-gotten could not be denied, and she soon became a frequent and valued customer at many of Washington's most expensive places of business. Success had made life one of ease and comfort for Trina and her loved ones lately, but not unlike other hustlers she soon grew eager to expand her reach into new territories around the city as well as the suburbs. Yuppies, many of them college students from Georgetown University, George Washington University and College Park's University of Maryland, were deeply into the recreational use of Ecstasy and Crystal Meth. Drugs which the preppy collegiate crowd claimed enhanced their ability to party, study and have sex for long, sustained periods of time.

Trina tapped into another lucrative vein of the illegal drug market and brokered a deal with Detroit Ecstasy dealer, Jeremy "Acid" Fawcett that until his 1992 arrest and conviction on drug smuggling charges proved to be quite successful for both her and the entire Go Hard Soldierz family. With the comfort of knowing that she had no current threat to her status as drug queen, Trina was ill-prepared for the events of December 11, 1990.

By the late 1980's, hundreds of Salvadorian immigrants relocated from their war-torn country to the shores of the United States landing in Los Angeles and later going east to Northern Virginia. Hardened by the horrors of civil war, the new immigrants formed gangs in order to protect themselves, originally from the violent street gangs in East L.A.. But within no time, the Salvadorian gangs morphed from loosely knotted cliques to a highly organized, incredibly violent super gang numbering well over 1,200 members in certain areas. They called themselves Mara Salvatrucha (street tough Salvadorians) aka MS-13.

The ruthless methods which this deadly menace employed startled and disturbed even veteran homicide detectives. Victims of the violent MS-13 gang had fingers or entire hands chopped off, machetes were used to decapitate enemies and headless bloody corpses were often dumped in front of police headquarters or the homes of the victims' families. They made their fortunes from drug trafficking, gun smuggling, prostitution, and welfare fraud. Now the gang had made its way into DC's Columbia Heights neighborhood. Rumor had it that the current gang leader of the Locos Vatoss 13, a local DC Chapter of MS-13, wanted in on drug business which had up until now been exclusively dominated by the Go Hard Soldierz, and they were not above resorting to bloodshed in order to take what they wanted. Trina shrugged it off just as she'd done the other reports of rivals moving in on her turf. Surely after dismantling the H Street Crew so handily no other group of drug dealing wannabes would dare attempt to challenge the power of her crew no time soon. Yet she'd welcome the chance to make an example out of anyone bold enough to jump out there with her. But the reports she'd read about in the papers and the programs covering MS-13 she'd checked out on T.V. could not prepare her for the afternoon of the 11th .

Trina had just left the Ghana Café in the trendy Adams Morgan community of Northwest Washington, after meeting with her two lawyers for a late afternoon meal and to sign a few legal documents in their presence. After her power lunch concluded at around 2:35 pm, Trina bid goodbye to her attorneys and proceeded towards her Suburban that she'd had parked about four blocks away in a quiet section of the neighborhood where nothing seemed out of place or weird. With the slew of Hispanic residents living in the area, Trina paid little attention to the short, ruddy complexioned Salvadorian man with a thick walrus-like mustache shadowing her for three of the four blocks that led to her truck. When at last Trina's suspicion kicked in and she turned to look back over her shoulder, the dark little stranger was gone . . . disappearing down one of the quiet side streets. She looked around her cautiously, clicked her car's remote lock on her keychain and entered the comfy confines of her SUV. Then time stopped.

A blue and white Ford Mustang carrying four tattooed Surenos came to a screeching halt next to her Suburban and began spraying the vehicle with semi-automatic gunfire. The windshield shattered and crashed raining broken glass all around the truck onto the street below; the clattering thud of bullets pelting the exterior of the Suburban was akin to the sound raindrops from hell. For two nightmarish minutes the Salvadorians peppered Trina's truck with gunfire while Trina crouched down low on the driver's seat. AK-47 slugs zipped and hissed mere inches above her as she huddled upon the fully reclined seat of the truck. Fortunately for Trina, at the urging of Kofi she'd added bullet proof sidings during her most recent detailing of her truck and now that discussion had saved her life. For what seemed like an eternity all Trina could hear was the deafening clatter of the AK's discharging the lethal contents of their clips outside her door. Then just as suddenly she the souped-up Mustang's tires scream as the swift car fishtailed away from the scene and down 18th Street Northwest.

MS-13 had now formally introduced themselves to her. And had it not been for the armored shell underneath the metal covering of the custom Suburban, she would not have escaped yet another attempt on her life. But unlike Trey Wills, Trina was not about to back down from anyone, regardless how fearsome their reputation might be. This was her city and she wouldn't allow any foreigners to take control of it without a fight. But MS-13 wasn't hardly done sending home their message of terror to the Go Hard Soldierz. Later during the same week two of her Northeast open air drug markets were attacked by several dozen assault weapon toting Surenos who shot to death eight of her drug dealers and wounded four customers. The tattooed gunmen also took drugs, money, and weapons.

Following the failed murder attempt on her, Trina was summoned down to the 2nd District Police Precinct for questioning concerning the Adams Morgan shooting for over three hours. She was grilled about the incident, which had caused uproar in the Adams Morgan community prompting a series of concerned citizen meetings where residents expressed their anger and outrage to the DC Police Chief, D.A. Francine Gonzolez and the Mayor himself. Instead of attempting to gain information about the Latino shooters, as always the boys in uniform seemed to badger her about her business dealings and whereabouts. Trina handled 2nd District with the same tight-lipped approach she used with 7th District cops.

After the three-hour interrogation ended, Trina had Kofi pick her up from the precinct and they went to their Shaw neighborhood home where she and Kofi relaxed out of sight for a time going out only to recover the damaged Suburban and to have it fully restored at a New York Avenue body shop.

The infamous couple had been eyeing the chic new homes within the upscale D.C. neighborhood, finally setting on a marvelous, Victorian style row house, back in early October, 1990.

Coming home from the grocery store on the weekend right before the holidays, Trina recognized the hunter green colored 1990 V6 Nissan M pulling up at the light from a gas station near her row house. There inside along with Bernard 'Big Stinka' Gibson was a familiar-looking woman. The woman seemed much older than the drug courier driving beside her. But they drove pass so fast that Trina could not get a particularly good glimpse of her. She thought about what she'd just seen. Then she made a quick call to Pooh when she got home.

"Hey, Pooh, y'all seen that nigga Big Stinka round here today?"

"Yeah, he 'bout to go take this bun to the telly and shit. Yeah, that's what he said he was 'bout to do."

"Oh yeah? What ditzy broad his lil' ho'n ass guttin' this go round?"

"He said he met this ole head out Maryland a coupla months back at Forestville Mall. He said since then he been hittin' that ass somethin' like two to three times a week. He s'pose to take the camcorder with 'im and get the bitch on camera today. Silly ass nigga talkin' 'bout sellin' them joints for $5 a pop after he gets them burnt. I told the nigga to hook me up with her old ass cause I'll fuck the shit out her!"

Trina was unusually silent on the other line which worried her friend Pooh.

"Whassup Trina . . . boo? Why is you so quiet? Thinkin' 'bout them dumb ass esays and shit?"

"Naw . . . just got a whole lotta other shit on may mind. That's all."

Trina was speechless. If only Pooh could've been there to see her face at that moment. It was the dumbfounded look of a person who'd seen a ghost! She fought to deny the bitter reality of her mother laying up with a man some thirty years her junior. She could not believe what she was hearing. Yet what she'd seen earlier and the confirmation given by Pooh was more than enough evidence that her beloved mother, Lucinda Ricks, had been sleeping with the nineteen-year-old drug dealer Big Stinka.

Big Stinka was one of the best earners—after Pooh and Lil' Ghetto who worked for Trina's crew. He, however, had a healthy sexual appetite which was bordering on addiction. He had little if any discretion at all when it came to satisfying his compulsive sexual desires. He bedded down crack whores, grossly obese women and still other undesirable females which other more discriminating men would not touch with a ten foot pole. He enjoyed threesomes and orgies, often with perfect strangers. This was a man who had contracted nearly every type of STD on record with the exception of HIV, though at any given time, his status was questionable due to his extreme sexual activity. He loved to videotape his conquests and show the X-rated footage later to friends of his, where he'd brag abut his prowess in bed and speak of his partners as if they were nothing more than dim-witted pieces of meat.

Though Trina liked Big Stinka as an employee of hers, she despised the nineteen-year-old thug as a person. For to her, he was very much similar in character to her late stepfather Maynard.

But what in hell was her mother thinking about? Of all the eligible men her age throughout the area, why in the world would Lucinda choose a young, sexual deviant like Big Stinka? Trina would not allow this relationship to continue. She cleared her throat and regained a bit of her lost composure. She called Laquita Smith, a long time family friend of the Ricks who often babysat Porsche whenever Lucinda had to work late nights or swing shifts. After speaking with Mrs. Smith for a few minutes and her daughter briefly, Trina hung up with the information that her mother had stepped out with a friend for a few and would return shortly. Still no info.

Then Trina found out 15 minutes later from Gibson's younger brother, Lil' Stinka, that he'd be at the Econo Lodge in Temple Hills. Trina thanked the kid brother of her henchman and drove Kofi's Lexus coupe out towards the Econo Lodge with anger boiling within her as she cruised down Suitland Parkway. She pulled up into the parking lot of the motel suite at approximately 11:45 PM.

There nestled between a White Acura Legend and a dark brown and beige Volkswagen Rabbit was Big Stinka's green Maxima. She would have recognized that car anywhere.

Her first thought was to bribe the young clerk at the desk with a couple of dollars and bust up into the room, but she tossed that thought out the window as too risky. She was no longer in DC and she had no illegal clout with the Prince George's County Police as she did with cops back in the District. Besides, P.G. County was still investigating the Crystal Skating Rink murders of the past year. So she killed the headlights and the humming car engine. Next, she reclined her seat comfortably enjoying the slow jams of WHUR's 'Quiet Storm' while twisting a thick blunt as she waited.

At 12:58 AM, Trina saw the two lovers emerge from their clandestine love nest, making their way down the winding stairs and down toward the Nissan Maxima in the parking lot. The vehicle now stood alone in the lonely lot with the exception of six other cars, one of which was Trina's. Arm-in-arm they strolled out toward the awaiting car with Lucinda Ricks laying her head affectionately against Stinka's shoulder as they walked. Trina was as sickened by the whole thing as she was outraged by it.

Big Stinka carried with him a medium-sized gym bag which must have held the video recorder. Trina fought to her desire to approach them right then and there. After locking lips with each other in a raunchy French kiss. Big Stinka started the engine, cruised out of the parking lot and backed out onto Branch Avenue totally unaware of the Lexus trailing two cars behind him. Trina parked about a block down the street from the 6336 Waterford Drive residence of Lucinda and Porsche Ricks.

She watched in utter disgust as her mother again passionately kissed the perverted drug dealer while he fondled her full breast and her plump behind under the dim yellowish glow of the porch light. Trina squeezed the steering wheel with a vice-like grip as she became increasingly more agitated with each lewd display of affection between the two. Then as Big Stinka drove passed her, a wicked smile of sexual satisfaction seemed to be frozen on his wide, heavy featured face. He'd no doubt relate unto his running buddies the intimate details of his latest motel romp with Lucinda Ricks. And this time he'd have proof of his sexual conquest on video for all to see.

Trina knew the types of unsavory bedroom perversions Big Stinka enjoyed with his clueless female partners and he was not above seducing underage females either. He'd been convicted of statutory rape in 1985 for impregnating a fifteen year old Suitland High student. Knowing this and considering the damage that her precious Porsche could potentially face at the sexual whims of the demented Big Stinka, Trina vowed to end a possible nightmare before it could begin. Trina shadowed her underling all the way back to his home on Bruce Place, Southeast, where at last she confronted him.

As Trina parked Kofi's Lexus on the dark curb directly behind Big Stinka's car, she reached for the Smith & Wesson nine-millimeter she had placed earlier inside the glove compartment. A clip filled with illegal Black Talon hollow tip shells was already loaded inside. She grabbed the weapon, cocked it, and sprung out of the vehicle in a huff. Though she was furiously angry when she emerged from the SUV, she knew that she'd have to be extra careful how she approached her equally hot-headed employee standing 6'2" and weighing a solid 237 lbs.

Big Stinka had the dubious reputation in his neighborhood

as a fearsome and violent ex-con who had once bludgeoned a neighbor with a metal pipe in full view of the man's horrified wife and children, who huddled together sobbing pitifully as Stinka, then a 15-year-old delinquent, continued to batter the man into submission. The 42-year-old man died of a massive brain tumor. He had simply asked that Stinka not walk on his lawn.

Because of the fear and hatred he instilled amongst so many residents of the ghetto, Big Stinka often wore a bulletproof vest whenever he ventured outside and stayed strapped with a semi-automatic. Thus, the reason Trina loaded her pistol with Black Talons. These were bullets designed to penetrate even protective vests.

Walking at a quick pace, Trina neared the rear of the M just as Big Stinka stepped out of the driver's seat with the music of Go-Go's Junkyard Band blaring loudly from the car stereo deck filling for a brief moment the late night stillness with sound. Turning off the ignition so the sound of street rattling Go-Go came to an immediate halt, Stinka placed one large Timberland boot out onto the pavement as he stepped into the cool, crisp December night.

"Stinka!" Trina snarled as she walked up on him from behind.

"What?" The ugly-looking thug retorted as he turned to face his boss with a half empty bottle of St. Ide's Malt Liquor dangling in his right hand.

"What! What! Nigga, you best know who the fuck you talkin' to, Slim! I'll tell you what! You better stop fuckin' with my peoples . . . that's what, muthafucka!" Trina snapped back viciously bringing the nine millimeter into view.

"What the fuck is you talkin' 'bout, young?" Big Stinka asked with indignation.

Stinka's wide, stubbly bearded face contorted in an angry frown which made his ungainly bulldog looking mug even more ugly. Trina aimed the Black chrome pistol towards her gunman sideways as she placed an itchy right finger on the trigger.

"You 'bout a triflin' muhfucka joe . . . fuckin' round with lil' babies and shit. Well, I'll tell you what, Slim . . . you ain't gonna fuck with my baby and shit. And you gonna stop seeing my mother, too. You understand? Fuck with somebody your own age, or somebody else's folks, but tonight is your last night fuckin' with Lucinda Ricks. You feel me?"

For a speechless moment in time, the two drug dealers stared each other down with equal venom in each other's eyes, each one daring the other to make the first move, which would initiate violence. Big Stinka glared at Trina as she held the weapon on him.

"Your mother sucks dick too good for me to let her go just yet . . . maybe you can hook up with us next week at the crib and we can all run a threesome. 'Cause I been wantin' to run up in your guts for a while now," Stinka remarked with a cutting bit of sarcasm.

With catlike reflexes, Trina clutched onto the partially drunk hoodlum and pressed the snout of the nine millimeter into his broad chest squeezing the trigger three times. Each powerful blast shook the young man's stout frame as the hollow tip slugs tore fist-sized holes out of his back. Slowly he gripped his blood-soaked chest and dropped to his knees. The malt liquor bottle fell to the ground shattering all over the sidewalk from Big Stinka's dying fingers. Glazing over, his eyes looked upwards as his quivering mouth failed to produce the words which he yearned to say. Stinka's strong hands clutched at Trina's legs for a brief minute before the final embers of life slowly faded from him.

As blood filled his bullet punctured lungs, a sickly gurgling sound rattled away within his throat as he gasped futilely for breath. Finally his eyes rolled back into their lids showing the pure whites just before he collapsed face first onto the street in death.

For a short while as Trina stared down at the still, cold body sprawled out on the pavement below, she felt a touch of grief that she'd resorted to killing a trusted drug runner and one time colleague. But considering Stinka's track record of past sexual depravity, she felt she was left with no other choice. Quickly, she searched the dead boy's ride rummaging through miscellaneous junk such as old grease splotched auto magazines, tools, and adult movie cassettes until she found the case which carried the video camcorder Stinka had used to capture the most intimate moments shared between him and Lucinda. Trina hurriedly yanked the camcorder out of the black nylon case and rapidly stepped out of the M and immediately moved back towards the Lexus.

Suddenly the door of Big Stinka's curbside rowhouse opened wide, and three individuals came running out. It was Big Stinka's mother and two younger brothers, Michael and Jerry Lil' Stinka Gibson. Trina sped passed the Gibson family as they knelt beside Big Stinka's bloodied corpse, wailing uncontrollably in their grief.

Once Trina had left Bruce Place, a number of curious onlookers and concerned neighbors took to the street in droves surrounding the Gibson trio as they continued to weep bitterly over the body of the slain Big Stinka. Trina tossed the camcorder into the dark, freezing water of the Anacostia River before driving back to the upscale Shaw neighborhood she now called home. Once she had gotten herself settled in, Trina called Pooh at his place in the Farms.

"Pooh, I got some fucked up news to tell you, young. I just shot Big Stinka . . . he's dead," Trina stated cold-heartedly. "I had to do it, Pooh. That woman he was talkin' to was my mother and this nigga would've had his triflin' ass around my baby. You know I couldn't have that bullshit, Slim! Look out for me, aiight, cause 7th District gon' be comin' round the Farms lookin' for answers and shit any day now. Tell the rest o' them young'uns to keep their mouths shut."

"I got you, Trina. You just do you. You know niggas round here know better than that. Don't nobody out the Farms be snitchin' cause muhfuckas don't wanna see me for real!" Pooh answered with murderous emphasis.

Trina thanked her lifelong friend kindly and gently placed the receiver down onto its cradle. She plopped down onto the living room sofa for a few hours, exhausted mentally and emotionally from the events. The early morning sun spilled its golden rays through the Venetian blinds of the spacious living room, giving birth to a fresh new day. Yet Trina curled up on the couch trying to catch up on some much needed sleep, which seemed to elude her as she tossed and turned about wrestling with her tormented thoughts and nightmarish visions that gnawed at her conscience. As she dreamed she couldn't shake the sight of Big Stinka's eye sockets rolling back into his head and the horrible sound of him chocking on his own blood. The nasty way in which his body jerked and twitched on the ground as death over took him played on her mind. She wanted to crouch down beside him, take him into her arms and hold him like a mother would a sick child. But now he was gone . . . gone forever.

And now she wept, long and hard. She wept for once—she hated the game, the pain she had no doubt given to so many others. She now felt pain herself. *Why? Why? Had fate chosen my mother to fall in love with Stinka, a dope boy?* She awoke dripping with perspiration and tears streaming down her cheeks. She had committed numerous murders in the past, killing her rivals without so much as a second thought about the matter afterwards. But this time, it was much different. Even Sophia Carlin's slaying did little to shake her. But she had known Big Stinka nearly as long as she had known Pooh.

Her two ferocious looking Akitas bounced over toward her and covered her face and hands with sloppy warmth as they licked her affectionately. She wrapped her arms around the huge guard dogs and nestled her head against their wooly coats as they hopped up onto the couch beside her. She then cried some more as the pain of what she had done became even more evident.

Trina awoke at 11:26 AM beside her dogs, who raised their heads alerted to the shrill sound of her ringing cell phone, which she used exclusively for fear of taps on the house phone. She wearily rose from between the massive Akitas and off the couch slowly taking the receiver into her hand, as she wondered who could be calling this time of day.

"Hello," Trina answered still groggy from sleep.

"Why? Why'd you have to kill Bernie, Trina. Huh? I can't believe that you would do somethin' like that! What's wrong with you!" Lucinda screamed over the phone.

Trina snapped out of her drowsy daze as soon as she recognized the voice on the other end. She wanted to escape from reality at that particular moment not wanting to explain her actions to her mother of all people, but she couldn't. She had to face the music.

"Ma, you just don't know what dude was about. I know dude. And trust me, he was on some other shit!"

At that point Lucinda broke down bitterly on the other end crying as if her heart would break. Trina listened to the mournful whimpering on the opposite line and remained silent throughout. Trina's own feelings of sadness returned and she gently wiped her red watery eyes free of tears. Sniffling she cleared her throat and spoke into the phone.

"Ma, Stinka was 'bout to sell tapes with you and him havin' sex and shit on it all over Southeast! He had a video camcorder hidden in the motel room y'all was in and he fucks with a whole rack o' broads. Shit, that nigga could o' had HIV or anything, Ma! That dirty dick bastard stayed with diseases and shit. Plus the bamma used to fuck with lil' kids too. And you had his triflin' ass around my daughter! Naw, I'm sorry, but I had to do it."

"Bitch, I hate you! I'm sorry that I ever gave birth to such a

nasty, hateful wench like you! All you do is sell dope, kill people and I hear people talkin' about you goin' both ways and all
kinds of weird shit. And you gonna fix your mouth to judge
folks? You ain't never gonna have no good luck. Never! 'Cause
God don't like ugly. I don't ever wanna see you again in life!
And don't worry about Porsche. You ain't been no kinda
mother to her any way except sending money and shit. Trust
me, she won't miss you. I'm gonna file for full custody this
coming week cause you are gonna end up in prison before too
long. Watch what I tell you! Get your life together before it's
too late!"

On December 20, 1990, 2nd District police raided Trina's
home. Over a dozen or more dark clad, heavily armed S.W.A.T.
officers stormed through the embroidered French doors at
919 S Street, NW. The clamorous racket created by the noisy
S.W.A.T. team, along with the fierce barking of the Akitas in
the back yard, awoke Trina abruptly from a deep sleep. As the
gangster diva arose from out under the warm blankets, she was
shocked to be staring down the barrels of multiple assault rifles held by a number of police sharp shooters. Off near the
side of her bed, 7th District Police Detective Billy Ray Turner
stood with 2nd District officials smiling as he tilted his ten gallon hat to the side.

"Darling, looks like you've gotten yourself in a whole heap
o' trouble this time. Trouble that even all o' your dope money
can't fix. The law states that you or no other drug dealers s'pose
to cause no kinda trouble that'll bring bad press to the City's
government and that includes murder, ma'am . . . You were
there at the meeting held by the D.A. and she stated plainly
that anyone who broke that statue would be arrested and pros-
ecuted to the fullest extent of the law.

Trina being nude pulled the quilt up around her breasts and
bare shoulders to hide her nakedness from the men surrounding her sleigh bed.

"I betcha I'll get to whoever snitched before my trial comes around. Trust me on that one!"

"I wouldn't make any threatening comments about anyone, if I were you, Ms. Ricks. You're in way too much shit already behind the murder of Mr. Bernard Gibson to allude to harming possible witnesses. Now, we're gonna give you the common courtesy to wash up and dress yourself. Then you are gonna be read your rights and taken down to the 2nd District Police Precinct for processin'. So let's get movin', sweetheart."

Slowly one by one, the S.W.A.T. team shuffled out of the enormous bedroom and into the even larger living room. Finally when Cowboy and the 2nd District Lieutenant departed, Trina calmly showered, dressed, and stepped out into the living room to the waiting lawmen.

"Aiight, I'm ready. I know y'all muhfuckas can't wait to lock me up. So c'mon then! What the fuck is y'all waitin' for?"

Cowboy smiled sarcastically as a 2nd District cop stepped towards her with a pair of shiny silver handcuffs.

"Don't worry though. I'll be out before the day is over with, once I get in contact with my lawyer and that's off the no bullshit."

Trina was handcuffed roughly and read her Miranda rights as she was escorted outside of her house and down the stairs, followed by the group of S.W.A.T. officers. As she came through her damaged front doors, she was greeted by scores of nosey neighbors some still in pajamas huddled together in the chilly early morning air, watching as the newly moved-in resident was brought out in cuffs before the entire community. As the blue and red flashing lights illuminated the neighborhood houses, Cowboy turned to Trina chuckling.

"You're big time now, sweetheart. So once you've been processed down at 2nd District, I'll take over from there and transfer you over to 7th District where you fuckin' belong!"

"You know what? I 'bout had enough o' you, Cowboy! You

one o' the main ones who's gettin' money from me on the low, yet still you stay fuckin' with muhfuckas! You full o' shit for real!"

"Imagine that! Me of all people taking bribe money from street scum like yourself. Where'd you get a crazy idea like that from?" lied the tall Texan sarcastically as he walked down the stairs beside Trina. "Besides, from what I'm hearin' you've been delinquent on your payments lately."

Trina frowned and mumbled under her breath as the arresting officer shoved her head as Trina was being forced into the back seat of a nearby squad car that was parked on the curb in front of her house. Ever since she had become the premier drug dealer in the city, she felt as though paying extra for a police partnership was no longer necessary. Nor would she continue to make the D.A. rich when she could now afford the best attorneys money could buy.

But the arrogance that had been brought on by her newly acquired power infuriated her corrupt business partners in law enforcement, which at last proved to be her undoing.

All over the day, news programs screamed the headlines "Breaking News . . . Southeast drug dealer and gang leader, Katrina Ricks, arrested today on charges for the alleged murder of fellow drug dealer Bernard Gibson of Bruce Place, SE. More details on this breaking news story tonight at 11:00."

Trina sat on her small bunk watching the television news program with silent simmering fury. The T.V. stations throughout the Beltway region showed her all across thousands of living room television screens being led out into the cold morning air by a mob of menacing S.W.A.T officers with drawn rifles at their sides. How embarrassing was this, for someone of her status to be treated by the cops and portrayed by the local media hounds in this way. Trina was crushed. She now hated the police more than ever before and as she sat alone in her lonely dark DC Jail cell contemplating everyone whom she had spoken to before and after Big Stinka's murder.

Someone had ratted her out big time and she pledged solemnly to find out who had snitched on her. The po-po had gotten a hold of her almost immediately after the killing of Big Stinka, a sure sign of the presence of a hater. As angry as Trina was sitting behind bars in the DC Jail, whoever had dry snitched on her, be they friend or foe, they had signed their death warrant.

Down at the 7th District Police Precinct, the Washington, DC, Police Chief Andrew Ellroy received a phone call from D.A. Francine Gonzolez directing him to pay a visit to Katrina Ricks down at the DC Jail. At 8:30 PM the Chief was admitted to jail cell 1313, which held the notorious queen bee of crime. Trina glared hatefully at the burly police chief as he waited for the jailers to escort her over to the lobby. Once there, the polished brass wearing chief picked up the phone before him and held it to his ear as he stared at the pretty, 22-year-old girl behind the plexi-glass window. Surely she had reached a level beyond the norm to have the pleasure of talking with the top cop himself.

Chief Ellroy was well respected among Washington's elite Capitol Hill society types. As a staunch, hardnosed lawman who had made the City a safer place to live for the residents and an attractive summer vacation spot for traveling tourists; however, in reality the heavy deep-voiced man with the salt & pepper beard and mustache had been on the Go Hard Soldierz' payroll ever since Trey Wills led the drug dealing outfit. Trina rolled her hazel brown eyes as she picked up the phone to talk.

"You have not held up your end of the bargain as we all agreed. Katrina, we thought that you were a woman of your word. But we've apparently thought wrong," he said in his typical booming voice.

"Nigga, fuck you! Y'all been gettin' loot up off me for years and shit. Thousands o' dollars and for what? Just to let Cowboy's redneck self pick with people all the damn time? Look where I'm at! You tell me who's fuckin' who!?"

"From what I hear . . . you've fucked quite a few folks over the years and I mean that literally as well as figuratively."

Trina's blood boiled after hearing the police chief's biting comment followed by a mocking grin.

"Yeah . . . well, guess what? Don't hate cause yo fat ass ain't never hit this and ya never will! Trina snapped.

The sarcastic smile immediately left the chief's face. And he leaned in closer to the plexi-glass.

"Watch yourself. You little Southeast trick! I can arrange it where you'll never spread those sexy legs of yours for anyone ever again, got it? And I'm talking 'bout taking a dirt nap . . . you do know what that is, don't you?"

"Yeah, whatever! You ain't gon' do shit but see me walk outta this bitch free like I always do. How 'bout that?"

"I see that I'll have to show you better than I can tell you. Too bad DC doesn't have the death penalty or else you'd be looking at death row right about now. But I'll take the life sentence for you just as nicely."

"Go for it! Cause with the law firm backin' me up, I'll not only walk free, but I'll have your badge, my nigga!"

"Alright, let's see if you're talking so big and bold come court day when Gonzolez's assistant D.A. prosecutes your little ghetto ass with premeditated first degree murder. Let's see your lawyers work their magic then. No one beats the system, young lady. Eventually, we get 'em all . . . Capone, Gotti, Escobar and now you . . . you're fucking going down!"

"I wanna talk to the District Attorney right the fuck now!"

"Why should Mrs. Gonzolez bother talking to your ghetto fabulous behind at this hour? You ain't hardly as important as you THINK you are."

"Yeah, well for the amount of dollars I'm givin' that chick every month, she better answer the fuckin' phone!"

"You think you're God Almighty, don't you? Well, hey . . . I got news for you. You, my dear, are nothing, nada, zero, a blip on the radar screen of importance in this city. We get bribe money from every lowlife dope dealing crew in the city. And when you and your gang of thugs disappear, yet another group of wannabees will come along with dreams of bling-bling dancing through their cornrowed heads and we'll eat off them just the same. You see, we're the poe-lice, we can do that!" the chief added bluntly. "Look, let's talk dollars and cents here, aiight?" Trina proposed. "How much more do I have to pay y'all to forget about all o' this bullshit? Cause for me, money ain't even an issue."

"As much as we'd love to continue doing business with you, we cannot due to the continued lack of discretion on your part. You've already forfeited your contract with me and my colleagues as far as we're concerned. Associating with you has become far too risky to carry on any further. So here it ends, all ties are now severed between us . . . for good. And this time around, you are totally on your own."

Trina's mouth dropped open with utter disbelief. *"This can't be happening"* she thought to herself as fought to keep her composure.

"Ya know what, Chief Ellroy?" Trina asked moving closer to the glass divider and glaring at the decorated Police Chief with a look of deep-seated hatred. "All y'all muhfuckas got me fucked up. I ain't scared o' none o' y'all fake ass bitches. All that shit you just talked don't mean a damned thing to me. And it don't put no fear in my heart. But I'll tell you what . . . if I got to go down, I'm takin' a rack o' y'all muhfuckas down with me. So you go run and tell that Mexican bitch that!"

"Typical behavior of you ignorant ghetto ass niggas. Don't you think? Trying to scare folks with veiled threats and hard looks. You all are a truly pathetic bunch . . . I'll tell you!" grinned Chief Ellroy.

"Keep sleepin' on me, Slim. You ain't never had to deal with a bitch like me before. And you ain't never gon' see another one like me again. I ain't no ordinary type hustler. Fuckin' with me will getcha in a world o' hurt. I'm tryin' to tell you."

"You're really funny . . . I'm serious. You're like fucking hilarious, really though! Anytime you can have the nerve to threaten the Chief of Police when behind bars and facing a major murder beef—you've gotta be an absolute moron to do such a thing. Now I know why your own mother took it upon herself to turn you over to us!"

"Say what?!" Trina asked with wide-eyed astonishment.

"Let me say it for you again . . . your mother, the woman who gave birth to you, Ms. Lucinda Ricks, dropped the dime on you that landed you here in the DC jail. She told us everything about everything. Your drug business, which of course we all knew about, a few of the murders you've committed, the ones she knew about or suspected anyway. She even threw in a bit about your bi-sexual relationship, which she referred to as quote 'fuckin' weird' and a whole shit load of other miscellaneous, but nevertheless quite interesting, tidbits about your life. Your mother was really pissed off about you killing her young stud boyfriend, you know. As a matter of fact, she's still salty behind Gibson's murder, said you killed her second husband, too, some guy named Maynard back when you were a teenager. She said that you were abused sexually by him and that she had no regrets after his death because you were only a kid back then and you didn't deserve to be violated. But she says that since then you've grown steadily each and every year into a monster with an uncontrollable lust for money, power, and revenge, and that you'd killed more people than she could shake a stick at. She said that she no longer knew who you were anymore and that her darling little Katrina left a long time ago. What can I say? The woman hates the very ground you walk on . . . talk about dysfunctional families, huh? Oh, by the way . . . your mom's six weeks pregnant . . . I guess you're gonna have a brand new baby brother or sister pretty soon."

Trina could not take anymore of the details which she had just heard. It had totally overwhelmed her emotionally as well as mentally causing Trina to drop the phone and walk away from the booth without looking back. She walked right over to the waiting guard who walked her back down the dark stuffy hallway towards the small, silent, and isolated jail cell at the end of cellblock 1300.

Once the steel bars closed behind her with a resounding metallic thud, Trina laid upon the musty smelling bunk and stared up at the ceiling blankly in the dark, for a long while before finally falling asleep.

Chapter 23
The Trial

On January 13, 1991, the floor of the Moultrie Courthouse at 500 Indiana Avenue, Northwest, Washington, DC, was crawling with camera-flashing paparazzi, curious spectators, local and national celebrities, and several hundred ordinary curious Washingtonians who showed up to either give support to or shout obscenities at the infamous thug diva. Never before had the photo of a drug dealer graced the illustrious covers of Time, People, Ebony and Newsweek magazines until Trina's was placed upon them all.

The murder trial gained national notoriety and soon became a regular featured news item on the evening programs of CBS, NBC and ABC. The trial became such a popular conversation topic around the water coolers of Washington's office buildings, that many people began organizing office pools, placing bets on the presumed outcome of the weekly proceedings. Ironically, the woman who had brought so much bloodshed, violence, and death to the city actually fueled the District with a huge spike in the city's revenue due to the high volume of outsiders entering the District in hopes of sitting in on the trial of the century.

The police presence was beefed up due to the numerous brawls which erupted in the crowd between groups of DC residents who sought Trina's freedom and those who longed to see her imprisoned forever. For many area residents, the name Katrina Ricks evoked a strong sense of loathing generated by the widespread murders that Trina and her Go Hard Soldierz hooligans had committed throughout the region, which had traumatized many families. Yet, still there was a great deal of Trina supporters, mostly ghetto youth who had benefited from her drug money in the form of generous handouts, rental assistance, child support, and employment as drug runners and police lookouts. They not only respected, but idolized, the sexy drug lord as one of their own who had overcome the poverty of the projects to achieve the American dream and a hero to be both admired and imitated.

The trial took a severe toll on Trina because of the betrayal which her very own mother had perpetuated against her. She also could not get over the fact that she had to remain behind bars in the DC Jail for the duration of the murder trial. Police Chief Andrew Ellroy got together with District Attorney Francine Gonzolez and assembled an aggressive team of prosecuting attorneys in order to hit Trina with the infamous 848 Kingpin Statute, a federal charge carrying with it nothing less than 20 years to life. However, indicting Trina would be no easy task for the city's prosecutors and they knew it.

Trina's two attorneys, Mark J. Burton, III and Carolyn Myers-Pierce, were the most successful and expensive criminal law attorneys on the entire east coast, whose highly sought after services were utilized by celebrities, business executives, and mob bosses to name but a few. Only the rich and powerful could afford them and they were worth every dime.

Lucinda Ricks agreed to take the witness stand for the prosecutors in order to testify against her youngest daughter. And for this decision, she had to be placed under twenty-four hour a day, seven days a week, police protection because of the high volume of death threats she had received over the course of the trial. The hood was livid with Mother Ricks's betrayal and considered her the worst possible dry snitch and sell-out there could be. Thugs and hoodrats from Montana Avenue to Shipley Terrace vowed to shoot Lucinda dead on sight. Many others living in P.G. County planned to invade her home on Waterford Drive and kill her that way. While cops discovered plastic explosives under her minivan, Trina surprisingly showed anger for the many threats against her estranged mother for whom she still had undying love for. Besides, she feared for the safety of her young daughter. She therefore paid several drug crews throughout DC and P.G. County a total of $80,000 to leave her mother alone during the trial.

Though the word went out from the various drug crew leaders throughout the hoods of the city and P.G. County for the youngsters to cease and desist with their murder plots against Lucinda Ricks, the orders were only partially heeded by the majority of trigger-happy thugs on the streets. Trina now had reason to appreciate the daily police protection that the P.G. County cops provided for her mother and daughter.

At approximately 1:00 pm on January 13, 1991, Lucinda Ricks took the witness stand before a grand jury in a packed courtroom, which had already endured an hour of tense, drama-filled testimonies, no-holds-barred cross-examinations, angry outbursts from amongst the jurors, and crafty attacks and counter-attacks between the prosecution and the defense teams. Almost all of Barry Farms were present as well as much of Valley Green's residents who came out to show support and solidarity for Trina who had been given the title 'Southeast Trina' in the media. Trina swelled with pride as she looked around the saw the number of drug dealers from around various neighborhoods in Southeast who had come to show her love. She had help put them on the map and now it was their turn to have her back for a change. And as Trina saw them seated throughout the courtroom audience, decked out in their glittering jewels and designer finery, she realized that they had indeed kept their word.

Trina's relatives had come from far and near and they all showed a variety of mixed emotions as they listened to witness testimonies, which for over an hour gave an eye-opening account of one woman's rise to power in the ranks of the District's drug world and the impressive wealth, as well as the unbelievable bloodshed resulting from her city-wide domination. While Trina sat between her two prominent lawyers, whispering with them and detailing notes during and between testimonies, she had occasionally made eye contact with her mother who had stared back at Trina with a dark look of contempt that no child would want to see from its parent. Trina's eyes watered and she quickly turned away to place a pair of Gucci sunshades on as her mother was called to the stand.

For the very first 15 minutes of her testimony, Lucinda spoke of the brief relationship she'd had with Bernard 'Big Stinka' Gibson whom she fondly referred to as 'Bernie', finally describing the events of the fatal night that he was killed. Once Lucinda had finished her testimony the prosecutor announced that he had no further questions and returned to his seat beside his partner. This is when attorney Carolyn Myers-Pierce approached Lucinda Ricks up on the witness stand in order to cross-examine her.

"Ms. Ricks, you claimed to have known Mr. Gibson a little over three months, is that correct?"

"Yes, Ma'am, it is."

"You said that the late Mr. Gibson was a wonderful friend and gentle lover. But did you realize that he sold narcotics and was a member of a notorious street gang?"

"No, I did not!"

"Hummm . . . I see. Were you present with Mr. Gibson when he was shot to death, Ms. Ricks?"

"No, I wasn't there, but I know that it was nobody but my daughter, Trina, who shot him."

"Did you see your daughter, Katrina, on the night of the murder at all?"

"No, I didn't. But . . ."

"So, what you're telling this court today, Ms. Gibson, is that you were not present with Mr. Gibson at the time of his murder, nor did you come into contact with my client on the particular night. Yet, you would have us to believe that Mr. Gibson, who had been to prison on more than one occasion, sold drugs, committed violent crimes himself, and associated himself with a dangerous local drug crew, could not have been murdered by anyone other than your daughter, Katrina; am I right, Ms. Ricks?"

"You're damned right! Cause you just don't know . . ."

"Thank you very much, Ms. Ricks. I have no further questions, your Honor," Attorney Myers-Pierce said quickly returning to the defendant's table. Trina turned to converse with Attorneys Myers-Pierce and Mark J. Burton, III, while audible murmuring and discussions among the jury and onlookers became so loud that the judge's wooden gavel was slammed down several times in an effort to return the court to order. Trina, along with her legal dynamic duo, smiled as they noticed the frustration and disappointment of the prosecuting team as they waved their witness off the stand.

It was quickly becoming evident that it may have been a mistake for the prosecution to place Lucinda Ricks on the stand. For after the blistering cross-examination was delivered by the defense, Lucinda rose up out of the chair and screamed obscenities at Trina and her lawyers in a bizarre outburst that caused her to be ungraciously escorted out by a pair of brawny bailiffs. Once again in the courtroom, the crowd chattered, taking the judge several minutes to bring the court to order. Other than the witnesses taking the stand, and the many recognizable faces among the jury, and courtroom spectators, Trina paid only slight attention to anyone else in the room except the dapper looking, smooth-talking young man seated on the first row to her far right. It was none other than her boyfriend Kofi. He was sitting next to two highly attractive females who were whispering and snickering softly in between testimonies.

For over two weeks, Kofi had not been at home and had not called since her arrest. He had claimed that his father's trucking company had opened up three new facilities up north and that his dad put him in charge of the hiring process. He had spent the two weeks between the cities of Boston, Buffalo, and Hartford. Trina had her doubts about the validity of his story as she had suspected infidelity. And as she observed him flirting boldly with the two sexy dimes on both sides of him, she silently fumed with jealous rage, believing it to be a final confirmation of her suspicions. Yet, she felt more anger at herself than at Kofi. She had promised herself that she would never fall in love with a member of the male gender in life, after having been raped and observing the callous way in which the vast majority of men handled their women's feelings in regards to commitment and faithfulness. And now she too, like so many other naïve women before her, had been played. As she sat staring at him behind the dark lenses of her $1,000 diamond-studded Gucci shades, Trina realized that there was nothing she could do.

FBI Regional Director, Rita Ann Ricks, had been a mainstay at 500 Indiana Avenue, Northwest, ever since the trial began. Trina's big sister had put on nearly twenty five pounds during her last pregnancy and still had not shed all of it. She looked much older than her thirty some years would suggest. And the increased facial sagging and crows feet at the corners of her eyes showed the signs of a life filled with bitter disappointments and hardships despite the high profile career in law enforcement.

At the evening adjournment of the trial on January 19th, Trina observed Rita Ann and Kofi laughing and talking with each other as they both exited the 4th floor and descended the steps out toward Indiana Avenue. There the two spoke for over 20 minutes more before leaving for their separate vehicles. Before they departed, they seemed to have exchanged handwritten phone numbers smiling like two school kids as they did so. Trina gritted her teeth angrily then turned quickly and stormed back into the building as the two police escorts with her cautioned the enraged drug queen about her sudden display of anger.

A day later the trial was again in session, lasting an additional two hours, during which at that time the jury deliberated for an hour. The prosecuting team had worked the jury with well documented arguments as to the many felonies Trina had been charged with in addition to the pre-holiday slaying of Bernard "Big Stinka" Gibson in a concentrated effort to sway the twelve member jury to convict. Charges of drug trafficking, prostitution, racketeering, money laundering, blackmail, armed robbery and murder were ranged against her. However, it was the charge of first degree murder which worried Trina. It didn't look good at all for Trina as she sat between her lawyers staring blankly behind her dark sunshades. Glistering beads of perspiration dotted her brow and Trina fidgeted with her half empty water bottle as she listened to the damaging final arguments delivered by the handpicked city prosecutors of District Attorney Francine Gonzolez and Police Chief Ellroy. A number of dry snitches came out of the woodwork to testify against Trina, about numerous allegations, claiming to be witnesses to her criminal activities. If only she could've taken it to the streets, they'd all be dead by now. But here in court, she was powerless. Trina seethed even more as she observed the smiling faces of the City's D.A., Police Chief, and Mayor.

"If only the courtroom audience could know just how corrupt these fake ass government officials were," Trina thought to herself. However, her brief anxiety soon turned to comfortable satisfaction once her dream team arose to take their turn to deliver closing arguments before the presiding judge and jury. Dis-

playing the amazing legal wizardry that had earned them both the fame and fortune to have become icons of modern criminal law, Mark J. Burton, III shredded the closing statements of the City's prosecutors as little more than hogwash. A case filled with unproven facts, hearsay and meaningless allegations delivered throughout the proceedings by questionable and inconsistent witnesses. The stinging sarcasm and witty innuendoes concerning the prosecution's legal credentials brought lighthearted laughter from the courtroom crowd, causing the Capitol Hill lawyer to receive a harsh word of reprimand from the judge before he took his seat.

As one half of Trina's dream team returned to the defense table, the other rose to take the floor. World-renowned, as well as thoroughly despised within Washington's legal community, the relentlessly attacking style of the Southern California born and bred Carolyn Myers-Pierce earned her the nickname "Wicked Bitch of the West" by her legal opponents. Myers-Pierce wasted little time in dissecting the prosecution's arguments piece by detailed piece, exposing major flaws in their presentation and attacking inconsistencies in the witnesses' testimonies upon review.

After thirty minutes of detailed summary of her own case findings of the Bernard Gibson's murder, as well as an exhaustive and remarkably convincing reexamination of the prosecution's blatant misrepresentation of the murder case, however, even more important than Trina's high-priced lawyers, were the presence of Pooh and some thirty members of the violent Southeast-based Go Hard Soldierz who stared across the room at the members of the jury, many of whom lived in or near low income housing areas themselves. With steady, hardcore thuggish gazes that caused more than one of the jurors to quickly avert their eyes in fear, the crew silently got their message across.

The presiding Judge Norman Broomfield had been bribed by Trina with $35,000 to influence the jury's final decision favorably for her. And he delivered by selecting only a large majority of easily manipulated ghetto dwelling residents to sit on the jury. At the end of the day, Trina walked free with a resounding courtroom victory. Nine of the twelve jurors found her not guilty. The three that didn't were white, upper middle class folks from the upper Northwest area. Though the government officials, cops, and reporters expressed disbelief and disappointment at the outcome of the much-anticipated verdict, the mood amongst the residents of the inner city was quite the opposite.

Following the end of the trial, Trina's victory was met with both celebration and bitterness. She got the ugly from certain individuals who were close to Mr. Gibson. Festivity and cheer filled the notorious hoods of Washington, DC, residents celebrated Trina's freedom with several days of wild, drunken parties, raucous gun blasting salutes and "Welcome Home" graffiti spray painted all across the city.

Trina's skilled legal team, bribed judge, and juror intimidation carried out by her mean mugging thugs had saved her ass, and subsequently crushed the prosecution's case. Trina celebrated with tens of dozens of jubilant well-wishers among the courtroom spectators. Trina smiled and winked at the jurors as she was led out of the courtroom by the bailiff who glanced once or twice at Trina in disgust. Trina noticed that several of the jurors, especially the older women, were somewhat shaken still by the fearsome looks directed at them by the Go Hard Soldierz hooligans earlier during the proceedings. Trina assured them that they had nothing to fear and promised to pay each juror's rent with the exception of the three White jurors, she was certain that they would turn the offer down. The week after the trial, nine of the twelve jurors had their rent paid up for an entire year and all nine received a 'thank you' card containing a thousand dollar money order within.

For thirty minutes after the "not guilty" verdict was read, Trina spoke with her attorneys, thanking them for their magnificent work in the courtroom, and planning a celebratory dinner date in which she would show her gratitude to her valued lawyers by paying for the entire meal. Yet still, Trina harbored thoughts of vengeance against those responsible for her recent hardships. As she exited the courthouse, she breezed passed her older sister, Rita Ann, who stood at the bottom of the steps speaking with several senators from the Hill. She also noticed Kofi's Lexus parked outside on the curb. He was sitting behind the wheel waiting for Rita Ann to come down the stairs..

"You're a fucking disgrace to our family. Do you realize that? Do you even care?" She said with hostility in her voice.

Trina rolled her eyes at her sister, but said nothing as she descended the steps. Right in front of the courthouse steps, Trina approached a truck that cruised up to the curb. It was her Suburban. Pooh had paid for it to be remodeled after the run-in Trina had out in Adams Morgan with the MS-13. It was painted a beautiful metallic gold and black, 22 inch gold rims accented the rugged Pirelli treads that were placed all around. The newly tinted windows allowed onlookers zero visibility into the SUV from the outside allowing Trina to engage in various illegal pursuits such as puffing marijuana within the presence of the cops without worrying about harassment.

A loud round of applause went up from a huge crowd which had gathered in front of the courthouse along Indiana Avenue when Trina walked out the building surrounded by her scowling roughnecks. Like a Hollywood star, Trina was mobbed by a host of paparazzi who thrust over a dozen or more microphones in her face urging her to give a statement or two regarding the verdict. As the throng of reporters grew and multiple cameras flashed brightly, Trina had to restrain her homies from striking out at the overly aggressive media hounds who continued to press their way into the crew leader's personal space for a quick snapshot or juicy scoop.

Trina cleared her throat loud enough to bring order and silence to the babbling group as she kindly requested of them to give her a little elbow room before she spoke.

"Today I was truly blessed, ya know? I just knew that I'd beat the case 'cause I had nothing to do with Mr. Gibson's murder. But when you're young, black, and got a lil' bit o' money, folks gon' hate on you . . . no matter what. But what makes it so hard is that haters, most o' the time, happens to be ya own folks. Ya own flesh and blood . . . now that's some hot shit. But it's all gravy though, I'm gonna keep it on the down low for a minute, spend some quality time with my daughter like a good mommy should. Take a trip or two overseas. Who knows? Shit, I might just move outta the country altogether cause I'm sick o' all this bull shit over here anyway. That's the simple fact why Josephine Baker left here in the twenties, and Marvin Hagler and Tina Turner . . . the U.S. Government don't want don't no black person to shine ever, 'specially not a black woman. The biggest crooks work on Capitol Hill and in the White House. Yet you don't see them muhfuckas on trial for shit, do you? As long as niggas keep gettin' fucked over by presidents like Bush and Reagan, we gon' keep on hustlin', believe that shit cause everybody ain't got the opportunity to go to no college and shit. And they already peeped that . . . they ain't dumb. So, I'm gon' say to niggas on the street . . . to do what you do to get that money. Feel me? I'm out!"

She hopped into her Suburban, along with her rowdy entourage and roared off down Indiana Avenue, connecting onto Pennsylvania and melting into the hectic Washington traffic.

The Queen Bee had returned.

Chapter 24

Vengeance is Mine

Trina arrived at her Shaw neighborhood residence at around 10:43 pm. As soon as she came through the recently repaired doorway, Trina tossed her white chinchilla fur coat onto a nearby loveseat and slumped down onto the plush leather couch in the stylishly furnished living room. Drained from the rigors of the trial and the post trial celebrations, she leaned back wearily closing her tired eyes for a quick catnap. She'd only slept for about fifteen minutes when keys rattled at the door noisily. Trina raised her heavy eyelids to see Kofi walk through the door, moving through the living room directly into the kitchen without so much as a hello said to her as she watched him walk past.

"No, you didn't just walk yo monkey ass pass me without sayin' shit!" she blurted out angrily.

Gone now was her fatigue replaced by irritation. Already she'd had a bone to pick with her man behind several of his recent fuck-ups and this latest offense pushed her over the edge.

"Look here, Kofi . . . I don't know who you think you fuckin' with, but I'm here to tell you I ain't the one!" Trina snarled, getting in between Kofi and the refrigerator. "I told you a long time ago that if you wanted to fuck around with other bitches, then you should not have tried to talk to me!"

"Girl, you lunchin' like shit! You stay fuckin' with a nigga 'bout other broads. You insecure than a muhfucka, young! You need to be thinkin' 'bout explainin' to niggas why you kilt Big Stinka, for real!"

"Fuck is you talkin' 'bout some explainin' 'n shit? Nigga, I ain't gotta explain a muthafuckin' thing to nobody!"

"Well that was fucked up. I don't care what you say . . . Big Stinka was like a brother to you. That nigga put in work for you, young. He kept your pockets oh, so swollen, and kilt a rack o' bammas for you, too. And you gon' go shoot my man just cause he been goin' up in yo' mother. Shit, your mother's a grown ass woman. She can fuck who she wanna fuck! You ain't had shit to do with that. That was their business!"

"Nigga fuck you! I got a lil' girl over there livin' with my mother aiight? And I'll be damned if I'm gon' let some child molester touch my baby. It ain't happen'n! I don't give a fuck who you is, you goin' away from here. I'm tryin' to tell you!"

Kofi's handsome face wrinkled in anger and his strong squared jaw tightened as his penetrating gaze bore into Trina's innermost being.

"You know what? You really need to take yo ass to a fuckin' psychiatrist. Know what I mean? You off that past shit like a big dawg, and you can't even see it in yourself."

"See, you can talk that ole' bullshit cause you don't know what type of gutter ass shit I had to go through, mutha fucka! That shit fucks with your mind, makes you feel dirty as shit. No matter how many showers you take, you can't wash that funk off. But you ain't the one to tell me what I need to do about this problem. I'll handle it on my own terms, in my own time. So, don't tell me what the fuck to do, aiight?" Trina retorted.

"You got a whole lotta young'uns confused and fucked up behind Big Stinka's death, baby. It's one thing to bust a cap in a bitch nigga like Roland or Nutt's ass, but you just can't go around shootin' ya peoples and shit cause there's gonna be some bad repercussions behind dumb shit like that."

"What kind o' repercussions, Kofi? You know some shit that I don't? . . . huh? Well fuck you, Kofi! And fuck all them punk ass niggas who been talkin' 'bout me behind my back and shit. Tell them niggas to come say that shit to my face and stop actin' like a bunch o' lil' gumps!"

"Look at you . . . girl, you gone!"

"If that's what you think then you need to get the fuck on!"

Trina spoke with a frank and serious tone in her voice that irritated Kofi upon hearing it.

"You never know . . . I might just take you up on that offer this time around 'cause you jive like got too much drama goin' on with you right now."

"Good! That's damn good! Cause I need a real nigga to ride with me. Not no fake ass wannabe gangsta like you!"

"Oh, you'll find plenty o' niggas to ride with you because you fine and phat than a muhfucka. So niggas gon' holla atcha regardless. But you ain't gon' find no real nigga whose gon' put up with all o' you bullshit like I do. Betcha that much!"

"You got a whole lotta nerve to be talkin' 'bout puttin' up with bullshit when just today outside the courthouse I saw you all up in my sista's face and shit. What's up with that hot shit? Huh, Kofi?"

"And?"

"Keep talkin' shit hear? You gon' fuck around and get the fire smacked outta you, watch!" Trina threatened.

"Yeah, right! You ain't stupid for real. You know better."

"Fuck that shit! Nigga, Whassup? You ain't like that!" Trina hissed pushing him backwards up against the far wall of the kitchen with all of her might. "What you tryin' to do? Cause I ain't scared o' yo big ass for real!"

Kofi stumbled slightly against a chair in the kitchen, but regained his balance immediately and advanced towards his angry girlfriend in a threatening manner. Trina who was no stranger to settling disputes with her fists, had already removed her 24 carat gold plated hoops from her earlobes and kicked off her high heeled boots into the corner of the room. She was preparing to defend herself against her muscle bound lover. Kofi took two steps forward then stopped abruptly in his tracks.

"You know what? . . . I ain't even gon' go out like that, young. I know you done went through a whole lotta drama with the trial and everything, and shit's been jive like hectic round this joint for a minute, so I' ma let that shit go. Cause real men don't hit on females and shit, no way." Kofi said in a more relaxed manner. "Trina, I've only known your sister since the trial and I keep tellin' you that when I go outta town, it's strictly business and that's all. Your sister was just kickin' it with me 'bout how it used to be when y'all was kids and shit. That 's all!"

"Whatever you say . . . I can't call it. Men gonna be men regardless. But I can't worry 'bout none o' that stupid shit right now cause I gotta take care o' some business my damn self before the month's over."

"What kinda business you talkin' 'bout?"

"You know Cowboy and that old ass Chief Ellroy was the muthafuckas who got me late and shit, right? Them two bastards do more dirt in the city than a little bit, but yet, still they gon' fuckin' with people for no reason. It ain't like I didn't pay their bitch asses, and I mean I broke them cats off with no less than three to four grand or more of our profits each and every month just like Trey used to back in the day. But see that don't matter to Cowboy's old redneck ass, he still be fuckin' with niggas on a regular and for what I don't know. I don't know if the muthafucka is racist, sexist, or what, but what I do know is that his White ass is 'bout to get his wig split. I don't give a fuck if he is the poe-lice and shit. Nobody fucks over me and stay breathin' out this bitch. Know what I'm sayin'? And as for

Police Chief Ellroy . . . his ass goin' away from here right along with Cowboy 'cause he been gettin' money from me also. So he coulda put a choke chain on Cowboy. He coulda told that muhfucka to slow his roll and shit, but naw . . . he gon' let cowboy do whatever he felt like doin'. So just for that he 'bout to catch them hotballs too."

Trina's eyes narrowed with intensity as she vented her pent-up frustration with the crooked cops.

"I hate all o' them muthafuckas, young! Especially that Mexican ho Francine Gonzolez. She the main one, the muth-fuckin' ring leader and shit! They coulda cared less 'bout Big Stinka gettin' kilt. All they wanted to do was get me caught up so they could send me to prison for life. And why was them jokahs schemin' on a bitch? I'll tell you why. Cause as long as I run shit in the city they're only gon' get what I been payin' 'em. Shit, maybe less now that my pockets stay on swole. But if they can get rid of me then they can straight bleed the rest of these lil' ballers on the come-up dry. You feelin' me? Dawg, the worst thing that coulda happened to them was me walkin' up outta 500 Indiana Avenue a free woman. Now it's payback time. And trust and believe I gots some young'uns that's ready to ride. All I gotta do is make a phone call and it's a done deal!"

Both Kofi and Trina hated the cops as did most hustlers. And they both soon squashed their beef in order to develop the murderous plans to eliminate those who were responsible for her arrest and attempted conviction. Yet, still they had not slept with each other for weeks and the romance between them, which had burned so brightly before, had long since cooled. It seemed to be but a matter of time before the gangsta couple severed ties completely.

On January 22nd, Trina took a few of her most hard working dope boys out on a moonlight cruise of the Potomac River aboard the "Spirit of Washington". She was pleased that Lil' Ghetto had managed to land a major marijuana deal with a Los Angeles street gang dubbed the "Reapers" who along with the infamous Crips and Bloods dominated the drug trade of South Central L.A. During the murder trial, Lil' Ghetto paid for over 100 pounds of high grade Mexican grown cannabis to be illegally smuggled into the District through the lower Midwestern States, into Ohio and up through West Virginia and Virginia on across the District borders.

While the group of criminals enjoyed the dining, dancing, and ladies upon the cruise ship, Lil' Ghetto, himself the honoree of the party, requested to speak with Trina alone on the sparsely traveled bow of the ship. She agreed and together they left the toasty interior of the vessel to go out into the frosty January night to converse privately. Once there, the slightly built, dread locked thug took a long drag on a freshly freaked Black & Mild cigar, exhaled the grayish white smoke into the biting chill of the windy night air and turned to face his boss.

"When is you goin' overseas and shit? Or did you just say that to throw muhfuckas off?"

"C'mon, boy . . . you brought me out here in the cold to ask me some shit like that? You coulda ask me that back inside where it was warm at. But since you all pressed and shit to know everything . . . I dunno. I'm aiight right now, you know? I mean, don't get me wrong, I like that paper just as much as anybody else. But I do gotta take into consideration that I'm a mother. Ya know what I'm sayin'? I got a child to think about. Smart muhfuckas get their hustle on, make that money while they can, save it—most of it anyway, like you s'pose to do if you gotcha shit together—and get out for good. If you save yo' money right, you can put it to good use later on in life. You feel me?"

"True, that . . . But you saw what happened to the H Street Crew after we bust Roland's head and shit. Them jokahs jive folded . . . fell off and shit. Now most all o' them dudes locked up down Lorton or dead. Niggas out the Farms and Valley Green ain't tryin' to go out like that, Trina. I know for damn sho I ain't. We wanna get pockets fat too, just like yours. You ain't get it by yourself. I know you realize that too. The Chronicles help put you on the map. We know you jive older than us and you do have ya lil' baby girl you gotta take care of. We feelin' you on that, but at the same time, we tryin' to floss too, ya know. So all I ask is that before you get out the game, make sure ya peoples is aiight."

Trina pulled her thick warm chinchilla coat around her and the matching fur hat down over her ears. She felt more than a little annoyed with Lil' Ghetto that he'd disturbed her mellow chill time to bring her out on the bow to discuss what she took to be an insulting proposition at best. But she continued to listen to Lil' Ghetto's concerns with reserved quietude, in spite of her growing irritation with the bold youngster. The increase of illegally gained cash and power would inevitably bring about trouble in the form of jealousy, greed, selfishness, and even betrayal. One could only trust close associates, but even those so much just when money came into play. As long as the cash kept coming in, loyalty would exist. But once drug money slowed up a bit, even so called friends could turn on you.

No one knew this ominous fact of the drug world better than did Trina herself. She had seen the overthrow of several ferocious drug lords in her teens, and she herself had contributed to the downfall of others over the dark and bloody years of the crack era. To these young boys who stood on the corners and in back alleys hustling from sun up to sun down, stacking dollars and making deals around the clock, looked up to her like a big sister or even an aunt. She provided for them, saw to it that they never ever went without, took care of their mothers and siblings whenever they landed in jail. Not to mention many thousands of dollars she had spent purchasing formula, clothing, pampers, and providing daycare for the numerous babies that many of them had fathered over the years. She would have to leave them cautiously or else she could very likely end up on the wrong end of a smoking revolver just as easily as any enemy if her young gunmen sensed that she had abandoned them.

"Is that what you think? Huh? That I'd leave y'all lil' niggas hangin'? I been takin' care o' y'all lil' nappy head fuckas all this time. Why would I just up and leave without breakin' ya off a lil' somethin', now?"

The two drug dealers hugged each other affectionately and hurried back down into the interior of the ship away from the frigid winter gusts blowing fiercely across the ship's bow.

The next day Trina busied herself with several important phone calls and trips across various neighborhoods of Southeast, DC, gathering up manpower and momentum for the execution of the ruthless task that lay ahead. She had learned secret espionage tactics from her association with the corrupt cops and Federal agents in the city and now had the money to buy the high tech equipment that she used to bug the home and vehicles owned by Billy Ray "Cowboy" Turner.

For the remainder of January, she compiled information on the daily movements of the big Texan via the strategically placed bugs, as well as two of the policeman's mistresses whom she bribed quite handsomely to both wear wires whenever they'd meet up with their lover for dinner dates and to betray his whereabouts and contacts. For the first week of February, Trina continued to pile up crucial information on the one cop that the hood loved to hate. Then by the beginning of week two, she had all the info she needed to move on Cowboy.

On February 11, 1991, at 5:52 p.m., Trina came back home from walking her pet Akitas around the Shaw area and stopped to chat with a neighbor who admired the beauty of the huge guard dogs. She talked with the long-winded old lady for about thirty minutes always looking down at her pager to check the time every so often. After 6:42 PM, Trina walked the dogs around back into her backyard where she fed them and gave them water before entering her home through the basement at the rear. Inside she entered the kitchen where she again glanced at the time, this time checking out the large-faced kitchen clock hanging on the wall. Finally at 6:51 p.m. as she prepared herself a hearty meal of baked chicken, rice pilaf and snow peas, Trina received the phone call she had been waiting for. It was Pooh.

Pooh let Trina know that he had acquired a Dodge Durango and had no less than seven guys with him, all heavily armed with semi-automatic weaponry. After revealing the details of Cowboy's alleged destination of that particular evening to Pooh, Trina hung the phone up returning to her delicious smelling meal, which simmered slowly upon the stove and within the oven, pleased by the fact that very soon yet another of her hated enemies would bite the dust. Meanwhile at the exact same time, Pooh and his truck full of trigger-happy hoods cruised toward Columbia Heights eagerly looking forward to the moment of gun play.

At 7:18 pm, Pooh pulled the Durango up to a dead end corner about a block and a half away from a sea green colored Mexican style hacienda which seemed dark and abandoned except for a single light illuminating the garage to the rear where the unmistakable sound of laughter and talking came out clearly. Pooh looked into the rearview mirror at his seven partners and nodded which gave them an unspoken signal to prepare for action. The tough looking kids, two of whom were no older than thirteen, attached silencers to their pistols and pulled leather gloves onto their hands as they simultaneously loaded clips into their hardware.

One after the other they exited the vehicle briskly walking down the partially lit street past several old rowhouses, a small Salvadorian church, and a dark empty playground before coming up to the house itself where Cowboy was visiting. Three gunman proceeded quickly around to the left side of the house, while three others flitted around to the right. Pooh and

Lil' Ghetto waited at the front with loaded guns drawn and ready.

Within a mere matter of nanoseconds, screams were heard as the men in the garage got mowed down by muffled gunshots fired from the surrounding darkness. Two minutes into the surprise attack, an unmarked police cruiser pulled up to a screeching stop just outside the front door. The unmistakable ten-gallon Stetson, snake-skinned boots and handlebar mustache of Billy Ray "Cowboy" Turner jumped out from behind the steering wheel, threw the door open, and bust off several powerful shots of his own in Pooh and Lil' Ghetto's direction, barely missing the right side of Lil' Ghetto's head as a bullet whizzed passed him shattering one of the hacienda's porch windows in the process.

In an surprising turn of fortune, the cop's police-issued service revolver jammed up on him for a quick second and the deadly bead he'd drawn on Lil' Ghetto, never reached its mark. Instead, the Texan watched in wide-eyed terror as Pooh's Desert Eagle recoiled sending a death-dealing slug speeding towards him, slamming into his left shoulder. Again, the big nine-millimeter kicked violently in Pooh's strong grasp, sending a bullet into Cowboy's upper right cheek. Bleeding badly, the tall, sinewy Texan, slumped forward dropping his gun to the pavement as he collapsed in the street.

Pooh walked up to the cop as he gasped for breath and gurgled on his own gore that pooled out in a huge crimson circle around his head. Pooh pointed the Desert Eagle down towards the man's helpless form and squeezed the trigger until he'd totally emptied the clip into Cowboy's body. Pooh spat upon the dead police officer and kicked him furiously for several seconds before Lil' Ghetto pulled him away from Cowboy's corpse and towards the Durango down the street.

The remaining six killers rushed away from the bloody murder scene, following Pooh and Lil' Ghetto back to the parked vehicle waiting along the dead end street. Once safely inside, the Go Hard Soldierz beat a hasty retreat away from Northwest back towards their Southeast stomping grounds leaving a grisly scene of eight bullet-riddled bodies behind in their wake, including that of Cowboy's.

Trina got the ecstatic call from Pooh bearing the news of a successful hit. She had just stripped naked in order to enter the bubbling water of her Jacuzzi bath. She joyously thanked Pooh for a job well done and promised him that she would reward them handsomely for their efforts. Hanging up the phone, Trina poured herself a victory glass of Moet before she slipped into the hot waters of the Jacuzzi. She closed her eyes and smiled broadly, content in knowing that now one less enemy existed on the streets of DC for her to worry about.

The department was not only embarrassed by the discovery of one of their own found slain so far away from his jurisdiction, but in a notoriously dangerous and drug-infested area populated by the menacing MS-13 cliques. With little in the way of an explanation behind the shady circumstances of Billy Ray Turner's brutal slaying and the 2½ kilos of coke found in the trunk of his squad car, as well as the briefcase filled with $3,000,000 of unmarked bills, the Metropolitan Police chalked Cowboy's murder up as a drug deal gone bad and closed the books on a case which had brought a black eye to the force.

With Cowboy out the picture, Chief Andrew Ellroy came up next on Trina's black list to be eliminated and she could not wait to carry it out.

Chapter 25

Dropping Just Like Flies

By February 23rd, the Federal Bureau of Investigation announced that it would assist the Metropolitan Police Department in the development of a special task force that would aggressively target drug dealing street crews and other violent criminals throughout the District. Regional Director Rita Ann Ricks would direct "Operation Dog Catcher". FBI Director Ricks held a national press conference that afternoon around 2:30 PM, where she stood before a large panel of reporters and photographers making it quite clear that the destructive nature of the City's drug crews was a blemish on the noble image of our Nation's Capitol that would no longer be tolerated by the Bureau and local authorities. She assured the assembled media that by the start of spring, the District of Columbia's streets would be cleared of narcotics and traffickers to boot. She especially made mention of the Go Hard Soldierz vowing to rid the area of their presence entirely.

Trina smirked sarcastically as she listened to the televised press conference. Lately the rift between her and Rita Ann had widened even more. The two sisters had never been that close, but at this point in both their lives, their distance had developed into mutual hatred for each other. Trina knew full well that she could not possibly do battle with her sister and the power of the FBI. However, if push came to shove, she would have no problem arranging for Rita Ann to have an unfortunate accident.

Trina treated herself out to dinner at Georgia Brown's on 15th Street, Northwest. She was seated immediately and a pitcher of ice water and menu were brought by a courteous young waiter who lightly flirted with her as she engaged him in small talk. Upon seeing this, a senior waiter called the young man over to the side reprimanding him severely for his unprofessionalism. The older waiter apologized for the actions of his co-worker and went into the kitchen to summon another server for her table. As she went through the various dishes of Southern style cuisine presented on the menu, Trina was approached by her new server, who announced her presence by introducing herself and asking for the details of her preferred appetizer and meal of the evening.

The voice that came to her ears was unmistakably recognizable and Trina immediately looked up from the menu that she held in front of her. Stunned, she could only stare long and hard as her eyes met those of her mother's.

"Ma?"

"May I take your order please?" Lucinda asked ignoring her daughter's recognition of her.

"Yes, I'd like to start with a tall glass of iced tea, an order of fried okra, and a plate of catfish nuggets."

When she folded the menu up and placed it down gently onto the table, Trina looked up to notice that Lucinda was nearly back inside the kitchen. Something wasn't right. She felt it strongly within her. *Her mother working as a waitress?* She'd quit her nursing career at the Greater Southeast Community Hospital two years ago and Trina funneled anywhere between $12,000 to $15,000 into a back account for her mother and daughter each month for the past four years now not to mention paying for the mortgage and car note as well. Why Lucinda Ricks would choose to punch a time clock in anyone's place of business was beyond her. It just didn't add up.

When her appetizer was served twenty minutes later, yet another waiter delivered it to her. When she inquired of him as to the whereabouts of her previous waitress, Trina was told that Lucinda had suddenly taken ill and had to leave early. Almost immediately Trina lost her appetite. She asked the waiter for the check and paid for the meal without eating. When the waiter asked if anything was wrong, Trina assured him that there was nothing wrong with either the food or the service. But instead she had forgotten that she had an important previous engagement in which she could not afford to miss. She apologized for any inconvenience on her behalf and left him with a $50 tip upon her departure.

When Trina exited the restaurant, she noticed a strange man walking away rapidly from her Suburban. She abandoned the idea of pursuing him as he disappeared down 15th Street and around the corner in between the buildings there. Trina surveyed her truck closely for several painstaking minutes noticing nothing out of line or any different with her SUV than when she first came to the restaurant. Then she got down on her hands and knees to look up under the bottom of the truck after finding nothing strange under the hood. After a search under the bottom of the Suburban for a little over five minutes, her flashlight's beam landed on a large electrical tape-wrapped bundle of dynamite wired in a detailed series of multicolored connections placed directly beneath the transmission. She had no choice but to contact the 2nd District Police to respond to 15th Street, NW.

Within 15 minutes, the lot was full of police squad cars, uniformed and plain clothes cops, barking bomb-sniffing German Shepherds and a heavily armored group of police bomb technicians. Trina, of course, was questioned for about thirty minutes about various details surrounding the discovery of the planted bomb. The bomb squad finally removed the explosive after a tense nerve-wracking twenty minutes.

Trina was informed that the power of the blast that would have resulted from the TNT, had she unwittingly turned the key in the truck's ignition, would have blown a huge crater 15 feet deep by 25 feet wide easily taking out several vehicles and buildings nearby, causing aftershocks to have been felt five to seven blocks away. Trina was not satisfied with the results totally and called a tow truck to take her truck to Branch Avenue Auto Repair Shop, where her favorite auto mechanic and body detailer could strip the SUV down and rebuild it once again.

She contacted Pooh who picked her up and took her back to the Farms. There she borrowed his Cadillac and made a beeline to Forestville, Maryland. Trina went up to the door of her mother's Waterford Drive home and banged furiously on the front door. Within two seconds her mother had snatched open the door and stood defiantly in the entrance before her enraged daughter. For a moment she just stared angrily back at her.

"Why the fuck are you doin' this shit to me? Trina cried out with tears welling up in her soft hazel eyes.

"It's for your own good child. You stay in trouble! It's bad enough that you out here selling dope, but now you just kill folks who cross you. I ain't raised you to be no hoodlum, selling that trash and shooting people all over DC and running around with dykes. C'mon now! What you need is Jesus!"

"What? I need Jesus? That's mighty funny comin' outta your mouth after all the years my drug money took care of you and your big time shoppin' habits. But now you wanna preach to me? That's real funny, ma . . . real fuckin' funny!"

"You need to get your mind right, Trina. And I think that by you being locked up that will save lives—both yours and other folks. This life is only a few short years . . . hell is forever!"

"Whatever! I ain't tryin' to hear all o' that. You had me set up! Your own daughter . . . I don't care what your say . . . that's crazy!"

"You damn right I had you set up! The police chief told me to shadow you so I had Laquita's son Larry, who works as a private investigator, follow you around ever since the trial ended last month. I'm tired of y'all lil' hoodlums now. All you do is damage the Black community with that trash you sell. You rob and steal from folks and even when you got their money, you turn right around and shoot them anyway. And what make it so bad is y'all killing your own people! Well I'll be damned if one of mine will keep on committing crime non-stop. You might have gotten away with murder last month, but I'm gonna see to it that you go to prison where you belong!" Lucinda exclaimed bluntly.

"I just can't believe what the fuck I'm hearin'! You'd sell out your own child, your own flesh and blood? And for what? Cause you got morals all of a sudden? Please . . . everything you own comes from my money! Even the goddamned under-wear you got on, you wearin' 'em cause o' me! I pay the mort-gage on this muhfuckin' house each month. I pay the note on that minivan! I keep money in your fuckin' bank account! You even got my baby! And this is how you thank me? It's bad enough that Rita Ann don't care 'bout me, which by the way don't bother me one way or another for real, but my own mother? Now that shit hurt me to my heart, Joe! How you gon' tell that bitch ass Chief Ellroy on me and shit? Do you realize that he don't wanna lock me up cause he already been there and done that . . . he know he's got no case. That old muhfucka wanna kill me . . . that's how he's goin'! Did you re-alize that shit? No, see you just think they gon' throw me in jail right quick and that's it. You must o' forgotten that even when they was tryin' to lock me up, they wanted to put me be-hind bars for life! You got me blown like shit behind this hot shit you did today! You're right, if you was anybody other than who you are, I wouldn't be up here fussin' with you. You'd be layin' on the livin' room floor with a bullet in yo' brain . . . consider yourself blessed. Big Stinka was a hustler aiight, one of the best who ever flipped an gram of coke, a pound o' green, or bag o' rocks, but as a person, he was a triflin', dirty, fucked up individual and I wasn't about to let him bring his child molestin' ass around my baby. And whether you wanna believe it or not, you wasn't nothin' but another piece o' ass to him. The bamma used to brag about all the broads he had sex with and I'm pretty certain you wasn't no different. I told you he was even 'bout to make homemade porno movies without you knowin', so he could sell 'em on the street. What do you think about that? Shit, if that was yo' man, he sure showed you love in a fucked up way!"

Lucinda's eyes brimmed with tears and she looked away from Trina as if contemplating the truthfulness of her daughter's words. Trina made a slight move towards her mother in an attempt to hug her, but stopped and backed away from the doorway.

"You ok, Ma?" Trina asked her mother with concern.

"You—you used to be such a sweet little girl, just like Porsche. You were so cute and cuddly . . . my sweet, sweet little girl. What happened to you, baby? What happened to you?"

Trina sniffed and dabbed a silk handkerchief across her tear-filled eyes. She could take it no longer and she rushed into her mother's arms and wept like a child. Her mother wrapped her loving arms around Trina. Lucinda pulled Trina in close to her bosom where she gently caressed Trina's head and cried along with her daughter.

"I love you, ma. I love you so much! I never wanted to hurt you! All I want is for you to be proud of me. I ain't gon' do this shit forever. I got a whole lotta money saved up, enough to take care of me, you, and Porsche for the rest of our lives, ya know? I know that what I do ain't right, but I gotta do what I gotta do to make it out here. Sooner or later I'll quit. I promise you that, aiight?"

"Don't make any promises that you can't keep child! You

and I both know how much you love doing what it is you do. So don't even go there with me." Lucinda said backing away slowly from Trina.

Trina smiled weakly and kissed her mother gently on her cheek, placing a thick rubber band wrapped stack of bills into her hand.

"No, Trina . . . not this time. You keep your money. You just come back here tomorrow and spend some time with Porsche. Take her out to the movies or the zoo or the playground or something. It doesn't matter. Your time spent with your child is more important than all the money in the world."

"You're right, ma. Tell my baby I'll see her tomorrow at 12:00 PM. We'll go out to Baskin Robbins and Chuck E. Cheese's, aiight? Then we'll do whatever she wanna do. I'll bring her back home around about 9 PM."

Trina waved at her mother and blew her a departing kiss as she walked back to the Cadillac. She drove away from her mother's feeling satisfied that she and her mother had finally settled their differences. No one else could've betrayed her and lived to see another day with the exception of her mother. All the way down the beltway, Trina thought about both the truthful words of her mother and her very own desire for vengeance against the crooked police force and other shady government officials. But as she traveled across the beltway, Trina had begun to heed the words of Lucinda. For too long she had relied on violence to handle all of her problems. She would have to learn how to solve her troubles through other less bloody means from now on.

Trina stayed up even after she arrived home an hour later. She dwelled on many things which had occurred over the past few months. She even picked up the Bible and read a few pages each day, understanding the possibility of death be-falling her at any time because of the heartless nature of the drug game. She remembered being in Church as a child, no

more than eight or nine years old, reading the Bible and praying each night before her Mother tucked her into bed. She
now needed GOD more than ever before.

She consulted with her attorneys and drew up a will as well,
leaving all of her earthly possessions to her daughter, Porsche,
in the event of her untimely death.

Trina still desired to bring all of the corrupt city officials
crashing down but she planned on doing it without weapons.
To blow the whistle on such government corruption would
definitely create a city wide scandal that threatened to throw
the entire political structure of the DC Government out of
whack. This would be a more satisfying bit of revenge than
any gangland hit would ever be. Trina savored the thought of
ruining her enemies' very livelihood. But nevertheless, she was
still a baller and gunplay, violence, and bloodshed simply went
with the territory. Others she would bring to justice through
the media, but as for the police chief himself, she continued to
harbor slightly more deadly plans.

On February 24th at 10:48 AM as Trina turned down her
street with the dogs for their daily morning walk, her pager
buzzed loudly upon the belt encircling her wide hips. As she
picked up the beeper and viewed the number of the caller, she
saw that it was Pooh and he had put 911 behind his number.
The call was urgent. She quickly walked to the house bursting
through the French doors with the Akitas bounding in right
behind her. Without hesitation she snatched up the phone's
receiver in the living room and rapidly dialed Pooh's seven
digits.

"Trina guess what I just found out, Shorty?" Pooh asked
with mounting excitement in his voice.

Trina listened carefully as her fellow Barry Farms thug
spoke on the cause of his enthusiasm. After they spoke for over
twenty-five minutes covering all bases concerning the plans of
the day, she got off the phone feeling more than a little satisfied with the pleasant news of the morning.

At 8:45 PM that night eight cars loaded with armed youths from various sections of Southeast's mostly deadly areas: Shipley Terrace, Potomac Gardens, Simple City, and Langston Lane came ready to put in work. They were the grimiest of the grimy which Pooh and Lil' Ghetto could round up for a few hundred dollars. The hustlers from the Farms and Valley Green also left the money making corners and dope spots in order to make the trip to Columbia Heights to handle Trina's light work. In a grim and murderous motorcade, they traveled toward the heavily Latino populated section of Northwest, Washington to pay a most evil visit. The all were aware however of the great numbers and equally fearsome firepower wielded by the ruthless cliques of MS-13. Also Pooh and company would have to watch their step with the newly FBI-formed dragnet going around arresting drug dealers and their respective crews. If they happened to be caught by the Feds or metropolitan police, they'd be in a world of trouble.

They parked their cars near a city park and Pooh exited his Cadillac along with Lil' Ghetto and Black Rick, who were followed by seven more pistol-packing toughs that were to act as back-up just in case their original plans backfired for any reason. Several younger hoodlums remained with the vehicles, sitting patiently behind the steering wheels smoking blunts and bobbing their heads to the music of their favorite Go-Go bands.

Near 18th Street the three Southeast gangsters noticed Police Chief Ellroy accompanied by a group of hardcore looking Salvadorians dining at the "Blue Parakeet", an Adams Morgan eatery specializing in fine Salvadorian cuisine. Pooh and Lil' Ghetto walked pass the window of the restaurant just to make sure that they were certain of the identity of their intended victim. As they watched Chief Ellroy discuss business with the members of Columbia Height's "Locos Vatos" Chapter of Mara Salvatrucha through the window of the eatery, they had no doubt that the well-dressed, middle-aged black man seated at the table among the muscle bound tattooed Surenos was none other than the police chief himself.

Satisfied with their findings, they then disappeared among the nightlife-loving Adams Morgan crowd. Once they crossed the street, Black Rick pointed out the police chief's stylish Rolls Royce parked on the curb of a dark, quiet side street adjacent to a large abandoned building. Together the trio approached the luxury vehicle and went to work placing enough C-4 on the chief's vehicle to blow up a moderate sized building. After a meticulous job of hotwiring, the plastic boxes containing C4 were firmly attached to Chief Ellroy's vintage 1954 Rolls Royce. They left just as quickly as they had come, once the job was done.

Chief Ellroy, like many other officers of the DC Metropolitan Police Force, saw the rapid rise of the MS-13 in both Northern Virginia and the Columbia Heights' neighborhood of Northwest, Washington. The highly organized gang brought in millions of dollars from drugs, prostitution, gun smuggling, and other criminal pursuits. Greedy as he was, he could not allow an opportunity to increase his finances considerably slip through his hands. So he chalked up a quarter of a million dollar cocaine deal with three equally well-dressed leaders of Locos Vatos, 36 year-old Chico Morella, 41 year-old Antonio Mandis, and Morella's dashingly handsome 22 year-old nephew Fernando Ruiz.

After discussing the particulars of the coke deal and enjoying a hearty Salvadorian style baked fish dinner, Chief Ellroy left the Blue Parakeet fully satisfied. He had just worked out a hefty deal that would earn him enough to retire from the force and live out the rest of his life in comfort and opulence. He opened the door of his Rolls Royce and sat down on the plush leather seat. He pulled the sun visor down to groom himself slightly before driving off.

As he placed the key into the ignition, the engine stuttered stubbornly once then twice. Chief Ellroy was perplexed; he'd always kept his prized automobile's maintenance needs on the top of his priority list. He sighed with frustration and tried his hand at starting the car's engine once again. This time the engine turned over, purred and idled to the satisfaction of the chief. Smiling, he put the car in drive in order to pull away from the curb. Then he smelled a strong acidic odor, almost like burning rubber or plastic. Then bluish white flames erupted along the dashboard, steering wheel, and windshield quickly spreading across the roof of the car's interior. The suddenly terrified police chief instinctively reached for the door handle, his very last physical action.

Within a matter of seconds the entire inside of the Rolls Royce was filled with red orange crackling flames that engulfed the now screaming Andrew Ellroy. The raging fire burned fiercely for a few minutes then the Rolls Royce was disintegrated by a tremendously powerful explosion, which set off car alarms and shook the foundation of area buildings many blocks away causing startled residents to come out into the cold night to investigate the source of the blast.

Trina awakened the next morning to the news blaring from her clock radio that a massive explosion had rocked a quiet residential neighborhood in Adams Morgan, sending frightened residents out into the cold. Trina pumped her fist in the air with triumph. For she, unlike the media, knew whose blackened shell of a car it was that sat, still smoking and surrounded by bright yellow police tape on the curb of the Adams Morgan neighborhood. Later in the day, the shattered, badly charred remains would be identified as those of DC Police Chief Andrew Ellroy. The car bombing death of Chief Ellroy made top story headlines for weeks around the greater Washington, DC, area and the Nation itself.

Trina was so overjoyed with the killing of the police chief who had tried unsuccessfully to kill her that she rewarded Pooh, Lil' Ghetto, Black Rick, and several other Go Hard Soldierz members to an all expense paid round trip, a weeklong vacation to sun-filled Rio De Janeiro, Brazil. Everyone who had previously dogged her out she had gotten even with so far. District Attorney Francine Gonzolez remained the only one left to be dealt with. She would have no need to actually have her murdered as she had done with the D.A.'s aggressively ambitious male peers. Instead she'd destroy her legal career through the exposure of her corrupt associations with known criminals throughout the city, which in turn would eliminate any chance of Gonzolez gaining a bid for the DC Mayoral office. That alone most definitely would send the arrogant, power hungry D.A. into a deep and long lasting depression, that could possibly lead to a life of alcoholism and/or suicide, knowing, as Trina did, how prone D.A. Gonzolez was to clinical depression. Then again, Trina could not forget about the MS-13, who also attempted to take her out and with whom she still had a major beef. They both would pay in time as would all others had who carried her but for now she would simply sit back, pop a bottle of Cristal . . . and chill.

Chapter 26
Respect My Gangsta

Despite the luxury, comfort and power that a huge bank account bestows on the hustler who reaches Kingpin status, nothing can prepare, much less bring solace to the baller on the unfortunate receiving end of betrayal by a loved one. It comes at you quickly, unexpectedly and hits you like a ton of bricks all at once. Recovery from this particular type of double cross is painfully slow and at times you never fully get over being sold out by your own. For District of Columbia's drug lord Katrina Ricks, March 1991, would bring just that type of drama to her life yet again.

On the 23rd of February, one of Kofi Whitman's top buyers of crack cocaine, Larry Smith, gave him photographs and other vital information which he had requested about his girlfriend Trina. Larry Smith, a full time private investigator for Raptor Technologies, Inc., was a crackhead with a $150.00 a week habit. He'd been promised $200,000 worth of rocks if he'd shadow Trina for two whole weeks returning with photos and information to Kofi's "Whitman & Son's Commercial Trucking" located on Rhode Island Avenue.

Each day between 12:00 PM and 4:00 PM, the gaunt, slack

jawed Larry Smith, who had ironically helped Lucinda Ricks spy on her daughter earlier, now brought Polaroid pictures and daily news to the attractive, square-jawed Kofi. Larry was provided with a $20 rock each time he delivered for his troubles.

Kofi and Trina's relationship had grown more sour month after month until at last Kofi moved out of 919 S Street, Northwest, never to return again. He had long since gotten tired of Trina's overly aggressive attitude towards him, not to mention the disrespectful way in which she'd speak to him, especially in front her neighborhood friends. He did not particularly care for the company of Trina's Barry Farm pals, especially Pooh, who seemed to be more of a soul mate to Trina than he was. Only their sex life kept any spark alive in what had become a painfully strained relationship which over time could not be saved by even a steamy sex life.

He had been involved with two women since dating Trina, an 18-year-old stripper from Georgia Avenue "Penthouse" Strip Club, and a 25-year-old pediatrician from Glenarden. He had always considered those two outside affairs as merely sexual flings that he would conveniently end after three or four trysts. But during the start of the murder trial he had met Trina's older sister, FBI Regional Director Rita Ann. They started off simply meeting up with one another in the courthouse cafeteria discussing details of the day's proceedings and reminiscing over past memories of the childhood innocence of Rita and Trina. Their mutual connection to the case's defendant and the chemistry between them brought a bond that soon blossomed into a full-fledged love affair, one which neither of them could hide from Trina any further.

Since moving out the house, Kofi had moved into an apartment complex in Laurel, Maryland, only two blocks away from Rita Ann. As a result of his breaking up with Trina, he completely abandoned the drug game, as well as the murder-for-hire business and stuck with his full-time career as a co-owner of "Whitman & Son Commercial Trucking". And now after spending so much of his free time in the presence of his new love, who happened to be the FBI Director, he began to view his ex-girlfriend much differently than he did before.

Trina now seemed to have become too big, too bold, and far too dangerous to remain on the streets of DC. Besides, the constant insight into the evil of the criminal mind and the vicious cycle of destruction resulting from it had changed his mindset forever. He and FBI Director Rita Ann Ricks conspired to set up Trina in the act of committing a felony, which would be the only way that the powerful drug queen could possibly be brought to justice. Kofi knew what moved Trina and he put his plan into action.

On March 9, 1991, 8:43 PM, Kofi called Trina at her home.

"Boy, why in the fuck you keep on callin' my muhfuckin' house? We don't talk no more and shit. So what the hell do you want from me, huh?"

"Oh, so you carryin' it like that now, huh? Well, I just wanted to tell you 'bout a big ass shipment o' coke comin' in outta California at 10:00 PM sharp. Them lil' Julio muhfuckas out Columbia Heights s'pose to make the drop and the pickup. Niggas told me we lookin' at somethin' like $500 G's, but you gotta get over to 18th Street Northwest before the Mexicans make the drop, aiight? Now if you don't want none o' that cheese, then shit, just stay yo' ass home."

"Who told you all that?"

"Don't worry 'bout it. This is your chance to rob them MS-13 bammas and air their bitch asses out. Know what I'm sayin,' 'cause they did try to hit your head just last December. Remember that? I would ride witcha tonight my damn self, but I gotta go buy a fleet of new 18 wheelers from down in Atlanta early tomorrow morning around 8:30 AM Which means by the time you and ya mob take care o' that light work, I'll be taking a midnight flight out to Georgia."

"What's the address where them Spanish niggas gon' be exchangin' this shit at?"

"They gon' be meetin' up at 1901 Kalorama Road, North-west, and remember be there before 10:00 P.M. that way you'll catch their bitch asses sleepin', aiight? Holla!"

Kofi slammed the receiver down on the phone's cradle be-fore Trina could respond. Kofi plopped down backwards upon his large waterbed and let out a huge sigh. He stared at the ceiling blankly for a long time after his phone call to Trina. He just realized the seriousness of what he had just done. He and Trina may no longer have been together, but he still cared about her and felt a bit of sorrow over his decision to set her up. He folded his strong arms behind his head as he shifted and turned on the pillow. Now that he had gone through with this plan, he needed for the FBI sting to be successful for if it failed for any reason at all, Trina and her numerous Go Hard Soldierz members would not sleep until they hunted him down and killed him.

As was the norm, Trina had Pooh round up as many drug dealers, ex-cons, and bad attitude-bearing thugs as he could gather to make the trip to Columbia Heights. Only this time Trina would take the ride out to Columbia Heights as well. After Pooh had everyone assembled, he and Trina rolled out in Trina's newly refurbished Suburban with six carloads of gunmen trailing behind them down the night streets of DC.

When they came up to the address which Kofi had given Trina earlier that night, 1901 Kalorama Road was a dark aban-doned building that had once been a Rite Aid Drugstore. Trina stepped out of the Suburban after parking along a broad curb; car after car lined up behind her Suburban. She slipped a full clip into a nine millimeter, which she drew out of the glove compartment of her SUV. She placed two more fully loaded clips into the pockets of her leather jacket and moved towards the darkened, boarded up structure with cautious, but steady steps as her gun-wielding entourage stepped quickly behind her.

As Trina neared the deserted building's door, she became

excited. Her heart raced with the anticipation of a huge score. She would have a chance to get revenge on the Salvadorian gang members who had riddled her truck with bullets only three months earlier. And she'd walk away with $500,000 and several kilograms of cocaine.

Once they were in front of the building the boys who had done jobs for Trina before instinctively spread out, with pistols drawn, around the sides and rear of the building searching for any lookouts that might be posted around the property of the old building. They reported back to Trina that the coast was clear. She then ordered two husky teenagers to kick the door in, opening fire, if need be, once the door gave way to their forceful entry. Once inside, they'd immediately spray the surprised Latinos with semi-automatic gunfire, taking the drugs and money after the shooting and leaving right away.

The two beefy thugs kicked in the door, which fell into the pitch black interior with a loud crash, sending a thick cloud of time-gathered dust into the musty, stale air of the building. The group of gangsters walked gingerly into the yawning, black space beyond the doorway. Suddenly, the dark interior of the room was illuminated brightly by dozens of blinding spotlights, which surrounded them.

"Oh, shit! It's the muthafuckin' Feds! Let's get the fuck up outta here! Run!"

In a crazed frenzy to get away from the trap which had been laid for them, the scene was one of chaos and confusion with kids yelling and running with breakneck speed for the doorway and dozens of armed Federal agents and DC police officers barking out orders to stop and giving chase after the criminals on foot.

Within minutes after the very first gunshot, the abandoned building and surrounding streets were filed with the terrible din of multiple guns blasting all at the same time. Trina turned as she fled down the street and squeezed off four thunderous shots in the direction of two DC cops who raced after her and

Pooh as they ran across the street toward the truck sitting at the curb in the distance. The two Barry Farm natives leaped into the SUV, started the engine and roared off into the night. Trina and Pooh's return fire had hit the two policemen.

Trina drove back towards her home like a bat out of hell, burning rubber at no less than 90 miles per hour down the streets running red lights, stop signs, and cutting off startled drivers who honked their horns at the reckless Suburban as it barreled across intersections and darkened crossroads en route to her Shaw neighborhood. Trina raced into her luxurious home, moving about the house as quickly as she could go. She gave Pooh orders to bring up a black crate filled with small packages from the basement. He obeyed and went down, coming up within a few minutes carrying it within his arms. Trina knelt down and took out two of the small but heavily weighted boxes, and lifted up her pretty hazel eyes towards Pooh and nodded towards him slowly. A gesture that caused him to nod back in agreement with his boss' silent orders.

After 15 minutes, the two drug dealers left the residence of 919 S Street, Northwest, along with Trina's two Japanese Akitas. Twenty minutes later, Trina and Pooh showed up at Lucinda's doorstep. When her mother approached the door, Trina looked over her mother's shoulder as if searching for someone.

"What's the matter with you, girl? Who are you looking for?"

"Ma, this don't concern you. I know Rita Ann is back there and she know why the fuck I'm here too!"

Before Lucinda could respond, she was brushed to the side by her older daughter who stood face to face at the doorway with her enraged younger sister.

"Excuse me, mama. I got this. What? I'm right here. Is there a problem?" Rita Ann said sharply.

"You low down, dirty ass bitch you. You and that pretty boy punk o' yours tried to set me up tonight, didn't you? Wait tell I let my lawyers know 'bout this shit. That's entrapment, now ain't it? You didn't give a fuck whether or not them peoples killed me tonight!"

"So what? You're a fuckin' criminal. You were a piece of scum then and you're scum now!" exclaimed Rita Ann yelling into Trina's face up close.

Without a moment hesitation, Trina drew back her right arm and landed a clenched fist hard against the right side of her sister's jaw followed by an equally punishing left, which caught the FBI Director on the top of her forehead, opening up a nasty gash as she careened backwards onto the hardwood floor of the living room.

Lucinda Ricks yelled at both of her children to stop fighting, but did not intervene for fear of causing harm to her unborn child. However, her tearful cries fell on deaf ears as Trina straddled Rita Ann pounding away at her face with such fury that Trina's fists dripped with blood as she stood over her big sister's battered form, breathing heavily with the front of her Prada sweater stained crimson with Rita Ann's blood.

Kofi Whitman rushed from upstairs where he had been tucking Porsche and Rita Ann's two children into bed for the night. When he reached the bottom of the stairs, he came to a sudden stop as Pooh stood at the stairwell with his face twisted in a savage snarl and the glossy chrome barrel of a Smith & Wesson nine millimeter aimed at Kofi's broad chest.

"Slow you muthafuckin' roll, nigga, before I unload this bitch into yo' ass!" Pooh growled at Kofi.

Kofi obeyed the orders given to him and made no further attempt to descend the stairs. Trina ran her fingers through her disheveled hair and pulled her silky, chestnut brown mane back into a bun. She then turned around towards Kofi.

"And you . . . you a bitch, young! How you gon' carry me like that? Huh? It's bad enough that you was fuckin' my sista behind my back and shit, but now since you talkin' to her, you gon' turn on me? Me of all people . . . don't nobody got love for a dry snitch, boo. You know that, and I know that. So you better get Rita Ann to place yo faggy ass in the muthafuckin' witness protection program 'cause after what you did to niggas tonight out Northwest, off that bullshit phone call you gave me earlier, you ain't gon' be safe no where on the streets o' DC. 'Cause you ain't nothin' but a straight up rat! I should just let Pooh put two in yo' skull just for pullin' some hot shit like that! But it's all good though, cause I got information on both o' y'all jokers that'll have you in some straight serious shit. And trust me, my two lawyers as you saw for yourselves ain't to be fucked with. So now Rita Ann, you gon' stop fuckin' with me one way or the other. 'Cause if you keep on, I'm sure the Bureau would like to know about your little relationship with my ex-boyfriend—a known killer-for-hire and a big time crack dealer. Humm . . . I don't think you'd keep ya' lil' gig with the Feds too long after news like that, now would you? And if you wanna go hard . . . I'll plant dope in your cars or wherever your boys in blue can find the shit and I'll make sure it looks just like it belonged to you. Don't fuck with me, Rita Ann, cause I ain't the one. I've been in this game for far too long and I know all the lil' tricks o' the trade 'cause I learned from the best—the police and the Feds. So right about now yo' lil' bitch ass agents is probably either on their way to my house or already in my fuckin' house tearin' shit up lookin' for me and evidence and all kinda shit. Well, you just betta get yo' ass up of the floor and call your dogs off or else I'm takin' everything I know 'bout everything to Nightline News. Wait 'til all them White folks hear Ted Koppel talk 'bout all o' this bullshit goin' on with you and your crooked ass runnin' partners in the DC government. Play pussy, you damned sure gonna get fucked. Now if your boys get to my house before I do, then that's gon' just be too bad for them cause me & Pooh here rigged that house with enough C4 to flatten half of S Street and some more shit. So if you wanna save the lives of your men, the police, and of course my poor innocent neighbors, you betta act the fuck like you know. 'Cause I got the number to the man with the detonator. Ya see he's a pyromaniac to his heart, a crazy Vietnam vet. He been buyin' heroin off me for a year or two. So he don't give a fuck! He's dying of Agent Orange any damn way. So he's fucked up with the Government ever since he came back to the states in '71. That high tech gadgetry he got is gon' tip him off to any physical presence in the house. That's cause it's some kinda computer-operated heat seeking shit. Anyway if anybody go up in the joint, he's gon' hit me up on the cell phone and from there, it's on me to say yea or nay. You think 'bout that and call me in ten minutes—no later. If I don't get a phone call from you by then, you can kiss your FBI career goodbye. And as for you, Kofi . . . you just betta hope that your NEW bitch do the right thing 'cause then maybe I'll think about lettin' you off the hook cause if not, you're a dead man. And you know it better than anybody else. C'mon, Pooh, let's dip!" Trina said stepping away from her bloodied sister. "Oh, yeah, Ma, I'm gonna come and get Porsche tomorrow. I'm gonna do some travelin' overseas like I told you. And just like you said to me, I need to be a mommy to my baby and that's what I'm gonna be from now on, the best mommy that I can possibly be."

Trina smiled at her still terribly shaken mother who helped Kofi raise the badly beaten Rita Ann off the floor and to her feet. As Trina and Pooh turned to leave, they were greeted by scores of P.G. County Police accompanied by just as many DC Metropolitan cops and Federal agents, all training their service weapons in the direction of the two young suspects standing in the doorway of Lucinda Rick's Forestville home.

As the police sirens chirped loudly and the blue and red flashing lights lit up the entire neighborhood, Trina and Pooh immediately raised their arms and assumed the position against the outside wall of the house. Dozens of curious and startled residents came out from the houses on to their lawns or peered through open windows to catch a glimpse at what drama was unfolding at Lucinda's place. Slowly Trina looked up and glared at her sister as she was helped to the door by her mother and Kofi. Rita Ann looked like hell, her usually well kept, neatly coiffed hairdo was wildly tousled and fell all over her head in lopsided, matted bunches. Her battered face was a mess— bruised, bloodied and bearing black and blue contusions all over. Blood slowly seeped from her left nostril and her right eye was swollen shut. It was plain to see that the Director of the FBI had gotten the ass whipping of a lifetime. As two Federal officers approached Trina and Pooh with handcuffs and opened billfolds bearing the official shield and badge of the U.S. Federal Bureau of Investigation, they were given the order to cease and desist by their commander.

"Do no take these two individuals into custody. They have committed no crimes that the Bureau is currently aware of," Rita Ann announced painfully through bloody and swollen lips.

Every officer within hearing distance stood looking on slack jawed with disbelief. "Excuse me, Ma'am, but I thought that you said—" "Agent Garrett, we don't pay you to think; I'll do that for you, thank you very much. Now back away from these citizens and allow them to leave without further interference. Thank you, gentlemen, this operation is now eliminated . . . that will be all for tonight. Thank you all for your prompt assistance. Good night."

Trina and Pooh rose up off of the wall and began walking out toward the Suburban. The large group of assorted P.G. and DC cops and FBI agents slowly and reluctantly cleared a pathway for the notorious felons as they walked defiantly through their midst and across the narrow street to the SUV. The angry and supremely baffled lawmen looked on helplessly as DC's most notorious criminal drove away, free as a bird into the night. The call from Trina's bomb expert never came in because the law enforcement officers went directly to her mother's home in Forestville, Maryland, after receiving a tip that Trina was there.

Trina apologized to her mother for all of the troubles she had caused her over the years and promised that she would work on being a kinder, gentler soul in the near future.

She placed Pooh, Lil' Ghetto, and Lil' Ghetto's uncle 8-Ball in charge of running the drug operations of the feared Go Hard Soldierz in her absence until she returned or whenever Trey Wills was released from prison.

She continued to forward a hefty stipend into her mother's account each month and left Lil' Ghetto, Pooh, and 8-Ball with a hundred pounds of "Sour Diesel", an extremely potent strain of marijuana usually grown under a 400 watt hortilux lamp along with 60 kilograms of cocaine. Everyone seemed satisfied, especially Lil' Ghetto.

Trina decided that now was the time to travel the world with her daughter who would be turning seven soon. Porsche was a school aged girl who had big, nutmeg brown eyes, soft brown skin the color of cocoa, a bright ready smile with a set of healthy white teeth and possessed a sunny, loveable personality and intense curiosity. Trina treated herself and Porsche to a luxury cruise around the globe aboard the magnificently gorgeous ocean liner Atlantic Princess. They toured Western Europe, the Mediterranean, North Africa, Southeast Asia, Australia, and finally the exotic islands of the Caribbean. Trina would one day return home, but for now she would simply cruise into the sunset forgetting about yesterday. She, along with her lovely Porsche, was eagerly looking forward to a brighter tomorrow.

Trina knew that one day she would eventually return to the nation's capital, the home she loved. But for now, she would travel the world and simply enjoy being the mother to the child she would no longer neglect, for anything or anyone ever again.